NEVER STAND ALONE

JANET MACLEOD TROTTER

Published by MacLeod Trotter Books

New edition: 2011

ISBN 978-0-9566426-7-7

www.janetmacleodtrotter.com

Janet MacLeod Trotter was brought up in the North East of England with her four brothers, by Scottish parents. She is a best-selling author of 15 novels, including the hugely popular Jarrow Trilogy, and a childhood memoir, BEATLES & CHIEFS, which was featured on BBC Radio Four. Her novel, THE HUNGRY HILLS, gained her a place on the shortlist of The Sunday Times' Young Writers' Award, and the TEA PLANTER'S LASS was longlisted for the RNA Romantic Novel Award. She has been editor of the Clan MacLeod Magazine, a columnist on the Newcastle Journal and has had numerous short stories published in women's magazines. She lives in the North of England with her husband, daughter and son. Find out more about Janet and her other popular novels at: www.janetmacleodtrotter.com

Also by Janet MacLeod Trotter

Historical:

The Beltane Fires
The Hungry Hills
The Darkening Skies
The Suffragette
Chasing the Dream
For Love & Glory
The Jarrow Lass
Child of Jarrow
Return to Jarrow
A Crimson Dawn
A Handful of Stars
The Tea Planter's Lass

Mystery:

The Vanishing of Ruth

Teenage:

Love Games

Non Fiction:

Beatles & Chiefs

CHAPTER 1

1976

Carol pulled a face in the mirror.

'I look about twelve!' she protested, staring in dismay at the way the hairdresser was yanking her shaggy brown hair out of its usual feather-cut into a high ponytail. 'And the dress - God, the dress!'

'Stop swearing Carol,' Nancy Shannon scolded her youngest daughter. 'The dress is a picture.'

'It's a nightmare,' Carol contradicted, tugging at the high lacy collar above the yards of flowery pink cotton and matching bolero that were to be her bridesmaid's dress. 'I look like summat out of a pantomime.'

'*Something* out of a pantomime,' her mother corrected automatically.

'If Kelly or my mates catch sight of me, I'll never live this down,' Carol continued, unabashed.

'Girls have friends not mates,' Nancy said, giving herself a sideways view in the vast bedroom mirror and smiling with approval at her trim figure in the cream silk suit. 'I don't know where you learned to talk like that.'

'The same place you did Mother,' Carol goaded, 'Brassbank Secondary Modern. Only you decided to go posh when Dad got the job as pit manager, didn't you?'

Nancy flushed, glaring at the silent hairdresser, defying her to show so much as a smirk at this remark.

'Now you listen here, you little madam-' Nancy broke off as her eldest daughter entered the room, looking pink and flustered in her mammoth white dress.

'Here comes Cinderella,' said Carol.

'Darling you look wonderful,' Nancy cried, jabbing Carol in the back. 'Your father is going to be so proud of you.'

Carol thought for one brief moment that her mother was going to succumb to tears at the sight of Fay in yards of Laura Ashley satin and lace and crown of false flowers in her permed brown hair. But she had never seen her mother cry, not even when Grandma Hutchinson had died, and it did not happen now. Nancy Shannon's heavily made-up face with its false tan and bright lipstick struggled successfully to compose itself under the stiff waves of dyed blonde hair.

Fay did not notice her mother's moment of emotion; she was fare too distracted with worrying about the day ahead.

'Do you think I've overdone it on the eye shadow? Vic prefers the natural look.'

'Is that why I've got to look like Little Bo Peep today? To please the wonderful Vic?'

'Shut up Carol,' her mother snapped. 'Fay, you look just right. Vic Proud's a lucky man to be marrying you and he knows it. Your father and I have been looking forward to this day for so long – it's worth all the expense.'

A good investment, Carol thought wryly. Her parents couldn't believe their luck that Fay was marrying Brassbank's most up-and-coming businessman with a fleet of coaches and two new travel shops opening up in Whittledene New Town. Fay had chosen one of the mock Georgian houses in the nearby village of Brassy as their marital home and had spent the past three months dragooning an army of decorators and joiners and landscape gardeners into producing the eight wonder of the world. Everything was split-level, built-in, shiny new and cream; from the kitchen cupboards to the Habitat furniture and deep pile carpets. They had a Jacuzzi in the bathroom and a fountain in the ground-floor lounge that lit up a lurid green at night. Carol had annoyed Fay by likening it to Santa's grotto. Yet the cost of this marriage and the wedding was staggering to Carol.

'Don't worry Mother,' she smiled impishly under her halo of pink flowers, 'I'll elope on the back of a moped to save you a bit of money.'

Nancy gave her a sharp look but Fay snorted, 'You'll have to catch a man first, and heaven help him when you do.'

Carol was dismissive. 'I'm not going to *catch* any lad. Girls don't need men as the only way to get on in the world any more. At least some of us don't.'

Fay's large-featured face turned crimson, her brown eyes watering. 'It's not like that with me and Vic. We're marrying because we love each other. I've got ambitions too, you know. Vic's going to help me set up a health food store in Whittledene with a sliming centre – wholefoods, herbal remedies – all that sort of thing.'

'Don't let her get to you,' their mother intervened. 'You and Vic have a grand future ahead of you. As for Carol, well, she's never going to get on in the world hanging around with the likes of Kelly Laws and the village boys. She wasted her time at school and refused to go to college. Now all she wants in life is a measly part-time job in a second-rate boutique.'

'I'm right here,' Carol smarted, 'you don't have to talk about me as if I'm out of the room all the time. And Bowman's isn't second-rate it's-'

'Excuse me, Mrs Shannon,' Margaret, the hairdresser, dared to intervene, 'it this how you want Carol's hair?'

Nancy stifled a waspish remark and glared at her daughter. It was the first time she had really *looked* at her youngest for an age. With her long wavy strands of shaggy hair pulled off her face, she could see the full features: the large mutinous mouth and wide nose, arresting and sensual rather than pretty. It struck her how alike she and Fay were, except the elder girl had her father's deep-set brown eyes while Carol's were large and green and fixing her with their perpetual defiant look. Those eyes, Nancy shivered, so direct and accusing.

'Cut the fringe,' she ordered and turned to help Fay with her veil and train.

'No, Mam, not the fringe,' Carol pleaded. Margaret hesitated, wishing this ordeal at the colliery manager's house was over.

'Yes the fringe. You're going to look smart for one day in your life. And don't call me Mam.'

Carol backed away. 'Don't bring those scissors anywhere near me.'

'It's just typical!' Fay suddenly screamed. 'You're deliberately trying to spoil my special day. Can't you do as Mother says for just once?'

With alarm, Carol saw her sister's eyes fill with tears. She had resisted assaults on her fringe for years, but seeing Fay in such a wound-up state, Carol capitulated. As much as she resented being paraded down the aisle in flounces of pink, she didn't want to ruin things for her sister, however over-the-top it all seemed.

'Okay, Margaret,' Carol said, 'do the wicked deed. I wouldn't do this for anyone else, mind, Fay.'

'Thanks.' Fay almost managed a smile and Nancy's taut face relaxed a little.

While Margaret snipped, Fay fretted again over which outfits to pack for her mystery honeymoon.

'Why such secrecy?' Carol asked. 'How can you pack if you don't know where you're going?'

'It's romantic,' Fay said in irritation.

'Bikinis in Alaska – yeah very romantic.'

'Very funny. But I wouldn't expect you to understand. You think romance is sitting on the back of a draughty motorbike or drinking beer on the beach. When you've seen a bit of the world like I have, you'll realise there's life beyond Brassbank.'

'You've been to Corfu twice and you're moving a mile away; hardly the world.'

'It's a step up from here,' Nancy snapped. 'Put them all in,' she advised, 'and if you need anything else Vic will buy it.'

After that there was no more time for argument. The wedding cars arrived: a cream Rolls-Royce for the bride and father while Nancy and Carol followed in a metallic silver limousine, with two small nephews of Vic's who were dressed in blue velvet pageboy suits. Carol felt some sympathy for them as they tugged at their stiff collars and pulled at the constricting breeches, while her mother ordered them to stop climbing on the front garden walls and get in the car.

'Make sure they behave themselves in church, Carol,' her mother fretted. 'Keep a tight hold on that David, he'll be climbing over the pews given half a chance.'

'Yes Mam,' Carol sighed, lifting the smallest black-haired boy off the wall.

'Don't let him get your dress dirty!' Fay shrieked. 'He's been jumping in the flower beds.'

Carol watched her sister growing more puce by the second under the canopy of white lace and flowers. It was already hot and not yet eleven o'clock. Her father's bald head was prickled with sweat and his bulldog face was an uncomfortable crimson above the starched collar of his hired morning suit. He had been standing outside for half an hour, not wanting to get embroiled in the bickering upstairs and concerned that the small pageboys might do permanent damage to his prized display of bedding plants, still blazing with colour despite the unusually dry summer.

Carol thought her father looked quite distinguished in his formal black jacket and pinstriped trousers that managed to hide his spreading paunch. Today he looked tall and benign and fatherly under his brindled moustache. The etched frown and shrewd brown eyes softened with pride for his eldest daughter.

'You look beautiful,' he kept repeating to Fay, 'I'm going to be the proudest man who ever took his daughter up the aisle of St Brandon's.'

'Dad, stop it,' Fay said with a mixture of laughter and reproach. 'You'll make me cry and smudge my make-up.'

'Do hurry up, Ben,' Nancy carped. 'We don't want to keep Vic waiting too long. Now into the cars everyone. Half the village will be out to see us. Let's

3

give them a sight for sore eyes.'

Carol winked at the small boy in her arms. 'Come on Davey, we're not allowed to escape till after the fashion parade.'

'Why've they got sore eyes, Auntie Carol?'

'It's just an expression. Mam wants us to look our best for the half dozen people who didn't get invited for the wedding.'

'In the car, Carol.' Her father gave her a warning look.

Carol bundled the two boys into the limousine. She breathed in the smell of leather; one of her favourite – along with petrol and coal fires in winter. Her family thought she was weird about smells, especially her father who prided himself on growing the best perfumed roses in Brassbank.

It took five minutes for the wedding party to arrive at the church gates, driving up the steep bank out of the mining village towards open fields and the squat towered medieval church of St Brandon in prosperous Brassy. Within the time it took her mother to slap the boys' knees twice for fidgeting, they had left the ranks of brick colliery houses, bustling high street, patchwork of allotments and busy park, and emerged into an oasis of ancient trees and ivy-bound walls. Gone was the incessant clank and throb and the mine, the haze of smoke that hung over the colliery even in summer, the blackened brick and overhead electric cables that reached between houses like giant washing lines.

On a hot sultry Saturday in Brassbank, people came to their doors to talk, grandmothers took children to the shops clutching hands and purses, and men padded out in slippers. But in Brassy, Carol noticed, the main street was deserted and still as a cemetery. Up here the air was cooler – catching a hint of sea breeze that set leaves softly rustling - and the houses set apart and hidden behind high walls. Brassbank hummed, chattered and sweated; Brassy breathed quietly and fanned itself gently in the heat.

A long line of cars was parked up on the verge either side of the old lych gate, including Vic's green Triumph Stag sports car which would be used to whisk Fay away after the reception at Brandon Castle to their mystery destination.

'Look at all those people at the gate,' Nancy exclaimed, pushing the boys out of the limousine and smoothing down her skirt. 'I see Val Bowman's come to have a gawp.'

Carol squinted against the sun to pick out her employer, who waved and smiled. Typical of warm-hearted Val to take time away from her shop on a busy Saturday to wish them well. She and Nancy were related on the maternal side and Carol felt Val should've been invite, but Val had gone beyond the pale when her sister Lotty had married into the Todds. The Todds and the Shannons did not speak; something to do with village history. The Todds were union people, while Ben Shannon had gone over to the management side many years ago, and they never met socially. To Carol, these petty divisions were baffling and she was constantly in trouble from her mother and sister for transgressing them.

'Carol!' a voice screamed from the throng on the footpath. 'Over here, you blind old bat.'

She turned and screwed up her green eyes. Kelly, unmistakable in a tight shocking pink t-shirt and orange shorts, was waving madly. Her red hair was tied up with a trailing Indian scarf that Carol had persuaded her to buy from Bowman's boutique, even though they both knew it wasn't her style.

4

'Hiya, Kelly,' Carol shouted back. 'Bet you wish you could be in this snazzy gear, eh?'

'Shut up and keep walking,' her mother hissed.

But before they could pass safely, Kelly was darting out and emptying a bag of rice all over them. Nancy shrieked as rice found its way beneath her silk jacket and into her strappy shoes.

Carol laughed. 'That's supposed to be for the bride after the service, you daft idiot.'

'Don't worry, there's more where that came from. It's pudding rice and it's on special offer at Marshall's.'

Nancy was still shaking herself down, her heavily tanned face turning a strange orange, when Carol's brother Simon appeared to usher them in. Simon looked handsome in his formal suit even though his blond hair was cut unfashionably short for the police force. His decision to join the force had pleased their parents and her mother was triumphant that he did not intend to follow his father into the mining industry.

He winked in encouragement. 'I know it's bad for your image, but you look fantastic in pink.'

Carol smiled. 'You look pretty good too, in spite of that terrible hair cut.'

Simon gave Fay a broad smile as she appeared on her father's arm, and led Nancy down to the front, while Carol held hands with the page boys and whispered, 'If you manage not to stand on Auntie Fay's train, I'll treat you to ice cream at Dimarco's.'

One squealed, the other said loudly, 'That's not a train, it's a sheet.'

Carol laughed low. 'Well keep off the sheet.'

Fay turned to hush them. Carol mimed zipping her mouth to the boys, who grinned, then the organ burst into the bridal march and they were setting off down the aisle.

Carol was mesmerised by the rich colours – crimson altar cloth and the psychedelic patterns from sun shot through stained glass – and the earthy smell of fresh flowers mixed with cold dank stone. This church had stood here for seven hundred years looking out on the temperamental North Sea, while deep below the layers of black coal lay waiting to be roused like a beast from sleep. She shivered to think that she was a part of it: the cycle of birth and growing up, of grafting and striving, of decay and dying that had gone on for centuries in this ancient corner of County Durham. What would her contribution be? *A measly part time job in a second rate boutique.* For a moment she yearned for something greater, something exciting that would make a difference.

'Come on Auntie Carol,' David said, 'we've got to go in the cupboard now.'

She had hardly been aware of the marriage ceremony and now it was over; Fay, Vic and her father were heading for the vestry. Guiltily she grabbed the boys' hands. Fay was so garrulous with relief and Vic his usual jovial self that Carol did not have to say anything or pretend it had been a wonderful moment. And yet, in a strange way it had been. Carol laughed at herself; must have had a touch of the sun.

Following the jubilant bride and groom out of the vestry and past the throng of floppy wedding hats and eager faces, Carol squeezed the hands of her new nephews and grinned in anticipation of the expensive reception at Brandon

Castle.

Mick Todd climbed from the diesel train that had taken him five miles from the coalface and got into the two-decker cage. With a signal from the onsetter, the men coming off shift rocketed up the shaft to the surface and emerged, hot and grimy, in the blinding sun.

'Out the night?' he asked his friend, Sid Armstrong, as they made their way towards the newly refurbished pithead baths. His head still rang with the underground noises of cutting machines and water sprays, diesel locomotives and the whir of the belt conveyors. His orange overalls stuck to his broad back and sweat trickled in rivulets down his blackened face. The thought of a Saturday night's drinking quickened his step.

'Aye,' Sid agreed, spitting dust out of his parched throat. 'Fancy a trip over Quarryhill? Or we could gan on the bike to Whittledene and drink round the pubs there.'

'I was thinking of a quiet pint at the club and a game of pool,' Mick snorted, as they trudged past the preparation plant, 'not driving you all over County Durham on *my* bike.'

'Where's your sense of adventure, Toddy man? We can take my Capri if you like. I know,' Sid's dirty face broke into a grin under his thin moustache, 'let's gan over to Brandon Castle and gate-crash the wedding.'

In front of them a train emerged slowly from the towering coal bunker, its trucks loaded with coal, and drowned out Mick's blunt reply. They continued to argue as they peeled off wet overalls and scrubbed off the day's grime in the showers.

'We might get a few free drinks out of old man Shannon – he's bound to be in a good mood with having Vic Proud's bank balance in the family,' Sid said, pulling on clean jeans and a short-sleeved t-shirt with a faded Genesis motif.

Mick rubbed vigorously at his long fair hair. 'You'll not catch me scrounging off the Shannons; just a bunch of jumped-up snobs whose family sold out to the bosses years ago.'

'Bloody hell, you sound just like your old man,' Sid laughed. 'I don't give a toss who's not speaking to who, as long as there's free booze flowing. All that carry-on between your dad and Shannon is ancient history anyway.'

'Not to my dad, it's not,' Mick answered with a stubborn look on his clean-shaven face. He laced up his trainers and pulled on his worn leather jacket, not bothering to comb his hair, waiting while Sid combed his dark hair in the mirror. Mick was resigned to his hair receding, but his workmate spent anxious minutes every day checking his temples for signs of premature ageing. Sid had done so since their days in secondary school, Mick thought with amusement, and would probably continue to do so until they came to cart him off to the old folks' home.

Sid inspected his comb for fallen hairs. 'Well if you won't come I'll find someone who's willing.'

'Oh aye,' Mick snorted, 'like Kelly Laws, you mean.'

'Maybe,' Sid flushed. 'At least that lass knows how to have a good time, which is more than can be said for you, you miserable bugger.'

Mick sprang over and ruffled Sid's hair, pulling him backwards. Mick was smaller but stocky and well-muscled and deceptively strong. They were on the floor and wrestling in seconds.

'Lay off us man!' Sid shouted, struggling off the wet floor. He grabbed a can of shaving foam and aimed it at Mick. Mick retaliated with a wet towel and brought him down again.

'Steady lads,' Stan Savage, one of the older face workers, warned them. 'I wish you showed half as much talent on the rugby pitch.'

Mick swore cheerfully at their team coach but released Sid from an arm lock. The men grabbed their kit bags and swung out of the mine gates together into the baked streets of Brassbank. The heat hung hazily over the village and the sea had disappeared in mist. The monotonous bellow of a fog horn competed with the merry jingles of an ice-cream van somewhere in the maze of terraced streets. Children were in the back lanes playing hopscotch and French skipping and banging footballs off yard walls where goal mouths had been chalked. Two girls sped by on roller skates, blowing balloons of bubble gum as puce as their hot cheeks. One of them waved but was gone before Mick realised it was his younger sister Linda. Doors and windows stood open gasping for air and bleached, bone-dry washing hung in yards.

As the men went up the street, they saw that a group of drinkers at the Red Lion, rosy-cheeked from sunburn and liquor, had spilled outside with their pints. The smell of hops wafted to them on the hot air and beckoned them to quench their thirst.

'Just one, eh?' Sid suggested, already dropping his bag from his shoulder.

Mick grinned, thinking this was how so many Saturday night binges with Sid had started in the past.

'Aye, just one.'

By the time Mick reached home, the intense heat had gone out of the day and he found his mother and Auntie Val sitting on the back steps of the neat yard, smoking in the evening sun. His motorbike leant against the wall, covered in tarpaulin and surrounded by pungent-smelling boxes of red and white geraniums.

'I've got to say, she was a lovely bride,' Val chattered. 'That dress must've cost a fortune - I'd say hundreds – and that's just for starters.'

'Yes,' his mother agreed. 'Think of the pageboys' outfits.'

'I wish she'd bought them at my boutique,' Val said ruefully. 'And the bridesmaid's dress was a picture. Funny seeing Carol Shannon in a dress – doesn't happen often.'

Lotty Todd gave a short laugh. 'Looked like butter wouldn't melt! But we all know better. I don't know why you let her work in the shop. You say she's always late or skiving off.'

'Carol's a nice girl underneath the wild image,' Val defended. 'And I bet she wouldn't act so daft if her parents paid her an ounce of attention.'

Lotty ground out her cigarette and stood up to greet her son, pulling at her short cotton skirt.

'Hello pet, tea's in the fridge; ham salad and potatoes. I didn't want it curling up in the heat. Been for a drink with Sid?'

Mick nodded and grinned. 'And you've been nosing at all the posh folk, by the sounds of it. Don't let Dad hear.'

Lotty fiddled with her fading fair hair. 'Oh, what's the harm in it? Anyway, your father's been up at the allotment all day. If I didn't know better, I'd think he was keeping a woman up there, the hours he spends.'

'Honestly Lotty,' Val laughed, 'he's making the most of the good weather.'

Mick kept to himself that his father spent most of his time with his feet up, reading newspapers and library books in his corrugated shed. He followed his mother into the kitchen. In the late sixties, when the Coal Board had installed inside toilets and bathrooms in the houses in Septimus Street, they had knocked the tiny scullery and kitchen into one. His mother got rid of the old range that she had battled with for over twenty years and installed a new gas cooker, as well as a fridge instead of the cold slab in the larder. Lotty was keen on any gadgetry going: an electric mixer two years ago, a telephone at the bottom of the stairs and a teasmaid in the bedroom last Christmas. Mick recalled recent skirmishes with his father over gas central heating.

'Nice and clean, Charlie,' Lotty had argued. 'No more coal dust or need to decorate every year.'

'We work down a pit,' Charlie had protested. 'Coal is a perk of the job – keeps the boiler red-hot. Whoever heard of a colliery house without coal?'

'We could still keep a coal fire for winter evenings,' she had bargained. But Charlie had refused to discuss it further and gone off to the allotment muttering, 'Gas, you bugger.'

Mick slung his leather jacket over the back of a chair and sat down while his mother fetched his tea. Val followed, tidying up from the table the Simplicity dress pattern she had brought to show her sister. She hung Mick's jacket on a peg behind the door, with a look that said he should have done it himself, then spoke.

'There's a new three-screen cinema opened in Whittledene, Lesley was saying.'

Mick knew his aunt was about to organise him into taking her. 'You and Mam should get yourselves over there and see something then,' he answered, starting on the buttered bread. 'Dad down the club now? Thought I might join him for a pint.'

Yes,' Lotty said, 'he's been over to fetch Grandda and take him for a game of dominoes.' She poured him a mug of tea. 'You're not meeting Sid again?'

'No, he's got this daft idea of going over to Brandon Castle and the wedding reception.'

Val gave a throaty laugh. 'He can't do that; he's not invited.'

'Anything for a free drink,' Mick grunted, tucking into his food.

His mother sighed, 'I worry for that lad. He used to be sensible at school, but since he started mixing with Kelly Laws and her type, he's gone off the rails.'

'He's just going to scrounge and drink or two,' Mick defended, 'hardly a hanging offence.'

'And there's that time with the motorbike,' she reminded. 'He had no right to take it without you knowing – could've killed himself or that lass.'

'All right, let's not drag that up again. Sid paid for the repairs.'

But his appetite faded with the reminder of Sid's recklessness. They'd gone drinking at neighbouring village Quarryhill and he'd decided to abandon the bike for the night. Somehow Sid got hold of the keys, driven it home with Kelly on the back and crashed into a ditch. Miraculously, both had walked away with only cuts and bruises, yet it had shaken Mick more than his friend, haunted by the thought that someone could have been killed. If he hadn't drunk so much he could have driven the bike safely home himself.

Kelly was bad-mouthed by many in the village – branded wayward and loose – but Mick quite liked her. She'd had a hard time, losing her mother as a small child and coping with a drunkard for a father. People didn't make enough allowance for Kelly having to grow up too quickly.

Mick pushed his plate away, noticing the look passing between mother and aunt. Was it so obvious that he avoided taking the bike out these days? Both Val and Sid kept thinking up excuses to get him out on it again. Well, he hadn't lost his nerve, he just wasn't going to take anyone for a spin when he'd had a few pints already.

'I said I'd meet some of the lads for a game of pool,' he said, getting up and grabbing his jacket. 'See you later.'

As he left he heard his mother say, 'I'll fetch Linda in and we can all go to the pictures. It'll have to be local – I don't want the bairn out too late – and Charlie'll want his supper later.'

Mick felt a stab of guilt and hesitated on the back steps. Lotty added, 'Thanks for trying, Val. I don't know why he's so sensitive about the bike; it's not as if he was even on it when it crashed. What's the use of having it standing in the yard unused?'

Mick strode across the yard without a glance at his neglected Yamaha, jacket over shoulder. Lotty watched him go from the kitchen window.

'Well, it's up to him what he does with it,' Val said.

Lotty sighed, saddened for her son. He had always been the easy one, unlike her forthright husband or rebellious cheeky daughter. Mick was uncomplicated and bashfully affectionate; popular with the other men because he fitted in. He would never be a leader like his father, but always a loyal and reliable follower and a good team member, as he had proved with the village rugby team. Until the motorbike episode, Mick had been as happy-go-lucky as Sid; now his youthfulness was dented and at twenty-three he seemed to carry the cares of the world. This sensitivity had surprised Lotty and she wondered if there was a side to Mick that had gone unnoticed in those busy years of rearing her family.

Just then, she heard someone whistling an Elvis song and Eddy Todd, her brother-in-law, went swaggering past the gate in his outdated winkle-picker shoes and velvet-collared jacket; his sideburns grey but dark hair still slicked back with Brylcreem. He caught her looking and blew a kiss. Eddy in turned-up, well-pressed jeans, ready for a night out, could always lift the spirits. She waved back. He was an irresponsible spendthrift, an ageing Teddy Boy whom kids on their chopper bikes would trail and exchange good-humoured insults, yet Lotty knew he was the kind of man who would do anything for anyone.

'There goes Eddy off to paint the town red.'

'Lesley with him?' asked Val, coming to the window.

'No, Lesley was invited to the wedding disco remember?'

'I think it was small-minded not inviting Eddy with her – they've been going out for donkey's years.'

'Yes, she deserves a long-service medal,' laughed Lotty. 'But it's no surprise;

he's a Todd. Shannons wouldn't want one of us within a hundred miles of their precious wedding.'

'It hurts you, doesn't it? Specially us being cousins of Nancy's. I shouldn't have dragged you up there to see it; I was just been nosy.'

'Course you were; so was I. You wouldn't think Nancy and I had been close - went to Sunday school together. But she's wiped twenty years of growing up from her memory. I can't stand that in people – being ashamed of where they come from. So don't worry, I wanted to be standing as near Nancy Shannon as I could and let her see that there's no getting away from the past – at least not from Lotty Todd.'

Val gave her sister's arm a squeeze; she always covered her hurt with fighting words. 'Let me treat you to the pictures.'

Lotty smiled, smoothing hands over her piled up hair. One day soon she really must get rid of her beehive hairstyle; Charlie had never approved of it even in the sixties when it was fashionable.

'Give me a minute to change skirts. Haven't been out to the films since that one with Robert Redford – *The Buzz* or something.'

The Sting,' Val laughed. 'It's time you had a night out; I'll go and fetch Linda.'

Lotty hurried upstairs, thinking defiantly that however much Nancy was lording it over Brassbank today with her expensive clothes and flashy cars, Lotty was the richer woman when it came to family. She loved her children with a passion. Not for the world would she swap them for the snobbish Fay or that wild, feckless one with the way-out clothes: Carol.

CHAPTER 2

The champagne had gone to Carol's head. She had allowed herself to dance to *Chirpy Chirpy Cheep Cheep* with Vic's spotty fifteen year-old cousin, Dan Hardman, and now he was dragging her out of her seat again for the *Bay City Rollers*.

She had long discarded her hairband of fake flowers and ankle-strap shoes, but Fay had insisted she keep wearing her bridesmaid's dress until after she'd gone. It was nearly nine in the evening and Fay and Vic were still here.

'Let's dance all night,' Dan shouted as he bumped into people on the polished dance floor.

Carol watched him play air guitar under the swirling disco lights, thinking it must still be light outside. The room, with its mock medieval tapestries and prickly velvet seats, was stifling. Her father was quick-stepping among the disco dancers, red face running with sweat, while her mother held court among Vic's family. She had been imprisoned in the banqueting hall for hours; two suits of armour at the door had cigars stuck through their visors and somehow her crown of silk flowers had ended up on a helmet.

When the music changed tempo, Carol extracted herself from Dan, bellowing in his ear that she needed the bathroom and would be gone ages because of the dress. Hoisting up her skirts, she ran past a room full of diners in medieval costume and bibs throwing food at each other and upstairs, searching in vain for the room where she'd left her white jeans and cheesecloth shirt. Giving up, she returned below just as her friend Kelly was trying to talk her way in at the entrance.

'But we're not wearing jeans,' Kelly was protesting, bulging out of a red skirt and stripy t-shirt.

'The gentleman is wearing a denim jacket,' said the doorman.

'He'll take it off then.'

Carol saw Kelly pull the sleeve of the man beside her, recognising the handsome miner, Sid Armstrong from Mafeking Terrace where Kelly lived. A few years their senior, Kelly had begun to see more of him since some incident with a motorbike about which her friend had been evasive.

'And no training shoes allowed,' the doorman added.

Carol thought Sid was about to lose his temper, so hurried forward, tripping on her hem.

'They're with me,' she cried, almost falling headlong into them. 'Shannons' wedding – they're evening guests.'

Kelly struggled to keep a straight face; Carol knew she must look like a dishevelled pantomime fairy. The doorman hesitated, then without a change to his superior expression, stood aside. 'On you go then,' he sniffed and turned his back.

'You look like you've been pushed in the pool.' Kelly giggled.

'I know, I'm lathered,' Carol said, feeling her damp hair, quite fallen out of its ponytail and linked an arm through her friend's.

'Been a canny do then?' Sid grinned.

'Just as expected – hot and hellish. I've been trying to get away from a kid with acne for the last hour.'

'Well show us where the action is,' said Sid.

'Sid's on the scrounge,' Kelly teased.

'I'll pay my way. I'm just interested in a late bar.'

'Any bar, you mean,' Kelly said, linking her other arm through his.

'This way to the dungeons then,' Carol said with a grin.

The evening picked up. Nancy was prevented from making a fuss at the uninvited guests by Carol's father immediately buying them drinks and Vic making a fuss of Kelly, whose father was one of his coach drivers.

Finally, Fay and Vic made a grand departure with the guests following them out onto the steps of Brandon Castle to wave them away.

'Look after Mum and Dad, won't you?' Fay urged Carol, growing suddenly tearful. 'I'm leaving home and you're all they've got now.'

'You're only going for two weeks; they can't get up to much trouble in that time.'

Fay grabbed her in a surprise hug. 'They need you, especially Mother. Don't do anything silly. I'll miss you, little sister. I love you.'

Carol squirmed. 'Hey, how much have you been drinking? I'll be up the road to pester you more than you'll want.'

Vic came over to extract his new wife. 'Come on doll; let's get this honeymoon underway.'

He winked at Carol and she wondered if she was the only guest thinking the same thoughts: would they do it tonight? Had they already done it? And what did big, bearded, hairy-armed Vic look like without his clothes on? She hoped his shrewd grey eyes didn't mean he could mind-read; there was something too knowing about him, too confident in his own charm. It made her stomach twist and she wasn't sure if she secretly fancied or really disliked him.

'Bye, little sister,' he smiled, leaning over and putting an arm about her. Very briefly, he kissed her full on the lips; a moist possessive kiss, and then let her go. Turning to hail someone else, his arm now firmly around Fay, he left Carol shaking.

'Well!' Kelly smirked.

'Well what?'

'That wasn't a very brotherly kiss.'

'He's kissing everyone like that.'

'Not me, mores the pity,' Kelly sighed and leaned on her friend. 'Hey, you're shaking.'

'It's chilly.' Carol watched her mother and Fay having a very public emotional parting; she would be hearing about this day for the next decade.

'It's the hottest night of the year,' Kelly said, dropping her voice. 'You're trembling with passion for Victor.'

'Get off,' Carol laughed, pushing her away.

'I know the signs. I don't half fancy him myself.'

'You fancy anything in trousers.'

'Or out of them.' Kelly gave a raucous laugh.

They waved at the revving sports car, bedecked with balloons, trailing cans and a message sprayed by Simon and best man, Pete Fletcher: *Now for a bit of son and heir.* Carol's insides fluttered again at the thought of sex. She was confused by her sudden interest in Vic and guilty towards Fay for even thinking it. Champagne made her randy about the wrong people; she'd stick to lager in future.

At the last moment, Fay shouted, 'Carol, catch this!' and hurled her bridal bouquet out of the open-topped car. It was a command to be the next one married, preferably to someone rich and responsible who would 'clip her wings', as her mother sourly put it. But Carol made no attempt to catch it. She didn't want all that; she wanted freedom and fun with no commitment or responsibility for anyone else – just a bit more of that funny feeling in her guts when a grown man kissed her.

'Look, I've caught it,' Kelly squealed, crushing the limp blooms to her large bosom.

Carol saw the look of disgust curling down the edges of her mother's mouth, before Nancy turned to wave her favourite daughter away with tears in her eyes. As the car roared down the drive, rattling cans, honking horn and spraying gravel, her mother gave way to loud sobs and even permitted Ben to put a comforting arm about her.

'My baby's gone for ever!'

Guests flocked around, offering tipsy words of comfort. Vic's old school friend and best man, Pete Fletcher, watched with detached interest. Tall and thin, with a sensuous mouth and wire-rimmed glasses – Carol heard he was a journalist – he gave her an amused smile and joined the group.

'She's in safe hands, Mrs Shannon, so lets go inside and toast the happy couple again before the bar closes.'

'Well said,' Ben Shannon agreed and the two men steered Nancy back up the steps.

Sid appeared at Carol's side. 'Sounds like good advice to me, eh girls?'

But Carol felt suddenly flat; excluded by her mother's scene in the driveway. Nancy would never be that upset for her – would probably set off fireworks in celebration at being rid of her. Carol couldn't fathom what it was about her that so irritated her mother, while Fay and Simon could do no wrong. Maybe all families were like that; some members were just harder to love than others and she was one of those that was lacking.

'Let's go somewhere else,' she urged, 'like down the beach.'

'Can we take some of your dad's booze with us?' Sid asked.

'Leave that to me – once I've got changed out of this fairy costume.'

'Pity,' he grinned, 'it suits you.'

Carol glanced at Kelly but her friend gave an exaggerated wink and didn't seem to mind Sid flirting.

'Well tough, it turns into rags at midnight,' she laughed. 'Come with me Kelly.'

The two girls set off at a run up the stairs; no one seemed to be interested in them. With Kelly's help Carol managed to find the room where she'd left her clothes and in two minutes flat she had discarded the dress and petticoats and was pulling on her jeans with relief. They felt like old friends, comfortably hugging her, fraying flares at the bottom tickling her bare feet.

As she buttoned up her shirt, Kelly said, 'I'm not going out with Sid, you know, we're just mates. Same street sort of thing.'

'Oh?' Carol kept her voice light. She grabbed a hairbrush and pulled it through her long brown hair, dragging on her cropped fringe to try and lengthen it.

'So he's yours if you want him,' Kelly spelled it out.

Carol laughed. 'Does he have any say in it?'

'Seems to me he's taken a shine to you already - all that pink frilly lace driving him wild.'

Carol hit Kelly playfully with the brush. But a spark of excitement lit inside. 'Let's be off then, before Dad puts a stop to it.'

They hurried downstairs to find Sid had already negotiated an armful of cans from her father and Carol was thankful she did not have to return inside the fetid disco and risk a confrontation with either parent. As they clattered down the steps and out into the warm night air, a figure wobbled in front of them. It was young Dan Hardman and from the look of his pasty face, he had just thrown up in the bushes. He caught sight of Carol and lurched towards her.

'Carol! Where you going?'

She recoiled at the smell of vomit on his breath. 'We're off to the beach,' she said, sidestepping.

He put out a hand to steady himself on her. 'Let me come.'

Kelly pushed him away. 'Sod off, zit-head, you're too young.'

Dan's ill-looking face looked offended then angry. 'I wasn't asking you, fat git. I was asking Carol.'

Carol realised Dan was about to get dumped in the bushes by an irate Kelly, but before she could intervene, Sid stepped in.

'Listen, lad, get yourself back inside. Carol doesn't want you hanging on, can't you see that? Looks like you've had a skinful, any road.'

Dan looked at them all with hostility.

'Aye, go back to your mam and dad,' Kelly needled. 'Don't want them worrying about you.'

He turned and spat at her and then threw Carol a reproachful look.

'I'll see you around, Dan - at the next family party,' Carol said, forcing a smile.

But Dan just sniffed hard and pushed past her. Kelly and Sid grabbed Carol and hurried her off towards the car park, chattering and laughing. Carol glanced back, hoping that Dan couldn't hear what was being said about him by the other two. She saw him standing illuminated on the gravel, wavering unsteadily and looking very ill. For a moment she felt bad about leaving him out, but smothered her guilt by telling herself that she'd cause no end of trouble in her parents' eyes if she let the fifteen-year-old go with her. She plunged into the dark with Kelly and Sid, too far away to see the look of bitter disappointment on Dan Hardman's wretched face.

Chapter Three

After drinking with his father and Grandda Bowman, Mick bumped into his Uncle Eddy and was enticed to The Ship for a drink - Eddy's favourite pub on account of the beer and the dated selection on the old jukebox. The Ship was run by a retired merchant seaman who had been on the convoys to Russia during the Second World War. The walls were covered in nicotine-stained photographs of old cruisers and frigates ploughing through rough waters. Captain Lenin, as he was affectionately named because he'd once been ashore in Murmansk, kept Eddy's tankard behind the bar and was pouring foaming beer into it from a hand pump the moment he saw his 'regular' at the open door.

'Good evening, comrades,' he called, in a voice that penetrated like a fog horn across the smoky interior.

'Evening, Captain!' Eddy replied. 'A pint for young Mick here an' all, please.'

'Coming up,' growled their host, in his deep tobacco voice.

Eddy sauntered over to the jukebox, not completely at home until he'd chosen a few favourites. They were all his singles anyway, brought to the pub over the last twenty years and installed as if in his own sitting room, which was largely how he treated the front bar of The Ship. Captain Lenin was a widower and happy to oblige, having no cosy private hearth to retreat to and no one to keep him company but a bad-tempered parrot who swore at him in Polish, Russian and Arabic.

As Nat King Cole's honeyed voice began to croon, 'When I Fall In Love', Eddy strolled back and claimed his pint, closing his eyes and taking a deep satisfying drink. He and the Captain fell to talking about football and the approaching start of the season and what Newcastle's chances might be. Eddy quizzed the Captain about his new dinghy and soon they were back reliving the days when Lenin had taken a youthful Eddy out fishing on his spells of leave and they'd returned with fish which his Polish wife Wanda had gutted and rolled in oatmeal and fried for their tea.

'Nowt like a fresh fish,' Eddy said, with a smack of his lips. 'Mind you, the fish stocks were always safe from me. Best thing I ever caught was a starfish, if I remember rightly. I'd not survive on a desert island, I tell you. Not without your beer either, Captain.'

His host took the hint and refilled Eddy's tankard. They talked more of fish and discussed the cod war with Iceland. Mick picked up his pint. Soon they would be off on more reminiscences around the high seas and he suddenly felt the urge for fresh air. He nodded towards the back and murmured he was going outside.

'Join you in a minute, Mick lad,' Eddy called after him.

At the back of the pub was a small uneven garden with a couple of weatherbeaten benches, a stone sundial and a weathervane in the shape of a ship. There was a row of salty-looking garden gnomes painted in naval uniforms sheltering behind a white fence. It was an eccentric, jolly garden, quite suited to its owner, and it was deserted, which suited Mick's strangely melancholic mood.

Mick breathed in the powerful scent of roses that hung in the warm air and, resting his elbows on the fence, looked out over the rough grazing land to the sea beyond. The haze of the afternoon had lifted to reveal a mysterious and molten sea, reflecting the last of the sun. Out in the depths, the lights of a passing vessel winked in the twilight and crept silently on. To his left lay the pit. Behind him wafted the strains of Ella Fitzgerald. Mick felt deeply at peace for the first time in weeks and, as he drank his pint in the evening calm, tried to work out just what it was that had been bothering him.

He sat on the bench for an age before the tranquillity was abruptly broken by the roar of a car churning up the dust along the main road behind him, accompanied by the jangle of tin cans. The unseen car was blaring its horn through the village and he could hear shouts from drinkers in the street as it sped past. Turning, Mick caught a glimpse of the sports car's headlights as it tore up the far bank, off towards Quarryhill and away to the south.

'Victor Proud and his new missus,' Eddy said, sauntering out of the back door.

'Aye,' Mick grunted. 'Who else would be showing off his expensive motor like that?'

'Good luck to him, I say,' Eddy said amiably, 'if he's found the right woman.'

Mick smirked at his uncle. 'And what about you, Eddy? Is Lesley Paxton going to be the next Mrs Todd?'

Eddy was quiet for all of three seconds, then laughed off the question. 'Lesley's far too good a lass for the likes of me - I keep telling her so.'

Mick grinned. 'So does Mam.' He thought of the cheerful, dark-haired Lesley who supervised the pit canteen and seemed to be able to organise everything in her life except the capricious Eddy.

'And what about you, bonny lad?' Eddy turned the tables on his nephew. 'Haven't seen you courting for a while.'

'Not interested.'

'Course you are.' Eddy nudged him. 'It's not like you to be hanging around with your old uncle. You should be out with the lads like you normally are. Where's that Sid Armstrong the night?'

'Gate-crashing the Shannon wedding,' Mick snorted. 'Drinking as much of old man Shannon's beer as he can get down his neck, most likely.'

Eddy laughed. 'Good on him! Hope he has one for all of us. Shannon gets enough sweat and toil out of us every day of the week.'

Mick looked at his uncle in surprise at the sharpness in his tone, but his face in the dusk looked merry.

'You should've gone too, Mick lad.'

'Not in a million years!' Mick answered stoutly. 'Not after what the Shannons did to the Todds.'

'By, you sound like that bugger Charlie sometimes.'

'Well, Dad's right,' Mick defended. 'We're the products of our own history, and the Todds and the Shannons have a long and bitter one. I'll not go licking Shannon's arse for any amount of free beer.'

'Perish the thought, bonny lad,' Eddy laughed, clapping him on the shoulder. 'Tell you what. You keep fighting for the rights of the Todds and the working man, and I'll fight me way to the bar for another round, eh?'

As Mick was about to answer, another car roared through the village, hooting out a jingle on its horn. Even before they saw the pale blue metallic Capri, Eddy and Mick looked at each other and chorused, 'Sid!'

'I've seen some strange sights,' Eddy chortled, 'but Sid Armstrong going off on

16

honeymoon with Victor Proud has got to take the prize.'

The Capri shot past the end of the pub, windows down and Status Quo blasting from its dark interior. Mick was sure he caught a glimpse of Kelly's grinning face and shock of red hair at the passenger window and felt a punch in his stomach. Revelation hit him like a giant wave breaking over his head and left him feeling sick.

Eddy saw his expression and said kindly, 'they'll be ganin' down the beach. Why don't you leg it after them?'

Mick could feel himself flushing. Did Eddy realise that he was jealous of Sid over Kelly Laws? He had told himself that Kelly was a daft overgrown kid, with a dangerous appetite for mixing it with the lads, and he hadn't cared a damn that Sid had taken her off on his motorbike without his permission to wherever they'd gone. But he realised now he had cared. He'd been trying to get off with Kelly at the disco in Quarryhill, but had got roaring drunk because she seemed more interested in Sid. And Sid had gone off on his bike with her and pranged it.

Mick tore his gaze away from where the Capri had disappeared from view. 'No,' he said, trying to sound unconcerned, 'let them get on with it. If Sid's playing Quo, he's already halfway to having his evil way with someone. I'd rather join you and the Captain in the Battle of Jutland, or whatever it was you were talking about.'

'Wrong war, Mick lad. For a working-class historian, you're bloody terrible on facts.' Eddy's lived-in face looked teasing. He grabbed his nephew round the neck and pulled him forward. 'Come on, who cares about Status bloody Quo? I feel an attack of Johnny Matthis coming on. Let's gan inside and liven up that jukebox. Did I ever tell you about the time I was in action during National Service?'

'You didn't see any action,' Mick laughed as he allowed himself to be steered inside by his slightly-built uncle.

'There was plenty action in the bars of Portsmouth, I can tell you!' As they re-entered the pub, Eddy began one of his colourful stories. 'Did I tell you about the time I met Elvis Presley?'

Mick had heard the story countless times before but he encouraged Eddy to tell it again. For a while, it made him forget what might be taking place on the beach below.

In the dark it was not so obvious that the sand was blackened with the dregs from the pit, spewed out further up the beach. There were those who collected small coals from the shoreline like beachcombers, but the only ones there at this time of night were Carol and Sid and Kelly - and Roxy Music blaring out of the car parked above them. They made a small fire and sat round it drinking from the cans that Sid had salvaged from the wedding party and smoking Kelly's Embassy cigarettes. Sid had a packet of cards and settled for a game of three card brag when the girls refused to play strip poker.

When the tape on the car cassette stopped, Kelly struggled up and said she wanted to put on something they could dance to. While she was away, Sid rolled closer to Carol and grinned at her beneath his dark moustache.

'I've always been a bit frightened of you, Carol Shannon,' he teased in a low voice.

Carol laughed. 'Oh, yeah? You look terrified.'

Sid put out a hand and pushed her hair behind her right ear. Carol felt herself tingle at the touch.

'I was! You being Shannon's daughter. A lot of the lads feel the same. But Kelly said you were just like one of us. Still, I never guessed I'd end up on the beach with you like this.'

'Like what?' Carol smiled, her green eyes laughing at him.

'Right cosy and dying to kiss that big mouth of yours,' Sid whispered. Then he leaned over and kissed her.

For the second time that evening, Carol found herself being unexpectedly embraced, but this time she relished the excitement inside and the feel of Sid's strong mouth on hers. He tasted beery and his moustache tickled as his kiss became bolder, but she responded happily. Sid was good-looking and fun and it was high summer and this was the best thing that had happened all day, perhaps all year, Carol thought dreamily as she relaxed back on to the black sand. Above them, the sound of 10CC pulsated out of the car and Carol thought she heard Kelly talking to herself in the dark. Then Sid's hands brought her thoughts back to the beach and she wondered how far she should let him go.

'He's down there. We've got some lager left.'

Carol became aware of Kelly's voice again and suddenly realised by the sound of heavy feet that her best friend was not alone. She pushed Sid away and sat up, her heart still pounding from the feel of Sid's mouth and hands on her. It must be her brother Simon or someone come to tell her off and drag her home and show her up in front of her friends.

Sid gave her a rueful look before glancing over her shoulder.

'Hello, marra! Come to spoil the fun at last?' he called.

'I found him lurking in the dunes,' Kelly teased as she pushed someone down the gully. 'Said he was on his way home.'

Carol had an impression of a stocky man with long fair hair, jumping down on to the beach.

'Me and Uncle Eddy are on our way home. I've lost Eddy somewhere having a leak. It was his bright idea to take a short cut along the beach.'

Carol could see his face now, illuminated by the firelight: a strong, square face with piercing eyes that seemed to be regarding her with a strange fierce look. It made her shift uncomfortably and draw her knees up to her chest, her long hair falling over her face in protection.

'Daft old Eddy,' Sid laughed, 'probably halfway to Hartlepool by now.'

'Haway and sit down, Mick,' Kelly insisted, plonking herself down on the cool sand. 'Here's a can.' She opened it for him and pushed it at his mouth, easing herself closer to him. Carol observed his awkwardness but thought he seemed quite pleased at Kelly's fussing. She certainly has a way with men, Carol thought in amusement.

Sid turned to her and put a casual arm around her back. 'Hey, marra, this is Carol - Carol Shannon.' Carol blushed with pleasure, realising Sid was showing her off.

'Aye,' Mick answered stiffly. 'Kelly told me who it was.'

Carol bristled at the way Sid's friend was giving her that cold stare again. What was his problem? Sid seemed not to notice.

'Carol, this is my mate, Mick. We work together down the pit. Wouldn't pass the time of day with the bugger otherwise,' Sid joked. 'He plays a shocking game of pool, and he supports Newcastle. All the Todds do - it's a family failing.'

'Supporting Sunderland shows your brain's failing, Sid Armstrong,' Mick quipped back.

Realisation dawned on Carol. This was Mick Todd, Sid's close friend, whom Kelly had talked about as one of the many blokes she fancied. Val Bowman, her employer and also Mick's aunt, had pointed him out before, passing the boutique window, but he'd usually been helmeted on a motorbike and Carol had not been interested anyway. The Todds had a grudge against her father's family for some reason and they were all too bolshie to speak to her. When the mother came into the shop she was stand-offish and insisted on being dealt with by Val. And as for the younger girl, Linda, she would stick out her tongue or screw chewing gum under the counter when Val was not looking and Carol would invariably get it on her hands or clothes after the kid had gone.

And here was the eldest of the tribe, giving her bonehead looks. She had a sudden desire to make him dislike her further. It was the devil in her, she was always being told, but if people had a bad opinion of her, it merely made her the more mischievous.

'One of the famous Todds, eh?' she said, unwinding her legs and leaning on Sid's shoulder. 'I've heard a lot about them from me dad. You'd fight with your own shadows, he says. But you don't approve of us Shannons, do you, Mick?' she challenged. 'Something to do with ancient history - so far back they don't even teach it in school.'

'Too recent to teach in school, you mean,' Mick snapped back. 'Nineteen twenty-six was only fifty years ago.'

'Long before I was born,' Carol smirked.

'Well, perhaps if you bothered to find out something about what happened before you were born, you might not sound so cocky. But then I wouldn't expect a lass like you to care a toss about the village or the pit or the people who support your comfortable life. Bet you didn't even notice the strike here two years ago!'

'Steady on, marra!' Sid intervened.

'You've no right to say that, you know nothing about my life,' Carol protested hotly. She stood up, quite ruffled by his aggression.

Kelly waved her down. 'Stop getting your knickers in a twist! You started it.'

Carol was unsure what to do. If she sat down, she would feel humiliated, like a reprimanded child. She was sure that was what Mick Todd thought of her anyway, a spoilt little rich girl; it showed all over his disdainful face. He sat there now, impassive and sipping at the beer Kelly had given him. Well, damn him for spoiling her evening with Sid and Kelly, the first real fun she'd had for weeks.

'I'm going for a swim,' she suddenly announced. When cornered, she usually did something daft to get her out of the original trouble, Carol mocked herself, and this seemed daft enough just now.

'Swim?' Sid queried. 'You're mad.'

'I mean it,' Carol laughed, pulling off her trainers.

'She's mad and she means it,' Kelly said calmly. 'I've seen her go mental like this

19

before, specially on a full moon.'

Carol had her jeans off and was heading for the sea before anyone could stop her. 'Last one in's a moron!'

Sid laughed and called after her, 'Haway, Carol, and wait for me!' He struggled with his laces and fell around in the dark trying to peel off his clothes. 'Come on, Mick, get your clothes o-off,' he hiccupped.

'No, ta very much, I'm staying a dry moron,' Mick grunted.

'Oh, haway, Mick,' Kelly coaxed, 'it's a smashing night for a dip. I promise not to look while you take your kit off.'

Mick looked with annoyance at the shadowy figure at the cold water's edge, her white legs gleaming in the moonlight and long hair loose, and cursed Carol Shannon for upstaging him. He knew it was a challenge. Her actions were saying, *if you Todds are so hard then prove it; follow me into the icy North Sea.*

'Oh, hell,' Mick muttered and struggled to his feet. Kelly giggled with glee and kicking off her high heels ran straight for the sea in her skimpy disco clothing.

Carol was already half submerged. She gasped at the shock of cold water about her legs, but made an effort not to cry out. She would soon be numb and not feel a thing. With a final plunge she struck out into the black water, ducking her head beneath a sluggish wave. She came up with a cry of delight.

'It's great, Sid, get yourself in!' She watched a dark figure weave its way towards the sea. Carol laughed as he threw himself into the shallow water with a string of oaths about the North Sea. He floundered around like a puppy, splashing aimlessly in three inches of water and it suddenly occurred to Carol that he might not be able to swim. He seemed quite content to sit in the gentle waves and shout abuse at the others. With satisfaction, Carol noticed that Mick was being goaded into the sea by a shrieking Kelly. Now let's see how brave you are, Mick Todd, she thought.

Carol turned and struck out a bit further. She relished the feel of the dark water about her and the bright moon above, making the cliffs and sand dunes gleam with a ghostly light. For a few moments she was completely free from the carping of her relations and the censure of villagers like the Todds who condemned her without even knowing her just because she bore her father's name. There was just the sea and the dark beach and in the distance the lights of the pithead like a friendly beacon - permanent, reassuring, the heartbeat of Brassbank.

Carol was aware that the tide was swiftly coming in and if she swam round the finger of rocks to her right, her favourite rock pool would be full enough to swim in. It was known locally as Colly's Leap because there'd been a tradition of colliers jumping the rock pool as a feat of strength when Brassbank had first been sunk nearly a century ago. As a child she had spent hours down there with Simon, searching for crabs and filling an old shopping bag with the flotsam and jetsam of the sea. Fay had found the whole idea of playing on the polluted beach disgusting and had preferred to lie in the garden with a pile of romance comics, listening to the radio.

Carol disappeared round the side of the rocks and let the tide lift her into the deep rock pool. The sound of the sea echoed around the natural chamber like giant whisperings and Carol thought with amusement of the mermaids she had conjured up in her childish imaginings. It was so calm here, so peaceful, so mysterious . . .

Suddenly, to her right, she heard a thud and a heavy splash. She turned, grinning, expecting to see that Sid had pursued her round to the romantic pool, but there was no sign of him. She swam over to where she had heard the noise and strained to see in the dark. There seemed to be nothing and she thought it must have been something chucked in from over the rocks.

'Stop carrying on, Sid! Show yourself.'

There was no reply but Carol just caught a muffled sound above the sighing of the sea. She swam further under the cliff and saw one of the rocks move in the pool. All at once she realised it was a dark coat or jacket floating on the tide like a slick. A sudden panic seized her and her first reaction was to swim as fast as possible out of the pool away from the sinister sight. What if it was a person? What if it was a dead person? Carol froze. Then she heard the noise again, like a primeval cry, and something inside her forced her to go to the rescue.

It was a man, and he was submerged, head down in the seaweed, weighed down by a heavy jacket. She grabbed a rock to steady herself and pulled hard at the coat, turning his head out of the water. But he was too heavy to hold and she felt him sinking back again.

'Sid!' she yelled. 'Help me, for God's sake, help!'

Carol knew if she let go of the man he would sink out of sight, so weighted down was his clothing now. She launched herself into the water again and swam round him, trying to turn him and lift him and hold his head out of the water. At this, the man struggled and began to thrash with his arms. Carol felt a moment's relief that he was still alive, but panic rose again as he knocked her in the face and she went under the water herself.

Spluttering, she emerged and managed to scream, 'Sid, help us, please Sid!'

Then she felt the man grab feebly at her and take them both under the inky water. As her nose flooded, Carol was certain that this man was going to drown them both. She had no idea who he was or why he was here, but he was going to take her with him and her short, unremarkable life would end in Colly's Leap.

As she spluttered and heaved and tried to force them both on to the rocks, Carol had a vision of the headlines in the local paper, 'Drunken teenager drowns in sea escapade after wedding'. Perhaps Pete Fletcher, the sardonic reporter, would write her epitaph. What a fitting end for Carol Shannon, they would all think.

Everyone knew she was never going to come to any good. 'I told you so' would ring around the village. It rang in her ears now like a death knell . . .

Then, inexplicably, the drowning man pulled away from her and she found herself emerging again into the night air. Someone had hold of the half-conscious figure and was dragging him on to the rocks. She could hear him being rolled over. Carol flailed for the side, coughing and sobbing.

'Is he breathing?' It was Kelly asking.

There was a sound of the man throwing up.

'The bugger's alive!' Sid said. 'Thank God.'

'Thank Carol!' was Kelly's riposte. 'Is she all right?'

Carol gripped the rocks, spluttering and gasping for air. As she looked up, she felt strong hands grip her under her arms and heave her out of the water.

'Are you OK?'

She leaned back into wet arms, expecting to see Sid leaning over her but with shock saw that it was Mick Todd. Carol nodded, nauseous from the sea water, yet overcome by a sweet wave of relief that she was still alive and not a subject for the weekly newspaper after all. She was trembling with shock. She had had no idea how much she wanted to live until, for a brief moment, she thought life was about to be snatched away from her early by the black water. Carol started to shake.

She became aware of Mick rubbing her cold limbs and was suddenly embarrassed by the feel of his muscled arms round her, his glistening wet body so close. His long hair was wet and straggly and tickled her shoulders and she could feel the warmth of his breath on her face as he bent to see if she was recovering.

Carol pulled away, unnerved by the unexpected intimacy. 'I'm OK,' she panted and cleared her throat of salt water. 'Who is he?' She nodded towards the groaning man, now supported in Kelly's ample lap. Sid was wiping bile from the stranger's face.

'It's me Uncle Eddy,' Mick told her. 'You probably saved his life, Carol. You've saved the life of a Todd.'

She gave him a sharp look but saw the teasing in his vivid blue eyes - and something else that hadn't been there before. Perhaps it was just gratitude.

Carol managed a laugh. 'Throw him back in then.'

Sid came over and put his dry jacket round her. 'Hey, pet, you're shivering. You're a brave lass. I'd have dived in myself but I can't swim that well. Mick here has his uses.' He gave her a squeezing hug and kissed her wet head.

Carol welcomed the warmth, but noticed Mick glance away and the brief moment of closeness between them was broken. Perhaps she had imagined it anyway, in her relief at being rescued.

She watched him walk over to Eddy and begin to talk to him in a gentle, concerned way. Carol flushed in the dark to realise he was only dressed in underpants and had been sitting so close to her moments before. He wasn't tall, but he was broad and athletic in build and when his face smiled as it was now with his uncle, it struck her how good-looking he was.

By now Kelly had reappeared from the beach with dry clothes and was standing close to Mick, his leather jacket draped round her own shoulders.

'Get that sopping jacket off him,' she said. 'He'll catch his death.'

Eddy groaned. 'Watch what you're doing with that, it's me oldest friend,' he said, hanging on to his beloved velvet-collared coat. 'Eeh, I think I drank something bad.'

'Aye, half a gallon of sea water, you daft bugger!' Mick chided him. 'That's the last time I let you lead the way home. What were you doing over there, any road?'

'I don't know,' Eddy said groggily, looking confused.

'Trying to beat the Colly's record, eh, Mr Todd?' Kelly joked.

'Na, he was taking a piss and fell in,' Sid conjectured.

'I - I was - I think I was flying,' Eddy said, quite seriously.

'Drunk as a skunk!' Sid laughed.

'Come on, Uncle Eddy,' Mick said gently, helping him to his feet, 'let's get you home and dried off. Sid's car's just up the gully.'

'Feel free,' Sid said. 'Soak my seats.'

Kelly suddenly screeched. 'Eeh, I can't gan home like a drowned rat, me dad'll have a fit!'

Carol looked at her own bedraggled state and groaned, 'me too.'

'We'll all gan back to Mick's place then,' Sid announced. 'It's the nearest and your mam'll have summat the girls can put on. Then I'll drop them off home.'

They all looked at Mick for confirmation and saw the reluctance on his face.

'Haway, Mick,' Kelly smiled, 'we're all freezing. Look at Carol, she's going blue.'

'Aye, OK,' Mick agreed. 'Eddy better sleep at ours tonight any road. I don't trust him on his own.'

'Stop fussing, I'm all right, man,' Eddy complained.

'Oh, aye? Flying home, are you?' Sid snorted. He steered a shivering Carol towards the gully, keeping a protective arm about her.

Back at the car, Sid put Carol in the front seat beside him, while the others squeezed in the back. Carol noticed how close Kelly snuggled into Mick's shoulder and wondered why it should bother her in the least. She had more or less paired off with Sid Armstrong; she fancied him and was happy that he was making a fuss of her. So stop thinking about his friend, Carol told herself severely. You hated him on sight half an hour ago!

It was only when they bumped up the back lane of Septimus Street that Carol came out of her stupor and realised with a lurch that she was about to go into the Todds' house - the lion's den. She had been too numb with cold and shock to take it in before. She should have insisted on being dropped off first. Even a telling-off by her parents might be preferable, to the reception she was likely to receive in the Todd household. And what a state she must look! But it was too late, Sid was steering her out of the car and into the back yard, from where she could see lights on in the kitchen.

The door flew open and Lotty Todd stood on the back steps peering into the dark, her blonde hair piled high on her head, her small, neat body wrapped in a quilted dressing-gown.

'What in the world - ?' she gasped, catching sight of the sodden Eddy being helped in by Mick and Kelly. She gave a sharp look at the buxom girl in the wet skirt and T-shirt and then at her son.

'We were coming home by the beach. Eddy fell in,' Mick explained. 'Everyone's a bit wet, Mam.'

Lotty quickly decided that fuller explanations could wait and she bustled them into the kitchen. Within half a minute she had the kettle on, towels fetched out of the airing cupboard, shoes steaming on the hearth and an open-mouthed Linda, woken by the noise, despatched upstairs for dry clothing. Lotty noticed with alarm that the other bedraggled girl was Carol Shannon, which confirmed her suspicions that where that girl and Kelly Laws appeared together, there was bound to be trouble. But at least Carol seemed to be with Sid Armstrong, she noted with relief. He was being very attentive towards her.

When she had shooed the girls upstairs to change in the bathroom, bundled the men's wet clothes into the scullery and administered mugs of piping hot tea, Lotty perched herself on the arm of Mick's chair and demanded details.

Carol and Kelly reappeared with a garrulous Linda, squeezed into a jumble of Lotty's clothing: flowery blouses, mini skirt and camel-coloured trouser suit. Carol thought they looked like sixties dancers from Top of the Pops and wanted to laugh. Mick was just finishing his story.

'Sit yourselves down by the fire, lasses,' Lotty ordered and thrust mugs of tea into their cold hands. 'What a carry-on! I hear we've you to thank for saving our Eddy.' She fixed Carol with her no-nonsense look. 'That was a very brave thing to do. Very brave! Thank you, pet. I've already told Eddy off for putting you in such danger, haven't I, Eddy?'

'Aye, as always,' Eddy muttered, looking very tired and ill. Carol felt a pang of sympathy for the wayward uncle being reprimanded in front of everyone.

'It was an accident, it could've happened to anyone. There's no harm done,' Carol insisted. She smiled tentatively at the bird-like woman balanced on the chair arm.

'No harm?' Lotty exclaimed. 'The pair of you nearly drowned! You were lucky my Mick was there to pull you out of the water, so I hear.'

Carol gasped in astonishment. 'I didn't need his help,' she began, but was cut short.

'Lasses your age shouldn't be out on the beach at this time of night, let alone swimming in the sea. I don't know what your mam and dad are thinking of letting you go out like that. And on the night of your sister's wedding! I certainly wouldn't let a daughter of mine carry on like that! More than likely your parents don't even know where you are, am I right?' Lotty fixed her with that look again and Carol flushed. 'I thought as much. Well, if you won't listen to your own mam, then listen to Lotty Todd, because I know what gets into you lasses on hot summer nights. High jinks, that's what! So don't let me hear you've been swimming at night time again, or it'll be you we'll be fishing out of the sea. Now, drink up your tea, lass, and Sid'll see you straight home, won't you, lad?'

'Aye, straight home,' Sid echoed obediently.

Carol was dumbfounded by the telling off. She had helped save the life of Lotty Todd's brother-in-law but here she was being ticked off more severely than by her own mother. Even more galling, it appeared that Mick was now taking the credit for the rescue! Why on earth had she even had an inkling of interest in him on the beach? Carol thought angrily. Glancing round the small kitchen, she saw by the quiet faces that no one was going to say a word in contradiction. It seemed that Lotty Todd ruled this household and what she said went. Even Kelly was mute and sipping sweetly at her tea. Carol bristled. It was bad enough being criticised on the beach by Mick, but what right did this outspoken, interfering woman have to tell her off as if she was her twelve-year-old daughter? She was nearly eighteen and a Shannon, and no Todd spoke to her like that.

'Would you rather I'd left him to drown then?' she demanded scornfully, putting down the tea untouched. Lotty blinked at her a moment, but Carol stood up before she had time to respond. 'It's none of your business what I do with my time and if I want to go swimming at night, I'll damn well do so!'

Lotty sucked in her breath and Linda giggled behind her. But Carol was too exhausted and annoyed and emotionally battered after the long wedding day to care what any of them thought.

Kelly put out an arm to warn her, but Carol shook her off. She caught sight of Mick's stony face and could read nothing in the direct blue gaze that held her own. Contempt, probably.

'Just because I'm seventeen, you think you can lord it over me and tell me what to do. But you're not me mam and you don't have the right to tell me how to behave! I'm off. I'll not stay for any more lectures, thank you very much. Not from you or any other Todd.' She said the name with as much disdain as she could muster. A stunned silence settled on the room.

Carol looked pointedly at Sid and wondered if he would stand up for her. After a moment's hesitation, he put down his mug and got to his feet.

'Better get you home,' he mumbled to the floor.

Carol's surge of relief evaporated the instant she turned to leave. There in the back doorway stood a small bullish-looking man in a suit, his tie pulled away from his thick neck and his top button undone. His dark eyes glinted in a lively face, hard and knowing, taking in the scene at a glance.

'Evening, Mr Todd,' Sid said, nodding at the man and standing aside with respect. 'We're just off.'

'Evening, Sid,' he replied.

'Charlie, there's tea in the pot,' Lotty told him, her voice betraying none of the fury she felt at the rude Shannon girl. 'Did you get me da safely home?'

'Aye, and the dog walked,' Charlie replied, moving into the room without taking his eyes off his visitors. A small West Highland terrier padded past his legs to the fire and flopped on the hearth rug. Carol was struck by the energy that emanated from Mick's father, dominating the cramped room as if it could hardly contain him, and she wondered with dread if he had heard the whole confrontation. No wonder her father called Charlie Todd a powerful man, she thought with a mixture of admiration and fear. They were a powerful couple.

She realised that they were not going to be provoked by her outburst; instead they were pretending she had not spoken or that what she said was too childish to be taken seriously. They were much too proud and secure among themselves to bother with her petulant rant. Carol was suddenly achingly tired. At that moment she envied them their togetherness, gathered around the cheerful fire, in harmony, related, content, not needing her there at all. Her envy clawed at her stomach like a physical hunger and she could no longer bear to be among them.

'I'll bring back the clothes, thanks,' Carol mumbled and dived for the door, keen to be gone, already regretting her fiery words. Her and her big mouth! She groaned inwardly.

Sid hurried after her and she could feel his embarrassment too. She had probably blown her chances with him now, having insulted his friend's mother and spurned her tea. Just as she was about to close the door, a voice called out, 'Carol.'

She glanced back to see Uncle Eddy standing, his craggy face still white and haggard from the half drowning but smiling at her.

'Thank you, flower.' He looked like a wizened imp, with his long sideburns and his twinkling eyes, but Carol saw the warmth in them and was grateful.

'That's OK.'

'I'll not forget what you did for me,' he said, his voice suddenly cracking. A moment later he crumpled into his seat and burst into tears.

'Pull yourself together, Eddy man,' his brother Charlie growled. 'Blubbering like a bairn! Too many pints at The Ship, I'll bet.'

Carol watched in consternation, upset by the sight, but Sid pulled her after him.

'Leave them to it,' he hissed. 'They'll not thank you for gawping.'

Minutes later they were back in the car and roaring up the sleepy back lane, down the hill towards Granville House and home. Sid was quiet. Carol sank back in the seat, utterly spent. He stopped on the road outside the wrought-iron gates and switched off the engine. Carol glanced nervously at the house. Her parents' bedroom light was still on. She didn't think she could face another ticking off.

'Would you like to come in?' Carol half pleaded.

But Sid had sobered up and was already wondering if he had gone too far with Shannon's daughter. He fancied her, but he wasn't going to get on the wrong side of the pit manager over her.

'Better not.'

'Another time maybe.'

'Aye, maybes,' Sid nodded. He leaned over and Carol thought he was going to kiss her, but he yanked on the door handle and pushed it open for her. 'Ta-ra, Carol. It was a canny laugh tonight, until. . . well, you know.'

I know, Carol thought, until everyone remembered I was a Shannon and not one of them. All she said was, 'Yeah, it was.' She quickly kissed his cheek and then climbed out. 'Ta for the ride home.'

She let herself in through the gate as quietly as possible, but Sid started the car noisily and by the time she was at the front door she could see that the landing lights had come on. It occurred to her that her clothes were still in a heap in the Todds' neat flowery bathroom and so was her door key. She was standing there dressed like one of Pan's People in orange flowers and a brown mini skirt. What would they think? She wavered for a minute on the doorstep, wondering whether it might be preferable to bolt now and run off to sea or join the circus.

Why was it that she kept wanting to run away from things? Fuzzy with tiredness, she leaned on the bell. She would come out with this sensible, heroic tale of her sea rescue and gain her parents' approval at last. But the thought of trying to explain how she was dressed in Lotty's dated clothing gave her the giggles, so that by the time her father yanked open the front door and was standing there glaring at her in his pyjamas, she was shaking with mirth. They would think she'd made up the whole story anyway. Best to say as little as possible.

'Forgot me key,' she chortled. 'Sorry.'

'Oh, for God's sake!' her father swore and dragged her in.

'Is it Carol?' she heard her mother ask in shrill concern.

'Yes, and she's drunk, Nancy. You can deal with her,' Ben said in disgust and pushed Carol roughly towards the stairs.

Carol walked into her parents' vast, mirrored bedroom with its gaudy Mediterranean paintings and decided to attack first.

'I stayed at the wedding until Fay was safely away and then I went off with my friends. We went to the beach and I went swimming. Rescued a drowning man. Clothes got soaked by the tide. Went back to Mick Todd's house and I'm wearing his mother's clothes. Oh, and my trainers are halfway across the sea to

Denmark. Now can I go to bed?'

Her mother was sitting up in bed in a flouncy blue negligee, her face pale and glistening with cream, her heavy make-up removed. Her mouth opened and closed several times before she could utter a word.

'Your trainers?' she gasped.

'The Todds?' her father barked.

'What drowning man?'

'On your sister's wedding day? How could you?'

Questions and accusations flew at Carol like pinballs. She flopped down on the red candlewick bedspread and tried to explain. But the more details she gave them, the more upset they became.

'What were you doing with Eddy Todd on the beach?' Ben shouted.

'Nothing. I heard him fall in Colly's Leap. I was with Kelly and Sid.'

'Is Eddy Todd all right?' her mother gasped.

'Aye, he is now,' Carol answered, 'and he was the only one of that terrible family who thanked me.'

'Sid who?' her father demanded, interrupting the diversion.

'Armstrong,' said Carol wearily.

'Is she seeing this boy, Nancy?' Ben demanded of his wife, as if Carol could not be trusted to answer.

'He just gave me a lift home, that's all,' Carol sighed. 'But if I want to see him again, I will.'

'You'll tell me first!' her father ordered.

'You've been to the Todds,' her mother shuddered. 'What was it like?'

Carol snorted to think her mother's curiosity was still razor-sharp. 'It was like any other house in Brassbank,' Carol answered, 'except ours.'

'What did Lotty Bowman have to say?' Nancy demanded querulously.

'You mean, Mrs Todd? Quite a lot actually.' Carol couldn't resist mischievously adding, 'She told me off for going on the beach at night and swimming. Said she would never allow a daughter of hers to do such a thing. I think she must disapprove of you two as parents.'

Carol watched the explosion. Her father glowed furnace red; her mother turned more of a nuclear white.

Nancy went off like a pressure cooker. 'The cheek of it! Lotty Bowman's one to talk. That revolting girl of hers, Linda, is always roaming the streets and calling out rude names. I knew Lotty at school and she was as common as they come - her mother used to clean for your father's family. How dare she tell me how to bring up my daughter!'

'We didn't allow you to go to the beach anyway!' her father thundered. 'We didn't know where you'd disappeared to. You went off without a word to either of us. We've been worried sick. It was thanks to young Dan Hardman that we knew you'd left the hotel and driven off. Otherwise we might have had the police out searching.'

Carol had had enough. She pulled herself up and glared at them both. 'Rubbish! You weren't the least bit concerned what I did tonight,' she accused. 'You were drowning your sorrows because the beloved Fay had driven off into the sunset with bags-of-money Victor. Don't pretend you were the least bit bothered about me, because I know you weren't. You never have been and you never will be. All I'm good for around here is being nagged at.'

Her mother began to wail. Her father whipped round the bed, took Carol by the arms and shook her hard.

'You ungrateful little bitch! We've given you everything the others have had but you've always thrown it back in our faces. You're wicked and destructive.' Carol winced at the pain of his hands digging into her upper arms, but she refused to cry out or show how much he was hurting her.

'Apologise now to your mother for saying those things. *Apologise*.' He shook her so hard that her vision blurred.

'Ben, be careful,' she heard her mother call from the far end of the bed.

Carol felt faint and sick, but she refused to utter another word. She wouldn't give him the satisfaction of an apology, she couldn't! He just wanted to show her up as weak, like her mother, to show that he was the one who must be obeyed and in control. She'd bet he was just like that at work as well. Well, she wasn't going to apologise for being a failure in their eyes, for not being the perfect daughter, for being unlovable. She was who she was, and if that wasn't good enough for them, then she would go.

Suddenly her father let go and she nearly dropped to the floor.

'Get out of my sight!' he bellowed.

Carol glanced at her mother. She looked haggard and wet with tears, but stayed silent, unable to come to her daughter's defence. Carol turned and stumbled out of the bedroom. Only when she was up the stairs and safely in her attic room did she give way to tears.

She lay on the orange bedspread and buried her face into her pillow so that no one could hear her distress. How many times had she done this in her orange room? she wondered bleakly, when the tears had subsided. It was stiflingly hot, even in the middle of the night with the dormer windows thrown open to catch the night sea air. The sloping walls were covered in posters of Led Zeppelin and Queen, Ilie Nastase and Omar Sharif. The chairs were piled with cheap clothes from the market and the boutique, scarves and homemade belts, while her desk and dressing table were a mess of shell jewellery and half-made sculptures, fashioned from driftwood and shells and dried seaweed. It was her haven in the eaves, the bedroom she had chosen, away from the grander rooms on the first floor.

Here she was left alone with her treasures; her mother told the old cleaning lady, Mrs Hunt, not to bother with the 'squalor'.

But now, looking around the overcrowded room, Carol felt it was no longer a sanctuary. It was too small and claustrophobic, too near to the scene of brutal bickering that had taken place below. With Fay now gone and Simon only around at odd weekends from his police training in Durham, she knew she would increasingly be the target of her parents' dissatisfactions. It was time to go.

Carol packed a backpack that Simon had lent her for a youth-hostelling trip in her last year at school. She stuffed in some clothes, shells, letters from a penfriend in Spain and Auntie Jean in London - who sent her joss sticks and exotic beads and didn't think being a teenager was a criminal offence - two paperbacks, her Biba make-up and a pack of sandalwood-scented toiletries from Fay for being her bridesmaid.

She had a sudden thought. Jean had offended the family for failing to come to the

28

wedding. Nancy had told her that starting a new hotel job and not being given time off was no excuse. Carol decided she would head for Jean's; they could be outcasts together, she thought wryly.

She lay on the bed until the dawn began to strike the orange walls and set them glowing. Getting up and putting on jeans and a sweatshirt, Carol shouldered her backpack and crept down the stairs. It was early Sunday morning and she knew her parents would lie in late after the excesses of the wedding day and the trauma of the late-night argument. She would be expected to fend for herself until lunchtime.

She scribbled a note of farewell and left it propped on the smoked glass hall table which she had always been terrified of breaking. She walked out into the fresh dawn of a beautiful summer's morning, with her father's roses heavy with dew and the birds singing their matins. In her sandals she tramped down the hill and past the cliff above Colly's Leap, thinking of the previous night's escapades and how the Todds had inadvertently triggered her flight from Brassbank. How Lotty Todd would disapprove of that!

But what had she to stay for? For a year, since leaving school, she had drifted along aimlessly, allowing other people to make decisions for her. Vic had got her the job with Val Bowman when she'd refused to go off to secretarial college; Kelly arranged her social life; her parents ordered and curtailed her every movement; Mrs Hunt cooked her meals and ironed her clothes.

Now it was time to take control of her own life for a change. And as she strode up the far hill towards Quarryhill, her spirits lifted at the thought of freedom. For an instant, as the sounds from the pit carried to her on the morning breeze, she wondered what the pig-headed Mick Todd would think of such rebellion. She could still remember his hard blue eyes on her last night. Mick Todd would probably think of it as another petulant, childish outburst from a spoilt Shannon. Or perhaps he wouldn't think of her at all. . .

Twenty minutes later, Carol was hitching on the road south. By half past six a lorry had stopped and she was on her way to London.

Chapter Four

1977

By the New Year, the scandal over Carol Shannon's disappearance had subsided and Brassbank returned to talking about football and VAT, the new craze in skateboarding and plans for celebrating the Queen's Silver Jubilee.

'Had a card from London,' Kelly told Val Bowman as they dressed the mannequin in the shop window one raw February morning. Kelly had taken Carol's job at the boutique as soon as Val had received a postcard from her telling her she had gone to London. Val had gone straight to tell Carol's parents so that they wouldn't be worrying, but Nancy Shannon had burst into tears and Ben had sent her away with the impression it was all somehow her fault. 'Didn't like me knowing more about her than they did,' Val had told Kelly when she'd asked her to work in the shop.

'Still with her Auntie Jean?' Val asked, arranging some Peruvian knitwear and thinking how Carol would have loved it. Sometimes she missed the lively Carol as much as Kelly did and the Shannon girl certainly had a better eye for clothes and fashion than her friend. The talkative Laws girl was good for custom, but bad for a fashionable image, Val thought wryly, glancing at Kelly's tight yellow skirt which showed all her bulges.

'Aye, she's helping her on her market stall, selling jewellery made out of old bits of bicycle and stuff. Says she's doing a course in arts and crafts. Sounds to me as if southerners will buy any sort of rubbish.'

Val gave a deep chuckle. 'Any word of her coming home?'

Kelly shook her head. 'Her dad's still refusing to speak to her but her mam rings up Jean on the quiet to find out how things are. Not that she'll speak to Carol - she wouldn't dare in case old man Shannon found out.'

'What a crying shame.' Val shook her head of permed curls. 'I'm not surprised she ran away, with parents like that. Never gave her a chance. Thought her working here for me wasn't good enough for her. It never occurred to them that she might actually enjoy it.'

'You've nothing to blame yourself for,' Kelly assured her. 'You did more for Carol than anyone around here.'

Val's pleasant, plump face looked pensive for a moment. 'Maybe. Still, I can't help thinking that my sister Lotty might have deliberately provoked her the night she ran off. I know some harsh words were said on both sides but Lotty was still sore at not being invited to the big wedding and she might have taken it out on Carol.'

'Oh, what's done is done - that was months ago,' Kelly dismissed her doubts. 'Carol probably would have taken off anyway. Once she's made up her mind, there's nowt can stop her.' Kelly was not going to criticise Lotty Todd. She had spent the last six months trying to get Mick's mother to like and approve of her and it was important now more than ever to gain the woman's blessing. Lotty tolerated her because she was going out with Mick but Kelly knew that she was not happy with the arrangement. Lotty was very protective of her Todd men, Kelly thought with annoyance.

Well, she's going to have to accept me sooner or later, Kelly told herself that evening as she hurriedly prepared her father's tea and draped a load of washing around the kitchen: she hadn't had time to hang it out before work. All her life she had done this - looked after her father and the house and dreamed of something better. When other kids had gone out to play after tea, she had always had some chore to do, while her father went to the club and drank away the memory of the wife he missed so badly and whom Kelly could never hope to replace.

'Now it's my chance to get away,' Kelly said aloud, as she applied her make-up in the mirror and doused herself in cheap perfume. She was half excited, half fearful at the evening ahead and how things would go with Mick. Tonight was Valentine's night and he was taking her indoor bowling in Whittledene. He was borrowing his dad's car because she said the bike was too cold at this time of year. Anyway, you could get up to more in an Escort than muffled to the eyeballs on a draughty motorbike, she thought with a red-lipped grin in the bathroom mirror.

Not that she felt much like romance just now as the familiar feeling of nausea rose inside her and she hung her head swiftly over the toilet bowl. She retched. She would feel a whole lot better once she had told Mick that she was pregnant and they could start making plans together for the future, for marriage, for a new home with a new baby . . .

Kelly was sick again. It left a metallic aftertaste in her mouth that she couldn't get rid of. It matched the fear that she felt in her stomach at telling Mick her news, in case he was not as pleased as she was. It wasn't that she wanted a baby straightaway; she would have preferred him to ask her to marry him first. But it had just happened this way and they wouldn't be the first in the village to have a hasty wedding. Then she thought of Lotty Todd's certain disapproval and the brave red-lipped smile she was practising in the mirror died. Kelly stared at herself for a long moment, wondering if the pale, full-faced girl staring at her would have the courage to tell Mick and his family what she had done.

Mick escaped out of the back door from his father's dire warnings about what would happen to him if he damaged the car and his mother fussing that he hadn't eaten half his tea. Sometime soon he must move out of the house, Mick promised himself. He'd get a flat like Eddy's and come round for meals at the weekend like his uncle did. He'd not move too far, certainly not out of Brassbank, but far enough to get some peace from his family when he wanted. The thought of taking off into the blue and heading for London like Carol Shannon had done was beyond his comprehension. Brassbank was home, his family, his job, his friends - his life - and he had no desire to leave it. But just occasionally he had a secret stab of admiration for the wild, outspoken, infuriating Carol for acting so rashly and defying them all by running off to London. Not for the first time, he wondered, as he started up the reluctant engine, whether he would ever set eyes on her again.

He was strangely reluctant to see Kelly that evening. She had wanted to go out for a romantic evening for Valentine's Day, but he'd managed to persuade her to go bowling instead. It unnerved him that it was a leap year and he half expected her to ask him to marry her or something daft. Mick liked Kelly, but he certainly wasn't in love with her - he'd realised that as soon as they'd started to go out. And he was pretty sure she wasn't in love with him, but he feared that she was in love with the idea of romantic marriage and settling down - getting out of that bleak house in Mafeking Terrace that passed for a home.

Kelly was cheerful and generous and eager to please and at times Mick felt sorry for her having to put up with a morose father who was either away on long distance hauls for Proud's Transport Company or laid up in bed with a hangover. On the few occasions that Kelly had dragged him into the house, he had found a blanket of gloom stifling the place. One Saturday, Kelly had planned a special tea and Ted Laws had been civil enough, but Mick had been unnerved by the tension between father and daughter. Kelly's over-eagerness for the occasion to go well had led to her father snapping at her short-temperedly and storming out the house, the meal uneaten. It was the only time Mick had seen Kelly cry.

'He can't stand me trying to make things nice, make things homely, like a family should be,' Kelly had sobbed. 'He should've died instead of me mam if he hates it here with me so much!'

'He doesn't hate you,' Mick had tried to comfort her. 'Your old man's just a bit of a loner. Perhaps it's me he doesn't like.'

But Kelly hadn't smiled. 'No, it's not you, it's me. You won't stop coming here because of him, will you?' she had pleaded.

Mick had felt sorry for her and promised it didn't bother him what her father thought. But after that he had made sure that Kelly got invited round for tea at his home and only went to Mafeking Terrace to pick her up or drop her off.

Tonight, as he pulled up outside her house, he could see her face peering out behind the sitting-room curtain and he hooted his arrival. Half a minute later she was out of the darkened house and yanking open the car door, her breath warming the frozen air in ghostly clouds. She immediately turned on the car radio and fiddled around for Radio Luxembourg. It crackled and fizzed and some foreign voice came loud and clear.

'It's too early,' Mick told her as he headed out of the network of terraces and on to the main street. Brassbank was quiet. The shops were closed, a solitary dog ran across the road on a silent mission and the pubs looked snug behind misted windows. 'Would you like to go for a drink - local like?'

Her face crumpled in disgust. 'You're kidding? It's Valentine's Day, Mick man! I don't want to sit in the pub watching you play snooker and chatting to all the old men.'

'It wouldn't be like that,' Mick said, hiding his annoyance. 'You could choose the pub, and I promise to talk to you all evening.'

'Very big of you!' Kelly pouted. 'What happened to the promise about bowling?'

Mike crunched the gears into third and accelerated up the deserted high street. 'It was just a thought,' he grunted.

They sat in silence as they sped out of Brassbank and up the road to Brassy. Kelly gave in first.

'That's the house where Vic Proud and Fay Shannon live.' She pointed out the mock Georgian mansion behind its wrought-iron gates. Mick glimpsed green lights lining the driveway and several cars parked outside the house. 'Must be having company. I'd love to live in a house like that.' Kelly sighed with envy. 'Carol said it's fantastic inside, like something out of a magazine.'

Mick snorted. 'If it was so fantastic, why did she run off to London? She could have had anything she wanted, from what you've said.'

'Aye, her old man was always trying to give her things. But that never seemed enough for Carol. She never wanted the things the rest of us graft for. She once told me the thing she had of most value was her collection of shells that she and Simon had found on Brassbank beach. Daft, isn't it?' Kelly laughed.

But Mick found this talk of Carol annoying. 'Only because she had the security of wanting for nothing. She was probably just saying it to make you feel better - you not having nearly as much.'

Kelly sparked. 'Just because you don't like Carol doesn't give you the right to slag her off to me! We've been good mates for years, and not because she felt sorry for me having less than her. That would never enter Carol's head. You've got a cheek saying she was only friends with me because she felt sorry for me!'

'I didn't say that.'

'You as good as did!'

'Look, why are we bothering to argue over Carol Shannon of all people?' Mick said in exasperation.

But Kelly appeared suddenly very upset. 'I can't believe you'd think that about me and Carol, that she was me friend out of some sort of charity.'

'Drop it, Kelly,' Mick sighed.

'No, I won't drop it,' she seethed. 'Is that why you go out with me, Mick Todd, because you're sorry for me? Poor old Kelly with no mam or family, just a foul-mouthed father who prefers to gan out drinking than stay in with me? Well, I don't need your pity. I only ever wanted your love!'

Mick was flabbergasted by the outburst. He pulled the car into a lay-by but left the engine running for warmth. His first reaction was to deny her accusations and tell her that of course he loved her. But it struck him as he looked at her angry, upset face that he couldn't say it. It would be a lie. And he saw in that instant that Kelly knew it too. She sank back in her seat with an anguished sob.

'I'm sorry,' Mick said, feeling helpless. 'I like going out with you, Kelly, that's all. Isn't that enough for now? You can't want anything more serious at eighteen, can you? You've always said you're just interested in having a good time. Can't we just carry on doing that?'

He could not fathom the look she gave him. It was desolate, almost desperate, and it shocked him. He'd had no idea she cared for him that much.

'No, we can't carry on like that,' Kelly answered in a low, bitter voice. 'We can't carry on at all. Not if you don't love me!' She looked up at him with fierce bright eyes that challenged him. He knew it was his last chance to make things better between them, to tell her that he did love her after all. But he couldn't bring himself to lie to her just to make her feel better for that moment, to let himself off the hook by taking the easy way out.

He shook his head sadly. 'No, Kelly pet, I don't love you. Not in the way you want me to.'

He expected her to shout at him, call him names, anything but this wounded silence. She wasn't even crying. Eventually he asked, 'Should I just take you home?'

Kelly rallied at this. 'No you bloody won't! You promised me a night at the bowling and you're not getting out of that.'

Mick laughed in relief at this sign of the old Kelly and they drove on to Whittledene while she fiddled with the radio channels. Mick enjoyed the evening more than he'd expected and was thankful there was no more heavy talk of love or hints at a more serious relationship. Kelly appeared cheerful again and he thought they would just carry on as before. But on the way home, she told him not to detour along the back lane to the allotments where they'd courted in the back of his father's car throughout the winter. And when he dropped her off, Kelly said with a tight smile, 'You're right, I'm too young to start getting serious about lads. I just want to have a bit of fun for a few years.'

'Aye, that's what I thought,' Mick smiled back.

Then, unexpectedly, she added, 'But not with you, Mick. I don't want to go out with you ever again. I'll go out with lads who want me, not pity me. Understand!' With that she got out of the car and slammed shut the passenger door.

Mick gawped at her as she let herself into the dark house, but she never looked back. For a moment he sat quite shamed. Somehow he had really upset her and handled the whole evening badly. Then he felt foolish. He didn't like the feeling and so got annoyed. She had rebuffed him. He had spent the last few weeks wondering if he should end their relationship and suddenly she had finished with him in a few seconds flat. His pride was hurt and he drove off angrily to catch last orders at The Ship. After a pint with the genial Captain Lenin he calmed down and by the time he got home that night, Mick felt light-headed with relief that he was no longer courting.

Kelly wandered numbly through the dark sitting room and into the glass partitioned dining area. The house was cold. In the kitchen, she almost made herself a cup of tea and then felt nauseous and abandoned the attempt. She pulled herself up the stairs without turning on any lights, a habit from childhood when she had grown used to them running out of money for the meter. How many nights had she climbed these stairs in the dark to her cold bedroom? she wondered in despair. The next minute she was crouched on her bed, head buried in her quilt, sobbing with unhappiness. She lay there an hour, knowing she could cry all she liked because her father was away for two days driving a group of pensioners to Edinburgh. And even if he hadn't been, he would have pretended he hadn't heard.

She wished fervently that Carol was still around to turn to. Her friend would have come and comforted her even at this time of night. Carol had never been afraid to visit Mafeking Terrace or risk bumping into her father, like the other girls from school had. Carol had never once said a bad word against her dad, and knowing how outspoken her friend could be, Kelly had always been grateful for that.

She crawled under the covers, not bothering to undress. But sleep wouldn't come and she began to torment herself with the awful thought that Mick might have been right - perhaps Carol had only ever been kind to her out of pity. No, she couldn't face that! Kelly shook off such a notion. She knew her friend far better than Mick Todd did and she knew she could always rely on Carol's friendship. If only she wasn't so far away.

Kelly cried out loud, 'I need you, Carol. Why don't you come home? *Please* come home.'

Yet, in the early hours of the morning, quite exhausted from crying and lack of sleep, Kelly realised she had to face this trial alone. She must get rid of the baby growing inside her. How could she possibly bring it into the loveless, unwelcoming world of Mafeking Terrace? Besides, she didn't want babies! she told herself brutally. And she certainly didn't want Mick Todd's baby when he thought so little of her. It had been a stupid mistake and she would take more care next time not to get pregnant. She'd go to the doctor's tomorrow and ask for an abortion. No, not the family doctor, Kelly blanched. She'd go to that clinic she'd read about in Newcastle and, if necessary, use the money she'd saved for a holiday to Spain. Yes, she'd go somewhere where no one knew her; arrange a couple of days off work when her father was working away. No one would need to know, not even Carol.

Loneliness weighed on her like suffocating bedclothes. Fleetingly, she wondered if her long dead mother was aware of her torment. Was she looking down on her with a heavy heart, full of disapproval or, worse still, pity?

'I'll not let anyone feel sorry for me,' she said, clenching her pillow. 'Never again!'

Finally, Kelly slept.

Chapter Five

It was the corgi toast rack that finally did it, Carol realised. London was swamped by Silver Jubilee memorabilia: mugs, aprons, T-shirts, chamber pots and even a £30,000 Jubilee bed. When her Auntie Jean suggested that she should paint her shell jewellery red, white and blue or stick medallions of the Queen and Prince Philip on to her lampstands, Carol knew she could take no more of it.

'They'd sell like hotcakes,' Jean had declared as she sewed silver ribbon on to her new range of Jubilee patchwork floppy hats.

'You've sold your artistic soul,' Carol teased. 'And the whole of London's gone crackers.'

'It's all a bit of harmless fun,' her aunt had defended herself and her adopted home, 'and you're enjoying all the partying as much as anyone.'

Carol had to admit that was true. She had been to several open-air parties and even one on the river, despite the unseasonably cold start to June. The carnival atmosphere was infectious, but it had left her feeling strangely restless and unsettled for the first time in the ten months she had been away. She couldn't help wondering what celebrations were being planned in Brassbank or imagining what everyone was doing. Kelly, her main source of news, had hardly written since February. Recently Auntie Jean had had several phone calls from Nancy, urging her to get Carol to return for the Jubilee.

'She's persuaded your dad to have a garden party on the day,' Jean had told her, 'and she thinks it would be the right time for you to come home. It's their wedding anniversary as well that week, remember. It's to be a joint party. Nancy thinks it would be the ideal time for you to patch things up with your dad.'

Carol had been adamantly against the idea at first; she couldn't bear the thought of being paraded in front of all her parents' city friends. Why was it that the only friends they seemed to have were from their early married days in Newcastle and not from Brassbank?

'Not a chance!' she had snorted. 'Dad will be hating the whole idea of a party in his garden - he can't stand entertaining and he'll worry the whole time about people trampling on his borders. He'll be in a bad enough mood without me appearing like Rumpelstiltskin.'

To Carol's astonishment Jean had burst into laughter. That's how you look these days with your orange spiky hair! Yes, you could be right about not going home just yet.'

Perhaps because her aunt had let the matter drop or maybe because talk of home had stirred up a buried yearning for Brassbank, Carol's longing for something other than the bustle of London grew daily until she could settle to nothing. Her evening craft classes had finished in the spring, she had grown bored with her cafe job and the Australian barman who had been taking her out had borrowed her brother's backpack and disappeared. Even her crafts weren't selling on Auntie Jean's Saturday market stall because of the tide of Jubilee knick-knackery.

On the eve of the Silver Jubilee, Jean came home with some news. Ted Laws was down with a coach tour that had booked into the hotel where she worked.

'They're here for a shopping trip, heading back tomorrow. They want to be home for their street parties. Why don't you get a lift with them? Ted said he'd squeeze you on. You could go back for a week or two and see how it goes.'

Carol was immediately excited by the idea. 'It's not that I don't like living here with you, Auntie Jean, it's been smashing. But. . .'

Jean swung an arm round her shoulders and squeezed them. 'I know. You're homesick, I can see that. Went through it myself when I first came down. Difference is, I wouldn't live anywhere else but London now. But I think you're too much of a northerner to settle here, Carol.'

Carol felt a wave of gratitude towards her aunt. Jean was right. She was homesick for Brassbank; that's what had been eating away at her these past weeks. As the days had lengthened, memories of the village in summertime had plagued her thoughts; the sound of the sea rolling up on to the beach and the cry of gulls, the children playing out in the back lanes and the shopkeepers winding out their faded awnings in the clear early morning light. She missed the smell of the sea and the waft from coal fires, the clank of the pit like a reassuring pulse and the quickfire chatter between neighbours across the street.

Jean helped Carol pack up her few belongings into an ethnic carpet bag and a tartan duffel bag and took her to the coach the next morning. Ted Laws greeted them with his habitual scowl, while Jean kissed her niece and wished her good luck.

'You can come back any time, there's always a home for you here, pet!' she called, waving Carol away. And Carol had found it hard to keep back the tears as she waved and the bus swung round and raced out of London. Jean had accepted her without criticism all those months ago when she'd turned up unannounced on her doorstep and had made her feel at home as if she really enjoyed her company. Carol realised she had never been made to feel like that before and it left an empty ache to know what being wanted and loved could really be like.

Then her pang of regret at leaving her aunt was interrupted by a tap on the shoulder and a friendly voice saying, 'Is that you, Carol?'

She turned to find Lesley Paxton smiling beneath a neat, dark fringe. She was a good friend of her old employer, Val Bowman, and worked at the pit canteen. Lesley had often come into the boutique for a chat and to try on dresses that she thought might galvanise Eddy Todd into 'popping the question'.

'Eeh, you look that different!' Lesley exclaimed, staring at Carol's punk hairstyle and darkly made-up eyes. Carol could see she was struggling not to comment on the safety-pin earrings and laughed.

'Go on; tell me I look a sight. I'll have to get used to the verbal abuse now I'm on me way home.'

'No, you look - well, trendy like,' Lesley stuttered. 'Anyways, it's grand to see you again. Val's missed you in the shop - Kelly too. It'll cheer her up no end you coming home.'

Carol was taken aback to think she might have been missed. 'How is Kelly?'

'Quietened down a bit, I'd say. Not like when you were around. She was courting Eddy's nephew Mick over the winter, but Val says that's been off for a while now.'

Carol felt herself blushing at the mention of the Todds and the unwanted memory of her final night in Brassbank.

'Suppose my name is still muck around the Todd household?' Carol grimaced.

'Not with my Eddy,' Lesley assured her. 'He thinks the world of you after what you did for him, and so do I. Eddy doesn't let family differences stand in the way of things like his brother Charlie does. And don't you worry about Lotty, she talks a good fight but she's soft as butter underneath. She knows what a good turn you did by fishing Eddy out the water and she'll not forget it.'

Carol felt encouraged by Lesley's words, but she couldn't bring herself to ask what Mick Todd's opinion of her might be. The journey passed quickly, as Carol talked about London and caught up on months of gossip from Lesley. Val Bowman was expanding her business to include bridal hire and her own sister, Fay, had opened up a second health food shop, this time in Brassy. Vic Proud was now running bus trips to the Rhine as well as Spain and Kelly had cut her hair into a short bob and lost two stones in weight.

It was early evening when the coach finally pulled into Brassbank, having meandered around the coastal villages dropping off tired shoppers. They alighted outside Proud's Travel Agency and Carol helped Lesley with her packages. She breathed in deeply, revelling in the smell of damp sea air, hot fish and chips and smoking fires. It was drizzling lightly, the air was cold and grey clouds frowned over the village. Marshall's general store was bedecked in Union Jacks above a new neon sign and the park gates had been freshly painted. But otherwise the streets looked achingly familiar, the shops and pubs and the vast redbrick Welfare Hall standing patiently like old friends to welcome her.

Carol refused a lift in Lesley's yellow Mini and on impulse asked Ted Laws if she could go home with him to see Kelly. He seemed surprised by the request but shrugged in assent.

'If she's there, but.'

Kelly was there. She was half dressed for a night out and shrieked in disbelief and delight to see her old friend. They hugged warmly and Kelly pulled Carol upstairs to her bedroom like old times.

'What the hell have you done to your hair? It shows off your face, but. And I love the straight-legged jeans - and the leather jacket. Not sure about the safety pins, mind. Long as you don't put them in your nose - Brassbank's not ready for that. Eeh, I've missed you, Carol man!'

'Me too,' Carol grinned. 'You're a lousy letter writer. Two postcards in three months. Too busy enjoying yourself, eh?' She looked at Kelly's new slim figure and trim bob of red hair. Her friend looked prettier and her figure-hugging clothes now fitted her, yet there was a drawn look to her once plump face. Carol decided she looked older.

Kelly turned away and busied herself looking for shoes under her bed. 'Yeah, well, I was never as good at writing stuff as you.'

'So who's the lucky lad tonight?' Carol teased.

'No one yet,' Kelly said breezily, retrieving a pair of wedge-heeled sandals. 'Still looking for Mr Special. All I've found so far is Mr Average, Mr Dead Loss and Mr Just For Tonight.'

Carol laughed. 'So Mick Todd wasn't the one then?'

Kelly's face went tight as she gave a bitter little laugh. 'He was a real dead loss. Mick Todd's idea of a good night out was a game of backgammon with his Uncle Eddy in The Ship. God, even the music there was rubbish! No, I was well shot of him. He was no good in the passion department either.'

Carol flushed. All at once she felt uncomfortable at such talk. She remembered how she had felt that time on the beach with Mick's arms round her, rubbing her warm. For some reason she didn't like to hear him being criticised so savagely.

'So what's on tonight, then?' she changed the subject swiftly.

'Disco at the Welfare, then the bonfire's being lit in the park at eleven. They're laying on fireworks and free beer,' Kelly said, with her old enthusiasm. 'You'll come along, won't you?'

Carol hesitated. 'I should really go home first - get the Spanish Inquisition over with.'

'Well, come later on then,' Kelly insisted. 'It'll be great. And tomorrow we're having a street party, whatever the weather. I'm really glad you're back for all this, Carol.'

'Hey, I nearly forgot.' Carol rummaged in her duffel bag and pulled out a tiny present wrapped in newspaper.

Kelly took it suspiciously. 'It's not a piece of bicycle chain to hang from me nose, is it?'

'Open it. It's just right for a Jubilee nutter like you!'

Kelly unravelled the newspaper to find two miniature corgi earrings with green jewelled eyes.

'Snazzy, eh?' Carol joked.

'Eeh, I love them!' Kelly squealed, rushing to the mirror to try them on.

'Thought you would,' Carol smirked and felt Kelly's excitement quicken her own. Tonight she was going to enjoy the start of the celebrations. Brassbank had accepted her back, she was home at last.

Trudging home from the pit, Mick stopped at the yard gate and chuckled. One half of the kitchen window was almost invisible under the dressing of bunting and miniature Union Jacks and silver tinsel. The other half was starkly plain, except for a hand-written poster proclaiming, 'Stuff the Jubilee.'

So his parents had reached a democratic compromise, Mick thought with amusement. For the past week, his mother had been itching to put up some festive decorations and had spent hours preparing and freezing cakes and scones for the street party. But his father had resolutely refused to have anything to do with such royalist indulgence and had stumped off to the allotment in disgust whenever the Jubilee was mentioned on the television.

Things had come to a head when Linda had returned home with a school essay entitled 'What would I do if I were Queen?' Charlie had come in from the pit to hear his thirteen-year-old daughter discussing trips to Disneyland on the royal yacht.

'All this preparation reminds me of the Coronation,' Lotty had said fondly. 'Remember the parties we had then, Charlie, before the bairns were born?'

Charlie had snorted. 'They're just a drain on the nation! All that ridiculous pomp and ceremony. We're paying for all those palaces and princes and cousins of princes and dogs and horses of princes. By heck, we should've got shot of them centuries ago like the French did.'

'Oh, Dad!' Linda had gone off in a huff.

'Well, I don't see the harm in it,' Lotty had replied. 'The Queen's a hard-working woman. She's done a grand job and raised four children at the same time. I don't begrudge her a party every twenty-five years.'

'Hard-working?' Charlie scoffed. 'She's got more staff and courtiers than she knows what to do with. All she does is gan round the country opening things. We pay millions a year for a royal wave and a royal handshake, that's what.'

'So you're not keen on having a bit of bunting in the window then?'

Mick had seen the disappointment on his mother's face and unwisely intervened. 'It doesn't mean anything, Dad. It's not as if the monarchy has any power over us these days.'

His father had exploded. 'Nee power? What Tory nonsense is that? The Queen's the head of state; she can dissolve parliaments and appoint prime ministers! And what about the honours lists? All part of a corrupt establishment pressing down on the people, that's what!'

Mick had exchanged wary looks with his mother and decided to say no more. Shortly afterwards his father had stormed off to the allotment (Eddy had nick-named it Toddy's Republic) and stayed there until dark.

But looking at the kitchen window now, Mick guessed that Val or Eddy must have mediated in the dispute. Usually solid in their support for each other, his parents had agreed to differ on this one thorny issue of royalty and the kitchen window displayed their opposing views. Mick heard his mother humming. Peace had been restored.

'Your father's agreed to take me to the party at the Welfare,' Lotty said cheerfully as he entered. 'As long as he doesn't have to stand for the national anthem.'

Mick raised his eyebrows at his father. 'Delaying the revolution?' he teased.

'Just for a night,' Charlie declared. 'Your mam doesn't get out that often.'

Mick grinned as Lotty winked at him.

'But I want it known that I go under protest,' Charlie blustered.

Mick nodded. 'We'll have it announced at the interval, Dad.'

Lotty laughed.

'What's so funny?' Charlie demanded.

Lotty went over and kissed him. 'You are. But come the revolution, I'll still love you. You get my vote for President.'

Mick saw his father blush at his mother's open affection but knew that he enjoyed it. They were so at ease with each other, like a worn pair of gloves, familiar and complementary. After twenty-seven years of marriage they still enjoyed one another's company, still loved one another. It was something to marvel at, Mick thought. He'd never gone out with anyone who he hadn't tired of before twenty-seven days were up, let alone found a woman he'd want to spend a lifetime with.

At that moment there was a clatter at the back steps and they all turned to see Linda appear with her friend Denise. There was a gasp of horror from around the tea table and a muffled expletive from her father. Mick looked in astonishment at his skinny sister, grinning at them. Her hair was sprayed blue and her face had been painted with the Union Jack. She wore a long blue dressing-gown and wobbled on high heels. Her friend shuffled in behind wearing black bin liners and her face blackened with boot polish.

'I'm Britannia,' Linda giggled. 'Denise is a lump of coal. Do you think we'll win the fancy dress?'

'Not if your father's judging,' Lotty said, stifling a laugh.

Mick chuckled, grabbing Denise and throwing her over his shoulder like a sack of coal. She squealed in protest and Linda screamed in delight. 'Haway then, girls, let's get along to the party!'

It was raining steadily by the time Carol reached the gates of Granville House. The delicate flowers on the rhododendron bushes in the driveway were being battered by the wind. In the evening gloom, Carol could see a marquee flapping forlornly on the main lawn and fairy lights strung in the trees. Her mother would be inside fussing over last minute details for tomorrow's big garden party, while her father grew agitated at the disruption to his routine. Carol almost turned and fled.

Then a car purred in behind her and caught her like a startled rabbit in its headlights. She jumped out of the way, but the car braked abruptly on the gravel and a window slid down on the driver's side.

'It is her!' a deep voice chuckled. 'The prodigal daughter returns, eh?'

Carol recognised Vic's bearded face, his lips very red as he smiled at her. Before she could answer, Fay had jumped out of the passenger side and was running round to meet her.

'Carol! You could have told us you would be here. Mum never said.' She brushed her younger sister with a cheek.

'Mum doesn't know.' Carol looked sheepish.

'Typical! You've caused no end of worry to us all, I hope you realise. You ruined our honeymoon in Barbados, you know. Mum was in a terrible state when I rang up. You really picked your moment, didn't you?'

Vic came to her rescue, abandoning the car on one of Ben's manicured verges.

'Hey, give her a break, doll. Carol's come back to us, full of repentance, I bet.' He leaned towards her and kissed her on the mouth. 'I like the hair, little sister.' He swept her with an appreciative look. 'Yes, very nice.'

Carol felt ridiculously gauche in their presence and doubted whether coming home was a good idea after all. But they swept her in with them, Vic grabbing her bags and Fay taking her firmly by the arm.

'Simon's bringing his new girlfriend. Just a small family dinner party. At least you've remembered it's Mum and Dad's wedding anniversary. I suppose you've brought them something nice from London.'

Carol thought of the corgi toast rack and winced. 'Not much really. And I'm not staying for dinner. I'm meeting Kelly at the Welfare later. I'll just dump my stuff and go.'

'Wishful thinking,' Vic murmured and winked at her.

As Fay's hold tightened on her arm, Carol felt her heart sinking.

It was very strange walking into her old home. It all looked much the same as when she had crept out ten months ago and yet it no longer felt like home at all. Her mother shrieked at her arrival in the sitting room and caused her father to spill sherry over a small blonde woman who turned out to be Simon's new girlfriend. Panic ensued as damp cloths were fetched and everyone gawped at and gave their opinion on Carol's outrageous appearance.

Simon at least remembered to kiss her in welcome and introduced Kate, a fellow police cadet from Durham.

'I told you she'd come back for the garden party, Ben,' her mother declared.

'You're not proposing she comes dressed like that?' Her father was still having

41

difficulty recognising her, Carol realised.

'She can borrow one of my dresses,' Fay announced, 'and a matching headscarf. She'll look fine once I've had a go at her.'

'Perhaps there'd be time to get Margaret in to do her hair,' Nancy thought aloud. 'I wish you'd given me some notice, Carol. It'll be difficult to arrange. And Mrs Hunt's made up your bed for Kate. We've got so many staying tomorrow.'

'That's OK,' Carol said hastily. 'I can stay over at Kelly's for a few days.' She was appalled at the prospect of wearing one of Fay's tent-like Indian dresses at the dreaded garden party and was madly thinking of how to get out of it all.

'Nonsense,' Nancy dismissed the idea. 'We need you here where we can keep an eye on you. You're not going to run off again. You've no idea how embarrassing it's been for your father and me.'

'She can stay with us,' Fay suggested. 'That's all right, isn't it, Vic?'

Vic gave a smile and a nod of consent. 'Fine by me, if that's what Carol wants to do.' Carol could tell he was highly amused by the whole drama but she was grateful that he was at least taking her wishes into consideration.

'Yes, OK,' Carol agreed with reluctance, thinking it was the lesser of two evils. Her parents were already driving her mad and she realised that she would find it very hard living at Granville House again as if she had never been away. Her mother was already reproaching her for having been away on her eighteenth birthday and telling Kate how they'd had to cancel the marquee and the caterers and the dance band.

Carol found it impossible to escape the family supper and sat through two hours of her mother and sister talking of foreign holidays and beauty treatments and health foods, while her father bored Simon and Vic with talk of the pit and the Coal Board. Carol sympathised with the glazed look that had crept into Kate's eyes and came up with an idea.

'Would you like to go and see the fireworks in the park, Kate?' Carol asked her loudly.

She gave an enthusiastic yes.

'We'd have to go now, or we'll miss them,' Carol continued. 'Anyone else want to come?' She stood up before anyone could scotch the idea and Simon soon followed.

'But what about coffee?' Nancy asked in disappointment.

'We'll come back for that,' Simon assured his mother. 'Kate wants to see something of Brassbank while she's here.'

'But there's nothing to see,' Nancy said with incredulity.

'Come on, it's the Jubilee,' Carol said impatiently and thought how Auntie Jean would have laughed to hear her sudden enthusiasm.

'Let them go,' Vic said with an easy smile. 'We'll stay and drink some of Ben's excellent brandy, won't we, doll?' To Carol's relief, Fay agreed and they were on their way out into the chilly night and heading for the park on foot.

Simon and Kate walked with their arms wrapped round each other and chattered all the way. Carol could tell they were eager to be alone together and once they reached the crowds of people in the park, she slipped away from them, saying she had spotted Kelly. That wasn't hard to do as her friend was in the centre of the action around the trestle tables of drink, her animated face lit by the glow of the bonfire.

'Here, have a beer!' Kelly called to her and waved her over, thrusting a plastic cup in her hand. 'Where've you been? You missed the party at the Welfare. Denise Wilson won the fancy dress as a lump of coal. It could only happen in Brassbank.'

'I couldn't get away. And tomorrow they want to dress me up for a garden party.'

Kelly gave a raucous laugh. 'Don't worry. You've never done anything yet that they've asked of you so why start now? Just stick with me, Carol man.'

Carol laughed and raised her drink. To the Jubilee!'

She took a long swig and watched a cascade of green lights pepper the night sky as the first fireworks were set off.

A couple of drinks later, Carol bumped into Lesley Paxton and Eddy Todd and she found herself warming to Eddy's banter. Val Bowman came up and gave her a huge, plump hug and told her to come into the shop the following week. After that, Carol realised that Kelly had disappeared in the crowd and she spent the next half an hour trying to find her friend to no avail and cursing her elusiveness. Just as she was on the point of giving up, Carol spotted Kelly heading away from the park with a tall dark-haired man. Squinting into the blackness she thought she recognised the shape of Sid Armstrong and instinctively stood back from the firelight so they did not see her. She still felt awkward about Sid because of the interest he had shown in her last summer. Good luck to him and Kelly, she thought. But it meant that she couldn't take refuge at Kelly's tonight and would have to walk up to Fay's house at Brassy.

Carol decided to set off, suddenly aware of how tired she was after the journey and the emotion of returning home. Leaving behind the sounds of celebration and the popping of fireworks, she set off in the damp. Passing the bright oasis of lights in the chip shop, Carol felt at peace as she strode up the hill and hummed to herself. She was surprised at how much she had missed the village and although she had no idea what she was going to do now she was back, she knew she was pleased to be here.

As she climbed past the allotments and felt the sea breeze, a memory came back to her of Mick Todd upbraiding her on the beach for not caring about the village or the pit. 'Or the people who support your comfortable life,' he had accused. How wrong he was! She cared about them all. But she had only come to this realisation since being away, so perhaps he had a point. She had been too content just to drift along, questioning nothing, making her petty rebellions against her parents but doing nothing to change her life. At least now she had proved she could stand on her own two feet. She had rejected the comfortable life that Mick had derided and whatever the future brought, she would make the best of it and rely on her own abilities, not her parents' money, she determined.

A motorbike roared past her and startled her thoughts in the tranquil night.

'Road hog!' she shouted after it.

To her dismay, the bike slowed further up the road, hesitated, then turned round. In panic, Carol wondered if the rider could possibly have heard her abuse and was coming back to take issue with her. Certainly, he was coming back.

The biker slowed down right beside her and put out a foot to balance himself. Carol couldn't help appreciate the smell of fuel. The man raised his visor and she found herself being watched by familiar unblinking blue eyes.

'Do you need a lift? It's late to be out walking on your own,' he said.

Carol peered closer, thinking she must be mistaken because he sounded just like Mick Todd. It was as if thinking about him had conjured him out of the night.

'I heard from Lesley you were back,' he grunted. 'Are you making for your sister's?'

'Er, yes, I was,' Carol stammered. Her heart was banging like a bass drum and she found it impossible to say any more.

He seemed suddenly unsure of her hesitancy and looked about ready to snap down his visor. 'Of course, if you prefer to walk . . .'

Carol found her voice again. 'No, I'd appreciate a lift. It's a long pull up to Brassy.'

She thought she saw him grin, but it was difficult to tell beneath the helmet. He reached for a spare helmet on the back of the bike.

'Here, put this on.'

He indicated for her to climb on the seat behind him. Carol swung herself over and gripped the seat as they moved off, wondering what had possessed her to accept the lift. For a few moments, she sat there rigid and terrified by the way the bike rolled with the bends in the road, but then she relaxed and bent with it like Mick was doing. As they sped towards Brassy, past the ghostly churchyard where her sister had been married, Carol felt a surge of exhilaration. What on earth had prompted Mick Todd to stop and pick her up? Whatever it was, it filled her with a new energy and excitement.

Too soon they reached Fay's house. Carol was surprised Mick knew where it was. There were lights on in the grand portico, but no sign of the car.

Carol shouted over the noise of the engine, 'Doesn't look like they're home yet, and I haven't got a key.'

'What do you want to do?' Mick shouted back.

Carol felt like doing something rash. 'Do you want to go to the beach? Walk for a bit?' she asked, expecting him to tell her to get lost.

He turned to look at her but she couldn't see his expression.

'Aye, why not?' he agreed and revved up the bike.

This time, Carol tentatively held on to Mick as they sped back along the coast. Breathing in the smell of leather from his jacket, she felt a strange thrill at being with him. Fireworks continued to light up the black sky and the village still looked the same as they cruised through it, but Carol knew something had changed, as if she had taken a momentous step in the last few moments.

Chapter Six

They abandoned the motorbike on the rough ground above Colly's Leap, but walked in the opposite direction as they both wished to avoid any reminder of the evening when they first met. The tide was out and they were able to make their way along the wet sand without scrambling across rocks. Mick asked about London and Carol spoke of her time away. She realised he was the first person she had talked to about her adventures, for none of her family had seemed the least bit interested. Her parents had made it plain that the sooner the escapade was forgotten, the better. Mick, on the other hand, appeared genuinely interested and laughed at her tales. As they meandered along the deserted shoreline he told her about his family, his job at the pit, about his parents' battle over the Jubilee. He found himself telling her things he never normally talked about.

'But the reason me dad spends so much time up at the allotment has nothing to do with gardening like Mam thinks. He goes there to read,' Mick divulged.

'Why doesn't he read at home?' Carol asked. 'Too noisy with your Linda around, I suppose.'

Mick chuckled. 'No. It's because he reads historical romances.'

'Never!' Carol exclaimed.

'Aye. He gets them from a second-hand stall in Whittledene, or the library. Says he's getting them for the wife, but Mam never sees them. She thinks he only reads the papers.'

Carol clapped her hands and laughed. 'I love it! Who would have guessed your dad's a romantic?'

'Don't you go telling anyone, mind.' Mick was suddenly unsure if he should have told her. 'Me and Eddy are the only ones who know - but Dad thinks no one knows.'

'Brownies' honour,' Carol smiled and did a mock salute.

Mick grinned. 'Don't tell me they let you in the Brownies?'

'Aye, I was an elf for nearly a year. But on bonfire night I set fire to my tie and they threw me out.'

Mick snorted.

'Well,' Carol defended herself, 'I'd seen them on the telly burning flags - something to do with Vietnam - and I thought I'd try it.'

They walked on, recounting tales from their childhood.

'I keep thinking it's time I left home,' Mick smiled ruefully. 'It seems that crowded and I never get any peace from Linda. But I'd never have the guts to take off like you did.'

Carol looked at him in surprise. 'It was nothing to do with guts,' she joked. 'I just couldn't stand being at home any longer. You're lucky, you've got a happy home where your mam and dad care about you. You shouldn't knock it.'

Mick suddenly stopped and seized her hand. 'I got it all wrong about you, Carol,' he said in a deep voice, 'but I was prejudiced against you, thought you were a snotty rich cow, if I'm honest.' He watched her, a little unsure.

'Ta very much!' Carol laughed.

'It never occurred to me you might be unhappy, not in that grand house and with all that money and your dad being Ben Shannon. You see, I've grown up with me dad telling me that your dad turned his back on the rest of them, going over to the management side. They used to be friends as bairns, you know.'

'My dad and your dad?' Carol exclaimed.

'That's what he says.'

'Then why is he so against my dad?' Carol asked. 'Is it just because he's management?'

Mick shook his head. 'It goes a lot deeper than that.'

'The recent strike, then?' Carol suggested. She remembered them having to use candles at home during the dark winter nights of 1972 and 1974 which she had enjoyed. But her father had been foul-tempered and her mother had moaned about the lack of heat in their draughty house.

Carol saw his reticence. She squeezed his hand. 'Tell me, please.'

Mick sighed. 'I don't know the full story, but it goes back to our grandfathers. They were both at Brassbank pit during the lock-out in twenty-six.'

'Yeah, Dad's always been proud of me grandfather working his way up to be overman.'

Mick drew his hand away and looked at her in sudden anger. 'Aye, but I bet he didn't tell you that he betrayed his own marras to get where he did?'

'What do you mean?' Carol demanded.

'Your grandfather Shannon was a scab!' Mick spat out the word. 'He went back to work for the bosses while his friends and their families stayed out and starved. It was because of men like him that the strike failed and the pitmen lost everything they'd been fighting for for years. But men like your grandfather were rewarded with good jobs for doing their dirty work.'

Carol flushed. She had never heard this before and was shocked by Mick's venom.

'He must have had his reasons,' she said.

The look of disappointment on Mick's face made her stomach leaden. 'Me dad would say there's no excuse good enough to turn your back on the men you work with and see them and their families hammered. If they'd stayed out, united, they would've got the conditions they were fighting for. Me grandfather Todd was branded a troublemaker and never worked again. He died at the age of forty-five. Didn't even live to see me dad get his first job down the pit or the industry nationalised. Me dad's very bitter about that, and that's why he resents what your dad's had in life, I suppose.' He gave her a sad look. 'Our fathers must've been about six or seven when the lock-out happened. Course, after that they would never have been allowed to be friends.'

'No,' Carol gulped, feeling the burden of shame for her family. She would never again be able to look at the proud family photograph in the dining room of her bearded grandfather and stoical-faced grandmother without thinking of his betrayal. 'I'm really sorry about your grandfather. There's so much I don't know about this place - never bothered to find out.'

Mick saw the unhappiness in her face and felt a pang of guilt for upsetting her. After all, it was hardly her fault she was born a Shannon. He did not know what had spurred him on to offer her a lift earlier; the impulse had taken him by surprise. But ever since Lesley Paxton had joined them at the Welfare and talked about Carol Shannon returning with her punk hairstyle, he'd not been able to stop thinking about her. So when he had found her on the road, it was as if they were meant to meet and he had been thirsty for her company and eager to prolong the evening with her.

He took her gently by the elbow and steered her towards a shelter in the rocks. 'I could tell you things - so could me dad. And Grandda Bowman's full of stories about the past - he's a walking history book about the village.'

Carol felt herself shaking at his closeness. 'Can't see your dad wanting to talk to me. And after what I said to your mam . . .' She blushed hotly.

'They'll feel differently once they've got to know you a bit,' Mick smiled.

She looked into his blue eyes and felt her heart leap. 'Do you think so?' she whispered.

'Aye, I do,' he said and leaned towards her. Cradling her head of spiky hair in his hands, he kissed her gently, tentatively, on the lips. Carol responded, her insides melting. They kissed more confidently, with increasing vigour, their arms going round each other in exploration. She buried her hands in his long hair and felt the roughness of his chin on her cheek, his hands waking her body to pleasant sensations.

They broke away and grinned.

'Wow, Carol!'

'I'm glad I came home after all,' she laughed. 'I think I've wanted to do this for months, if I'm honest.'

'Me too,' Mick chuckled. 'It drove me mad when Sid said he'd kissed you on the beach. I kept imagining it was me.'

'Mick Todd! Go on then, imagine some more.' Carol laughed low and pulled him towards her.

They lay for hours on his leather jacket, kissing and hugging and talking until they became suddenly aware of the tide at their feet, Already there was a watery pale light seeping into the sky over the North Sea and it came as a shock that the short night was waning.

They scrabbled up the rocks and shook the dirty sand off their clothes. Carol shivered with cold, but nestled into Mick's arm as they made their way back along the top of the cliff to where they had left the bike.

He fondled her spiky hair again and hugged her to him. 'Where to now?'

Carol groaned. 'I'll be hung, drawn and quartered for not turning up at Fay's. You've really got me into trouble this time, Mick,' she teased.

'And I've enjoyed every minute of it,' he laughed, nibbling her ear.

'I don't think I can face my sister just yet.'

'Don't then. We'll ride over to the motorway service station behind Quarryhill and have a big breakfast. Then we can decide what to do on a full stomach.'

'Spoken like a true miner,' Carol kissed him and felt her desire for him sweep over her again.

They ordered a huge cooked breakfast and mugs of tea and after that they decided to carry on towards Durham, neither wanting their time together to end. The city was waking from a deep sleep, its cathedral tower languidly tolling the hour and the rooks and wood pigeons breaking the quiet among the thickly wooded river bank. The River Wear shimmered below as early morning rowers skimmed silently across its pewter surface. Carol had never seen the city look so beautiful or peaceful.

Leaving the bike in the town, they walked along the riverbank until they were out in the countryside again. Mid-morning they stopped at a village and

47

bought cans of Coke to quench their thirst and Carol could not believe she still had energy left to walk further. Retracing their steps, they explored the cobbled city, then mounted the bike once more and took off in the direction of Weardale. They stopped for a drink and sandwich at a pub, high in the folds of the Durham hills, and as the sun broke through, they climbed over a dry-stone wall and lay down in a sheltered field with only sheep for company.

'My parents' garden party will be starting about now,' Carol said, with a guilty pang.

'Just tell them you were abducted by a Todd,' Mick laughed and rolled over to kiss her.

'Oh, that would really make things better,' Carol snorted.

'Well, if it makes you feel less guilty, I'm missing the Septimus Street party right now, and me mam and sister will never forgive me for that.'

'Aye, but you'll have pleased your dad. He'll think it's a republican protest,' Carol joked.

They had talked so much about each other's families that she felt she knew all about the Todds. She had never imagined how close she could grow to someone so quickly. She marvelled at the strength of these new feelings as she gave herself up to the pleasure of embracing Mick.

During the afternoon they fell asleep and woke to a gentle rain making them cold and stiff. They took refuge in a tea shop and thawed out with hot drinks and cream scones. Afterwards Carol said she felt really wicked and she wished she didn't have to go home.

Mick drew her on to an old wooden bench in the rough open field that passed for a village green.

'Let's not go home,' he suggested nervously. 'We could stay somewhere for the night. I'm not back at work till tomorrow afternoon.'

Carol felt herself go hot as she realised what he was implying. She was not sure.

Mick took her hands in his. 'I don't want to push things, but I've never felt like this about any lass before. I just want to be with you, Carol.'

She took a deep breath. All she wanted at that moment was to be with him too. She couldn't bear to be apart from him or see beyond the day. She didn't want to think of her family's reaction to such a relationship, so she blotted them from her mind. All she was sure of was her overwhelming longing for the man beside her. She didn't care what either of their families thought of them, she decided defiantly.

'That's what I want too,' she answered quietly.

Then Mick's handsome face was smiling in relief and she knew it was going to be all right. They made their way to the cottage advertising Bed & Breakfast at the end of the lane and booked in for the night.

Chapter Seven

'You stupid, selfish little bitch!' her mother screamed and slapped Carol across the face. 'How can you bring such disgrace on your father and me?'

Carol stood frozen in shock as her puce-faced mother berated her in the empty hall.

'Thank goodness all our friends have gone and won't have to see you like this - like some scruffy tramp! How dare you waltz in here, bold as brass, after disappearing for two nights? You disgust me! And with that Todd boy. Carol, how could you? I don't know what your father is going to say.'

It did not take long to find out. Ben Shannon stormed back from the pithead offices as soon as the incoherent Nancy called him on the telephone. By this time she had pursued her daughter up the stairs where Carol was trying to lock herself in the bathroom and have a shower. But Nancy dragged her out again and pushed her into the guest bedroom, from where Carol could see the marquee being dismantled on the south lawn.

Mick's tender parting still played in her head, protecting her from the vitriol of her parents. 'Let me come in with you,' he had urged, 'so you don't have to face them alone.' But she had made him go, telling him he must not be late for work. She had not wanted him to hear the abuse that she knew was in store. She would rather have faced her sister first, but she knew Fay and Vic would be out at work and she had no choice but to go home.

Ben Shannon's cold rage was worse than her mother's hysterics. He threw her in a chair and questioned her mercilessly about where they had been, what they had done, prising the information out of her until she was close to tears. When he had finished with her, Carol felt quite humiliated and degraded. What had been for her the most important, intense, tender two days of her life was reduced by them to an underhand, sordid affair.

'Your mother and I will never forgive you for this,' her father blazed. 'Your behaviour has been contemptible. From now on we'll decide who you mix with and where you go. Vic has offered to take you on in his office. It's just clerical work, but it's a start and it's certainly more than you deserve. You'll attempt to do something useful with your life, Carol. This is the last chance we're giving you, do you understand? And you're not to see Mick Todd again - I forbid it!'

Carol was shaking with misery. She accepted that she deserved a rebuke for disappearing without letting them know where she was, but not this terrible outpouring of bile from her father. His hard brown eyes glared at her now with real hatred and her insides gripped with fear. Never before had he said such awful things to her; it was as if his resentment and anger had been building up for years and had finally exploded. Going off with Charlie Todd's son had obviously been too much for him.

When Carol thought of the futile bitterness between the two men, she felt suddenly angry too. Not only had the hatred between them poisoned their own early friendship, but it had nearly prevented her friendship with Mick. All at once Carol was determined that her father would never be allowed to ruin the love she had just found. It had come as an unexpected gift and was too precious to be stamped out by her father's bitter pride. She had never thought to find someone who loved her as intensely as Mick had these past two days and it gave her the strength to stand up to her father.

She sprang out of the chair. 'You've no right to tell me who my friends must be and you can't stop me seeing Mick. We're in love and we're going out together. I shall carry on seeing him.'

Her father grabbed her and shook her hard. 'No you're not! You're my daughter and you'll do as I say. And I can make things very difficult for Todd at the pit,' he threatened.

Carol lashed back. 'No you can't! This isn't nineteen twenty-six any more. You can't treat people as if they don't count.'

Ben gripped her tighter until her arms throbbed. 'What do you know about the past?' he demanded with scorn. 'You learned nothing at school. All you've got to your name is a couple of useless CSEs!'

Carol was stung into replying hotly, 'Maybe I wasted my time at school, but I'm learning things fast now! I know that me grandfather betrayed the people of Brassbank by scabbing and that's why you're where you are today.'

She heard her mother gasp and thought her father was going to strike her. Instead he dragged her out of the bedroom and on to the landing.

'Get out! I'll not hear my father maligned by a little whore like you! That Todd's filled your head full of filth,' her father bawled. 'Get out of my house!'

Carol struggled to free herself from his bruising grip and her mother hovered in the doorway, her pretty face fearful and haggard.

'Ben, please,' she wailed.

A moment later, Ben pushed his daughter over the top step and Carol felt herself stumble and lose her grip. She grabbed the banister, but tripped and somersaulted down the wide, red-carpeted stairs. It all happened in seconds. She landed at the bottom, winded and shocked, but still conscious.

Looking up she saw her parents staring down like figures in a tableau, their expressions frozen.

'Carol?' her mother's voice quavered. 'Carol?'

Carol pulled herself to her feet, feeling relief that she could still stand, though her head was pounding. Scrambling for the door, her only desire was to escape from the house and the darkness that seemed to engulf it. She never wanted to see her father again.

'Go on, go!' he shouted at her and chased down the stairs. 'And don't come back!' He picked up her duffel bag and her carpet bag, which still stood by the umbrella stand where she had left them on the night of her arrival, and kicked them after her on to the front steps. 'And don't bother running to your sister's house, because she doesn't want to know you either. She's just as ashamed of you as we are!'

Carol fumbled for her bags and stumbled down the uneven stone steps, a sob choking her throat. She ran as fast as her bruised legs would carry her up the drive, past a startled workman carrying guy ropes, and out through the iron gates. She ran on blindly for several minutes and then collapsed at the side of the road, heaving for breath. Two children gawped at her as they passed on bicycles and Carol made an effort to stand up, trying not to draw attention. But she was shaking too much to carry on; her legs buckled and she sat down again.

A wide yellow car appeared round the bend, passed her and then stopped, its pointed tail lights showing red as the driver braked. Carol thought vaguely it looked like something out of an American film. It reversed and pulled up beside her, the driver opening his door.

'Are you all right, flower?' a man asked in concern.

Carol looked up and saw the gaunt, lively face of Eddy Todd peering down at her. She burst into tears.

'Hey, we can't have that,' Eddy fussed, springing out of the car and pulling her up. He held on to her awkwardly but gently and waited for her crying to subside. 'Can I give you a lift somewhere?'

'I - I don't know where to go,' Carol wept. 'They've thrown me out of the house.'

Eddy steered her round to the passenger side and bundled her in. He offered her a checked handkerchief which smelled faintly of coal dust. After a few minutes Carol was able to explain what had happened. Eddy listened, visibly upset.

'It'll be all round the village soon, I bet,' Carol said miserably and wondered if Mick would disown her too. The thought was too painful to contemplate and she felt tears well up again.

'Don't worry about village gossip,' Eddy reassured her with a hug. 'I've had plenty of that in the past and no one dies of it. What you need is somewhere to stay. How about your friend Kelly?'

Carol nodded. 'If her dad doesn't mind, I suppose.'

'I can have a word with Ted if needs be,' Eddy promised.

Carol smiled for the first time. 'Thanks a lot.'

'I owe you one, remember?' Eddy smiled back and started up the Dodge.

They found Kelly at Val's boutique and Eddy went to have a quick word with Val while Carol explained her predicament to Kelly.

Kelly was silent at first and Carol feared her friend was going to refuse; she looked quite shocked by the news.

'Please, Kelly, just for a few days,' Carol pleaded.

Kelly rallied. 'Aye, of course you can - till you get this all sorted out, anyways.'

Before they left, Val insisted on giving Carol a cup of tea and Eddy pressed a ten pound note into her hand and was gone before Carol could protest.

Back at Kelly's house, Carol had a soak in the hot bath while her friend made fish and chips. They ate them together in front of the TV and then Carol dozed off.

She did not hear the doorbell, but Kelly shook her awake. Carol looked up to see Mick standing in the doorway. She felt waves of relief sweep over her at the look of concern on his face.

'Eddy told me what happened,' Mick said. 'I knew I should've stayed with you.' He crossed over and sat down beside her, giving her a tender hug.

'You can't stay long,' Kelly said abruptly. 'Me dad'll be in from the club soon and he'll not want to find you here.'

Carol saw the look of resentment on Kelly's face and remembered that she had taken a dislike to Mick after they stopped going out. Carol did not want to cause any bad feeling between them.

'You better go, Mick,' Carol said reluctantly, kissing him quickly. 'Are things all right for you at home?'

Mick pulled a face. He was not going to tell her of all the angry words that had been flung at him on his fleeting appearance at home to get ready for work. He had been reproached for missing the street party by Linda, castigated for going off on the motorbike by his mother who thought he had had an accident, and reprimanded by them all for having spent the time with Carol Shannon. They had been spotted returning to the village on the motorbike and news of it had preceded Mick's arrival.

'Don't worry about me.' He smiled and kissed her back.

Kelly made a noise of disapproval and marched into the kitchen, making a great clatter as she washed the dishes.

Carol and Mick exchanged looks.

'She doesn't like me,' Mick whispered.

'Can't think why.' Carol grinned and kissed him again.

'I'll come round tomorrow before me shift,' Mick said. 'We can get away for a few hours.'

'Good,' Carol agreed. Seeing him but not being able to be with him was torture to her and she let him go with reluctance.

After he had gone, Carol tried to talk to Kelly about him, but her friend cut her off bluntly.

'Listen, Carol, I don't like all this business with Mick Todd. You shouldn't have gone off with him without telling anyone. I was worried when you didn't turn up at our street party.'

Carol snorted. 'The last time I saw you was at the bonfire going off with Sid Armstrong. You didn't seem particularly bothered about me then.'

Kelly blushed. 'Sid's different. He's just a friend. You know where you stand with Sid. But Mick Todd leads a lass on and you're a fool to trust him. He'll use you and then dump you like he did with me.'

Carol flinched at the accusation. 'I thought you finished with him?'

'What does it matter now?' Kelly snapped. 'I'm just telling you that he's bad news.'

Carol stared at her friend, puzzled by her hostility, and wondered if she could be jealous of her new relationship with Mick.

'Kelly,' she said quietly, 'I'm really in love with someone for the first time. I'm sorry if you don't like Mick, but I'm going to carry on seeing him no matter what anyone thinks, even you.'

Kelly glared at her, her face crimson. 'Have it your own way but don't say I didn't warn you.' She went and turned off the TV, then added tersely, 'And you can't stay here long either, not if Mick keeps coming round. Me dad doesn't like him and it'll only cause trouble.'

Carol looked at her sadly. 'Just give me a few days and I'll be out of your way.'

They went upstairs without speaking another word to each other.

The next day, after Carol had seen Mick and heard him declare that no one was going to stand in the way of their seeing each other, she went to speak to Vic Proud. She found her brother-in-law in the scruffy, nicotine-stained office above his bus depot, arguing sharply with someone on the telephone. He saw her and rang off.

'Hello, Vic. I've come about the clerical job,' she came straight to the point. 'Is it still on offer?'

Vic eyed her. 'Well, you've certainly stirred things up around here, haven't you?'

'So you've heard?' Carol went red.

'Surprised it wasn't on the regional news. Naughty, naughty Carol,' he teased.

'Please, Vic, I need a job. Dad won't give me anything now - and I wouldn't want him to,' she said stubbornly.

Vic laughed. 'Yes, OK, I need someone to answer the telephone and contact drivers. My last YOP's just left. You can start Monday.'

Carol smiled in relief. 'Don't suppose Fay would consider having a lodger for a month until I get paid, would she?'

'I don't think even I could swing that one at the moment, Carol,' Vic said, offering her a cigarette. She refused. 'No, your sister's really upset by it all, and she takes your parents' side as usual.' He lit up. 'You'd have been better off staying in London, if you ask me.'

'No,' Carol was adamant, 'then I would never have met Mick. This is where I belong. I know that now.'

Vic shrugged and the telephone rang again. While he was answering it, the other one rang and Carol picked it up. She took a message. Vic came off the line and told her he had to dash over to the travel shop in Whittledene.

'Can you stay for an hour or two? It's just I'm short-staffed at the moment.' He gave her his disarming smile.

'Course,' Carol replied and found herself working there for the rest of the day.

The summer passed quickly working at the coach depot. The hours were long and badly paid, but Carol enjoyed getting to know the drivers and chatting to the customers and feeling responsible for running the office. Even at Val's she had never been entrusted with so much and it gave her a special thrill to be relied upon and have her opinion valued.

Vic, she was not so sure about. He was charming and friendly one moment and then moody and losing his temper the next and she often found herself intervening between him and other members of staff to prevent a row. She was not surprised that he had lost a string of youth opportunity trainees and noticed that he was reluctant to take on full-time workers to whom he would have to pay a proper wage.

Still, she was happy. Thanks to Eddy, she had found lodgings with Lesley Paxton and left the strained atmosphere at Mafeking Terrace, although she met Kelly regularly for a lunchtime sandwich at Dimarco's cafe. It was almost like old times, as long as she kept off the subject of Mick, which she found difficult to do.

Carol lived for the times when she saw Mick after work when they would take off on the motorbike and roam the Durham countryside together. From the Dales in the west with their pale stone villages to the lush farmland in the east, they explored places Carol had never even heard of and time and time again they returned to Durham City, Carol's favourite spot. They rowed on the river, walked the riverbank and drank in old pubs. On Miners' Gala Day, Carol danced through the Durham streets with Kelly in front of the Brassbank lodge banner and met up with Mick and Sid at the fair, dragging the men away from listening to Eric Heffer and Arthur Scargill. For that day Kelly seemed to forget her animosity towards Mick and the four friends celebrated around the town together. Yet Carol enjoyed it most when she had Mick to herself.

The only blight on their relationship was the attitude of Mick's parents. Carol was acutely aware that they did not approve of the amount of time he spent with her and she felt awkward when she was at his house. Only Linda - who followed her around like a puppy - seemed pleased to see her and asked her questions about clothes and punk rock, which only annoyed Mick's parents the more.

'Why don't you move out?' Carol constantly urged Mick. 'Get yourself a place of your own like you said you would. It would be so much easier for us to see each other and you could afford it.'

But she felt Mick's resistance to the idea and she silently cursed the hold his family appeared to have on him, the clannishness that excluded her. Sooner or later, Carol determined, he was going to have to make a choice.

For his part, Mick had rediscovered his enthusiasm for the bike since going out with Carol and also his interest in everything around him. The countryside, Brassbank, the sea, his work, all took on a new vibrancy. He looked back on the time before Carol and thought how dull and aimless his life had been without her. But increasingly he worried about his family's suspicious attitude towards her. Whenever he brought Carol home, his father would swiftly disappear to the allotment while Linda would flock like a vulture to question her and gawp at her punk clothing. But the worst was his mother's stiff politeness, offering her refreshment but nothing more, keeping her well at arm's length.

Mick always felt uneasy around the house when Carol was there, frightened she would react to the hostility and cause another scene. Increasingly he made excuses for her not to call round, preferring to pick her up from Lesley's and not have their every move scrutinised by his family. She began to badger him about moving out, which annoyed him, because she could not understand how much it would hurt his mother. His desire to leave home had always been half-hearted. He just wanted to leave well alone and let things go on as they were, keeping everyone happy.

But towards the end of the summer it provoked a major row. It was Linda's fourteenth birthday and she was having a special tea before going out to the pictures with her friend Denise. Mick had arranged to meet Carol later after the birthday tea, but she turned up unexpectedly on their doorstep, brandishing a present.

'It's for Linda,' Carol said brightly as Mick answered the door. She saw his look of alarm. 'I am allowed to say happy birthday, aren't I?'

'Aye, it's just everyone's here,' he mumbled.

'One big happy family,' Carol mocked. 'And me coming in is going to spoil it, I suppose.'

'Carol,' Mick gave her a desperate look, 'I thought we were meeting later.'

'I came to see Linda,' Carol reminded him, 'but if I'm not welcome, forget it.' She pushed the present at him and stormed off. 'And you can forget tonight an' all!' she shouted back.

Mick closed the door on the shouts of inquiry from inside the house and ran after Carol, grabbing her arm in the street.

'Don't walk off like that!' he said angrily.

'Get off me!' Carol struggled to release his hold.

'I thought you understood,' Mick accused.

'Oh, I understand! It's obvious you're ashamed of me. I'm not good enough for your precious family, am I? That's what they think and now you're beginning to think it too.'

'That's not true,' Mick answered, pulling her into a side alley away from the inquisitive stares of neighbours. 'Why are you so bothered about a bloody tea party? It's only for Linda.'

'It matters because Linda's the only one who gives me the time of day. At least she speaks to me when I come round. Your parents treat me like a bad smell. I wanted to give Linda something and see her on her birthday. Is that such a crime? Have you any idea how I feel being snubbed by your family, being the only one not invited? For goodness sake, Mick, we've been going out for three months and I'm not even invited round to tea. My own family aren't speaking to me - you're the only family I've got!' Carol glared at him in desperation.

'Carol man, they'll come round to you in time.'

'No they won't,' she answered fiercely. 'We could give your parents a hundred years, but they're never going to accept me. So what are you going to do about that, Mick?'

They stared at each other unhappily, but Mick seemed lost for words. Carol knew then that he was not prepared to stand up to his family for her sake.

'You're a coward, Mick Todd,' she told him harshly, 'and I don't want to see you again.' When he slackened his hold on her she ran off up the street, fighting back her tears of frustration and anger. She had come round on the spur of the moment, wanting to force the issue with him. It made her so angry that she was not included in the Todd household when she was Mick's girlfriend and she thought by bringing a gift she could ingratiate herself with the family. She yearned to be accepted by them; if not loved then at least liked. What a fool she was!

Perhaps Kelly had been right all along about Mick. He was not to be trusted; he had used her. Commitment frightened him and he would rather finish with her than risk his family's censure. Torturing herself with her doubts and fears, she ran on.

Eventually she found herself making for the beach and the consolation of the crashing, sighing waves. If he did not stand up for her over the small issues, what chance was there of him supporting her over the big ones? she thought miserably. If they were to part, Carol had no idea where she would go or what she would do. All she knew was that she would be unable to face Brassbank, with the constant reminders of what might have been. She would not be able to bear her parents' triumphant reaction that they had known all along that Mick Todd was no good for her. Carol buried her face in her hands and let the sound of the sea drown out her tormented cries.

When Mick returned, the room fell silent. Their faces told him they knew what had been going on.

'Here,' he muttered, thrusting the wretched present at his sister.

Linda tore off the wrapping paper to find a pair of tartan trousers with zips in the legs, just like Carol's.

'Eeh, they're lush!' she squealed. 'Look, Mam!'

Lotty gave a despairing look. 'You're not going punk too,' she told her youngest. But Linda had already rushed from the room to try them on. She came back in the figure-hugging trousers.

'I love them! Why didn't Carol stay to tea? Will you tell her I really like them?' Linda enthused. 'I'm going to wear them tonight.' She pogo-ed out of the room to answer the door to her friend Denise, who came in dressed all in black.

'You come straight home after the film, mind,' Charlie warned.

The girls promised and clattered out of the room.

'She's a strange one, that Denise,' Val commented. 'Fancy wearing black all summer long.'

'It's your niece I worry about,' Lotty sighed. 'She's wanting to wear everything that Carol wears. It'll be the hair next - blue or something terrible.'

'Not in my house she won't,' Charlie snorted, folding up the evening paper.

Lotty eyed her silent son. 'Are you going out later?'

Mick shook his head. 'Not any more.'

Knowing looks were exchanged around the quiet kitchen.

Lotty brightened. 'Well, you could go over and fetch Grandda, take him for a game of dominoes.'

'Aye,' Mick agreed without enthusiasm. He was furious with Carol for having put him in such an awkward position and angry with himself for handling it badly.

But suddenly Uncle Eddy piped up, 'I think you should come for a drink with me. We haven't been to see Lenin in The Ship together for weeks. How about it?'

'Go on then,' Lotty waved them away. 'Your dad can fetch Grandda. You get yourself out, son. You've been neglecting your family and friends around the village these past months.'

Everyone knew it was a criticism of Carol and the way she had monopolised him over the summer.

Mick hauled himself up, suddenly eager to be away from the stifling kitchen and the stares of his family.

'You deserve better than Carol,' Lotty called after him, 'and there's plenty more fish in the sea, as Eddy always says.'

Mick gave her a hard look and left.

There was silence a moment when he and Eddy had gone, then Charlie said, 'I told you not to worry. It was all bound to blow over sooner or later.'

Lotty gazed out of the window after her son. 'I'm not so sure,' she murmured. She had expected to feel relief that things between Mick and the Shannon girl were heading for the rocks; she had actively encouraged the break-up, for she disliked Carol. She hated the way she looked, the way she tried to worm her way into the family, the hold she seemed to have over Mick. It annoyed her, too, that they were beholden to Nancy Shannon's daughter for coming to Eddy's rescue. And that, Lotty suddenly realised, was the problem. Carol was Nancy's daughter. Nancy, who had once been one of them, Nancy Hutchinson, schoolfriend and neighbour, was now high and mighty Nancy Shannon who thought herself above them all and had forgotten where she came from. Every time Lotty looked at Carol she was reminded of that; she could not help herself.

Now watching her unhappy son stride away down the back lane, Lotty felt a pang of guilt and wished she had not been so critical or hard on young Carol.

Then she turned and saw Val clearing the table to show her some new dress patterns and felt her resolve return. If Carol had been as sensible and hard-working and obliging as Val, she would have had no qualms about Mick courting her. Her son deserved someone who would look after him properly and in time make him a happy, comfortable home to come back to after a hard day's work at the pit. And Carol Shannon, Lotty knew, was quite incapable of that.

Chapter Eight

'Go and find Carol,' Eddy ordered. 'You can't let other people stand in the way of your happiness.'

Mick was surprised by Eddy's urgency for he had not thought his uncle had noticed the undercurrents of hostility at home.

'Why can't she just accept things as they are?' Mick argued. 'Everything was going fine. Mam and Dad just need more time to get used to her but Carol can't see that.'

'You know that's not true.' Eddy fixed him with his bright eyes. 'Your mam and dad don't approve of her. How do you think Carol feels about that when her own family have kicked her out an' all?'

Mick shrugged uncomfortably.

Eddy put a hand on his shoulder. 'I'm the last bugger should tell anyone about commitment, I've run away from it all me life. But if you care for the lass,' he said gently, 'then don't miss your chance of happiness with her. She needs you to stand by her, Mick man. No one else has.'

Mick saw the compassion in his uncle's eyes and felt a leap of encouragement. He set down his pint on the round wooden table.

'Aye, maybes you're right,' he murmured. He was too shy to say just how much he did care for her, but he suspected his uncle already knew.

Carol stubbed out her fourth cigarette and went for a swim. The tide had come in and the sea seemed to beckon her in with its whispering spray. She left her clothes on the rocks and plunged into Colly's Leap. Already the sky was darkening, marking the end of long summer days, and the water was icy cold. Black thoughts took hold of her. No one knew where she was and who would notice if she slipped under the freezing waters and never came up again? No one would come looking for her until she failed to turn up for work on Monday, or maybe Lesley might grow concerned if she was not there in the morning.

Maybe she should return to London. Why not admit coming home had been a terrible mistake, for where now was home? Carol plunged her head underwater to rid herself of defeatist thoughts. When she re-emerged she thought she heard something.

With a gasp she made out the shape of a man standing on the cliff above her. Then he disappeared from view. Carol swam for the rocks and heaved herself out, feeling suddenly vulnerable and very alone. She pulled on a T-shirt and struggled into her jeans and was reaching for her leather jacket when the man reappeared out of the gully. He came towards her and all at once she recognised the square shoulders and long hair in the semi-dark.

'Mick?' she whispered.

'Carol!' As soon as he spoke her name she knew it was all right. They rushed to each other and his arms went round her in a fierce hug. 'I'm sorry,' he said.

'Me too,' she admitted.

They kissed urgently and clung to each other, Carol shaking with relief. 'Don't let's fall out again,' she cried. The thought of being without you, being alone ...'

'You'll never be alone again, I promise,' Mick said, kissing her tenderly. 'I want to marry you, Carol.'

She searched his face. 'Is that what you really want, Mick?'

'Aye, it is.'

'But your family?'

'It doesn't matter what they think. It's you and me that matter. I'd like them to wish us well, but we'll do it anyway. How about it, Carol?'

Carol kissed him in reply. 'Oh, Mick, I love you so much. You know that, don't you?'

'Aye, bonny lass,' he grinned at her, 'I do.' He pulled her tight against him and kissed her hard once more.

It was the following week before Carol plucked up the courage to go and tell her parents. In the end she could not face going to Granville House but she knew her mother would be at Fay's on Wednesday after her aerobics class in Brassy church hall. She got a lift with Vic who took the news with his usual amused detachment.

'Well, break it to them gently,' he pleaded. 'I don't want my wife miscarrying.'

Carol knew that Fay was expecting their first baby in December. The news had at least served to distract her parents from her affairs. Carol thought with optimism that they might be pleased she wanted to settle down.

But their reaction was one of shocked indignation.

'You're far too young,' Fay scolded, distractedly pacing up and down the conservatory. Nancy was rooted to a cream leather chair, quite speechless.

'I'm nineteen. You were going out with Vic at the same age,' Carol pointed out.

'That's different,' Fay said, waving her hands about as she did at her shop assistants. 'We went out for four years before we married, we really knew each other.

'You can't possibly know this Todd boy properly. It's a passing phase. You're only doing this to shock us, as usual.'

'He's not a boy.' Carol was indignant. 'He's older than you, Fay. And I know him well enough to want to marry him. I'm not doing this for anybody's sake but mine and Mick's.'

This galvanised Nancy out of her speechless state. 'You're pregnant, aren't you? That's why you've got to get married. Oh, my God, what am I going to tell everyone? What's your father going to say?'

Carol turned on her in annoyance. 'Why is it always so important what Dad thinks? I'm not pregnant!'

'Then why have you got to marry him?' Nancy asked in perplexity.

'Because I love him!' Carol said in exasperation.

'Fay's right,' Nancy continued, dismissing the explanation, 'you're much too young to know your own mind. You're just doing this to get at your father and me - being childishly rebellious as always. Well, if you must see the boy, then carry on until you grow bored, but don't frighten us with talk of marrying a Todd. It's just not suitable. Your father would never agree.'

Carol had had enough. She walked over to the open conservatory door, shaking with anger at their scornful rejection. 'I just came to tell you, not to ask permission. We're going to marry as soon as possible. I'm not asking for any help, or a big white wedding. It just would've been nice if you'd managed to wish me well.'

She left them among the humid houseplants, gawping at her. Swallowing her disappointment, she made her own way back to Brassbank.

Mick was half expecting a summons and it was almost a relief when it came. He entered the pit manager's office still dressed in his working overalls, hidden behind a mask of coal grime. Ben Shannon nodded for him to sit down. Mick remained standing, awkward but defiant.

'This is just an informal word,' Ben smiled, clasping his thick fingers together on the large desk. 'Man to man.'

Mick looked warily at the shrewd brown eyes studying him, the mendacious smile under the bushy grey moustache. Although he disliked Ben Shannon for who he was and for the way he had treated Carol, Mick respected him as pit manager. Shannon worked hard on behalf of the pit and was always bullish but fair in his dealings with the men. The pitmen knew where they stood with their manager and although he was a hard bargainer, he was always willing to listen. Even Mick's father had grudgingly admitted that Shannon would do anything for Brassbank. But they were not here now to talk about the pit and Mick knew he must be on his guard in the face of Shannon's ruthlessness. He waited and listened.

'You're not one for traditions, you youngsters, are you?' Ben said with false joviality. 'In my day when we wanted to get married we asked the girl's father first.'

Mick said nothing. Ben's smile died.

'You haven't known my daughter very long, have you, Michael?'

No one had called him Michael since school, Mick thought with irritation. It made him feel juvenile.

'I've known Carol all her life, Michael, and I can tell you she's not easy to live with,' Ben grunted. 'In fact she can be exceedingly difficult. Moody, rebellious, never sticks at anything. Oh, I'm very fond of the lass, naturally, but she's still very young, got a lot of growing up to do.'

The two men regarded one another with suspicion.

'What is it you want to say to me, Mr Shannon?' Mick asked stiffly.

Ben leaned forward. 'What I'm saying, Michael, is that she's too young to get married. She'll have changed her mind in a few months' time and then it'll be too late. You'll be landed with her.'

'Landed with her? How can you say that about your own daughter? We may not have been going out long but I think I know Carol better than you think. She'll not change her mind. Me neither.'

'Listen, Todd,' Ben snapped, 'you have a good job in the pit, good prospects for the rest of your working life if you want it. Don't throw it all away on a girl like Carol. She'll never make you happy.'

Mick stopped himself giving his boss a mouthful of abuse. He was incensed by Shannon's high-handed meddling in his personal life and astonished at the bitterness with which he talked about his own daughter. But Mick heard the menace in the remarks about his job in the pit and knew Shannon could make things difficult for him.

With restraint he replied, 'This thing with Carol and me has got nothing to do with me job. It won't affect the way I work down the pit. I'm sorry if you don't want me for a son-in-law, but we've decided to get wed no matter what anyone thinks. We'll make our own mistakes, Mr Shannon.'

They glared at each other, Ben going red in the face at Mick's intransigence. He could see that nothing, not even veiled threats, would change the young man's mind. He stood up abruptly.

'I think you're making a big mistake,' he growled, 'but I can see you're both as pig-headed as each other. Carol will continue to do what she damn well wants, but she'll have no help from me, financial or otherwise. I wash my hands of her.'

Mick flushed with fury. 'That's what you've always done, isn't it, Mr Shannon? I've seen pet dogs tret better. Well, we don't need your money, we can manage just fine. We're not having a big white wedding at Brassy or a posh reception at the castle. We don't want to show off to anyone, we just want to get wed.'

'Get out, Todd,' Ben seethed. 'You don't deserve my help. And you're not welcome at my house either, son-in-law or not. As far as I'm concerned, Carol's no longer mine, so you can both go to hell!'

Mick gave him a disdainful look and marched out of the office without another word, leaving his boss shaking with rage.

Charlie Todd was secretly laughing at him, Ben knew it; he bet the whole village was laughing at him. Because for all their airs and graces their daughter was marrying a 'common pitman', as Nancy called Mick Todd. And there was absolutely nothing he could do about it, despite all his carefully built power in the village. It mattered little to Ben that Mick was one of his ordinary miners, but it mattered a great deal that he was a Todd.

He whipped round and yanked the photograph of Carol off the wall where it hung below his other children. He glared at the broad smiling schoolgirl face with the shaggy brown hair and mischievous green eyes that looked back at him.

'You silly little bitch, Carol!' he roared and threw the framed photograph into the metal bin, where the glass shattered with a deafening crash.

Outside his window he watched the broad back of Mick Todd as he strode away across the pit yard and felt overwhelmingly alone.

Chapter Nine

In late September, Carol and Mick were married at the Methodist chapel on Good Street, where the Bowmans were regular attenders. It was to be a small affair of close family and friends with tea afterwards at the Comrades Club, where Charlie Todd was secretary. Right up until the last minute, Carol was unsure who, if any, of her own family would attend. As her parents were not speaking to her, she had asked her brother Simon to give her away, but he had made excuses about going on holiday with his girlfriend, Kate. Simon would be safely in France and so could avoid having to take sides. At Mick's suggestion Carol had asked Eddy to stand in.

Eddy had looked at her in astonishment and Carol had thought he might refuse, but then he'd squeezed her arm and nodded. 'I'd be pleased to, flower,' he said, his voice full of emotion and Carol was not sure if he was delighted or embarrassed.

One thing had delighted her though; Kelly had agreed, after protest, to be her bridesmaid.

'I'm too old,' she had grumbled at first.

'You're nineteen, same as me,' Carol had laughed. 'And I promise not to dress you up in frills and petticoats.'

In the end, they had had a happy afternoon trawling through the boutiques and second-hand clothes shops in Whittledene, putting together their traditional outfits.

'Val will never forgive you for not hiring one of her new bridal dresses,' Kelly said.

'Seeing as I'll be leaving the chapel on the back of Mick's motorbike, I think she'll understand.'

Carol saw the expression change on Kelly's face like a sudden shadow and quickly changed the subject. They settled on a cream denim knee-length skirt and matching jacket for Carol with black boots and a shocking-pink dress for Kelly. Both chose black berets.

'The chapel won't have seen anything like it,' Kelly giggled. 'What will Lotty Todd say?'

Carol grimaced. 'Probably sigh with relief I'm not turning up in me leather jacket and jeans.'

On the wedding morning, Lesley gave Carol breakfast in bed and Kelly and Val Bowman came round with a bottle of sparkling wine to wish her luck and calm her nerves.

'We've brought a surprise visitor for you,' Val told her with a throaty chuckle, 'an old school friend of mine.'

'Someone else who used slates and pencils?' Carol teased.

'Cheeky!' Val gave an affectionate swipe.

Kelly opened the door with a flourish and there standing behind it, clutching a huge bunch of flowers and dressed in a floppy Jubilee hat, was Auntie Jean. Carol screamed with delight and rushed to her aunt, throwing her arms round her.

'I'm staying with Val,' Jean told her, smiling. 'Wouldn't miss the punk wedding of the year.'

'I'm dead grateful you've come all this way,' Carol said. 'You might be the only family there, you know.'

'I gathered that.' Jean gave her a rueful smile and another hug. 'But we'll make it one to remember.'

Vic stepped out of the Jacuzzi and rubbed himself down with a huge jade-coloured towel.

'I'm going anyway,' he told his heavily pregnant wife, 'and I think you should too.'

'Why do you have to do this?' Fay cried petulantly. 'You know I can't go. It would be disloyal to Mother and Dad.'

'Carol's one of my employees,' Vic said, dousing his beard with aftershave.

'I've got nothing to wear,' Fay complained. 'Nothing nice fits me these days.' She eyed her husband's tall, hairy body and felt unattractive.

'It's hardly the social event of the year,' Vic laughed.

'Oh, God, the Comrades Club! I can't face it.'

'Just come to the chapel service then,' Vic suggested indifferently.

Fay gave him a suspicious look. 'You've got close to Carol working with her, haven't you? Do you find her attractive?'

Vic wrapped the towel round his waist and padded across the deep pile carpet to their bedroom door. 'Carol's like a little sister to me, nothing more,' he said without turning round.

Fay was not convinced. 'You're not growing tired of me, are you, Victor? It must be difficult to fancy me when I look and feel like a beached whale.'

Vic hid his irritation at her constant carping about her pregnant appearance. He turned and strolled back across the room. He bent down and kissed her swollen stomach.

'I love you like this,' he grinned and put his hands on her enlarged breasts. 'Let me show you how much,' he said softly, nibbling at her neck.

Fay was mollified, but pushed him away. The thought of sex made her feel tired. 'There's no time,' she replied, 'not if I've to get ready for this wretched wedding.'

Carol arrived in a taxi with Kelly and Lesley and Auntie Jean and saw with a racing heart that Mick's motorbike was parked outside the chapel. It gave her courage, as did the small band of onlookers at the steps. She recognised some of the drivers from work and their children, and two of Lesley's friends from the pit canteen, Dot and Sid's sister Joanne, both of whom had come to the hen night the week before.

'Good luck, Carol!' they called to her good-naturedly.

A squall of rain battered the wedding party and threatened to streak Carol's black eye make-up. Kelly and Jean pushed her inside. The neat, plain chapel was decorated with yellow and white roses that filled the large building with perfume.

'Lotty did those,' Lesley whispered, nodding at the tasteful displays.

Carol raised her eyebrows in surprise. Her in-laws-to-be had been civil and co-operative over the wedding arrangements, but Carol was sure they had little enthusiasm for the match.

She saw Eddy in a smart suit and wide tie that must have been borrowed, but was amused to see he still wore his old winkle-pickers. He winked at her in encouragement and put out a tentative arm for her to take as the music struck up for their walk down the aisle. She was touched to see he had tears in his eyes.

In the blur of excitement, Carol noticed the Todds and Bowmans clumped together behind Mick's strong shoulders. Beside him, his best man, Sid, stood with gleaming brown hair still wet over his collar, both of them self-consciously formal in hired suits.

The bride's side of the chapel was virtually empty, save Auntie Jean and Lesley and a couple of girls from work. Then Carol heard the tap of heels behind her and turned to see Vic and Fay arriving late. She smiled at her sister, overjoyed that one of her immediate family had turned up, and wondered for a dizzy moment whether her parents had relented and come to support her too. But there was no one else and Carol swallowed her disappointment.

She turned forward again and was greeted by Mick's loving, smiling face. He was waiting for her, impatient to start their future together, and she had no shred of doubt that she wanted him too. Never again would she stand alone in the world. Carol smiled back and felt Eddy squeeze her arm with encouragement as he let go and Mick stepped forward to be at her side.

Nancy Shannon looked out of the long French windows at Granville House and watched her husband in his grubby gardening clothes, methodically digging out the last of the annuals. The first frost had bitten last night and killed their fading blooms. He worked on as if it was an ordinary Saturday afternoon, as if nothing of note was taking place in the village that day.

Nancy stifled a sob and went to pour herself another gin. She thought of her youngest daughter at that very moment being married to the Todd boy and took a large swig, hoping to drown the pain she felt inside. She turned on the television at full volume, wanting to deafen the awful thoughts that plagued her mind, but still they haunted her. How dare Carol deny her the small pleasure of seeing her married, of being able to make the arrangements and choose a new outfit and be at the centre of the occasion. She was filled with bitterness and fury at her daughter for having chosen so badly.

Yet as the alcohol numbed her senses, she dared to blame her husband. With it came a surge of bravery. She would defy Ben and rush round to the chapel to see Carol. She yearned to know what she looked like, who else was there, what they were all saying and doing. Carol was her baby. He didn't have the right to stop her!

Then her husband straightened from his digging and turned to look at the house, as if he could read her thoughts, and Nancy jumped back guiltily out of sight. Of course she could not go there without him - she was incapable of doing anything without Ben Shannon.

Nancy flopped down on the flowery patterned sofa, sloshing her drink over her pale yellow trousers, and broke into racking sobs. She was contemptible! She was a coward and a drunkard. She had been a useless mother and a disappointment as a wife. All she had to show for twenty-five years of marriage was this Gothic, draughty house filled with expensive pretty furnishings but echoingly lonely now her children were gone. Nancy felt crushed by the burden of her failures. All through the afternoon she sat drinking and weeping and wishing she was somewhere else.

It was time to leave. Sid had given an amusing, irreverent speech about

Mick, and Mick had said a few brief, tenderly shy words about his new wife. They had eaten the pies and salad tea and ice cream laid on by Dimarco's genial proprietor Paul and the club bar had been flowing generously with drinks provided by the Todds. Now people were coming up to the newly-weds and kissing them goodbye and good luck as they prepared to leave.

'Have you still not booked anywhere after the first night?' Lesley asked incredulously.

Carol laughed, thinking how sensible and organised Lesley's honeymoon would be if she ever got Eddy to the altar. 'No, we're just going to take off on the bike and see where we end up,' Carol grinned, her insides churning with impatience to be off and away with Mick.

Sid came up and kissed her, and her new father-in-law broke off his argument with Captain Lenin on the protracted strike down at Grunwick to give her a peck on the cheek in an astonishing display of affection. 'Take care, lass,' he growled.

Kelly threw her arms round Carol and burst into tears. 'It's never going to be the same now!' she wailed.

'I'm only away for a week,' Carol teased her and gave her friend a hug. 'I'll come round as soon as we're back. And once we get moved into Dominion Terrace, we'll be in the next street to each other.'

But this just seemed to upset Kelly more and she howled louder. Val stepped in and prised the bubbling Kelly away. Carol caught Mick's look across the room and they both made towards the door. Lotty stopped her.

'Make him happy, Carol,' she said in a low but firm voice. The two women regarded one another for a moment. Until their colliery house was ready, they were going to have to live under the same roof as Mick's parents, Carol thought without relish. She was going to have to be careful not to clash with her mother-in-law over Mick.

'We will be happy,' Carol replied with conviction.

Lotty's concerned face suddenly lit with a smile. She patted Carol's arm. 'Aye, well, any road, you're family now. We'll take care of you, pet. So off you go and enjoy yourselves while you can.'

Carol felt an unexpected flood of warmth towards the fair-haired woman and on impulse leaned forward and kissed her on the cheek. 'Thanks, Mrs Todd.'

Lotty said in a fluster, 'Call me Lotty, or call me Mam, but no more Mrs Todd, do you hear?'

Carol grinned and nodded and felt she had passed through some invisible barrier on the way to being accepted as a new daughter. And she was more than grateful. Her own mother had never turned up to wish her well and Fay and Vic had left early with excuses about her sister being exhausted. Carol had the impression Fay had been bullied into coming by Vic and would rather not have been there at all.

They emerged into the fading afternoon light and prepared to mount the motorbike, their few holiday clothes bundled into the panniers on the back. As Carol pulled on her helmet, Eddy lurched up to her and gave her a hug.

'Lovely lass,' he slurred and Carol thought he wanted to say something else but was either too overcome with emotion or beer to form the words. She gave him a kiss and then straddled the bike behind Mick.

The guests fell back to the club doorway as the bike revved and kicked into life and they were off with grins and waves, roaring up the steep high street and past the park gates. Carol clung to Mick's back, suffused with happiness, watching Brassbank fade behind them as they made for the open road. Tonight they would spend their first night of marriage in Durham, the city of their summer courtship, and after that. . . Carol could not think beyond the bliss of the night ahead.

She felt Mick's gloved hand rest on her leg and give it a possessive squeeze. He shouted out and set the startled rooks around Brassy Church screaming in alarm.

'What did you say?' Carol shouted back.

'I love you, Carol!' Mick bellowed above the engine's roar.

Carol laughed and hugged him tight. It was the first time he had actually said it, though she had known the truth of it all along.

Sid found Kelly outside the club, smoking in the dark.

'That's where you've got to,' he said, plonking himself down beside her on the cold steps. 'I thought you must've gone home.'

'What and miss a party?' Kelly said sarcastically.

Sid threw his arm round her shoulders and gave her a squeeze. 'I know you're missing Carol, but she'll be back soon. Life goes on, pet.'

Kelly winced and ground out her cigarette. Life, she thought bitterly. She could never tell Sid that she had once carried the start of life inside her - her baby, Mick's baby. Bloody Mick Todd! She had got rid of their child because she could not bear the thought that he had never really wanted or loved her. She could have used being pregnant to trap him and make him marry her, but for what? He would have despised and resented her and sooner or later he would have rejected her and the baby anyway, she had told herself.

Kelly dug her long pink nails into her palms to halt her tears. She would not let herself think about it. She was only nineteen and who wanted to be tied down with a squalling baby at her age? Mick Todd had done her a favour really. Carol was welcome to him. The man she ended up with would love her and take care of her and they'd have all the babies she wanted in time.

She turned and smiled at Sid. 'Give us a kiss, Sid man,' she ordered.

He tasted of pickled onions and beer, but she enjoyed the warmth of his embrace, the quickening of desire that he always aroused in her. Sid would probably do.

They never went back into the club, but slipped away and ended up in one of the shelters round the bowling green. Later, a little drunk on beer and lust, Sid said to her, 'Why don't we get wed, Kelly? I've always fancied you. How about it?'

It was hardly the romantic moment she had dreamed of, chilly and rain-spattered on a bench by the bowling green, with an inebriated Sid struggling back into his trousers. Still, it would be something to boast to Carol on her return from honeymoon. And it would mean escape from Mafeking Terrace and cancel out for ever the mistake she had made with Mick Todd.

'Aye, go on then,' Kelly agreed.

Sid looked at her in surprise as if he had not expected such a quick victory.

Kelly gazed at him dubiously. 'You'll not forget what you've said in the morning, will you?'

Sid laughed. 'Come here and give us a kiss, Mrs Kelly Armstrong-to-be!'

Kelly giggled and snuggled into his hold, liking the sound of her new name. Maybe this was what she had been looking for all along, she thought with rising optimism, and kissed him back.

Chapter Ten

1979

Carol lumbered to the door of their colliery house in Dominion Terrace and turned her face to the early May sunshine. Mick had gone over to Grandda Bowman's to drive him to the polling station in their new red Cavalier. They had kept the motorbike for old times' sake, but it stood in the yard, shrouded in tarpaulin and unused for months. Mick had said, 'We'll not be needing it any more now the bairn's on the way. It's time we had a family car - fill it up with little Todds.'

Carol rubbed her aching back and felt the baby stir restlessly. She looked down at her inflated body and laughed. 'There's no room in there any more, is there, little pet? Well, don't think of coming today, 'cos your dad's busy with the election and politics comes first in this family - you'll soon learn that.'

'Who you talking to?' Linda startled her from behind. She had let herself in the back with her silent friend Denise, who followed like a faithful shadow. They were tall, bare-legged fifteen-year-olds with bored, stroppy expressions and Carol knew she would have them hanging around the house all day as the school was being used as a polling station. On several occasions recently Linda had been playing truant and she was impatient to leave school at the end of term when she would turn sixteen, though to do what, Carol had no idea.

'I was having a conversation with your nephew or niece-to-be,' Carol smiled.

'Weird. Do you think it can hear?' Linda asked, stretching out green-painted fingernails to touch Carol's bump. Linda was into heavy metal now and was growing her fair hair long and shaggy to cover the love bites she acquired on weekends at the pub discos she and Denise sneaked into without their parents knowing. 'Eeh, I felt it move! Denise, have a feel.'

But her friend just stood there mutely uninterested, her wrists jangling with bracelets as she pushed back her jet black hair in an impatient gesture.

'You go on in,' Carol told them, 'and put the kettle on. You can help me with the jewellery later.'

They padded back into the terraced house in their bare feet and Carol heard the blare of the television as the girls made themselves at home. She sighed and sat on the step, rubbing the neck of Magpie, their stray black and white cat that had turned up over a year ago and found the place to his liking and so stayed. Mick had been optimistic that the black and white cat was an omen of good fortune for both them and Newcastle United and so had given him the club's nickname. Magpie appeared to have done more for them than for Mick's favourite football team, Carol thought, as she sat out of the sea breeze feeling lazy and content like a becalmed vessel, not wanting to move.

She and Mick were happy together in their own home, which they had decorated in fresh yellows and blues and whites: seaside colours, as they had explained to a sceptical Lotty. Carol had decorated the bathroom and kitchen with collages of shells and driftwood and pieces of old fish netting that Captain Lenin had given her. She had painted fish and crabs on the tiles and now she was selling her hand-painted tiles and shell jewellery in Val's shop. It was a side-line she intended keeping going once the baby was born and now that she had finally finished at Vic's office.

Her brother-in-law had offered to take her back on in six months' time but without offering her any maternity benefits in the meantime and Carol had thought it a good excuse not to go back. Even the fact that she was noticeably pregnant had not stopped Vic's attentions - nothing that could be really complained about, just a touch here, the lingering of a hand there, the standing too close and the suggestive remarks. She did not need to put up with Vic's innuendoes any more; Mick was making decent money at the pit and she would soon have their baby to love and look after.

Fay was a different matter. Since the wedding, Carol had kept in touch with her sister and offered to help out when Fay gave birth to twin girls shortly afterwards. At first she had been rebuffed and the designer-dressed babies, Jasmine and Ngaio, had been cared for by a succession of young live-in nannies. But none of them had stayed more than two months and Carol had wondered if this was owing to the interference of a fussing Nancy or the unwelcome attentions of Vic. Probably both, Carol sighed.

The outcome was that on the days when Nancy was occupied with aerobics and coffee mornings or shopping in Sunderland and Newcastle, Fay now frequently dropped off the young toddlers at Carol's small house while she rushed off to her successful healthfood shops.

Occasionally Carol met her mother at Fay's, having pushed the twins back up to Brassy in their de luxe double pushchair, but they had avoided any personalconversation by fussing over the girls. Her father she had not spoken to for nearly two years.

Carol heard the loud-hailer of a campaigning car reach the top of the street and stood up to see if her father-in-law was in it. There was talk of the Conservatives getting into power after the industrial unrest of the winter and the mood in Septimus Street had been gloomy for weeks. Even an amusing letter from Eddy working in the Midlands did not seem to have cheered them up and Carol wished Mick's friendly uncle had not suddenly up and left last year to work away. It appeared Eddy was never going to settle down. Poor, faithful Lesley had finally tired of waiting for him. At Christmas, Paul Dimarco had begun to court her and by Easter they had married. Lesley had left the pit canteen to help her husband in his cafe.

Suddenly a sharp twinge gripped Carol's belly and she cried out in pain. The campaign van sped past and she saw her father-in-law wave grimly, but she could not wave back as she clutched herself.

'I need Mick!' she shouted instinctively, but the blare from the loud-hailer drowned out her cry and the van passed.

The jab of pain subsided and Carol felt foolish for panicking. She turned and went inside. Denise was riveted to the TV programme, but Linda was messing about with some shells and card and glue on the new blue sitting-room carpet. Carol was about to sit down when another spasm clutched her stomach and she gasped aloud.

'I haven't spilt owt!' Linda cried defensively.

'Ohh!' Carol groaned again. 'I'm not worried about that.'

'What's wrong, Carol?' Linda demanded in alarm. 'Bloody hell, you're not going to have the baby here on the new carpet, are you?'

Carol laughed through the pain. 'I think I get more warning than that, Linda man.'

Linda scrambled to her feet and gave Denise a shove. 'Haway, our Carol's going to have her baby! Let's go and find Mam, she'll know what to do.'

Denise stirred reluctantly and got up, shaking the crumbs off her lap from the last of Carol's biscuits.

'Linda,' Carol stopped her. 'Just go and tell Mick to get himself home while I ring the hospital, will you?'

'I don't like to leave you on your own,' Linda said, looking unsure.

'I'll be all right. I'll ring Kelly at the shop if I need anyone.'

The girls fled and Carol went upstairs to pack some things for the hospital, glancing in at the small bedroom they had done up for the baby in blue, because she was convinced it was an energetic boy she was carrying. By the time she got downstairs again, the contractions were fierce and more frequent. Carol was alarmed that it was all happening so quickly; everyone had kept telling her that she would be in for hours of labour with the first one.

Half an hour passed, but there was no sign of Mick. Then Lotty arrived, followed quickly by Kelly because the girls had gone flying into Val's boutique and babbled about Carol's pains.

Lotty saw the agony Carol was in already and shooed her on to the settee.

'I think this one's ready for off,' her mother-in-law announced. 'Call an ambulance now, Kelly.'

When Linda returned, having failed to track down Mick, Carol began to weep. She attempted to stand up, but at the movement a gush of liquid poured between her legs. Linda screamed and Carol flopped down, feeling faint.

'It's just your waters. Don't go getting upset,' Lotty chided. 'You'll need all your breath to get this baby out. Linda, upstairs and get some sheets and towels.' Both Carol and Linda stared at her in horror. 'Just in case the ambulance is too late. Gan on, Linda!'

'I'm off,' Denise said abruptly and disappeared. They were the first words Carol could remember her saying for weeks and this unnerved her more than anything.

'Well, fat lot of use she is when she's needed,' Linda complained and clattered upstairs. Carol lay breathing hard, listening to Linda banging cupboard doors in search of sheets.

'Take them off the bed!' Lotty shouted up. 'Breathe deeply, pet, until you feel the next contraction.'

Carol relaxed a little at her mother-in-law's calm directions as she bustled about. Kelly came out of the kitchen, saying the ambulance was on its way. She took one look at Carol's agonised face and retreated. 'I'll put the kettle on.'

Ten minutes later, Lotty had Carol stripped of her maternity dungarees and underpants and lying on a bed of towels over bin liners in an attempt to save the new settee, and was giving instructions to pant and not push. At this point Linda lay down on the floor, complaining of faintness and left Kelly to hold Carol's hand.

Carol panted and roared and sobbed as the labour took hold and engulfed her body in waves of pain. She could feel the baby's head now between her legs, tearing at her flesh.

'Time to push now, when you feel the contractions,' Lotty ordered gently. 'Go with it, pet.'

Carol pushed and felt relief she could now flow with the pain rather than be battered by it. As she yelled and pushed, she was aware of someone else in the room behind her.

'You get yourself next door to Evelyn's,' Lotty commanded sharply.

Carol stretched round to see Mick standing in the doorway, stunned by the scene.

'Carol?' he gasped in concern, rooted to the spot.

'Stay,' Carol croaked. 'Please.'

Mick looked between his mother and wife, quite paralysed by the unexpected sight of the frantic women and the smell of blood. Carol was seized by another contraction and started to push again.

'Come over here, you soft bugger!' Kelly ordered. 'Take Carol's hand and help her bring out the bairn.'

Mick moved quickly to his wife's side and let her grip his hand hard, not daring to look at what was happening at the other end of the settee. Lotty and Kelly shouted encouragement, while Linda rolled over and switched on the TV to drown out the noise.

Carol was vaguely aware of a commentary about the election as her baby thrust into the world on to the gold Dralon settee. They were interviewing voters coming out of a polling station.

'What is it?' she croaked, still panting. Mick craned over cautiously.

Lotty was bundling the slippery infant into a towel. 'A girl,' she said, with a relieved smile. 'Look, her eyes are already open.'

Mick took the bundle and held her close so Carol could see. 'She's sharp, just like her mam,' he said hoarsely and kissed Carol tenderly.

Carol held her daughter and felt tears of triumph and emotion flood down her face. Her baby had dark eyes that seemed to hold her gaze as if to say she had not been able to wait any longer to be with her.

'She's bonny!' Mick boasted.

'She's bald,' Linda pointed out, having crept forward to look.

'She's both,' Carol laughed and hugged her closer protectively and kissed her sweet, puckered face. She was ready to smother this baby with the love she had been denied as a child. For the first time in her life she felt gripped by a strong sense of purpose and it made her deliriously happy.

'What are you going to call her?' Linda asked.

'Anything but Margaret, please,' Lotty winked, 'or Charlie'll not speak to you both.'

Carol and Mick exchanged looks.

'She's Laura Kelly,' Carol announced with a tired smile and looked over at her oldest friend. 'Laura 'cos we like the name and Kelly 'cos we'd like you to be godmother.'

For a moment Kelly stared at her with a strange look and then she laughed, a little hysterically. That instant, they heard a siren blaring outside as the ambulance arrived.

'I'll let them in,' Kelly said, still laughing, and rushed from the room.

Carol sank back, too exhausted to think of Kelly's reaction as strange.

It was only Lotty who, two hours later, finding the red-haired Kelly in the back yard crying her eyes out, pondered on it. Afterwards she told Charlie that she

71

thought it odd and wondered what had really gone on between Kelly and their son. 'Do you think the lass could be jealous of Carol being so happy with our Mick?'

But her husband was not listening, for by that time it was clear that the Conservatives had won the election and that Margaret Thatcher was making history as the first British woman Prime Minister.

'Margaret Thatcher, the milk snatcher!' Charlie growled with disgust. 'Now we're about to find out what else she wants to snatch from working people.'

'Come to bed,' Lotty yawned, too weary with the day's events to worry about tomorrow.

'Aye,' Charlie said, deeply despondent, 'we might as well get some kip now, for we'll not dare sleep for the next four years.'

Chapter Eleven

1983

In the autumn that Laura started school, Carol went back to work for Val Bowman. She and Mick had finally bought their own house, but Carol felt achingly lonely when she returned from seeing Laura safely into school, her new winter coat unbuttoned and hung on its peg and her sandshoe bag hanging next to it. Where had her babyhood gone? Carol wondered tearfully, gazing at her daughter's chuckling baby face and mass of fair curls in the photograph on the mantelpiece. Since the startling birth, Carol had immersed herself in caring for Laura. But now her daughter did not need her as much, would never be as dependent on her again, and she had taken Val's offer of a job to fill the great void in her life.

What a companion Laura had been these past four and a half years, Carol thought tenderly, and what a bridge builder. For Laura had been the catalyst for the truce with her parents. They could have gone on for years not speaking. But Lotty gently chivvied her into going round to see them with Laura.

'Seems a shame for them not to see what a bonny grandbairn they've got.'

'They're quite happy spoiling Jasmine and Ngaio,' Carol had answered, fearful of the idea.

'Those little terrors!' Lotty had snorted. 'Let your mam and dad see what they're really missing - a granddaughter to be proud of.'

So Carol had plucked up courage and gone one Saturday afternoon when Mick had been playing rugby away at Horden. She found her father alone in the garden. Laura had tottered over to see him, fallen into a tray of new bedding plants and Ben had reached her before Carol could. Laura had put a pudgy, soily hand into his mouth and grinned at him with her gummy smile and Carol had seen her father's stern face soften.

He had become quite boyish and taken his granddaughter round to the side lawn where an array of garden swings and slides and climbing frames had been erected for Fay's girls. Ben put Laura gently into a baby swing and chuckled at her enjoyment.

'Jasmine and Ngaio spend about five minutes on all this and then say they're bored,' he confided.

He asked Carol polite questions about her house and her jewellery-making, until she could not bear the falseness of it all and said she would have to go. All her pent-up anger at his violent rejection of her and her new family, his refusal to come to her wedding and the wasted years of not speaking, threatened to boil over. She was so furious with him! But she bit back angry words so as not to upset the unsuspecting Laura. With the innocence of a baby, Laura accepted everyone she met with the same uncritical warmth and trust; Carol wished she could protect her daughter from the pain of growing up.

'Tell Mam I came round,' she mumbled.

'Stay till she comes back from shopping,' he urged and Carol had the impression he really did not want her to go.

'She'll be hours if she's gone into Newcastle,' Carol joked and scooped up Laura from exploring a flowerbed.

'You'll come again then? And bring Laura?' he asked, his usually stern face unsure. Carol thought he had aged a lot, his hair and moustache quite silver, his eyes sagging in the once confident face.

How had she been able to hate this ageing man so much? Then she remembered the injustices he had done to her. She wanted to scream all her angry questions at him. Why had he not been able to love her like he did Fay and Simon? What had she done that had been so terrible? Why could he not have delighted in her company as he now did in Laura's? Instead she said bitterly, 'Why the hell should I? You didn't even come to her christening!'

They stared at each other as if across a chasm, neither prepared to cross it first. Carol saw his face harden once more into set, uncompromising lines. That stubborn jaw was so familiar. Her father would never admit he was wrong about anything; he would die rather than show such a sign of weakness.

So she turned to go, annoyed with herself for coming. It had been a futile mistake.

'Carol. Wait.' She heard the uncertainty in his voice and glanced back. She could see him struggling. Finally he said in a stumbling way, 'I'm sorry we fell out like we did. There are things, well, I wish I hadn't said. You know it's not easy for me to admit that but, anyway, I'm glad you came today.'

It wasn't much, but Carol knew how difficult it was for her father to humble himself to her and she felt that terrible knot of anger and bitterness inside her ease a fraction. In the past she had always been quick to speak before thinking, had never been lost for fighting words to fling back at him, but now she could think of nothing adequate to say. So she had merely nodded and turned away, her eyes stinging with tears.

But it was the beginning of a cautious reconciliation. She allowed her parents to make a fuss over Laura on subsequent occasions, but Mick would never go with her to see them. She did not blame him; she knew the hurt that her parents' snobbishness had inflicted on him.

After a couple of months, Carol found herself enjoying working again. Val was doing a booming trade in bridal hire and Carol, under Val's guidance, discovered she had a talent for dressmaking and did most of the alterations. She enjoyed the bustle of the shop and meeting the young women who came to plan their spring weddings. At lunchtime she would meet Kelly and go for a sandwich at Dimarco's.

'How's Laura getting on at school?' Paul Dimarco called over the counter one day. Laura's biggest treat was to go to the cafe for a Knickerbocker Glory served in a tall glass with a long spoon. Paul had dark good looks like his father, whose photograph hung above the counter - a young soldier in uniform standing beside his Italian parents outside their cafe in Whitton Grange.

'Grand, thanks,' Carol smiled. 'She brought back her first reading book this week. And the paintings she's doing are fantastic.'

Paul chuckled. 'Tell her if she can read the whole book to me she can have a free ice cream on Saturday.'

Carol could have gone on talking about her daughter all day, but she sensed Kelly's restlessness and stopped herself. Kelly and Sid were still childless, although Carol knew they had been trying for a baby for years. For a while Sid had persuaded Kelly to finish work, blaming her for doing too much, but Kelly had just got bored sitting around at home waiting for Sid to come off shift and had got herself a job at Proud's travel shop.

Kelly gave Paul a bold look. 'And what do we lasses have to do to get a free ice cream?'

Paul was used to her flirtatiousness and laughed it off. 'Be under six years old,' he teased back, wiped the table and moved on swiftly to chat to another customer.

'I can't understand how Lesley got her hands on him,' Kelly said, stirring her coffee dreamily.

'Because she's canny.' Carol gave her friend an impatient smile. 'And you're happily married too, remember?'

'No harm in just looking,' Kelly grinned.

'He must be twice our age,' Carol whispered.

'He's thirty-nine.'

Carol raised her eyebrows.

'Val told me.' Kelly looked smug. 'She's known him ever since he moved from Whitton Grange when the pit closed. They're a story and a half, the Dimarcos.'

'Well, you can tell me another time,' Carol said, stubbing out her cigarette. 'I've got a bridesmaid's dress to finish before I collect Laura.'

Kelly looked at her friend in disappointment. She would have liked to stay and gossip about the Dimarcos and drink more coffee and eye up the proprietor. Carol was no fun these days; all she cared about was bridal dresses and darling Laura and rushing home to be there for Mick. Kelly's stomach twisted with resentment. Where was the rebellious Carol with the dyed orange hair and black make-up who had thought nothing of running off to London in the seventies? Now her hair was back to long brown waves and her green eyes shone in an unmade-up face. She looked more like a schoolgirl than she had at school, Kelly thought and glanced away to be met by her own sallow reflection in the wall mirror.

'I'll see you in here tomorrow then,' Kelly said and began to clear up their cups. But after Carol rushed off with a wave at Paul Dimarco, she settled back into the mock leather bench seat and caught Paul's eye. 'I'll have another coffee, please,' she smiled and flicked her red fringe out of her eyes.

Carol worried about Kelly and Sid. It had been a while since they had all gone out together socially, but last week had been Mick's thirtieth birthday and she had organised a party for him at the Welfare. The place had been full of family and friends and there had been a nice buffet and a disco with lots of nostalgic seventies hits, but Carol had not enjoyed it. The men had stood in sombre groups at the bar talking about the overtime ban at the pit and Charlie had fulminated about the new NCB Chairman, MacGregor.

'He's stirring things up with the union, not consulting us about matters. He's even talking about encouraging foreign investment in our mines.'

Sid and Mick had begun to argue about the hit list of seventy-five pits that NUM President Arthur Scargill had warned were threatened with closure.

'It makes nee difference to us, Mick man!' Sid had said. 'Brassbank's got millions of tons of coal in reserve - it'll not affect us. Pits have been closing for decades. They get worked out and the pitmen move on.'

'But what if they start closing pits that have still got plenty reserves in them, like Arthur says?' Mick worried. 'Just say they're uneconomic and close them anyways? Then where do Durham pitmen move on to?'

'Well, it's not going to happen here. Super pits like Brassbank are the future of mining. There'll be jobs here till we're long dead and gone, they've told us that.'

Sid slurped his beer. 'Haway, birthday boy, let's get the beers in.'

Carol had tried to get Sid on to the dance floor with Kelly, but he seemed more interested in working his way through the free kegs of beer, while Kelly flirted with his friends in the corner. Then she had found herself in the middle of another crisis, trying to calm down a furious Lotty who had found her precious daughter wrapped round a young miner in a committee room upstairs. Linda had been marched home in tears and Carol had missed Mick's speech and the cutting of the cake. When she had gone outside to stand under the chill November stars and smoke a peaceful cigarette, she had seen Kelly sneaking off with someone.

She was so preoccupied with worrying about Kelly's marriage that Carol did not notice at first what was happening under her nose at home. Linda, who was now working part-time at the pit canteen, was constantly round at their house. There was nothing new in this, as she spent more time with them than at home these days and loved to mother Laura, but as the weeks drew nearer to Christmas, Linda began to offer to babysit more and more rather than go out, which made Carol suspicious.

She was seeing the young miner she had met at Mick's birthday party, but he always arrived after they went out and was gone before they got back from their night out.

'Why don't you want us to meet him?' Carol teased. 'Is he too respectable?'

Linda had blushed. 'I want you to, Carol, but Dan's shy - not one for company.'

'Where does he live?'

'Whittledene.'

'With his family?'

'Aye, but he's getting his own flat shortly. Stop asking questions, Carol, you're worse than Mam.'

Carol tried talking to Mick about the mysterious Dan.

'Do you see him at work?'

'No, he's on a different shift - never set eyes on the lad.'

'Do you know his family?'

Mick shook his head. 'They're not from the village. Sid says they're not a mining family at all.' He laughed at her concerned face. 'Carol, you're getting as nosy as me mam. Who would've thought you'd worry about such things.'

That night they had planned to take Grandda Bowman out for a drink but had arrived to find him full of cold and not wanting to leave his fireside. It looked so cosy and inviting that Mick suggested, 'Let's gan home and cuddle in front of our own fire, eh?'

Carol had agreed at once and they had returned to find the lights out downstairs. Coming in through the kitchen, they thought the sitting room was empty, until Mick snapped on the lights to find Linda and her boyfriend illuminated on the Dralon settee, struggling to do up buttons.

Carol stared at them and then at Mick's shocked face and burst out laughing.

'Well, I don't think it's funny,' Mick spluttered. 'It's the last time you take advantage of us like that, Linda. You're supposed to be looking after Laura, not having it off on our settee!'

Linda was a flustered puce, but the lean-faced Dan stood up aggressively and said, 'The bairn's fast asleep. And from what Linda tells me, there's a lot worse gone on on this settee than what we were doing.' He turned and glared at Carol.

She blushed to think he was referring to her giving birth on their couch and was suddenly cross with Linda for telling this stranger such personal details.

'Linda!' she chided.

Linda sparked in defence. 'Well, don't you get so high and mighty all of a sudden. You were no angel with our Mick. All the village knew about you going off with him when you hardly knew him.'

Mick sprang forward. 'Don't you speak to Carol like that, do you hear?'

Dan gave a harsh laugh as he reached for Linda's hand and pulled her away. 'Linda's right. Even I knew Carol was easy.'

Carol gasped in shock at the insult and gave him a blazing look. There was something familiar about him ...

'That's it. Get out, Dan Hardman!' Mick thundered. 'Get out before I give you a good kickin'!'

Dan sneered, 'Think you're so hard, you Todds, don't you? Well, you're a bunch of tossers!' He pulled Linda with him. 'Come on, you're not stopping here. I've had enough of sneaking around trying to avoid your precious family. From now on we go out in Whittledene with my mates.'

Linda looked frightened and undecided. The petulant jut of Dan's chin and his resentful eyes triggered a memory for Carol.

'Dan Hardman? Aye, I remember you now. You're Vic's cousin. You were at his wedding.'

She saw him flush at the reminder. Then, he had been pimply and gauche and had wanted to tag along with her and her friends. He had been only fifteen and she had not let him; he had taken offence. But that was no reason to be so insulting to her and the Todds now.

Carol said quickly, 'Don't let him bully you, Linda. You don't have to go with him at all. You know you can stay with us any time you want.'

For a long moment Linda agonised between rushing to Carol and hugging her tight or going with her boyfriend. She loved Carol, had thought she was wonderful since the time she'd come into the family and stirred it up with her punk rock and her forceful ways. But she was in love with Dan. He was glamorous because he wasn't one of the village lads and he had a car and friends who had money, and he had a lovely body and was making a fuss over her now, wanting her to come with him. She wasn't going to be made to feel small by her overprotective brother.

'I'm going with Dan,' she said defiantly and tossed her long fair hair.

Carol was reminded of herself for an instant and put out a restraining arm to prevent Mick from stopping his sister going.

'Let her go,' Carol said quietly. 'But Linda, you know we won't turn you away any time you want to come back.'

'She'll not be coming back,' Dan snarled, grabbing his jacket, and pushed Linda out of the room.

Carol found Laura shivering on the stairs and was instantly worried about how much the child had overheard.

'Why was Daddy shouting?'

'It's nothing, pet.' Carol bundled her back to bed but lay awake that night anxious at what had been said in the heat of the moment.

The next day, Lotty sought her out at the shop, beside herself with worry.

'Is Linda at your house? She's taken her things and gone. I'm that worried!'

Carol left work early and went round to be with Lotty.

'She'll be back in a few days - she'll miss her home comforts too much,' Carol tried to reassure her distraught mother-in-law.

'Charlie's furious. He might not have her back.'

Carol thought ruefully how similar this was to the rift with her own father. But the difference was, Carol knew, that however much Charlie Todd disapproved of his daughter's carrying on, he would never cast her out of the fold. For although her father-in-law was not a man to be crossed, he was staunchly loyal to his own kind and he loved his family above all.

But Linda did not come home and she lost her job at the pit canteen for not turning up for work. As Christmas approached, Carol knew she must go and find her, for her absence was breaking Lotty's heart. Mick had confronted Dan at the pit gates, but the surly young man would tell him nothing about his sister.

In the end, Carol went to Vic and asked him to find out where his cousin lived.

Vic shrugged. 'Why interfere?'

'I won't if I find Linda's happy with him. I'd be the last one to tell her what to do with her life. But it's the not knowing. She's cut herself off from her family and they're worried sick.'

A couple of days before Christmas Vic phoned Carol with an address on a new estate on the fringes of Whittledene.

'It was a bit tricky,' Vic warned her. 'Dan's parents don't approve of his living with your sister-in-law. In fact they thought a job in the pit was beneath Dan as well. Apparently he only took it because he couldn't get anything else. So they don't really know what's going on either.'

Val gave Carol the day off work and she took Laura into Whittledene on the bus. The girl chattered excitedly about Santa and gawped at the gaudy street lights and the decorated shops thronged with Christmas shoppers. Carol felt a secret thrill to know how overjoyed her daughter would be when she came downstairs on Christmas morning to find a bulging stocking and the piles of presents waiting for her by their Christmas tree. Laura had helped her decorate the tree weeks ago; Carol loved everything about Christmas and couldn't wait for all the rituals to begin.

She grew nervous as they boarded another bus and headed into the maze of Whittledene Rise Estate, wondering what she would find. After half an hour of searching for the right block of flats and asking directions, Laura was fractious and wanting to go home. Carol placated her by promising something to eat when they got to Auntie Linda's.

Eventually she found the impersonal block of flats and buzzed on the intercom. Linda's disembodied voice answered and, after a shout from Laura, she let them in.

Linda looked pale, her hair lank, she'd been slopping around the flat in leggings and a baggy jumper of Dan's. The flat still smelled of fresh paint and new carpets and there was MFI furniture in the sitting room. But it was all quite bland and impersonal, like the estate itself; there were no homely touches or signs of Linda's belongings save her radio cassette player by the window and a pile of Mills & Boon on the cane coffee table. The TV blared in the corner unheeded and Carol noticed a video machine beneath it. Linda was a visitor here, Carol thought, this was not her home.

She bided her time while Laura explored the small flat and gabbled to her aunt about being in the Christmas play at school.

'I was a mouse in the stable,' Laura said proudly.

'That sounds like a star part,' Linda teased, her thin face lighting up with the banter.

'It was,' Laura nodded. 'I wasn't the only mouse, mind. There were ten of us. Me and Sarah and Louise and Tracey and Mark Taylor and Gillian and Ali Jabbar and Lorraine and - I can't remember. Who have I said?'

'I think she gets the picture,' Carol laughed.

'Why didn't you come and watch, Auntie Linda, like you said you would?'

Linda looked uncomfortable and let her long hair fall over her face.

'Why don't you see what's on the telly, pet?' Carol said to distract her daughter. Laura went and lay down on the floor quickly, not used to being allowed to watch TV so early in the day.

'Linda,' Carol asked quietly, 'are you all right here?'

Linda shook out her hair. 'Course I am. Look at this place, it's lush. I can do what I want, get up when I want, watch what I want. Dan gets me everything, he's a good spender.'

'So you're not working?'

'Dan likes me here when he gets home,' Linda said, as if it was something worth boasting about. 'Anyway, who wants to work in a grotty canteen?'

Carol bit her tongue. 'Don't you find it a bit lonely out here?'

'I've got Dan for company.' Linda was defensive.

'But when he's at work . . .'

'We've got a good social life - he's got stacks of mates round here. He's always out - we both are, I mean.'

Carol's dismay increased. 'And I suppose you see his family, do you?' she asked lightly.

Linda's mouth tightened. She could not admit to their hostility towards her.

'Your mam's dying to see you. Couldn't you just come home for Christmas?' Carol pleaded.

'Dan and me have planned a special dinner, it's all booked at the local pub - after he's been to see . . .' Linda hung her head.

Carol stretched out a hand. 'You could pop home and see your family too. Come tomorrow, Christmas Eve.'

Linda flinched and moved out of her reach. 'I can't.'

'You can,' Carol urged. They won't give you a hard time; they'll just be pleased to see .you.'

Linda's look was harrowed. 'I can't face them, Carol.'

Carol began to lose patience. She could not bear to think of the lively Linda cooped up in this soulless flat, killing empty hours waiting for Dan to return. And if he cared for her so much, why did he spend all his time with his other mates?

'Look at yourself, Linda man! You've cut yourself off from everyone who cares for you. If Dan really loves you, why is he afraid of letting you see your own family?'

Linda suddenly burst into tears. Carol leapt across and hugged her. Laura looked up, startled.

'Tell me what's wrong,' Carol urged.

'Oh, Carol,' Linda sobbed. 'It's me who's afraid of seeing them. Oh, God, Carol, I-I'm pregnant!'

Chapter Twelve

1984

'What do you mean he won't marry you?' Lotty was scandalised.

'We don't want to get married,' Linda told her mother, her look stubborn. The family were gathered in the cosy sitting room in Dominion Terrace, but tempers were growing hotter than Carol's roaring coal fire behind its protective glass screen.

'I'll see that the bugger weds you!' Charlie bellowed. 'Nobody treats a daughter of mine like that.'

'It's not for you to say, Dad,' Linda rounded on him. 'Dan thinks we're too young to get married yet.'

'And maybe he's right,' Lotty said, 'but you've a bairn on the way so things are different.'

Linda rocked dangerously on two legs of her chair. 'We've decided to live together for a bit. You don't have to get wed any more because there's a baby.'

'Oh, aye?' Charlie thundered. 'And you think this Dan Hardman is going to stand by you once the bairn is born if he won't marry you now? You're living in cloud cuckoo land, Linda.'

Val tutted. 'I don't know what you see in such a lad. He obviously has no respect for you. Can't you see the way you're upsetting your mam and dad?'

Linda lashed out. 'You're just jealous of what I've got because you've ended up a sad old spinster!'

Val threw up her hands with impatience.

Lotty wagged a finger. 'Don't you speak to your Auntie Val like that. She's done far better for herself than you ever will. You're a silly, selfish lass! Fancy running off and getting yourself pregnant. It's not just your life you've got to consider; what about the poor bairn? What sort of home is it going to be born into with a dad who doesn't even want to give it his name?'

'And where is he?' Charlie demanded. 'He hasn't even got the decency to face us!'

Linda threw Carol a desperate look and Carol wondered if she had done the right thing by bringing Linda to face her censorious family. She was thankful that Mick had taken Laura over to Grandda Bowman's to avoid the row, but it was almost dark and she wished Mick would hurry back. What could be keeping him?

It was that bleak time in January when the Christmas decorations had been put away and the days were short and dark and lifeless. And here were her in-laws bickering among themselves over the hapless Linda and her unborn baby. Whatever she said she would be condemned, Carol thought, because they resented her, the outsider, for knowing about the baby since before Christmas. But they were all turning to stare at her now.

'What's happened has happened and we just have to make the best of it,' Carol said stoutly. 'None of us can make Dan and Linda marry if they don't want to. Perhaps when the baby comes along he'll realise that it's best if they do, but until then we just have to support Linda. We can't do any more and all the arguing in the world isn't going to change a thing.'

Linda smiled in gratitude. 'See, Carol understands.'

This seemed to incense her parents and they started to shout at the same time. 'That's typical!'

'Take the easy way out, is that it, Carol?'

'The lad has responsibilities!'

'You've always encouraged Linda to go her own way - now look what's happened.'

Linda suddenly leapt up. 'Shut up, both of you!'

An astonished silence fell on the room as they gawped at her livid face.

'You've no right to attack Carol like that. She's the only one who's really bothered about what I want. The rest of you are just worried what the village gossips will say. Well, I'm going to keep me baby and care for it just as well as any of you would, and I'm going back to live with Dan 'cos I love him and that's where I want to be.'

The room seemed to echo with her words and they all sat in stunned silence, as if they had run out of steam.

With a surge of relief, Carol heard Mick and Laura clump in at the front door, their chatter lively. The door swung open and Laura raced in and rushed straight to Lotty. Her grandmother put out eager arms and at once her strained face was beaming.

'Nana, nana! I've got a surprise for you.' Laura announced breathlessly, still wearing her coat and woolly hat and scarf. Her cheeks were pink with cold and excitement.

'What's that then, pet?' Lotty laughed. 'Have you brought me something from Grandda's?'

Mick came in grinning. 'You could say that. We found him at Grandda's, any road.'

Everyone craned to see. Laura sprang across the room again and dragged the mystery guest through the door.

'Eddy!' The screech went round the room.

Carol was overjoyed to see Mick's uncle standing there, an impish smile on his craggy face, with Laura scooped up into his arms.

'You're back!'

'Are you back for good?'

'You should've said. We could've come to meet you!'

They all crowded round him, showering him with hugs and kisses and handshakes.

'Laura's already told me off for missing Christmas,' Eddy laughed. 'But I'm back now and I'm staying put. I've had enough of working in that Midlands pit.'

'Well, I'm glad to hear it, pet,' Lotty smiled. 'But let's get you home and the tea on.'

'Why don't you all have your tea here?' Carol offered at once, and before Lotty could refuse, Mick insisted too.

'So what are you going to do?' Charlie sat down with his brother. 'There's an overtime ban at the pit and things are looking dodgy.'

'Don't let him put you off with his doom and gloom,' Lotty scoffed. 'You'll find summat here.'

'Aye, I already have,' Eddy said with a pleased look. 'Start Monday in the workshops.'

'Well, that's champion,' Mick said, giving him a pat on the back. 'Think we might go down The Ship later and celebrate with the Captain, eh?'

'Took the words out me mouth, bonny lad,' Eddy chuckled. He smiled over at

Carol. 'That's if you don't mind, flower?'

Carol laughed. 'Learnt some manners towards the lasses while you've been away, Uncle Eddy? Have we the southerners to thank for that?'

'Thank them for nothing,' Charlie grunted. 'They sent the bugger back to us.'

Eddy laughed the loudest. 'By, I've missed these family get-togethers. It's what's brought me home, if I'm honest. All us Todds together again.'

'Oh, aye?' Val chortled. 'And now Lesley's married off, it's safe to come home?'

Eddy winked at her and grinned. 'So, tell me, is it something special? Have I forgotten someone's birthday?'

An awkward silence descended as looks were exchanged round the room.

'Well, Eddy,' Lotty cleared her throat. 'Our Linda's got something to tell you.'

Uncle Eddy's surprise arrival put an end to the family squabble over Linda and she returned to Whittledene knowing she could rely on her family if she needed them. As February came and work grew busy at the hire shop, Carol felt happier that things were going to turn out all right for them all - for Linda and the baby, for Eddy who did not seem the least upset at Lesley marrying Paul Dimarco in his absence, and for her and Mick. Laura was happy at school, Mick was content with his rugby and a quiet pint with his uncle or Sid, and they hoped one day for another baby. They had never planned for Laura to be an only child, but it looked increasingly as if she would be. But when she thought of Kelly, who had never managed to become pregnant, Carol knew she was lucky to have her precious daughter.

Perhaps it was because she had been so preoccupied with Linda's troubles and Kelly's dissatisfaction with Sid, or too busy at work, or so content with having the amusing Eddy back in the village that Carol had not seen trouble coming. But then no one seemed to have foreseen the tidal wave of trouble rolling towards them with such momentous strength, until it broke and came crashing over their heads in early March.

It was a cold Thursday evening when Carol made her way from the shop to Septimus Street to pick up Laura

She had been working late for Val, doing a final fitting for Stan Savage's daughter, Angela, who was getting married at the end of the month, and Lotty had picked Laura up from school. Entering the warm kitchen, all seemed normal. Laura looked up from her tea of ham steak and vegetables and grinned in welcome.

'Hello, pet,' Carol said, kissing her daughter. 'What have you done today?'

'Can't remember,' Laura smiled. 'Can we go swimming on Saturday?'

'She started a new reading book,' Lotty prompted, peering over her sewing glasses. 'And she's doing a project on grandparents, aren't you, Laura?'

'Oh, yes,' Laura said absently. 'Please, Mam, can we go swimming?'

'Perhaps after Daddy gets back from work,' Carol half promised.

'Yeah!' Laura clapped her hands with glee.

Suddenly Grandda Bowman appeared at the partitioned doorway that led into the sitting room, wheezing hard. Carol had been vaguely aware of the TV grumbling away in the far room and the old man shouting for it to be turned up. Carol saw the look of concern on his weathered face.

'What's wrong?' she asked.

'They're closing Cortonwood in Yorkshire - it's just been announced on the telly.'

'Isn't that where your cousin Geoff works?' Carol asked, turning to Lotty.

Lotty nodded.

'But Cortonwood's one of the super pits,' Carol said in astonishment. 'I remember Geoff saying in his Christmas card they've just had new pit baths put in and—'

Charlie came storming into the kitchen. 'There must be some mistake!' he cried. There's been nowt said about this as far as we've heard. They can't just say a pit's going to close in a month's time without it going through the proper procedures. There's a rabbit off here.' He grabbed his jacket from the back of his chair. 'I'm off to the Welfare to do some ringing around.'

He left immediately, leaving the women troubled. Carol had a gnawing anxiety in the pit of her stomach, but didn't know why.

'What's wrong with Grandda Charlie?' Laura asked, puzzled.

Lotty went and put her arms round the girl's narrow shoulders and Carol instinctively felt it was to comfort herself rather than the child. 'Oh, just union business, pet.'

Carol exchanged glances with her mother-in-law. 'You're not just worried for Geoff, are you?' she murmured. 'There's more to this, isn't there?'

Lotty shrugged.

'Charlie thinks so,' Grandda Bowman fretted, gripping the back of a chair. 'Cortonwood's not a pit that's worked out, it's got plenty stocks of coal.'

'So why are they closing it without any warning?' Carol asked, baffled. 'They must know the Union won't stand for that.'

'Aye,' Grandda Bowman agreed, sucking in his cheeks, 'and maybe that's why they're doing it - forcing a confrontation. Who knows?'

Carol shivered. 'Well, it's just the one pit - it's a matter for Yorkshire, isn't it?'

Lotty gave her a strange look and shook her head. 'No, Carol, you should know by now that when it comes to the crunch, we all stick together. The union won't stand by and see pits picked off one by one.'

Carol felt her throat go dry. Up until now, her greatest anxiety for Mick had been that of any miner's wife - fear of the danger below ground. She had become used to glancing at the clock and listening out for the buzzer at the end of his shift and the lightening of her spirits to hear him tramping through the front door and calling out her name. But now she was beset by a new fear of uncertainty. She didn't know what this announcement really meant, none of them did, and it was the not knowing that sent her hurrying home, clutching Laura's hand tightly in hers and praying that it was all a fuss about nothing.

She hardly had time to talk to Mick about it as he hurried off for the late shift and by the time he had surfaced the next day and she had returned from work, there was a further announcement of the closure of Bullcliffe Wood, near Barnsley. Rumours were rife around the school gate when she collected Laura that Friday and Mick and the other men spent much of the weekend hanging around the Welfare and the clubs, trying to find out more.

By Monday it became clear that the Yorkshire NUM were calling a strike for the Yorkshire area, to begin on the last shift on Friday. The following day, MacGregor announced that twenty more pits would close.

'That's a loss of twenty thousand jobs!' Mick fumed when Carol got in from the shop. 'And he's refusing to say that there won't be compulsory redundancies.'

'But does it affect Brassbank?' Carol asked anxiously.

Mick looked at her sharply. 'It affects all the NUM whether it's our pit or not.'

Carol still did not understand. 'But Durham hasn't voted to strike or anything.'

'Listen, Carol,' Mick said urgently, making her sit down, 'this is very serious. It matters nowt whether we've taken a vote or not, they're already striking in Yorkshire. It's just a matter of time before we're all picketed out - that's the best way to start a strike.

There's one thing you can be sure of, no union lads are going to cross a picket line 'cos loyalty to the union gans first. That's how we won in seventy-two and seventy-four.'

The following day, Carol could see that Mick was right. Two Scottish pits went on strike and by the Thursday all of Scotland, Wales, Yorkshire and Kent were granted official area disputes by the national executive in Sheffield. By Friday the pickets arrived in Brassbank and Mick went up to the pit as a formality, knowing that he would be turned away from work.

'Guess who I met at the picket?' he grunted. 'Me cousin Geoff. Mam's putting him up, along with a couple of the other lads.'

'What's their news?' Carol asked as she folded up the ironing. She was tired after a week's work and the anxiety over the pit, yet it all seemed so unreal. She could not imagine what it was all going to mean to them. There had been threats of strikes three years ago, but the Government had backed away and everything had settled down as before, so perhaps it meant very little. Business in the streets of Brassbank seemed as brisk as ever and she had a feeling of being cocooned from outside events as if it was all going on far away. But now the possibility of a strike was lapping at their door and she had a sudden chill feeling of fear.

'They reckon half the coalfield's out already,' Mick replied, settling to watch the evening news.

'So it might all be over quite soon, then?' Carol asked with a surge of optimism.

Mick's face was sombre. 'Nottingham's the sticking point though; they're going to take some convincing.'

'Why should they be any different?' Carol could see the worry on her husband's face.

'They're happy making good bonuses in big, modern pits,' Mick snorted. 'There's a lot of lads come into the Notts pits for the money, who've never been pitmen before - not from mining families. They don't have the same loyalty to the union as we do in the old mining areas. We've seen how the union has fought for us over the years. We'd still be working in dodgy private pits with piss poor wages and nee holidays if it hadn't been for the union.'

Carol came and put her arms round his neck as he sat tensely on the settee. 'You don't have to convince me about it, Mick love.' She kissed his cheek.

Mick smiled up at her, but his blue eyes were searching. 'Carol, if it comes to all-out strike, it won't be easy for us. Will you be able to . . .?'

'Support you?' Carol asked. She gave him a look of annoyance. 'Do you still think that because I'm the boss's daughter I'll not be able to stick it if things get tough? Well, you should know me better than that, Mick man. I'll always back you, however hard it gets.' She bent again and whispered in his ear. 'Loving and doing go together - and I love you very much.'

For an instant she saw his eyes glisten with emotion and then he was pulling her over the back of the settee on to his lap.

'Give us a kiss!' he grinned.

Carol laughed and kissed him tenderly and then he pulled her up and suggested an early night.

'What you doing back here?' Kelly demanded when Sid returned twenty minutes after leaving for his shift.

'Pickets turned us back,' he explained and threw down his bag. He had hardly kicked off his boots when she rounded on him.

'What do you mean by that? They can't stop you, you're not on strike. You should've gone in. We can't manage on just my wages, so don't think you'll be stopping work.'

Sid gave her a baffled look and noticed for the first time that she appeared to be dressed up to go out. Her short red hair was gelled and there was a smell of fresh nail varnish in the room.

'Where are you going?' he demanded, going on the attack too. 'You never said owt about going out.'

'I'm meeting Carol,' Kelly replied curtly, 'and don't go changing the subject.'

'You must be daft if you think I'd cross a bloody picket line,' Sid snapped. 'Life wouldn't be worth living around here if I did, you know that as well as I do.'

'The sooner this is all settled the better.'

'I agree with you there,' Sid sighed and put his feet up on the coffee table. He flicked on the TV while Kelly reached for her bag and checked it for cigarettes. 'Where you going? I might join you later.'

Kelly waved a hand vaguely. 'Oh, we haven't decided yet.'

Sid gave her a bleak look. 'I'll probably go down the club later and see what's happening.'

'Aye, do that,' Kelly answered and hurried out.

Sid went into the kitchen and helped himself to a can of lager, wondering why Mick had never mentioned that Carol was seeing Kelly that evening. The sweetness of Kelly's perfume still hung in the room and Sid felt suddenly very alone and empty. He would have to put a stop to Kelly's disappearances and the money she seemed to spend too easily, whether there was a strike or not. Sid banged down his full can on the coffee table where it frothed angrily. He would go and seek company at the club, he decided, since he couldn't find it here. Pushing on his boots, he stormed out of their quiet semi-detached house. They had bought Number Six, the Birches, two years ago on the small development after the 1920s Coliseum cinema had been pulled down, but he had never thought of it as home.

That Saturday, loud-hailers were heard around the close streets and back lanes of Brassbank, announcing a meeting at the Welfare that evening. Carol knew from Mick that his father was going to speak as union branch delegate and she was curious to hear him.

'Come and help me in the kitchen,' Lotty suggested when Carol raised the matter of going. 'We'll put tea on afterwards. Our Val can stop in with Laura.'

Carol was pleased that her mother-in-law had suggested it, but she was quite unprepared for the sight that evening. People had come in from the surrounding villages and the car park was overflowing, with cars lining the length of the high street. As she helped Lotty fill the large urn, she glanced out at the packed hall and said, 'This'll never make enough tea for all that lot.'

'They'll not all want tea,' Lotty laughed and busied herself putting out cups and saucers.

When the meeting began, Carol squeezed into the hall, noticing the overflow of people listening through the open doors at the back. The branch secretary had already spoken, but there was a lot of calling and grumbling from the assembled miners. Then Charlie Todd got up to speak and Carol could see her small, thickset father-in-law standing with fists gripped like a fighter. His voice carried across the restless crowd.

'Comrades! This is going to be the most important meeting of your working lives, believe me. This isn't just to decide about Cortonwood or any other pit, it's a fight for the union - our union!'

'He's telling lies!' someone shouted from the depths of the heaving mass.

'Not a word of a lie!' Charlie shouted back and stabbed the air with his finger. 'Cortonwood is just a test for us to see if we'll stand up for our livelihoods. If they can close Cortonwood saying its coal is too expensive then they can close any pit on economic grounds.'

'Never Brassbank!'

'Aye, even Brassbank! They're testing our loyalty to the NUM, and if we fail we might as well close down the morra. 'Cos if you don't back the union, why should management listen to us?'

'We should only strike for pay, like we did in seventy-two and seventy-four,' another member shouted. 'That's what the union's for. This doesn't affect us.'

'By God it does! This is more important than striking for pay,' Charlie insisted. 'We're fighting here for the right to work - for us and for our sons and our grandsons! Cortonwood was closed overnight with no review and no consultation - no redundancy notice. Men had been transferred there only in December and told they had a secure future. Now they're out on their ear in a couple of weeks' time. And that's just the start of it, the beginning of a massive pit closure programme, just like Arthur Scargill told us. Don't trust their promises that your jobs are safe, it means nowt. The only thing you can rely on is what our leadership is telling you.'

'We should have a ballot to decide before we strike,' one miner grumbled, 'not be forced out by Yorkshire's flying pickets.'

Charlie dealt with him sharply. 'We had a ballot back in eighty-one to take strike action if any pit was closed for reasons other than seam exhaustion - eighty-six per cent in favour. That's our mandate and a bloody overwhelming one!'

'That was then,' the dissenter persisted.

'Listen, comrade,' Charlie urged, his face passionate, 'we'll be up against the whole establishment just like in twenty-six and seventy-four - not just the NCB, but the Government and all its muscle. They want to break us because we miners stand up for ourselves and have the most effective union in the country. We have two centuries of struggle behind us, remember. We had to fight the coal owners for every improvement in wages and conditions and we finally beat them when we got nationalisation thirty-seven years ago. And why did we win? 'Cos we had a bloody good union who fought for us all the way! But the Government would have us back to the bad old days, given half a chance. The Tories still hate us for bringing them down in seventy-four. Privatisation is already creeping into the industry by the back door, giving over contracts to private firms where union men would've been employed before.'

'That's rubbish,' the heckler scoffed. 'They'd never privatise the mines again.'

'Shut up and let him speak!' another jostled.

'If the NUM is broken, that's what you'll get,' Charlie insisted. 'Privately owned mines and profit put before the safety of the men. And don't think they'll have anything to do with union members either. Listen, you daft bugger, it's only a generation since the coal owners ruled our lives. Look around the graveyards of County Durham and see how many men were killed in their pits, the names on the monuments - our forefathers - thousands of them! I tell you now, this generation of union men is never going to allow privatisation back!'

Carol noticed a shift in the crowd; they were listening now. It was as if Charlie had struck a sudden chord of unity, conjured up the memories of their collective past. Carol could almost sense the ghosts of their forefathers standing amongst them, willing them to take heed. She felt a prickle down the back of her neck as she listened with them and Charlie intoned like a prophet at the far end of the hall.

Tonight the choice is yours,' he told them. 'If you vote against strike action you'll be throwing away everything your fathers and grandfathers fought and died for. You'll be the murderers of our industry, not just killing your own job but those of the men beside you. And there will be no jobs to pass on to your sons. Think what that will mean to our communities - you'll be killing them off too. Make the wrong decision now and you'll spend the rest of your life on the dole regretting it. But endorse the decision of Council to strike from Monday and we stand a chance!' he urged. 'Scotland and Wales have already agreed, Kent and Derbyshire will be joining too, and the rest will be picketed out. Don't let our enemies trick you into demands for more ballots when we already have our mandate. The one real bond of comradeship we all share as union men is that we never ever cross the picket line, and that's how we'll get the others to join us, those who think they don't need to fight for their jobs and who can't see beyond their next pay packet. We'll picket them out quickly and bring the strike to a swift end. Remember the victories of seventy-two and seventy-four.'

Charlie lifted his fist in a salute that reminded Carol of the picture of Lenin on the Brassbank lodge banner that hung on the wall behind him, rallying the workers to action.

'Brothers, your jobs - the very future of our families and villages - are at stake. Like it says on our banner: "Never Stand Alone!" Well, we won't, we'll be with our pitmen comrades. The fight-back has started, lads, so let's get into it!'

The hall burst into a thunder of applause and whistling and Carol felt her heart beating fast. She was quite overwhelmed by his words. All her life she had lived in this village, but it was as if she had gone around with her eyes closed, oblivious to its realities.

The pit had always been there, humming and clanking away, and the pitmen had come and gone from it like the tide lapping in and out on the beach below. She could not imagine Brassbank without it and it had never really occurred to her that such a catastrophe could come about. But now she saw how important it all was to her and Mick and his family - to Laura and her generation now growing up in the pit's shadow. It was their lifeblood, their prosperity, their inheritance - their future. Carol knew then that she was going to have to fight for it too.

The men were taking a show of hands and Carol could only count five or six miners out of the hundreds there still opposed to strike action. She was dismayed to see that one of them was Sid Armstrong. But there was overwhelming support for Charlie and the other officials. As the hall broke into a cacophony of excited talk, Carol turned to look at Lotty and saw the older woman's bright eyes swimming with tears.

'Oh, Carol!' she cried.

They stepped towards each other without a word and hugged each other tight. Carol realised with surprise that the wetness on her cheeks was from her own tears. She was fearful yet exultant. For the first time, she felt like a Todd - and proud of it.

Chapter Thirteen

The first week of the strike seemed unreal to Carol. Mick no longer went off to the routine shifts underground. The locker rooms and lamp room remained silent and the cutting machines idle as the men stayed at home or gathered at the Welfare Hall. Mick took Laura to school the first day, but by the second he had volunteered for picket duty and was out early in the morning. His father spent every waking hour at the Welfare, trying to organise picketing and sorting out the miners' benefit problems.

'The lads on strike can't claim owt,' Mick told her, 'but the Social are deducting fifteen pounds from the benefits the families are claiming.'

'What on earth for?' Carol asked, dumping down a bag full of groceries and debating what to make for tea.

'Cos the Government are saying we're getting fifteen pounds each in strike pay,' Mick growled.

'But none of you are getting any strike pay!' Carol flopped down.

'Exactly. If we paid that amount out, the union would be bankrupt in weeks. But that's what the DHSS are saying,' Mick sighed. 'Some families will be living on next to nowt, once their savings are gone.'

'Good God!' Carol said in annoyance. 'Do they really intend to starve people back to work like they did in twenty-six? It's barbaric.'

'The union will do what they can to help out,' Mick answered sombrely, 'but it's going to be hard.'

'Thank goodness for me job at the shop,' Carol said and got up. Mick didn't answer, but switched on the TV news.

As she busied herself in the kitchen, Mick shouted in, 'Can you make up some bait an' all?'

'What for?' Carol asked, coming into the sitting room and seeing pictures of dozens of police arrayed around the gates of some pit. The newscaster was announcing that the NCB had successfully sought an injunction against 'flying pickets'. From now on pickets had to be confined to their own pits. *"The Nottingham-shire police are being reinforced by men from five other areas . . ."*

'I'm driving some of the lads down to Ollerton tonight,' Mick said quietly.

Carol looked at him worriedly. 'But they've just said—'

'The union in Nottingham have asked for our help,' Mick interrupted. 'They think we might be able to persuade some of the lads who are crossing the picket line to stop. There's a lot of Durham pitmen went down there in the sixties who we think'll listen to us.'

'That's if the police let you anywhere near them,' Carol snorted. 'And that doesn't look likely.' She waved at the television.

'We've got to try,' Mick insisted. 'There's only a handful of pits still working anywhere, and we've not been on strike a week yet.'

Carol felt the old tension inside that she experienced when Mick went underground. 'I wish you could just picket locally - there's no bother at all with the police here.'

'Aye, that's why we can let Grandda and the other pensioners picket in Brassbank while we go further afield.'

'Are you enjoying this?' Carol asked in surprise.

Mick's look was boyish. 'It reminds me of when I first went picketing in seventy-two - kipping on people's floors, listening to "Maggie Mae" on the radio. All the lads together.'

Carol sighed. 'I just remember the telly going off early and filling me bedroom with candles. I hope this one's over as quickly.'

Mick took her hand. 'Well, we're never going to win if we stay at home, pet,' he said and smiled in reassurance, 'and we are ganin' to win.'

That night Carol lay awake after Mick had crept out of the house at 2 a.m. She heard the car engine start up and listened as it grew fainter down the back lane. She imagined him meeting up with the other young men on the chilly steps outside the Welfare, sharing a cigarette, whispering jokes and encouragement. Lotty might be there making them hot drinks before they set off, for Carol knew that her mother-in-law was spending all her free time down at the hall, helping her husband. She had astonished them all by buying a moped so she could come and go on errands and bring Charlie meals while he spent long hours organising the men.

Mick had laughed. 'She's always had her eye on a motorbike since I got mine.'

Carol tossed and turned in the empty bed and was finally on the verge of sleep when a small, ghostly figure appeared in the doorway.

'Laura?' Carol called softly.

The little girl padded quickly to the bedside and pulled at the covers.

'Where's Daddy?' she demanded.

'He's gone to meet some of his friends, pet.' Carol put out a comforting arm. 'They've got work to do.'

'But Louise Dillon says our daddies aren't working any more,' Laura said, puzzled.

'Not at the pit, but they've got plenty to do still.'

'Can I sleep in your bed tonight?' Laura asked. 'There's a dinosaur under mine.'

Carol smiled in the dark. 'Won't Teddy be lonely?'

Laura waved her battered bear in triumph. 'He wants to sleep in your bed too.'

Carol relented and pulled back the covers. It was probably the wrong decision and she might find Laura in their bed every night from now on, but at that moment she wanted the comfort of her daughter's warm body beside her as much as Laura wanted her reassurance.

They snuggled down together with Teddy and sleep came quickly.

By the time Carol went to collect Laura from school, Mick was home, tired and foul-tempered.

'They turned us back at the county border - couldn't get anywhere near Ollerton! There were van loads of them and roadblocks everywhere,' he fumed. 'It was unbelievable. We even got stopped on the Al and questioned. One copper told me he'd take me car keys off us and we could all walk home if I didn't turn round and eff off back to Durham right then. It was like something you see on the telly about a police state - I couldn't believe it was happening just a couple of hours away from our own doorstep! What happened to freedom of movement and citizens' rights all of a sudden?'

Carol listened to him vent his frustration until the evening news came on.

'Listen, they're saying something about Ollerton,' she interrupted.

They watched in amazement and then with mounting horror as they saw the angry rows of pickets, arm in arm, attempting to block the hundreds of police bringing in the day shift. There was jostling to and fro and a lot of shouting and then snapshots of violence that made Carol's stomach churn. This cut to an announcement from the Home Secretary, Leon Brittan, that three thousand more police were on standby from seventeen different forces, who would be given what power they needed to stop vehicles and people coming into Nottinghamshire.

Carol and Mick looked at each other as the ominous words sunk in.

'They're so organised,' Carol said, quite stunned. 'It's as if... Oh, Mick, I'm glad you didn't get through today.'

He looked at her with steely blue eyes. 'Maybes not today, but by heck we'll try again!'

For the next few days, Mick was sent on picketing duties to pits in the area and to the power station at Blyth where they had success in turning back union drivers. The rail unions rallied to their support and were severely hampering the movement of coal stocks.

'Just like in twenty-six,' Grandda Bowman told Carol when he stopped by for a cup of tea after picketing at the pit gates. She would hear him whistling through the gaps in his teeth as he came in the back yard, bent over his stick like the crooked man in Laura's nursery rhyme book. He seemed to be thoroughly enjoying himself. The banter with the local police appeared friendly and he sometimes came away with bars of chocolate and sandwiches for his dinner.

'That brother of yours - what's his name?' he wheezed.

'Simon?' Carol queried.

'Aye, Simon. He gave me a packet of tabs yesterday. Canny lad.'

Carol thought cigarettes were the last thing the old man should be receiving with his bronchial chest, but she was pleased by the gesture. She had not seen her brother since the strike started; in fact she had avoided seeing any of her family, knowing how awkward it might be for Mick. But she knew that sooner or later she would have to face them all.

The second week into the dispute was one of watching and waiting to see how the ballot of Nottinghamshire miners would go. If they came out on strike then the Board would be forced to withdraw the pit closure programme and the whole thing would be over. Carol hoped fervently that it would, for things had already gone quiet at work and orders for summer wedding dresses were being put on hold until the future became clearer.

They watched the evening news tensely at Septimus Street when the results were announced.

'Three to one against striking! The bastards!' Charlie fumed. For a moment Carol wondered if her father-in-law was going to cry, he was so puce in the face. It was as if the working miners had delivered a personal slap in the face.

Lotty put a hand on his arm. 'It's not the end of the world, Charlie man. We just carry on picketing them out until they see sense. They'll come round in the end when they see it's to safeguard their jobs too.'

But Mick's face was downcast. 'They've said no pits will close in Notts - they've set out to divide us from the start.'

Carol exchanged looks with Lotty. They were not going to let their men become despondent. They had to help boost morale and keep each other going now that the strike looked set to harden.

'Then it's our job to unite us all,' Carol said. 'Most miners are supporting the action and the transport unions have rallied round, just like old times - the Triple Alliance.'

Charlie gave her a look of surprise. 'By, you've been learning your working-class history.'

'I've been drinking a lot of tea with Grandda lately,' Carol smiled.

Before they left, Lotty took her aside and asked her, 'Would you fancy helping out at a social we're organising - raise a bit of money for the strike fund?'

'Course I would,' Carol agreed at once.

'The thing is, I feel we should try and get more of the wives involved in helping out - take a bit of the burden off the lodge. They've got their hands full organising the picketing and that. We could start something at the Welfare - soup and sandwiches for the men at dinnertime, maybes. There's some of .the young lads have nothing to live on at all, now their pay's stopped. We could make sure they get something in their stomachs once a day.'

'I'd like to help out,' Carol assured her, 'and maybes Val would let me come down in me dinnertime - we're quiet enough, I'm afraid.'

'That would be grand. But what I really need is for you to get the young wives interested. We don't want to frighten them off with talk of meetings and commit-tees, but we're going to need all the help we can get to keep the village together.'

Carol thought about it on the way home. The next day she spotted Lotty's moped outside Dimarco's and caught her corning out.

'That canny Paul has said we can have two crates of pop and a box of biscuits for the social, and he's donating a big box of chocolates for the raffle an' all,' Lotty beamed as she buckled on her helmet. Her old beehive hairstyle had been sacrificed for a short cut that gave her an impish, youthful look and allowed the wearing of her crash helmet.

'I've been thinking about getting the wives together,' Carol told her. 'Why don't we have them round for coffee one evening, say it's to give advice about claiming benefits, how to budget, that sort of thing? Then see who's interested in doing more.'

'Champion,' Lotty agreed. 'We can have it at our house.'

Carol smiled. Her mother-in-law was a born organiser, but Carol didn't want her taking on too much. 'You'll have enough to do with this social. Let me have the meeting round at mine.'

Lotty smiled beneath her visor. 'If you think you can manage.'

'Aye,' Carol said. Just let me show you, she added silently.

She could not put off seeing her family any longer and accepted the invitation to lunch one Sunday at the beginning of April. Mick was reluctant, but Laura's anticipation at seeing her cousins and playing in Grandpa's large garden persuaded him to go.

At first Carol thought they were all going to get through lunch without a mention of the strike. There was a bizarre unreality about Vic's false heartiness and Fay's incessant talk about her health club and wholefood shops and her mother's brandishing of holiday brochures and her father's attempts to entice Mick outside to look at the daffodils. Carol knew he wanted to talk about the strike but dared not, whereas the others were avoiding it like the plague. She felt as if someone in the family had died, but no one wanted to talk about them.

Laura was itching to run outside, despite the squalls of rain, but her cousins Ngaio and Jasmine elected to sit in front of the new video and watch cartoons. Mick saw his escape and took Laura out to play, bundled up in wellies and waterproofs.

'I could do with some fresh air too,' Ben grunted and followed them out.

As soon as they were gone, Nancy asked, 'Are you managing all right? You can take what's left of the joint for your tea and help yourself to what's in the freezer.'

'You don't have to, Mam,' Carol smiled tightly. 'We're doing fine.' She was not going to tell them that last week they'd had to use their savings to pay the mortgage and the quarterly electricity bill and that they had an appointment to see the bank manager about how they were going to pay for things this coming month. Carol could not believe how quickly they were dipping into debt without Mick's wages; her modest pay from Bowman's bought the groceries for the week but little else. She could not imagine how they would manage if she were to lose her job.

Fay was all concern. 'I've brought a bag of the girls' clothes for Laura - things for the summer.'

Carol felt uncomfortable. 'Thanks, Fay.' She turned to Kate, attempting to change the subject. 'I haven't seen Simon for weeks. How's the decorating coming along?' She knew that her brother and sister-in-law were busily doing up the solid semi they had bought on the outskirts of Quarryhill. It was a former colliery doctor's house with high ceilings and marble fireplaces and a large, overgrown, walled garden.

'Oh, it's come to a standstill,' Kate complained, 'with Simon being away.'

'Away?' Carol queried, having assumed her brother's absence meant he was on duty.

Kate's fair face flushed pink and she shot Fay a nervous look. 'Yes, I hardly see him at the moment.

'Working all this overtime. Still, the extra pay's handy and it'll mean we can renovate the kitchen as well as the bathroom this summer.'

'Coffee in the lounge?' Nancy asked, her voice nervously high.

'You mean he's away on picket line duty?' Carol asked.

Kate nodded. 'It's a worry, of course, the violence . . .'

Carol had a sudden image of the easygoing Simon, brandishing a baton at the pickets. It came as a shock. He would see it as his duty, she realised, and yet he was being set against the miners - against men like Mick - other people's husbands, sons and brothers. Was this what Charlie had meant when he'd said the muscle of the establishment would be used against them? Peaceable, unquestioning, apolitical young men like Simon who had mortgages to pay and houses to improve? The trickery of it suddenly incensed her. The police should be there to protect the miners and their families too, but they were being used as strike breakers for the Coal Board.

Fay was agreeing with Kate. 'It must be terrible for Simon, with all those hooligans you see on telly chucking bricks and causing as much trouble as they can.'

Carol sparked. 'You mean the miners who are standing there in jeans and T-shirts and trainers against police protected with helmets and weapons?'

Fay pouted disapprovingly. 'I don't know why you're trying to defend them - not the troublemakers who act like thugs towards the police.'

'Yes,' Kate joined in, 'and it's not just the police they hate, but their own kind. Simon says they treat the other miners like dirt - swear and spit at them and beat them up, given half a chance.'

'The miners who are working and trying to cross the picket line, you mean?' Carol asked. 'Well, of course the pickets are angry with them for not striking. And the police are making it ten times worse by forcing them through the picket instead of allowing the union members to reason with the working pitmen. That's what's causing the violence.'

'Reason?' Fay scoffed. 'They're animals. How can you stick up for them against your own brother?'

Carol winced at the insult to the pickets. Her own husband was one of them, but Fay was too insensitive to realise the hurt she inflicted. 'They're fighting for their jobs, for God's sake!' Carol fumed. 'We all are.'

'I hope you're not going to go picketing, Carol?' her mother asked in alarm.

'If it comes to it, I will,' Carol said at once. The thought had never occurred to her, but why shouldn't she begin to get more active?

'Don't worry,' Vic laughed, 'the miners are too protective of their women to allow them out on dangerous missions, Nancy.'

He was treating it as a joke and his flippancy riled Carol more than Fay's prejudice.

'The women will do what's necessary, whether the men want them to or not,' she snapped.

Vic gave her a patronising smile. 'I'm sure they will. But it'll all be over before long. Scargill will have to settle and accept that some pits are going to close. If I was Mick I'd be happy that Brassbank's not on the closure programme and isn't likely to be.'

'Yes,' Fay agreed. 'I don't see why they're striking here at all. Actually, I think they're being selfish putting their families through all this worry over money. You would think Mick would put you and Laura first.'

Carol jumped up, furious. 'That's exactly what he is doing! If the union doesn't make a stand now over all these other closures, then no pit and no job is safe, Mick's included. I'm just glad he's outside and doesn't have to hear what you really think about him!' She pushed back her chair and stormed towards the door, but Fay was determined to have the last word.

'Irresponsible as ever, aren't you, Carol?' she accused. 'I certainly wouldn't risk the roof over my daughter's head for the precious union. You should be hanging on to what you've got and doing the best for Laura, not throwing it all away. I hope Daddy's out there now telling that to Mick, because someone ought to.'

Carol spun round, almost choking with anger and frustration. Her sister would never understand that the strike was about justice and decency for ordinary working people who wanted the best for their families and communities. How could she make Fay see that they were prepared to make sacrifices now so that they and their children would have a future? The injustice was that they had to strike for such things at all, but there was no other way. Living with the Todds she under-stood that now, but Fay might as well have been living on the moon for all she grasped of the crisis.

Vic tried to temper his wife's attack. 'It's not that we think you'd ever let Laura suffer, but we think you're mistaken - this whole strike's a mistake. Scargill just wants to take on MacGregor and Thatcher. He's using you all to bring down a Conservative government, because to him this whole thing is political.'

Carol gave him a look of contempt. 'You've been reading too many right-wing tabloids,' she mocked. 'One man can't start a strike. It's the thousands of miners all over the country who have decided enough is enough. They're the men who risk their lives to make this country prosperous - keep little businesses like yours going, Vic, with the money they spend. And they want to go on working and risking their lives for us, that's all they're asking. If this strike fails, we'll all be losers.' She looked at them, willing them to understand, but their faces were stony, disbelieving. All except her mother's. Nancy had an odd, tearful expression and Carol was not sure if she was upset with her or touched by what she had said. But she said nothing in support.

Vic shook his bearded face. 'Mick will pay for his loyalty, I'm afraid.'

'Carol and Laura will, you mean.' Fay was scathing.

Carol caught a sudden glimpse of Laura dashing past the French windows, her long wavy hair lifting in the wind, mouth open in excited laughter. Seconds later, Mick appeared round the corner, chasing her, his fair hair wet and curling down the back of his neck. Then they were gone.

Carol spoke with quiet conviction. 'We're nothing without loyalty,' she told them. 'Loyalty and respect for each other - and love. That's what this dispute is all about. And if you can't see that, then I feel sorry for you all, because they're the things no one can take away from us.' With that, she turned away from them and their arguing and hurried from the house.

She found Mick and Laura sheltering in the old summerhouse, while her father continued his solitary gardening in the larger of the two greenhouses. She wondered if they had argued too. She looked at Mick and did not have to explain anything; the pain must have shown in her eyes. He leant forward and kissed her mouth tenderly.

'Let's gan home then,' he said.

Chapter Fourteen

The following week, Val began to drop hints to Carol that her business was in trouble. Once the Nottinghamshire miners had voted to stay at work, there had been a flood of cancellations for wedding dresses. 'No one can afford a big white wedding this summer,' Val had moaned, her usual sunny disposition dampened. 'Stan Savage's daughter was the last on the books, and they've asked to pay the balance in instalments.'

Carol could not reassure her. Even the boutique side of the business was dead. People came in to browse and chat and see what had been discounted, but no one was buying. Carol's shell jewellery lay gathering dust in the window and eventually she took it away and gave it to Lotty to raffle at the social.

By the middle of April, Val reduced Carol's hours to three mornings a week.

'I'm really sorry, Carol, but at this rate I can't see me keeping the shop open at all. I'm buying in no new stock and I've no dressmaking work for you, just the odd repairs.'

'I know, Val,' Carol tried to be cheerful, 'don't worry about it.'

'Well, I do worry about you, you've Laura to take care of,' Val said, her face creased in concern. 'But at least you've got parents and family who can help you out financially, not like some of them round here.'

Carol nodded and turned away. She had told no one except Mick about the row with her family and she was not going to add to Val's anxiety by telling her that she could not turn to them for help. After Mick had confided that her father had tried to bully him out of strike action too, Carol had neither spoken to her parents or sister, nor taken Laura to see them. She doubted that Mick would ever step willingly inside their house again.

She had been deeply hurt by their criticism of Mick and their lack of concern for the plight of the other miners and their families. The shaky relationship that had been re-established with her parents since Laura's birth was once again in tatters. The differences between them that had been ignored for a while now yawned like a chasm, deep and unbridgeable.

But Carol buried her hurt and decided not to worry about money, instead spending her spare hours helping Lotty at the Welfare.

'Where do we start?' Carol asked, looking dubiously at the ancient gas cooker in the Welfare Hall kitchen, which was to produce food for dozens of men.

'You start by going round the shops and asking for food - anything for free,' Lotty directed. 'I'll be responsible for turning it into a gourmet meal,' she said with a wink.

So Carol trawled round the local shops asking for contributions for the social raffle and also for donations of food to get their soup kitchen going. At first she felt awkward about asking for charity, then reminded herself that it was not for her, but to ease the burden of those who were struggling on benefits as meagre as six and seven pounds a week and whatever they could sell. A month on strike and people were already having to cancel their summer holidays, return their rented video machines and sell their cars.

Carol was astounded by the response of the local traders. From two of the butchers they received mince and cheap cuts of meat for pie fillings, from the fish and chip shop came a sack of potatoes and from Marshall's Carol got tins of soup and beans. One of the bakers donated the previous day's bread and

Dimarco's gave enough tea bags and coffee to last a fortnight.

'That's very generous,' Carol thanked Paul Dimarco.

He smiled disarmingly, looking much younger than forty. 'My grandfather did the same for the pitmen in twenty-six. He had a lot of respect for the miners of Whitton Grange and they stood by him, too, when things were tough,' Paul reminisced. 'Aye, we Dimarcos have survived strikes before, and a world war. We'll get through this one, an' all.'

That week, Carol got Kelly to photocopy a leaflet on Vic's copier inviting miners' wives to an evening at her house.

'Can you do me forty?' Carol asked.

'You'll have me shot,' Kelly complained.

'Not unless Vic finds out,' Carol pressed her.

Kelly did the job with reluctance and brought them round to Carol's.

'Great,' Carol thanked her. 'Would you like to help me stick them through doors this evening?'

Kelly pulled a face. 'I'm not that desperate for summat to do. Mind you, it'd make a change from arguing with Sid about what we watch on telly. It's driving me crackers having him around every night. The sooner he gets back to night shift the better.'

Carol studied her friend. She had a strong suspicion that Kelly was up to something, perhaps seeing someone on the quiet. She'd been uneasy about her since Mick's birthday party last November. And she knew the signs when Kelly was keen on a bloke: the frequent hair cuts, faddy diets, a flood of new clothes, despite the shortage of money, and that smug cat-got-the-cream look in her eyes.

'Cramping your social life, is he?' she asked quietly.

Kelly flushed beneath her short red hair. 'What's that supposed to mean?'

'Come on, Kelly man, you've been like the vanishing woman these past few months,' Carol challenged. 'And I bet you tell Sid it's me you're coming to see when you gan out. So where have you been going? And don't tell me you've taken up night classes in flower arranging.'

Kelly just laughed. 'Nothing so exciting. I work hard and I sometimes work late, and just as well for Sid that I do. At least we've got money coming in. You're as bad as he is with your suspicious mind.' Kelly hauled herself out of her chair - she hadn't bothered to take her coat off since she'd come in. 'Mind you, I've started evening classes in Spanish.'

'Spanish?' Carol gawped. 'What on earth for?'

'If I learn a bit of Spanish I might get a job as courier on Proud's bus tours to Spain,' Kelly grinned. 'Better than being stuck in that grotty office all day, eh?'

Carol was amazed. Kelly wasn't the travelling type; she had never been further than Blackpool before. 'Aye, I'm sure it would. What does Sid say about it?'

Kelly gave an impatient huff. 'He's not interested in what I do at work. He'll just have to lump it, 'specially if I'm the one bringing in the wages. Anyway, he's getting to travel all over just now with picketing. Doesn't it piss you off that the lads are away having a good time, playing footy on the picket line, and we're stuck at home trying to get by on the little we've got?'

Carol was taken aback by Kelly's resentment.

'I don't think it's a bundle of laughs being chased by the police and that,' Carol answered, but felt strangely unsettled by the criticism.

'Bollocks!' Kelly sneered. 'They love getting up in the middle of the night and sneaking off around the country trying to outdo the coppers. They haven't had such fun since they were bairns playing knocky-nine-doors.'

'Cynic,' Carol accused, getting up to see her friend out. But she wasn't going to let her get away easily. Even if Kelly was not in favour of the strike and was giving Sid a hard time about it, she knew her friend was loyal to their own kind and just needed a little persuasion to help.

'You'll come along and support me meeting then?' Carol insisted.

'Oh, Carol man, you know I hate meetings. Five years ago you would have a run a mile from all this boring committee stuff too.'

'Five years ago there wasn't a need to get involved. Now there is,' Carol pointed out.

Kelly took the leaflet she held out and stuffed it in her coat pocket. 'Maybes I will. If I've nowt better to do,' she said, her round face puckering in a smile. 'But I'm not going to sit around knitting socks for strikers or owt like that.'

'No knitting, I promise,' Carol laughed.

When the night came, Carol packed Laura off to bed and Mick down to the Welfare and spent a nervous half-hour pushing back the furniture and re-arranging the crisps and nuts, until Lotty arrived with a large bottle of wine.

'No one's turned up,' Carol said in panic.

'They will,' Lotty reassured.

'What if too many come and there's nowhere to sit them all? And what are we going to say to them? Is it warm enough in here?'

'Sit down,' Lotty ordered, 'and stop your fussing while I pour you a drink.'

Carol perched on a chair arm, but was on her feet in seconds when the doorbell rang.

Lotty winked. 'They must've heard the bottle opening.'

In the end, fifteen women gathered in Carol's cosy sitting room, squeezed on to chairs or kneeling on the floor by the fire. There were Stan Savage's wife Maureen and their newlywed daughter Angela; Lesley Dimarco and her friend Dot, Sid's older sister Joanne, along with two of her neighbours, May and June, from the new estate at the top of the bank. May and June were sisters; large, big-boned women with pale frizzy hair who argued and laughed in equal amounts. May's cheerful dumpy daughter Louise was in Laura's class at school. The rest of the women Carol only knew by sight or from serving in the boutique, except for the most surprising guest of all, Linda's silent best friend, Denise. She had probably been dragged along by her mother, Evelyn Wilson, who lived two doors away.

It was like old times having Denise squatting on the floor, black leggings and heavy black boots crossed under her black skirt, her pale face sullen under the cropped black hair. Carol thought it seemed an age ago that she had given birth on the settee with Linda sprawled on the floor trying to watch television, while Denise rapidly withdrew.

'I haven't seen you for months,' Carol said. 'Are you still working in that shoe shop over Whittledene?'

Denise shook her head. Her mother translated. 'They laid her off after eleven months so she couldn't be classed as permanent staff. Probably take her back on for the summer. But I thought she could make herself useful in the meantime.'

'It's good of you to come, Denise,' Carol encouraged. 'Seen anything of Linda lately?'

'Na,' Denise mumbled.

'Used to be her shadow, our Denise,' Evelyn said. 'Doesn't know what to do with herself with Linda living away.'

'If she comes to visit me,' Carol answered, 'I'll let you know and you can come round.' In fact, she rarely saw Linda these days. Last week, she and Dan had appeared for Sunday lunch round at Septimus Street for the first time in months. Linda, now obviously pregnant, had been cheerful, but Dan had looked pale and surly. He had tucked into the roast chicken and spring vegetables from Charlie's allotment as if he had not eaten for a week. Discovering that Dan had spent the last month sitting at home watching TV, Mick had encouraged him to go picketing and Dan had shown interest when told he would get a pound a day for his trouble. Carol had tried to take Linda aside and ask how things really were, but she brushed her away with the assurance that everything was fine.

Denise's head drooped further at the possibility of seeing Linda and Carol was not sure if this was a nod of acceptance or a rebuff to mind her own business. She escaped to the kitchen where Lotty was pouring wine into a selection of glasses and tea cups. Her mother-in-law gave her a reassuring wink and said, 'Ready, steady, go!'

At first everyone was a bit awkward, but by the time the wine had been drunk and the coffee and snacks handed round, the room was buzzing with talk and May's loud cackle, and Carol had to open the window for air. Laura appeared in her nightie like a small pink-cheeked sprite.

'I can't sleep, you're making too much noise,' she accused, before Carol had time to send her back to bed.

'Come here, pet,' May Dillon insisted, pulling Laura on to her ample knee, 'and tell Auntie May what you and our Louise have been getting up to at school.'

'Why are you called May?' Laura demanded. 'And Mrs Burt's called June.'

May chuckled. 'Cos I was born in May and me sister was born in June. Imagine if we'd been born in November?'

It took Laura a moment to work this out and then her impish face broke into a grin.

'Or February!' Laura giggled. 'Or March, or August, or—'

'That's enough,' Carol warned.

Laura ignored her mother. 'Or what if you and Mrs Burt had been boys,' she tittered. 'Would you still have been called May and June?'

May's face wobbled like blancmange as she laughed with the girl. 'No, we'd have been called Monday and Friday!'

Laura went into a giggly heap.

Lotty saw Carol's cross look. 'Let her stay. She doesn't like to miss out and we'll not be much longer.'

Carol could see that the women wanted to make a fuss of Laura and gave in. She went and made more coffee and by the time she returned, Kelly had turned up.

'Hope I've missed the boring bit, have I?' She laughed and squatted down beside Stan Savage's daughter, Angela. 'Saw your wedding picture in the paper - dress looked fantastic.'

Thanks,' Angela beamed. 'Carol helped make it.'

'Clever-clogs Carol, eh?' Kelly grinned at her friend. 'Got any lager? Coffee makes me wee all night.'

Lotty gave her a disapproving look and Carol intervened quickly. 'I think there's a can in the fridge.'

Once Kelly had been quietened with her drink, Lotty took control again and was soon organising a rota for the soup kitchen.

'What about the ones living out of the village?' Joanne asked. 'Maybes there're families living too far out to come to the Welfare every day.'

'Or too proud,' Kelly added.

'This isn't charity,' Lotty bristled. 'It's the least the men deserve.'

'Aye, but people have their pride,' Kelly insisted, 'and some would rather sit at home and starve than be seen coming for free meals.'

'She has a point,' Carol agreed. 'We don't want families suffering more than they have to, and some lads might stay away whatever we tell them.'

'Aye, it's the families miss out if the men are too proud,' June nodded. 'It just means what little they've got has to go round further.'

'And I'll tell you something else. My Marty still expects his bit of pocket money for a pint at the social and his packet of fags,' May complained. 'But he says we can't afford Easter eggs this year for the bairns.'

'Your Marty says that every year,' her sister June scoffed.

Carol waited for May to explode, but she just laughed. 'Aye, Marty's a miserable bugger, isn't he?'

'Well, I've a husband and two sons on strike,' cut in Evelyn Wilson, 'and Denise here is unemployed. I get nothing for the lads from Social Security. Apart from what Denise gets, we've to manage on six pounds forty-five a week. And me with five grown-ups to feed!'

The room suddenly broke into a heated discussion on benefits and the DHSS and how some were being paid a week in arrears because of the backlog of claims. Carol looked at Lotty for help, thinking that the whole meeting was going to degenerate into a grouse about their husbands and the DHSS. But Lotty let them carry on for several minutes while they aired their problems and shared their worries. Then she told Evelyn to go and see Charlie at the Welfare in the morning.

'He can help sort out your late payments and see what else can be done,' Lotty said. 'And that goes for any of us who're in trouble. Go to the union or come and tell one of us. Don't sit at home worrying and letting things get worse. We've all got to help each other out. Now let's get back to Joanne's point about the families who can't use the soup kitchen.'

'We need to make a register of families - how many kids they've got, that sort of thing,' Carol suggested. The others agreed and Lotty swiftly delegated the job to Carol and Joanne.

'What we need to do is make up food parcels for them,' Lesley suggested. 'We could try and do it weekly.'

'Aye, and we could put bits of toiletries and baby stuff in for the young families,' Angela added. 'Every bit helps.'

Kelly nudged her. 'Have you something to tell us?' she teased.

Angela blushed. 'I hope not! Can't afford a bairn this year.'

Carol gave Lotty a wary look, knowing she would be thinking about Linda whose baby was due in July.

'We'll have to do a canny bit of fundraising,' June Burt commented. 'One social isn't going to help very much.'

'We could go round the pubs collecting,' Carol suggested.

'Eeh, Marty wouldn't let me do that!' May said.

'I'll volunteer,' Kelly laughed.

'The idea is to make money, not spend it,' Lotty said tartly.

'Let's decide on fundraising at the next meeting,' Lesley intervened.

'Where shall we have it?' June asked.

Carol and Lotty exchanged glances, encouraged by the women's enthusiasm to carry on.

'I'll book a room down the Welfare,' Lotty decided, 'so no one has to put themselves out. Then we can have a drink in the bar after.'

'I might just come again then,' Kelly whispered loudly.

'There's one other thing,' Lotty continued, ignoring her. 'There's a bus going from the village to a rally in the Midlands. Our men are getting criticised in the media and the union want to show the country that most of us are behind the strike. I think some of us women should go to show our support for the lads - let the ordinary people of this country know what we're really fighting for. Anybody want to come?'

There was a buzz of interest. Lotty had already mentioned it to Carol, but she had dismissed the idea because she had Laura to look after.

Just then her daughter piped up, 'Can we go on the bus, Mam?'

Carol looked at Laura's excited face and then at Lotty.

Her mother-in-law shrugged. 'It's a day out, I suppose. Why not take the bairn?'

'Please, Mam!' Laura pleaded. 'It'll be like the Big Meeting.'

Carol thought of the great annual gathering of miners in Durham with its carnival atmosphere and was carried away with excitement too. There might not be a gala in Durham this year if the strike dragged on into the summer, so why not take Laura to the rally?

'If your dad agrees,' Carol said.

'Great!' Laura squealed. 'He will.'

At that moment, Carol was engulfed by a sense of togetherness and optimism for the future. There was such a will among them to pull together and help each other that anything seemed possible. With neighbours and friends standing up for what was right, the country would soon see the justice of their strike. How could they not win? Carol thought happily.

Chapter Fifteen

In the end, Mick could not go with them because he was sent on picketing duty to a local power station, but Carol and Laura went with Lotty and some of the new women's support group on the bus. Kelly's father was driving and they enjoyed the journey down, singing local songs and swapping news. Some, like Carol, had not been out of Brassbank all year and there was a holiday atmosphere on the coach.

'Look at that, Denise is wearing grey instead of black today,' Lotty whispered. 'It must be spring.'

The night before, Joanne and June had come rushing round to Carol's, saying they should have a banner to wave at the rally. Carol had fetched an old cot sheet and sent Joanne round to Val's flat to borrow some marker pens. Mick had come in late to find them crouched on the floor designing their banner.

'What are we calling ourselves?' Carol asked.

'Miners' Wives Support Group?' June had suggested.

Carol had thought of Denise. 'We're not all wives. Some are daughters, girlfriends . . .'

'Women's Support Group, then,' Joanne had said.

'We should say something about miners,' June had argued, 'so they know what we're supporting.'

'Miners' Women's Support Group?' Carol had said.

'Brassbank Miners' Women's Support Group,' June had said, her round face pink with enthusiasm.

Mick had laughed. 'You buggers, you'll need a king-size bedsheet for all that.'

Carol had given him a playful push. 'You could make yourself useful and find us some poles to tie the banner to.'

By midnight they had the banner marked out in black pen and glued to two old fence posts that Mick had scavenged from his father's allotment in the dark.

'That's another job for the women's group,' Joanne had said, as they eyed the makeshift banner. 'We'll make a banner to be proud of for the next rally.'

Now the banner was draped across the back window of the bus and some of the overtaking cars hooted their support, giving Carol a thrill of pleasure. As a young teenager she had danced with Kelly in front of the lodge banner at the Durham gala, wearing a kiss-me-quick hat, when her parents had thought her safely in the charge of Auntie Jean. They would have gone into orbit, Carol thought, if they'd known that Jean had encouraged her to join in and had herself worn a hat declaring 'Kiss me slowly, squeeze me tight'. But her aunt had assured Carol that Nancy had danced into Durham behind the Brassbank band as a girl and they were just keeping up tradition. Even now, Carol found it impossible to imagine her mother dancing under anyone's banner and wondered when it was that she had changed into the insecure woman who hid behind her rich friends and possessions, frightened of standing up to her husband on anything.

But today Carol resolved not to think of her parents as she marched with the banners again, this time under one of her own making, with her young daughter clutching her hand in excitement. However crude or ill-made the banner was, it was the symbol of the women around her, showing that they were active too. For a day they had left their homes and mundane chores, turned their backs on worries about money and mortgages and were going to march through the streets of a

Nottinghamshire town to show the world that they cared.

'Give us a B, give us an M, give us a W, give us an S, give us a G,' Joanne and June chanted at the back of the bus. 'Brassbank Miners' Women's Support Group!'

'Give us a can of pop, June man,' May cackled. 'I'm gasping.'

Carol laughed and hugged Laura in excitement.

Mick stood ranked with the other pickets across the roadway leading into the plant. They waited in their dozens, their jackets discarded in the warm spring sunshine, sharing cigarettes and jokes with the miners who had travelled from Scotland and Yorkshire. Mick and Sid argued about football while Eddy eulogised about Kevin Keegan.

'He's the pride of Newcastle United,' Eddy declared.

'Aye, Stan's hoping he's going to give away the trophies at the sportsmen's dinner next month,' Mick said.

'Oh, aye?' Sid ridiculed. 'Bet that's been in Keegan's diary all year. Dream on, Stan Savage.'

Mick was glad he and Sid were back to their old joking friendship. He had had words with Sid for voting against the strike, but Sid had been adamant. 'I didn't want to strike, but you should know I'll not gan against the union. Nowt will make me cross a picket line, Mick man.'

Two police vans drew up and extra constables climbed out. Murmurs went around that a delivery was due soon.

'It's non-union drivers are the problem,' Eddy muttered. 'They'll cross the Red Sea if the bosses tell them.'

Dan Hardman shifted nervously and asked Mick for a cigarette. It was his first time on picket duty and Mick wondered if they should have brought him along. It might have been better to let him picket at home to start with, but now it was too late. The number of police was growing by the minute and they looked set for a confrontation.

'How's Linda?' Mick asked him.

Dan shrugged. 'OK.' Mick thought that was all he was going to say, but he suddenly blurted out, 'I can't afford to keep the flat on. I'm going to have to move back in with my parents.'

Mick watched him. 'What about Linda?'

Dan gave him a defensive look. 'She'll have to go back to her mam and dad. I can't see what else we can do.'

'What does Linda want to do?' Mick asked, trying to keep his voice level.

'She wants to get wed, of course. On at me all the time,' he grumbled.

'Well, she is going to have your bairn,' Mick reminded him.

'Aye, that's all I ever hear about,' Dan complained. 'And how am I supposed to pay for it? I told Linda I didn't want her to keep it.'

Mick bit back a sharp reply. Instead he said, 'We'll help you out where we can, that's what families are for. Don't go doing anything daft without telling us first.'

Suddenly a shout went up and Mick found the men around him surging forward. Within seconds he was separated from Dan and the others. Above the noise of the crowd he could hear the roar of a lorry approaching at speed and the cordon of police began to push them back. They jostled and shoved and Mick heard Sid shouting in anger somewhere nearby. The lorry drew closer, but the rows of police were too great to break through.

All at once, Mick saw Sid drop his shoulder and charge at a constable as if on the rugby field. He barged the policeman out of the way and ran out into the road, followed by several others. They tried to flag down the lorry, but Mick could tell it was not going to stop.

'Get out the bloody way!' he shouted at his friend.

Just as Mick thought Sid was going to be knocked over by the coal lorry, two policemen grabbed him from behind and wrenched him backwards, flinging him to the ground. Then Mick lost his footing as they were shoved backwards and the lorry sped past through the gates with a belch of exhaust.

'Shite!' It was Eddy beside him, pulling him up. 'Look over there.'

Mick stood just in time to see Sid being bundled into the back of one of the white vans along with two others and then he was gone from sight. Mick felt a surge of anger and frustration at the arrest of his friend. What right had the police to prevent them from trying to speak to the drivers? They were being treated like criminals. He was about to rush after the van when Eddy put a restraining hand on his arm.

There's nowt we can do just now,' he told him, 'and I think you better see to the Hardman lad.' Eddy nodded over his shoulder.

Hearing a groan behind him, Mick turned and saw Dan bent double over the dirty verge. He rushed up to the young miner.

'Are you hurt, lad?' he asked in concern.

Dan did not answer as he retched into the ditch.

Eddy came up beside them. 'Nerves, is it?' he grunted, putting a comforting hand on the boy's shoulder.

Dan shoved him away and glared at them both. 'I wasn't scared! Someone hit me in the stomach!'

Eddy said, 'Aye, of course.' But Mick could tell by the glance he gave him that he did not believe Dan.

'Come on, I'll give you a lift home,' Mick offered. Then someone'll have to break the news to Kelly.'

'It's not like the Big Meeting, Mam,' Laura said, her small face worried. 'I don't like it here.'

Carol tried to smother her own fear. The march had started well enough and the speeches had been rousing, but now on their way back to the coaches, the onlookers were openly hostile. A grey-haired woman shook her fist and spat at Lotty and Evelyn as they went by carrying the banner. Two men beside her shouted obscenities and when Carol looked round they stuck two fingers up at her and swore again.

'Don't use language like that in front of my little girl!' Carol had broken step to round on them. Laura clung to her hand like a limpet.

'Haway,' Joanne said, pulling her arm, 'just ignore them.'

'Bloody whores!' one man bellowed. 'Think you can come down here interfering.'

'Yeah, let's see your tits! That's all you're good for,' the other leered.

Carol was incensed, her face turning puce with embarrassed indignation. But before she could speak, May Dillon elbowed her way in front and rounded on the heckler.

'Well, if that's all you've got to say for yourself, you're a poor excuse for a man!' she scorned, prodding him with a large finger so that he had to step back. 'We're down here to show our support for real men - men who want to work hard for a living and take care of their families and treat their lasses with respect. I wouldn't walk to the kerb and back for the likes of you!'

June came to her sister's side, ready to back her up. The man took a look at the bulky women standing aggressively with fists on hips, swore at them foully and moved away. His friend followed, but the grey-haired woman was not so daunted.

'Call them real men, do you? Well, that's a laugh! Your men are a bunch of sheep following that communist Scargill. He's the one what's ruining the coal industry. If they had any guts about them, they'd go back to work tomorrow and be grateful for what they get. Our men are making good money down here and we're certainly not going to give it up for the likes of you. So just leave us alone!'

Carol was stunned by the woman's invective, far more than by the men's childish abuse. She had come here thinking they could all be united, that all they had to do was march together and others would follow. But here were mining people who had not only disagreed with what they were fighting for but despised them so much they had come out to harass them.

'Haway,' Joanne told her friends, 'she's not worth arguing with.'

Aye, got the brains of a pea,' May ridiculed.

'A wizened one at that,' June laughed.

The marchers were moving on and soon they would be separated from the others. But Carol was desperate to convince the angry-faced woman. Charlie or Mick would've done the same; Todds didn't run from an argument when they knew they were right.

'You might have good money today,' Carol said, stepping forward, 'but for how long? It might be your husband's or son's pit next year. It doesn't matter how much they're investing in it now, tomorrow it could be called uneconomic just like Cortonwood. And then where will you be? You won't have the help of the thousands of miners on strike now, because they won't be miners any more. The only way you can safeguard your own jobs is to join the strike and help save the jobs at the threatened pits now, before it's too late. Arthur Scargill's right about a hit list.'

The woman looked at her uneasily but would not be swayed. 'Scargill! You're scaremongering, just like him. No one's going to get compulsory redundancy. The Yorkshire miners will be offered jobs in other pits.'

'Where?' Carol demanded. 'In Nottinghamshire? In your husband's pit? Is he going to give up his job for one of them?'

'Well, they've nothing to complain about,' she blustered. 'The Coal Board are offering the best redundancy pay in the country.'

'So they pay them off with taxpayers' money - our money - and the pit closes. They can't open it up again. And when the pit goes, the work goes and the life of the village goes down the plughole an' all!' Carol cried.

'Aye,' May shouted. 'If it happens to us, our husbands might never work again!'

'Our village would be a dead place without the pit,' June added.

'You should be the other side of this rope standing up for all miners,' Carol told the woman and swept her arm to include all the stony-faced onlookers. 'It'll be your families one day!'

But the middle-aged woman waved them on angrily. 'Not in my lifetime! Go back home where you belong and stop making a nuisance of yourselves. We don't want your problems here and we're not going to give up our good living for anybody. We've worked hard for it and deserve every penny. So just shove off!' She spat at them again and her gobbet of phlegm landed on Carol's cheek.

Carol gasped in disgust, too stunned to react. The crowd grew more menacing with aggressive words and rude gestures.

'Mammy, I want to go!' Laura tugged at her hand in fright. 'Nana's gone. I can't see her. Mammy, please.'

Carol saw with shock that her daughter was in tears. She was furious with the woman for frightening her child and guilty that she had brought Laura in the first place.

'Haway, Carol,' Joanne took her arm, 'let's get out of here.'

She turned away humiliated, clutching Laura close, and followed her friends.

May shouted a last insult. 'Don't die of anything trivial, will you!'

The others made a show of laughing but Carol was shaken as they hurried to catch up with Lotty and the women who had disappeared ahead with the banner. How naive she had been to believe that most people thought the way they did. After all, her own family lived in a striking village and yet were opposed to the cause. How much more difficult it was going to be to convince an apathetic or hostile public who thought the strike had nothing to do with them, she thought bleakly.

All at once Carol could not wait to get out of the town and back north on the bus. As they approached the line of coaches, parked along the side of the road, she became aware of another line of white police vans. There had been a police presence in the town but there had been no trouble apart from an exchange of insults with some of the men. Now people sat about on the grass verge smoking and chatting and waiting to board the coaches. Carol noticed two teenagers sharing a can of beer, laughing over something. At least the march as a whole had been peaceful and no one could call them troublemakers.

'Where've you been?' Lotty rushed up to them. 'I've been that worried.'

'Nana, you went without us,' Laura accused, throwing herself into her grandmother's arms. 'Mam was shouting at this old woman. So was Auntie May. She was nasty - spat on Mam. I was scared, Nana!'

Carol was about to explain when shouting broke out right behind them. She turned to see the two teenagers in dispute with a group of police. The uniformed men were pushing them around, accusing them of drinking under age.

'I'm eighteen!' Carol heard one youth insist.

'Bloody liar!' the policeman answered and shoved him backwards. The boy tried to fend him off, but a second officer grabbed him.

'That's called obstructing a police officer,' he taunted. 'We'll have you!'

A moment later, his truncheon was in the air and then he brought it down on the boy's head. His friend kicked out in defence. The miners standing nearby, who had watched the teenagers being baited, rushed over to help them and suddenly the place erupted.

It was as if a signal had been given, for abruptly the doors of the white police vans burst open and dozens of uniformed officers jumped out. They swarmed like dark wasps on the miners and began to grab bystanders indiscriminately, punching and kicking and hauling them away. Carol gaped at the violent scene, quite frozen in horror.

One moment there had been a scene of tired marchers waiting for stragglers to catch up and board the coaches, the next there was a pitched battle. Fists flew and boots were kicking men on the ground. She heard the sickening crack of truncheons and the howl of the police in pursuit of the scattering miners. The fighting spread like a fire about to engulf them all. Carol looked into the grinning face of one officer as he beat a man on the ground and saw that he was enjoying himself, intoxicated by violence. The man on the ground was curling up under the blows to his head and all she could do was watch.

Carol felt sick with terror and wanted to run but could not move. She knew she should try to help the miner. What if this was Mick?

'Leave him alone,' she screamed. 'You'll kill him!'

But no one seemed to hear her. She pushed her way towards the attack and put a hand out, grabbing the policeman's arm. He stopped for a moment and stared at her.

Suddenly Carol was aware of Laura screaming beside her and Lotty pushing her towards the bus.

'Get away!' her mother-in-law commanded.

Kelly's father was on the steps pulling the women and their children on as fast as he could.

'Let's get the hell out of here!' he shouted at them. People were shouting and crying out to each other, banging on the windows in anger and fear at the scene below. Carol scrambled on board, shoving Laura ahead of her.

The doors slammed shut and the coach began to move while everyone was still swaying in the aisle. Ted Laws reversed over the verge and swung the bus round, away from the fighting. Carol strained to see what had happened to the miner on the ground but could not find him among the sea of struggling men. She saw someone clambering over a wall being pulled back into the fight and then the bus was accelerating fast down the road.

'There's May,' June screamed. 'She's not on the bus!'

'Stop for her!' Joanne shouted, turning to Kelly's father.

Ted slowed, unsure what to do. Laura howled as she knocked her head against the back of a seat. Carol grabbed her and clung on, trying to soothe the distraught girl and protect her from the sights beyond the window. For an instant she wanted them to keep moving, to take her daughter and herself and the others to safety. Let May follow on the next bus out. Carol hated herself for her cowardly feelings, but they engulfed her.

Then Laura began to scream in agitation.

'Auntie May! Auntie May's left behind. Don't leave her!'

All at once, Laura's distress spurred Carol out of her paralysing fear. They were running away like terrified animals, but they were not going to leave their friend behind.

'Hold Laura,' Carol ordered Lotty. She lurched to the front. 'Get the doors open!'

Ted obeyed. Carol stood on the steps with the bus still trundling forward and held out a hand to May. She panted towards the open door, her coat gone and anxious face perspiring. She was so out of breath she could not speak. Carol leaned out further and May grabbed her hand. The heavy woman nearly yanked her out of the bus, but June was there behind and hung on to Carol. May tumbled on to the steps like a beached sea lion. The doors slammed shut and Ted accelerated once again.

Between them, Carol and June hauled May up and gave her a hug. Carol could feel her friend sobbing with relief. A cheer went up on the bus as they sped out of danger. A roundabout loomed up ahead, but Ted hardly stopped as he rushed across it.

'Are you all right, Auntie May?' Laura asked, looking at her flushed, damp face.

May nodded, too distraught to speak.

'We'd have left you, no bother,' June teased her sister, 'but Laura made us stop.'

'Aye, now that's the end of peace and quiet,' Joanne grinned and hugged May.

But May was still too overcome to say anything and the bus fell silent. Carol glanced back at the struggle still going on in the distance and worried about the man on the ground. They had all had a terrible fright and Carol wondered if the women's group might collapse before it had properly started. None of them would want to face that again.

A police van tore past them, its siren screeching, and Carol saw the anxious looks on the faces around her.

Suddenly, May spoke. 'He'll not sell many ice creams going that fast,' she declared.

It was an old joke, but with it the tension broke and the women laughed.

'He'll be wanting to get home to see himself on the telly,' June quipped.

'No,' Lotty joined in, 'his wife's told him not to be late for tea.'

The jokes continued. After several minutes, Ted shouted out, 'Anybody know which way to go?'

'Home'll do, Ted man,' June called back.

'None of this looks familiar,' Ted grumbled. 'I lost me bearings back there.'

'Your ball bearings, Ted?' someone shouted. There was ribald laughter and a startled exclamation from Evelyn Wilson. 'Our Denise!'

Carol looked in astonishment at the normally mute Denise and saw her grinning under her long black fringe.

'Let's have a whip-round for Ted's bearings,' May suggested.

'It's all your fault, any road,' June joked. Ted would still have 'em if we hadn't stopped for you.'

'You bugger, I wish I'd caught another bus,' May replied. 'I'd have been home by now.'

'We could always stop at the friendly local police station and ask for directions,' Carol laughed.

'Remind me never to go on a trip with her again,' May grinned.

'Give us a B,' Joanne began.

'B!' they chorused back.

'Give us an M . . .'

As they sped through the unknown Midland landscape, chanting at the tops of their voices, Carol knew their group was not going to fizzle out. Travelling away together and experiencing the shocking events of the day had knitted them more tightly than any amount of committee meetings ever could have.

Chapter Sixteen

Carol could not sleep, so she got up and went downstairs to make a cup of tea. She squeezed a used tea bag into a mug and poured on boiling water. Sometime soon she would get used to black tea without sugar, she thought, grimacing at the bitter hot taste. Mick had resorted to a drop of condensed milk to sweeten his tea, as they saved their ration of real milk for Laura.

Carol sat in the dark, wrapped in her dressing-gown and thought of their daughter, buried under the covers of their double bed where she had insisted on sleeping.

Mick had lost his temper when he discovered how close they had been to the violence at the rally.

'I knew you shouldn't have gone!' he shouted. 'It was a daft idea.'

'It wasn't daft,' Carol protested, 'and you never tried to stop us going. It wasn't our fault anyhow. There was no trouble until right at the end.'

'I saw it on the TV,' Mick fumed. 'It was worse than anything on the picket line. You should leave the marches to the men. You're stopping at home next time.'

'I'll do whatever the Women's Support Group wants me to do,' Carol flared back. 'And if that means marching, I'll damn well march!'

Mick paced around the sitting room like a caged animal, pulling at his collar-length blond hair. 'You'll not take Laura again! And what's all this the bairn's been saying about you shouting at an old woman in the crowd? It sounds like you went looking for trouble.'

'I don't know how you can say that!' Carol protested. 'We all went to support you and the other lads. I was just trying to talk some reason into the people there. You wouldn't believe the foul things some of them were saying to us. But I couldn't care less about that; I'd do it again if I thought it might change some folks' minds.'

'A bunch of lasses chanting and waving a sheet will change nowt,' Mick answered dismissively. 'The pitmen who only think of themselves have to be picketed out and kept out by the rest of us. It's a hard fight and one for the men. You stick to the food parcels in future.'

Carol fumed with indignation, but she could see that Mick was in no mood to reason. She had no intention of staying at home while others took on the fight, but she still felt guilty at subjecting Laura to the ugly scenes at the rally and decided to say no more.

They sat in stony silence awaiting the late news. When Carol saw how the fight at the rally was portrayed as being provoked by drunken miners, she was incensed.

'It's all lies!' she shouted. 'There wasn't any trouble until the coppers came tearing out of their vans. They went berserk! The lads had nothing to defend themselves with. Oh, God! There was this man lying on the ground being kicked in the head and I kept thinking I should do something.' Carol began to shake. 'But I was too scared to move, I just wanted to run away. Oh Mick, I kept thinking what if it was you?' Carol burst into tears.

At once Mick reached over and pulled her to him in comfort.

'It's all right, pet,' he murmured into her hair. 'Have a good cry.' He held her for several minutes while she sobbed into his shoulder. Finally he said, 'I'm sorry, Carol. I shouldn't have lost me temper with you. I was just worried when I saw the news - felt I should have gone with you. And after Sid being arrested . . .'

Reminded of Sid, Carol made an effort to stop crying. 'Look at me, crying like a baby when none of us has come to any harm. And there's poor Sid in the cells. I should go and see Kelly.'

'Not now,' Mick answered. 'She's stopping over at Auntie Val's tonight. She didn't want to be on her own. You can go round tomorrow when you've had some sleep.'

But, exhausted as she was, Carol was unable to sleep. She finished her tea and got up and fetched her coat and boots from the hall, tiptoeing through the kitchen to let herself out of the back door. She stepped out into the sharp night air. The black sky was littered with stars, unusually bright, and Carol realised that there was an absence of smoke from people's fires. Instead of the pungent smell of burning coal, she was hit by bracing, tangy salt air straight off the sea. She could hear the distant hum of the pit, kept going by the deputies' union, Nacods. But there was no clatter of boots down the streets for the early shift or the noise of miners arriving by car. Gone was the sound of the coal trucks clattering along the line, disturbing the night.

Carol walked on to keep herself warm and thought about Kelly. There would have been a time when her friend would have come to her first when she needed support, not Val Bowman. She knew that Kelly had drawn close to Val since working for her years ago, but it saddened her that Kelly no longer turned to her. There was a reserve between them these days that Carol could not explain and she wondered what it was that Kelly was keeping from her. Years ago, to have had secrets from each other would have been unthinkable. But now, Carol could see that they had drifted apart - had begun to ever since she had married Mick. And now, with her time increasingly taken up with helping the strike, Carol saw even less of her old friend. She was forging new friendships through the Women's Group and new interests. Still, Carol thought, she must support Kelly in this crisis over Sid's arrest, for she was not sure how much pressure their rocky marriage could take.

She diverted down the back of Septimus Street, certain that the house would be in darkness but hoping that someone else might be sleepless too. Her spirits lifted to see the kitchen light burning. Peering in at the window she could see Lotty talking to Eddy. Carol tapped lightly on the glass and went in at the back door.

Lotty showed no surprise. 'Come in, pet. There's some tea in the pot, though it might be a bit stewed. I was just telling Eddy about the rally.'

'I'm glad I'm not the only one who can't sleep,' Carol grinned.

'No one sleeps at the right time around here any more,' Eddy answered, 'and we're used to getting up at all hours, any road.'

Carol accepted the mug of tea he held out to her and sat down on the settee beside him.

'Eddy's moving back in with us,' Lotty told her. 'The rent on his flat is too much.'

Eddy's thin face tinged with embarrassment. 'Just temporary, mind. I've still got a bit put by, so I can help with the bills here.'

'Don't you worry about that,' Lotty said.

'So what's keeping you awake, flower?' Eddy changed the subject quickly.

Carol sighed. 'I can't stop thinking about the rally. I had a row with Mick about it earlier. He doesn't want me to go away again.'

'I'll speak to him,' Lotty assured her. 'He'll come round.'

'Lotty tells me you tried to stop a lad being kicked on the ground,' Eddy said with admiration. 'Said you were arguing with the crowd like a leader.'

Carol blushed. 'No, I just said what came into me head.'

'We need speakers,' Lotty insisted, 'women who'll go out and put people in the picture about what's really going on in the pit villages. Tell them what the families are suffering; help raise a bit money for them to live off. You could do that, Carol.'

'I couldn't speak in public,' Carol protested.

Lotty snorted. 'You've never been backward in coming forward before.'

'Aye,' Eddy encouraged. 'Anyone who can answer back to Charlie or Lotty can take on the world.'

'Cheek of it!' Lotty took a swipe at her brother-in-law.

'I don't know.' Carol was cautious. 'Mind you, I feel so angry about the way the rally was shown on TV. We were treated like thugs, not ordinary decent families. Nobody seems to want to show the strike from our point of view.'

'There you go then,' Lotty answered. 'Think of ways we can get our message across. We're not just going to leave this to the men; we decided that when we formed the support group. I can ask Charlie about contacts in other unions who might want to help us, or local councils. We'll put the word about. Now, do you know any local press who might be sympathetic?'

Carol was astonished by the speed of Lotty's thinking and wondered if she had already been discussing it with Eddy before her arrival. She found herself excited by the prospect of becoming more actively involved, even though the idea of standing up and speaking to strangers terrified her.

'There is someone,' Carol suddenly remembered. 'A friend of Fay and Vic's. He was their best man. Pete . . ? Pete Fletcher, I think they called him. He was a jour- nalist on a newspaper in Sunderland, but that was a while ago. I could find out if he's still around.'

'Would he be on our side?' Lotty sounded doubtful.

Carol shrugged. 'He's local. He might at least be impartial.'

'Worth a try,' Eddy said. 'And if our Carol can't win him over then he's not worth the bother,' he grinned.

Carol smiled. 'I'll get on to it in the morning.'

Lotty yawned. 'That's not long. I think you should be off home before Mick starts sending out a search party.'

Carol got up and Eddy rose too.

'I'll walk you up the street,' he offered.

Out in the dark again, Eddy said, 'She thinks the world of you, you know.'

'Who? Lotty?' Carol exclaimed. 'Don't be daft.'

'She does,' Eddy insisted. 'She might never say it to your face, but she's proud of the way you're standing by the family and the village.'

'Surprised, you mean. Because I'm the Shannon girl,' Carol mocked herself. 'I think if I live to be a hundred, I'll never shake off that name.'

Eddy slung his arm over her shoulder. 'Names don't matter a bit,' he declared. 'You are who you are, and you should never be ashamed of it. We come into this world without a say about who our parents are or what family we'd like to belong to. We just have to get along with the buggers we're landed with.'

'Or not get along, as the case may be,' Carol said wryly.

Eddy stopped her and made her look into his craggy face. She could tell he was serious for once. 'I'm sorry if you've not been happy with the Shannons. They must be mad turning their back on a daughter like you. You're a special lass, Carol. But the Shannons' loss is the Todds' gain. So stop doing yourself down. We all think the world of you.'

Carol felt her eyes sting at his generous words. For so long she had striven to be accepted by her in-laws and now here was kind, funny Eddy telling her that she was. She could not be sure. She would probably never know what Charlie really thought of her, because he was not the sort of person who could easily show his feelings. She still felt a reserve between them, despite coming closer since the strike started. Nevertheless, she felt a wave of gratitude and tenderness towards Mick's uncle for his kind words and for his understanding that the Todds' approval was important to her.

'You're a good, kind man.' She smiled and kissed him on the cheek. She thought she saw his eyes glisten.

'Well, I've never been accused of that before,' he joked. 'Now don't go spoiling me James Dean image, will you?'

Carol laughed and linked her arm through his. They walked up the quiet lane, lit by a bright moon, in easy companionship.

'Did I ever tell you about the time I met Elvis?' Eddy asked, squeezing her arm.

'Presley or Costello?' Carol teased, knowing he had never heard of Elvis Costello.

'Elvis the Pelvis, there is no other,' Eddy protested.

'You have, but tell me again,' Carol grinned.

'Well, it was during me National Service . . .'

The following day, Carol went to the library and searched through the back copies of the newspapers.

She read everything she could find about the strike and became increasingly angry and dismayed by the stories she read. There was little explanation of what the strike was all about, just coverage of any bit of trouble with the police or in the courts. In the tabloids there was gossip about pickets making money from picketing and exaggerated claims about the wages miners earned. She had never read newspapers regularly before or paid much attention to news in the outside world. Current affairs in school had been viewed by her and Kelly as an opportunity to skive off and go down the beach or into town.

Carol combed the serious broadsheets that she had never touched with a barge pole before. There had been a debate in Parliament on 10 April in which the Opposition had accused the Government of using the police in the strike and putting them in an intolerable dilemma. 'Police force is not an arm of the state but the servant of the community. . . confidence in them has been eroded. . .' Carol murmured as she read.

She noted the names of politicians who spoke on the miners' behalf; the

Shadow Home Secretary, Gerald Kaufman, and Tony Benn who accused ministers of authorising police to harass miners and blamed magistrates for working hand in hand to make possible the butchery of the mining industry.

Carol thought of Sid and two others coming before the magistrates' court that very day and wondered what would happen to them. Mick and his father had gone to support him, but Kelly had been sharp with her when she had suggested they go together.

'You can go if you want,' she had said tartly, 'but as I'm the only one keeping a roof over our heads, I'm ganin' to work.'

Carol was sure Kelly was worried about Sid but she was not going to show it to her or anybody else. Carol took her mind off gloomy thoughts about Sid and Kelly by absorbing herself in the newspapers. She searched for a mention of Pete Fletcher but could find none in the recent past. There was nothing for it but to contact Vic about his friend.

She called in at Proud's office on her way home, but he was not there and Kelly was in no mood to chat. 'Try him at home,' she said shortly.

Plucking up courage, Carol decided to take Laura up to Fay's house in Brassy. Even if she and Fay were estranged, there was no reason why Laura should not have contact with her cousins, Jasmine and Ngaio. Brassy village was looking springlike with daffodils and tulips lining the main street and the trees burdened with pink cherry blossom. Laura scampered up the pink gravel drive in anticipation of playing with her older cousins, but Carol's stomach twisted at the sight of the opulent house with its vast Grecian tubs full of pansies guarding the portico. Resentment filled her as she thought how a few days ago she and Mick had visited the bank once again to sort out their looming financial crisis. They had taken out a loan, to be paid off once the strike had ended, to cover their mortgage and essential bills, which had given them a reprieve. But Carol knew this would not cover new shoes for Laura or unforeseen repairs or the weekly groceries that were a constant drain on their dwindling resources. They had never been in debt before and Carol had never had to cope with life without money. She had never craved money and possessions as Fay had, but having to worry about how to make ends meet was new and very frightening.

'We can't afford the HP on the car much longer,' Mick had said, 'though I've been trying to hang on to it for picketing.'

Carol knew, but did not say, that what would really break his heart was the thought of having to sell the motorbike. It stood unused in the back yard under its tarpaulin like a reproachful beast. How unfair it was that her whole world was under threat while Fay lived in prosperous security just because she had married Vic Proud. But Carol had chosen Mick and she knew that even had she been able to see into the future, she would not have chosen differently.

Laura had already rung the bell and Carol tried to quell her anger before Fay came to the door. But it was Mrs Hunt, her mother's old cleaning lady, who answered. Carol was amazed to see the pensioner still working.

'Fay's at her shop,' Mrs Hunt explained, 'but the girls are in. I'm looking after them for the Easter holidays. Come in, pet.'

Laura rushed ahead. 'They're in the playroom watching a video,' Mrs Hunt shouted after her, but Laura was already halfway up the stairs. Carol knew what a treat it was for her daughter to play with her cousins and she felt a pang of guilt for not having brought her sooner. Still, it was a relief that she did not have to confront Fay. She wondered if the ancient Mrs Hunt had been brought in because her brother-in-law had frightened away all the young nannies in the area, then chided herself for the unkind thought.

'It's really Vic I was hoping to catch,' Carol said.

Mrs Hunt gave her an inquiring look before answering, 'Oh, well, you're in luck, he's working in his study. You go on up and I'll make a cup of tea. Do you still take it with milk and two sugars?'

'Ye—' Carol stopped herself. 'No, I take it black now, no sugar, thanks.' No point getting used to the taste of sweet tea again, she told herself. She would like to have gone into the kitchen and chatted to Mrs Hunt, who was a neighbour of Grandda Bowman's and kept an eye on the old man. But she was keen to get her request to Vic over with and escape.

Vic was in his large airy study, fitted with mahogany shelves and a large desk at which he was seated, absorbed in front of a computer screen. The air was stale with the smell of cigarettes and made Carol suddenly crave a smoke. She had given up four times in the last two weeks and had held out for five days this time.

'This is a nice surprise,' Vic smiled and came to greet her. Carol turned her face quickly so that his kiss landed on her cheek.

'Just a quick visit,' she said, suddenly nervous of him. He had always had the ability to make her feel like a gauche teenager, she thought in irritation. Mick would probably go mad if he found out she had come to see him on her own, for he used to complain that Vic was always trying to make a pass at her. Carol would counter that Vic flirted with any female under ninety, but she knew Mick disliked him.

'Cigarette?' Vic offered. Carol, in a state of sudden nerves, could not resist. He lit it for her and she inhaled deeply.

'So,' he smiled, 'I hear you've been getting into scrapes in Nottinghamshire.'

'Says who?' Carol asked, cautious.

'Ted Laws was full of how you tried to tackle the police at the rally. Pulling women on to buses, that sort of thing. Not sure I want my buses used for political purposes,' Vic teased. 'Never took you for the radical type either.'

'I'm not,' Carol answered. 'This isn't about politics, it's about justice. We went on the march to draw attention to the way the miners and their families are suffering. We just want people to listen to us, not hound us off the streets like criminals.'

Vic began a slow hand clapping. 'Spoken like a true Todd.'

'Don't mock me,' Carol said with an angry look. 'I mean what I say.'

Vic was suddenly serious. 'The best way to stop the suffering, as you call it, is to get back to work and save your own necks. Why throw everything away for a few bolshie Yorkshiremen?'

His sudden aggression took Carol by surprise. She gave him a hard look and saw the deep worry lines on his brow and the dark smudges below his eyes. He was looking older, tenser; his fingers were nicotine-stained.

'It's affecting your business, isn't it?' Carol said quietly.

Vic slumped back into his worn leather chair. 'Of course it damn well is! Half my business was ferrying men to work at the pits around here, good regular runs. Now it's gone. I'm relying on holiday tours to Spain. But the problem is no one's going on holiday around here either. The number of cancellations ...'

His look was despairing as he ran his fingers through his receding hair. Here was a glimpse of the unguarded Victor, Carol thought, the man beneath the confident exterior whom no one normally saw. For a moment she felt sorry for him.

'Then you know what it's like for us,' Carol said gently, perching on the edge of the desk. 'I really don't know what we're going to live on if the strike goes on all summer.'

Vic did not seem to hear her. He was immersed in his own worries.

'I don't want to have to lay drivers off,' he continued, staring at the computer screen, 'but what else can I do? Things were going so well up until now. Do you know we'd started a property business? Renovating old houses, converting large terraces in Sunderland into flats - that sort of thing. Now all that's under threat.' He waved a hand around the room. 'All this is under threat.'

'At least Fay has her business,' Carol pointed out.

Vic snorted. 'Yes, and a very successful one, as she never stops telling me. But as you know, your sister has extravagant tastes. She spends money as fast as she makes it. Not that I mind, as long as it's coming in, but this house costs a lot of money and we've the girls to educate. We have more to lose than—'

'Than the miners?' Carol fizzed with annoyance. She stubbed out her cigarette, her patience at an end. Vic was only concerned for himself as usual. 'There are people in this village who are likely to lose the very roof over their heads, Vic. People who will have to spend the rest of the year paying off their debts, even if they go back to work tomorrow. You're worrying about school fees when families down the hill don't know what they're going to feed their kids come the end of the week!'

He reached across the desk and grabbed her round the wrist. 'Then the sooner they stop pratting about and get back to work, the better for all of us,' he hissed.

Carol tried to pull her hand away, but he kept a tight grip. 'Let go,' she told him.

He ignored her, thrusting his face close to hers. 'Why are you here, Carol? You've kept away for such a long time - too long.'

She could smell the stale tobacco on his breath, warm on her face, his beard brushing her skin. She tried to control the panic she felt.

'I want to contact Pete Fletcher, the journalist,' Carol answered, leaning away.

This seemed to take him off guard and he loosened his hold in surprise. Carol whipped her hand away and stood back out of his reach.

'Why?' he asked in suspicion.

'The Women's Group want some publicity. Is he still working in the area?'

Vic withdrew across the desk. 'He's freelancing. Doing radio stuff. Living in Newcastle. Doubt he'll be interested.'

'But you've got his address?' Carol persisted.

Vic studied her. 'I could arrange a meeting for you.'

'Just a phone number would do, thanks,' Carol answered, knowing his game.

Vic grunted and turned to his computer, tapping at the keyboard until a list of addresses appeared on the screen. He scribbled an address and telephone number down on the multi-coloured pad next to the telephone and tore off the top sheet. Coming round the desk, he waved it at her.

'Here you are then.' He smiled at her once more.

She took it quickly. 'Ta. I'll be off then,' and turned to go.

'You must come again soon.' Vic slipped in front of her, blocking her escape to the door. 'Family get-togethers are very dull without you, little sister.' He put a hand on her shoulder. 'And any help I can give you, I will. All that talk about the business in difficulty, take it with a pinch of salt. I was just playing for your sympathy.' He laughed, his self-assured demeanour back in place. 'I work at home a lot at the moment,' he said in a low voice full of invitation. 'We've always got on so well, you and I, haven't we, doll?'

'You'll tell Fay I called, won't you?' Carol said, feeling her face burn. She tried to step past him. 'I must go and find Laura.'

But Vic caught her arm. 'Goodbye kiss then?' he smiled, and holding her firmly, pressed his mouth over hers.

Carol stiffened as his wet lips sucked at hers, his tongue trying to force its way inside her mouth. For an instant she was stunned and then revulsion engulfed her. She parted her lips and then bit him sharply on the tongue.

Vic howled and recoiled from her. She gave him a push and glared in fury. 'I'll not be back here again.'

Vic could not speak as he clutched one hand over his mouth, but with the other he swiped at her as she passed, hitting her face. Her cheek stung with pain, but she did not cry out or hit him back. The look that she gave him was full of disgust and contempt.

'You're pathetic, Vic.' Carol walked calmly to the door, opened it and went out without a backward glance.

Once out of the study, she hurried to the playroom to find Laura, but the room was empty. Rushing downstairs, she saw them playing out in the garden on a new climbing frame. As she stepped outside, she caught their chatter.

'Will you get one of these for your birthday?' Ngaio asked.

'I might be,' Laura answered excitedly. 'It's a surprise.'

'No, you won't,' Jasmine told her brutally. 'Mummy says Uncle Mick doesn't have any money, so you won't be getting anything for your birthday. You're *poor.*'

Carol's stomach churned at the cruel words and she saw Laura's face fall. She wanted to weep for her daughter, but instead hurried over.

'Come on, Laura,' she said briskly. 'Time to go.'

'Oh, Mam, I want to stay and play,' Laura protested.

'We're going out shopping soon anyway,' Jasmine said, 'so you can't stay.'

Carol resisted the impulse to retaliate and put out her hands to Laura, lifting her down off the climbing frame and praying she would not make a scene.

'You can see the girls at your birthday party,' Carol promised rashly.

Laura's face lit up. 'Am I having a party, Mam?' she cried.

'Course you are,' Carol said, cursing her impulsiveness. If Jasmine had not annoyed her so much, she would never have said it.

'Goody!' Ngaio squealed, clapping her hands. 'I like going to your house, Auntie Carol.'

'Yes, we can make a house under the bed again,' Laura said in excitement. 'And have lollipops!'

'Sounds boring to me,' Jasmine complained, feeling left out. 'I like discos better.'

Carol said quickly, 'We can have a disco too. We'll borrow some of Auntie Linda's tapes.'

'Yeah!' Laura and Ngaio cried together.

'And can we have a clown like Ngaio and Jasmine did?' Laura asked, skipping along at her side.

Carol groaned inwardly. 'We'll see.'

'Yeah, a clown!' Laura grinned, as if her mother had agreed to the idea.

Carol waved to Mrs Hunt as they passed the kitchen window and marched her daughter smartly down the drive, before she dreamed up any more expensive birthday treats. Then remembering Laura's perplexed, hurt look at Jasmine's unkind words, Carol squeezed her hand tighter and determined to give her the best birthday ever.

Chapter Seventeen

Carol looked nervously at the clock. The reporter was fifteen minutes late. Joanne was in the kitchen boiling up the kettle again and Carol could hear Laura and Joanne's son, Mark, jumping off the beds upstairs.

Laura was on a permanent high, thinking about her birthday party the next day. At Lotty's suggestion, the Women's Group had decided to hold a party for the children on the afternoon of the fundraising social, which happened to be Laura's fifth birthday. So Carol no longer had to worry about laying on a birthday party, as her daughter thought having one in the large Welfare Hall was far grander than anything she had previously had at home.

It had taken the heat out of her argument with Mick over the foolishness of promising Laura a party at all and for Jasmine's spiteful words which Laura had relayed to him.

'How dare she go on about us like that?' Mick had fulminated.

'She's just repeating what her parents say,' Carol had defended her niece.

'Well, she'll not go upsetting Laura like that again. I don't want you taking the bairn up to Brassy any more.'

'I won't be,' Carol had said.

Then they had rowed again over her going to see Vic about this journalist, which was why Mick had refused to stay in the house to meet Pete Fletcher and why Carol had begged Sid's sister Joanne to come round and give her support instead. Carol hid her hurt at Mick's parting words that she was getting involved in something she knew nothing about. She suspected he was really angry that she had gone to see Vic without telling him, so she had spared him the details of Vic's unwanted advances.

'Mick's just suspicious of journalists,' Carol told Joanne, 'and I can't blame him after the way the media's been reporting the strike.'

'My John would be the same,' her friend assured her. 'Anyway, the men are busy organising for the visit tomorrow.'

Carol nodded, thinking how pleased Mick and his father were that Arthur Scargill was to be visiting nearby Quarryhill and how they were all to attend the rally through the village. 'We might get to meet Arthur in person this time,' she said excitedly.

'That's if we're not too busy organising the kids' party and the social,' Joanne reminded her.

There was a ring at the door and Carol jumped.

'Go and answer it then,' Joanne laughed.

A tall man with short reddish hair stood on the doorstep. His face was boyish behind a pair of wire-framed glasses and he wore jeans and an old tweed jacket. Carol had forgotten what the journalist looked like, but he held out his hand with a smile and assured her that he was Pete Fletcher.

'Let him in then,' Joanne called behind her and Carol flushed and stepped aside. She had a sudden pang of misgiving at what she was doing. Perhaps Mick was right and this man would twist what she said to fit some sensational story for the tabloids. She should be down at the Welfare helping Lotty prepare food parcels . . .

'I was pleased to get your letter,' Pete said easily. 'The idea of doing a piece about the Women's Group really interests me.'

Carol nodded.

'I'm Joanne. Sit down and I'll make some tea while Carol finds her voice. She's not usually tongue-tied.'

'No, I don't remember her like that,' Pete smiled. 'How are your family, Carol? I've been out of touch.'

Carol laughed shortly. 'So have I. In fact we don't speak any more, not since the strike. They never really approved of me marrying a miner anyway.' She stopped suddenly, wondering why she had told him that. She must be cautious; there was no telling what he might do with such information. 'But that's not what you've come about,' she added swiftly.

Pete sat down. 'I thought I might hang around the village for a day or two, cover what's going on. Perhaps you could suggest some people to talk to? I'd like to do a feature for one of the nationals.'

Carol felt more at ease at the switch in conversation. 'Well, you've come at the right time. Arthur Scargill's in the area tomorrow. And the women are organising our first big fundraising social - and there's a party for the kids.' Carol found herself launching enthusiastically into the subject.

Joanne brought the tea. They had splashed out on milk and a precious bag of sugar, not wanting the reporter to think them inhospitable. Carol found him easy to talk to and her nervousness evaporated. Within twenty minutes they had told him all about the group and the soup kitchen and the generosity of local traders and about the rally in the Midlands and Sid's arrest.

'Me brother's very upset about it all,' Joanne said. 'Been bound over to keep the peace for nine months, and all he did was shove a copper out the way. Now he can't do any picketing at all.'

'It's the way they're trying to beat us,' Carol added, 'arresting as many miners as possible for the slightest thing, so picketing gets disrupted. Men who've never been in the slightest bother before are finding themselves with criminal records.'

Pete nodded in understanding. Just then, the children came bounding in, red-faced from trampolining on the beds, and rushed at the stranger.

'Are you the man from the telly?' Mark asked, fiddling with Pete's black camera bag.

Pete laughed and asked them their names.

'You're a friend of Uncle Vic's, aren't you?' Laura said, showing off her knowledge. 'Mam told me.'

Pete glanced at Carol. 'I went to school with Uncle Vic, but I don't see much of him now.'

'Can we be on the telly too?' Mark asked, hopping on the spot.

'Just me,' Laura insisted, "cos he's my mam's friend, not yours!'

The children began a squabble which their mothers attempted to silence with threats of being smacked and sent upstairs again. Pete intervened.

'Would you like me to take a picture of you both?' he asked, delving into his bag.

'Yes!' they chorused.

Pete got them to pose on the chair opposite and took several shots.

'I'll give you copies if they come out well,' he promised the women.

Carol was touched but embarrassed. 'We can't pay for them.'

Pete waved his hand. 'They're for the kids.'

Joanne said it was time she took Mark home. Pete packed up his camera.

'I'd really like to talk to you some more,' he told them. 'Can you suggest somewhere in the village I could stay perhaps a night or two?'

Carol and Joanne exchanged looks.

'A bed and breakfast would do,' Pete said, not wanting to embarrass them.

'You can't do that,' Joanne protested. 'You can stay with us.'

'Great!' Mark whooped.

'Oh, Mam,' Laura complained. 'I want him to stay at my house.'

Carol knew Joanne was struggling to make ends meet since John's younger brother had moved in with them, made homeless by the strike. And the thought of a tantrum from Laura spurred her on to say, 'You've got a houseful, Joanne. We've more room here - if you don't mind kipping on the settee, Pete?'

'Not in the least,' he smiled. 'Would you like to discuss it with your husband first? I could call back . . .'

'Mick won't mind,' Carol said, hoping she sounded convincing. 'Not if it's going to further our cause.'

Pete got up. 'I'll take a walk around then. Come back tonight. I'll eat at the pub, of course, so please don't go buying any extra food.'

'There's no need for that,' Carol said proudly, 'we can take care of visitors.'

In the passage, he hesitated before opening the door. Joanne had gone into the kitchen with the dirty cups.

'You've turned out differently than I'd expected,' he mused. 'Fay was always going on about her badly behaved younger sister - the wild thing, Vic called you.'

The mention of her brother-in-law aggravated Carol. 'Well, I can still get wild about things that really matter.'

'Good,' Pete said with approval, 'because Vic and Fay seem to have lost sight of that somewhere along the way. The last time I saw them they bored me rigid with their money-making scams.'

Carol laughed. 'Sounds like them.' And suddenly she had the feeling that she could trust Pete Fletcher. He was not here to exploit them, she was sure of that. But how was she going to convince Mick?

If they had not been so busy preparing for the events of the following day, Mick might have protested louder. Unexpectedly, Lotty came to Carol's rescue as they busied themselves sorting out raffle prizes and food for the children's party at the Welfare Hall.

'Why's he got to stay with us?' Mick demanded.

'He's doing a story on the Women's Group,' Carol said, curbing her annoyance. 'It's just for a couple of nights.'

'It might lead to something important,' Lotty interrupted, 'and Carol's just being neighbourly. You let her get on with her work for the Group. Now, these food parcels are ready for delivery, so make yourself useful.'

A disgruntled Mick was dispatched on delivery duty and it was late before they returned to the house with a sleeping Laura to find Pete sitting up with Eddy.

'I found your reporter having a crack with Captain Lenin down The Ship,' Eddy explained his presence. 'Discovered he's an Elvis fan.'

Mick grunted. 'That'll be useful for his article.'

Carol blushed and introduced Mick to the journalist. Pete offered his hand with a friendly greeting which Mick took awkwardly. Laura stirred in his arms.

121

'I'll get the bairn to bed,' he said quickly and headed for the stairs. Carol knew he would not reappear and felt embarrassed by his lack of hospitality.

'I'll make some tea,' she offered. 'You'll stay for a cup, won't you, Eddy?'

Eddy saw her pleading look and agreed. While the kettle boiled, Carol went upstairs to find bedding for their guest. Laura had woken up and demanded to sleep in their bed. Mick had already given in and was settling their daughter in the double bed.

'I'll sleep in Laura's room,' he told Carol, glancing away, 'so we all get some kip.'

Carol felt a stab of hurt. 'Mick—'

'I'm too tired to argue about it,' he snapped. 'Better get back to your reporter.'

Carol flushed. 'Stop behaving like a bairn,' she hissed at him in the corridor. But to her annoyance he said nothing more and closed the door to Laura's room. Carol swallowed her frustration and went downstairs to make tea. Eddy gave her an inquiring glance as she re-entered but she ignored his look. She turned to Pete.

'Well, what else do you want to know about the Group?' she asked briskly.

'Look's like you're on duty,' Eddy grinned.

Pete smiled and pulled a tape recorder from his bag, placing it on the coffee table. He handed round his cigarettes and they all lit up.

'Well,' he said, balancing his cigarette on the ashtray, 'why don't I start with you?'

It was after one o'clock when they finally stopped talking and Eddy left for Septimus Street. Carol lay awake beside Laura for a further hour, thinking about their discussion. She had talked and talked as she had not done for years, about growing up in Brassbank and her schooldays, life at Granville House and her time away in London, then marrying into the Todds and having Laura and how things had changed so dramatically for them all since the start of the strike. Pete had listened and smoked and nodded and led her in different directions with his soft questioning.

Eddy had listened too as if he had heard none of it before and now Carol went hot in the dark to think she might have said too much, given too much of herself away. Why had she spoken of her past like that and to a virtual stranger? It was as if all these thoughts had been piling up over the years like the waste on a spoil heap, unspoken until the man full of questions had arrived and caused a verbal landslide.

'It's like I was living inside the wrong skin,' she heard her words echo again in her head, 'like I never really knew who this Carol Shannon was. It wasn't until I broke free and went off to London that I began to realise who I wanted to be, where I wanted to be. I had a chance to step back and look at all the time I'd wasted battering against my parents. It wasn't Brassbank that I hated, it was being forced to be the sort of daughter that I could never be. So I came back. And then I met Mick and everything began to slot into place at last. I'd never been so happy. And we had Laura. I had her right there on the settee where you're sitting!' Carol.blushed again to think that she had even told him that. 'So this strike,' she had concluded, 'it's not just about saving jobs for the future, it's about saving everything we stand for, everything that makes life in Brassbank worth living - our families and homes and friends, our traditions. It's all under attack. And we women are prepared to fight for that to the bitter end.'

She had sat back and for a long while the men had been silent. Pete had watched her closely, the tape recorder finally switched off, and Eddy had reached over and squeezed her hand but said nothing. Carol had seen the tears in his eyes before he hurried into the kitchen with his tea cup.

After that no one seemed to feel like talking any more and they had said their goodnights. Now Carol lay, beset by doubts about the wisdom of having talked so frankly. She had said too much, embarrassed Eddy and given Pete Fletcher too much ammunition to fire off at whatever targets he chose, just as Mick had feared.

Oh, Mick! Carol thought of her husband lying in the single bed on the other side of the wall. She wanted him here beside her to snuggle against, to feel his heavy arms round her and hear his breathing. But if she moved now she might wake Laura and then everyone would be woken. And what if Mick should reject her? Since the strike had started their time alone together in bed had been disrupted by early morning picketing and Laura's nightly visits and their lovemaking had been sporadic. She would have to be firmer with Laura about sleeping in her own bed. Smothering her loneliness, she buried down under the covers and fell into an exhausted sleep.

The next day was bright and blustery and Carol's spirits were lifted by the optimism among the marchers heading for Quarryhill. The women had stayed up late all week, making a proper banner with material donated from Val Bowman and curtain tie-backs joined together for the cords. It was austere but stunning in its simplicity - black and red lettering on a white background with motifs of a pick, miner's lamp and red heart.

Laura woke as soon as it was light and raced around excitedly shouting about being five years old. They gave her a special breakfast of her favourite cereal and allowed her to eat sweets as there were few presents to open. But Mick had managed to fix up a second-hand bicycle which he had painted purple and Laura was ecstatic. She dragged him outside and Mick spent the next hour pushing her up and down the back lane.

'It doesn't have any stabilisers,' Carol explained to Pete. She felt embarrassed that he had witnessed their meagre attempts and knew that Mick resented him being there on Laura's birthday. But he seemed not to notice.

'Better not to have them,' Pete said, 'she'll learn to ride all the quicker.'

Eventually Carol called them in to get ready for the march to Quarryhill.

Pete came along as an observer with Charlie's permission and on the understanding that he did not make a nuisance of himself. There were delegations from pits around the county and some had travelled from Northumberland to support their leader.

Just before they left Brassbank, the local lodge surprised the women. Charlie Todd stood forward.

'In appreciation of the hard work of the Women's Group,' he told the crowd, 'we'd like to have a dedication of their new banner. They've never stopped for a minute. The kitchen's feeding two hundred men a day every dinnertime and scores of food parcels go out every Friday. Today they're laying on a party for the bairns and a fund-raising social for us after. Now we want to show our support to them for supporting us.'

Charlie smiled at Lotty and the young vicar Stephen Copeland stepped forward. He blessed their new banner and prayed for them all. Carol looked on in quiet gratitude for this gesture by the men and she slipped her hand into Mick's, while heads were bowed, and squeezed it. She felt an answering grasp from him, which made up for his bad mood of the past week.

The miners of County Durham and their families marched proudly through Quarryhill, behind 'Coal Not Dole' posters, their children riding high on shoulders, and ended up in the municipal park near the old bandstand. There were few police around and the mood was buoyant, with rousing singing and chants of, 'Arthur Scargill, Arthur Scargill, we'll support you evermore!'

'There's Auntie Kate!' Laura cried, waving at Simon's wife who was on duty and standing by the park gates. Kate waved back and Carol wondered where her brother was. She knew the police were on constant duty, working massive overtime, and wondered if he saw anything of Kate these days. If she ever found time she would call round . . .

The NUM president stood relaxed on the bandstand, sharing jokes with those around him and then spoke passionately to the crowd. Carol was exultant to be standing so close to the leader they usually saw only on TV. He spoke with far more humour and compassion than the brief clips on television ever showed. Scargill praised the women for their superb support and talked of asking for a levy of fifty pence from other trade unions to the hardship fund. Then he promised that there would be a national demonstration soon, probably in Nottinghamshire. At the mention of the county, Carol felt a chill go down the back of her neck. Her mind flashed back to the hostility of the crowd and the ruthlessness of the policing there.

'Why aren't the media reporting that there are twelve thousand miners in Nottinghamshire on strike? Why don't they show the police going berserk against our members? Well, we will show them at this national demonstration that we support the strikers. If the paramilitary police attempt to stop us going in, we shall walk in! If it means getting arrested, we shall all be arrested!'

The crowd cheered and clapped their approval and Carol chided herself for her cowardice. The men around her were willing to go to any lengths to support each other and she should show the same fortitude. Something made her look across at Mick and for a moment she saw grim determination in his face. Carol was awed by it. She knew then that her husband would risk everything for their cause. And if ordinary, peaceable men like Mick were prepared to fight, then they all would, in their thousands. The enormity and scale of their protest hit Carol like a wave for the first time. They were on a road of no return. They had to succeed: defeat was now unthinkable. Defeat could mean the annihilation of the whole mining industry and their way of life. The thought was apocalyptic.

Carol stared at Mick and knew that he felt the same weight of destiny; that he would have to do something, however small, to make a difference. Perhaps he had been feeling guilty that it was Sid who had been arrested outside the power station instead of him and that was why he had been so short with her recently. She felt suddenly anxious and wanted to go over to him and stand close, hold his hand and let him know that she understood his burden. But she was standing with the other women, holding on to one of the cords, and she could not move from her position.

The moment passed and soon they were all making their way down the road to Brassbank, chatting about arrangements for the evening.

Laura came bounding up with her friends Mark and Louise. 'Can I change for the party now, Mam? Can Louise come with us? She wants to wear my purple disco skirt with the black bow. Can she, Mam?'

Carol grinned at her daughter, thankful for her bursting enthusiasm.

'Course she can,' she agreed, hugging Laura to her side. But the girl broke away impatiently and skipped ahead with Louise, chased by Mark. To her this was just another march and the real excitement was the party to come. May, Louise's mother, laughed.

'That's the way to be,' she nodded at the children. 'No thought beyond where the next ice cream's coming from.'

'Aye,' Carol smiled. But she wondered how long they would be able to go on like that: innocents with the storm brewing about them.

Chapter Eighteen

In the last week of May, Carol found Val in tears at the shop.

'I'm sorry, Carol, but I'm going to have to lay you off.'

Carol had never seen her so upset before and she went and put her arms round her. 'I understand,' she said, trying to comfort her, though she felt sick at the thought of her meagre wages coming to an end. They had been a lifeline these past twelve weeks, helping her put enough food on the table for anyone who came.

There had been a steady stream of visitors at different times of the day; Grandda Bowman after the morning picket, Uncle Eddy dropping in to share a cigarette, May and June and Joanne for a chat or a moan on their way to and from the Welfare, Sid following Mick around like a forlorn shadow, not knowing what to do with his empty hours, and even the taciturn Denise would be found squatting in front of the TV, leafing through Carol's out-of-date magazines.

After school the house would be invaded by children from Laura's class, demanding biscuits and jam sandwiches and to be taken to the park. And there had been Pete Fletcher. He turned up from time to time with his camera and tape recorder, stalking around the village like an anthropologist observing them all. She knew that he got on Mick's nerves, but she still believed he was on their side and was going to give them sympathetic coverage. No national paper had yet taken any of his pieces, but he said it was just a matter of time and gathering more in-depth information. Besides, Carol liked his company - his easy conversation and broad range of interests - and she was not going to turn him away.

'It means I can spend more time with the Women's Group, any road,' Carol assured the distressed Val, but she seemed not to hear.

'Business has never been so bad,' she fretted, 'not in all the years I've had the shop. Perhaps I should never have expanded into wedding hire.'

'You weren't to know,' Carol sighed. 'And maybe it'll all be over in a few weeks.'

But they both knew how unlikely that was. The latest round of negotiations had just broken down and MacGregor had withdrawn from the talks. Carol went home full of gloom and when Laura was out playing, she told Mick her bad news. He tried to console her, but she was overwhelmed by sudden fear and doubt for the future.

The news that evening reported arrests at the coking depot at Orgreave where non-union drivers were being brought in under heavy police guard.

'Where is Orgreave?' Carol asked, feeling tearful and depressed at the lack of good news.

'Near Sheffield,' Mick replied, his face brooding, and then abruptly he switched off the television. 'Let's got for a walk along the beach,' he suggested, 'with the bairn.'

Chivvied by Mick, Carol roused herself and they fetched Laura from down the street where Denise was teaching her hopscotch.

'Can I have an ice cream?' Laura asked in excitement.

Carol glanced at Mick, feeling guilty and suddenly angry that they had to deny their daughter such a simple pleasure.

Mick took hold of Laura's hand. 'I've got summat for you in me pocket,' he said mysteriously.

'What is it?' the girl demanded, hopping on one foot.

'You'll find out when we get to the beach,' Mick grinned.

Laura squealed. Tell him to show us now, Mam!'

She kept up such a noise of protest that Mick gave in before they had reached the end of the lane and fished out a small, bright red lollipop. Laura grabbed it. 'Ooh, my favourite colour!'

Mick took off the wrapper and soon their daughter was sucking happily and skipping along between them, all thoughts of ice cream forgotten.

Carol smiled at her husband, realising how he must have planned the surprise in anticipation of Laura demanding something more expensive.

'That was thoughtful of you,' she murmured and slipped her arm through his.

He smiled back. 'No point in worrying over money, pet. We'll manage without your wages. I'll gan to the Welfare for me dinner if you like.'

Carol knew how difficult it was for Mick to say that. He had held out from attending the soup kitchen, saying it was meant for men who were worse off then he was and he would not take food away from the needy. Now he was swallowing his pride and admitting that they themselves needed the help they had been giving to others.

Carol squeezed his arm, thankful that he was there to support her and lift her spirits. It felt good being close to him again, touching him. For the past month they had hardly been alone together and even at nights he had been off early on picketing duty or slipping off to Laura's bedroom when their daughter monopolised their bed. Carol had been unable to deny Laura the comfort of snuggling up to her in bed, for the child had nightmares about a bus leaving her behind and being chased by an angry man and Carol knew the rally still haunted her. It haunted them both. The picture of the miner being beaten on the ground kept plaguing her mind.

But tonight, Carol determined she and Mick would make love again and make up for the distance of the past month. As they cut through the allotments and down the steep cliff path to the sea, she felt Mick relax, chattering with Laura and talking confidently to her about how everything was going to work out in their favour.

She no longer felt disheartened. The evening sun shone warm on her back and she breathed in the salty sea air. For a moment she stood and watched Mick chasing after Laura along the beach, his blond hair shining, his face and arms faintly tanned from being above ground every day. Then she was running after them to catch up.

'Hey,' she shouted. 'I love you!'

They turned and looked at her in surprise.

'I love you both; I love you both to bits!' Carol yelled, grinning, and caught up with them, pushing Mick over on the sand and grabbing Laura in a hug. They fell in a giggling heap on top of him.

'They'll lock you up one of these days,' Mick laughed.

'As long as they lock you in with me, I don't care,' Carol answered and kissed him.

'Kiss me! Kiss me!' Laura squealed and planted wet kisses on both their cheeks.

'You're soft, the pair of you,' Mick smiled, but hugged them fiercely to him.

'Dad, mind me lolly,' Laura protested and pulled it off his T-shirt.

They spent the evening throwing stones into the sea and filling their pockets with shells. Wandering home via the allotments, they found Charlie reading on an ancient deck chair, taking a rare evening off. He gave them rhubarb and a cabbage and pressed ten pence into Laura's hand to buy sweets. They chatted about the garden and the family, but only later did Carol realise there had been no mention of the latest strike news or plans for the next day, as if the men had already discussed them.

They strolled home in the twilight with a sleepy Laura in Mick's arms, and Carol felt content and revitalised and ready to face another day.

That night, Laura slept soundly in her own bed. Mick took Carol in his arms and they made love before falling into a deep dreamless sleep, drugged by tiredness and sea air.

Something woke Carol shortly before dawn. The space in the bed next to her was empty and chill. Mick was gone. Then she noticed the note scrawled on her bedside table.

'See you soon. Don't worry. I love you. Mick.'

Carol went cold inside. She had a gut feeling that Mick was in danger, like women had about their men going underground. The day stretched ahead of her, long and anxious. Her question of the previous evening rang in her head, *'Where's Orgreave?'* Mick had said near Sheffield but had not wanted to talk about it. Had he known, as he turned off the ugly pictures of confrontation on the television, that soon it would be him on the front line?

At breakfast time, Charlie appeared at the kitchen door, looking tired. Laura rushed up to him for a hug and began making a fuss over his terrier, Dougal, who was jumping around her legs. It pained Carol that she no longer asked where her father was, having grown used to him not being there in the morning.

'I just came to tell you, Carol, that Mick's away to South Yorkshire. There's a few of the lads gone, Eddy included. Local families are going to put them up, they'll be well looked after.'

Carol felt a swell of resentment, wanting to know who would be caring for her husband and on whose floor he would be sleeping that night.

'How long?' she asked, feeling her eyes prickle.

Charlie shrugged. 'As long as it takes. Maybe a couple of days, maybes longer. If they stay local, then they'll not be harassed by the coppers on the road. There's been that many roadblocks. You wouldn't believe the trouble there's been just trying to reach picket lines - smashed windscreens, car keys confiscated, the lot. The police are abusing their powers all the time.'

Carol stiffened. She knew that some of the police had acted with brutality but she was not going to suffer one of Charlie's tirades against them. Her brother Simon was no bully and she was sure the majority were decent men like him, forced to carry out unpleasant work. She would not risk having Simon criticised in front of Laura either.

'Go and get your hairbrush,' she told her daughter firmly. When the girl was out of the room, Carol rounded on her father-in-law. 'You should have told me last night where he was going. You knew and you never said. I never had a chance to say goodbye properly.'

'He's just gone picketing, pet.' Charlie dismissed her worries with a laugh.

'Don't treat me like a kid. He's heading into trouble; else there wouldn't be all this secrecy.'

Instantly Charlie was serious. 'Listen, Carol, the fewer people who know where the lads go the better. There's a dirty war going on out there against us, believe me. Thatcher and the Tories want us beaten. Our phones are being tapped. There are undercover coppers mixing with the lads, ready to shop the activists. They're finding out our plans and then stopping us on the road before we even get there. Thousands of pitmen have been arrested already. I just came here to put your mind at rest - thought maybes Mick wouldn't have told you he'd be off for a few days. No doubt he'll ring you when he gets there.'

Carol looked at her father-in-law. They had always been wary of each other, but just now she felt he had confided in her as never before. He was carrying a huge burden of worries yet had found time to come here and make sure she was all right. His face was stern and knowing, but his eyes shone with compassion.

Impulsively, Carol stretched out her hand to touch his. 'I'm sorry for biting your head off. It's just I worry so much for Mick.'

He gave her a small, bashful smile. 'I know you do, pet.'

To the relief of both of them, Laura bounded back into the room and set Dougal jumping and barking with delight.

'Stay and have a cup of tea with us,' Carol urged. But Charlie shook his head.

'I must get back.' He whistled to the dog and Dougal raced to his heels.

'I'll see you later at the hall, then,' Carol said, then forced herself to add, 'Thanks for coming.'

Charlie nodded and was gone.

'Can we have a dog?' Laura asked.

Carol sighed. 'Not this year, pet.'

'When then?' Laura persisted. 'For Christmas?'

'We'll see.' Carol knew she should scotch the idea straightaway, but didn't have the heart. Every day she seemed to be saying no to anything Laura asked for.

'Great, a dog for Christmas! I want a black one with a red collar.'

'Laura . . .' Carol tried to protest, but the girl was already out of the door and shouting out the news to Denise who was passing in her long black skirt and heavy boots.

The older girl stopped and waved at Carol to come out. Surprised, Carol went out to see what she wanted.

'Linda's back,' she said without expression.

Carol was stunned. 'She can't be. Her dad's just been round here and he never said anything.'

A faint smile of triumph played around her pale lips. 'She turned up at ours last night.'

'With Dan?' Carol asked, nonplussed.

Denise shook her head. 'Dan's gone back to his parents but Linda was scared of ganin' to hers. She's been living on her own for a week. Don't think she's eaten in a couple of days.'

Carol was shocked, thinking how wounded Lotty would be that her youngest had not gone straight to her for help. But her heart went out to her lonely, unhappy young sister-in-law and she felt a pang of guilt for not having made more of an effort to keep in touch.

'Oh, poor Linda! Well, your mam can't be expected to feed an extra mouth, she must come to us,' Carol insisted. 'Tell our Linda I'll be round as soon as I've taken Laura to school.'

Denise nodded and grinned. Carol was amazed at the effect it had of enlivening her pallid face.

'I knew you'd stick up for her,' Denise said with approval. 'I told Linda you would.'

It was early morning. Mick and Eddy sat in the makeshift canteen of a miners' hall, eating bacon sandwiches. A cheerful man sat opposite munching on his roll and swapping stories about his family and children with the men from Durham. Bob told them he was from the north-east but now living and working in Yorkshire. Eddy chatted happily about their village and Mick found himself drawing out a photo of Carol and Laura and showing them off.

'Canny,' Bob said with a nod of appreciation and got out one of his children sitting on a beach. 'That's when we went to Corfu. Not be doing that this year, more's the pity.'

Bob's chatter took Mick's mind off the day ahead. They had stayed the first night on the floor of a social club, some of them lying out on the pool tables to sleep, but last night they had been farmed out to different homes of striking miners to try and make their presence less obvious. Mick and Eddy were staying with an elderly couple whose son-in-law and grandsons were strikers. The stooped, retired miner, John Kirkup, had sat up late reminiscing about his days in a Durham pit before the war. Eddy's easy chatter had drawn the old man out of his reticence.

'I remember picketing in nineteen twenty-six. Me brother-in-law, Sam Ritson, got sent to prison. You've maybes heard of him? Red Sam they used to call him. Aye, Whitton Grange,' he whistled through false teeth, 'that's where I was born and brought up . . .'

His wife had told them that John rarely talked about the old days. 'It tore his family in two, did the lock-out. I was glad when we moved away. Seeing all the trouble on the telly, well, it brings it back to him. It's hard to believe it's all happening again. Breaks me heart to see me grandbairns suffering like we did. So we want to help where we can.'

Mick thought again of his own father's stories of 1926, of the friendship with Ben Shannon which was poisoned by Shannon's father scabbing for the coal owners.

'My grandfather went to prison too,' Mick told the Kirkups, 'for putting a brick through a scab's window. Even though me father says he never did it. He never had a proper job again after that. Died in his forties, broken, very bitter, me dad says.'

Eddy nodded and added sourly, 'The scab went on to become overman at the pit. His son's the manager there today.'

Mick was surprised by Eddy's bitter tone and felt the injustice of the situation swell in him again. Well, Carol had married him, he thought in harsh exultation. At least Shannon's daughter had been taken from him, as if in some recompense for the wrongs of the past.

The Kirkups had shaken their heads in pity and understanding and retired to bed late. Mick had lain awake listening to the old man coughing through the night and thought of Carol alone at home and wished he could be with her. His ancient hosts had no telephone and so he had not been able to ring her as he had hoped. Tomorrow he would find a kiosk and ring home and hear the voice he missed so much . . .

Breakfast over, they boarded the mini vans that were to take them near Orgreave. A mile or so from the plant, they disembarked and trudged along the road in the early morning light. Birds choroused and the green wheat fields around them rustled and whispered like the sea, making Mick long for home. Beside him, Bob was engaging Sid's brother-in-law, John Taylor, and Marty Dillon in conversation. Marty, a red-faced barrel of a man, was keeping their spirits up with a stream of jokes and outrageous statements about everyone from politicians to the local vicar. By the time they came within sight of the coking works, their mood was buoyant.

They skirted a large post-war housing estate and crossed a railway bridge. Below lay fields and then the long grey tarmacadam road leading to the depot. Grey light glinted on metal storage tanks around the squat buildings and blackened chimneys of the works, belching white smoke into the lightening sky. It seemed to taunt them with its activity.

'We're going to stop the bastard scabs bringing any more in!' Bob shouted as they marched forward and there were cries of agreement around him. 'And no effing copper's going to stop us!'

After that, the jokes ceased and they hurried on purposefully to join the other pickets. At Mick's side, Dan Hardman kept close. Mick could tell the lad was nervous and wound up and he thought he smelt liquor on his breath even at this early hour. He had been camping out in someone's back garden and looked unshaven and unkempt and Mick wondered how well he and Linda had been managing for the past month. No one had seen them for a fortnight and Dan had shrugged off his questioning with blunt denials that anything was wrong.

Suddenly Dan swore at the sight up ahead.

Through the gloom they now saw rank upon rank of police amassed at the depot gates. All traffic had been stopped from approaching the plant but there were motorcycle outriders buzzing like drones up and down the road and lines of transit vans, their windows darkened from prying eyes, parked at the ready. More police with dogs were gathered in a nearby field, waiting.

'There's bloody thousands of them!' Eddy said in awe.

'Canny of so many to turn up just for us,' Marty joked grimly. 'I mean, they could be out catching thieves, but no, they'd rather be here with us. Touching, isn't it?'

They walked on, joining the other pickets that were appearing in gathering numbers down the road and in the opposite field. As the lines of police drew nearer, Mick told Dan, 'Stay with me and don't do anything daft.'

For a while the two sides stood off from each other, with just some harmless name-calling. Then Mick heard a noise in the distance - the deep, rumbling roar of heavy lorries on the move. The convoy hove over the hill and down towards them. At once the pickets began to push towards the entrance, trying to get close to the plant, but the sheer numbers of police held them off. The pushing and shoving increased.

Arms linked, the cordons of police moved forward, propelling them off the road. The shouting became more hot-tempered as frustration set in. Mick could feel himself stumbling back towards the ditch. The lorries careered past and hurtled safely through the gates.

All at once, a loud-hailer boomed above the shouting and Mick thought he heard it bellowing for prisoners to be taken.

Before he could react, Mick saw the lines of police open up nearby and through them, running at the double, came a score of men, wielding truncheons. The pickets began to scatter and run, hurling themselves over the walls into the fields. But miners around Mick were grabbed and kicked by the pursuing police and dragged off by the snatch squads who disappeared behind the cordons of police as quickly as they had come.

'They've got Marty!' Dan shouted.

Mick turned long enough to see his friend being hauled away and repeatedly kicked in the legs as he tried to stay on his feet. Then Marty was gone. Mick pushed Dan over the wall and followed, scraping his elbows. Somebody hit him in the throat and he fell down among the young wheat, gasping for breath. He saw Dan running, dodging crazily through the crop, and braced himself to be grabbed by his pursuers.

But the arms that got to him first and hauled him up were those of John Taylor and Eddy.

'Haway!' Eddy panted.

'Back to the bridge, lads!' Bob ordered.

Dan joined them and they set off at a run, routed by an organised force and snapped at by vicious-looking dogs, straining at their leashes.

Finally stopping at the railway embankment, Mick felt his insides heave. He was ashamed at having run away so quickly and angry at the overwhelming numbers against them.

'They're like an army, it's bloody ridiculous!' he ranted. 'And we're no better than a Sunday School outing with nowt but our trainers to kick with and our fists as weapons.'

'Didn't even have the chance to use them,' Eddy scowled. He was sweating and grey-faced and looked ill from running.

'What do we do now?' John asked.

No one spoke. They were shaken and unsure. Mick had never before seen such opposition ranked against a mass picket or such a ruthlessly swift response to their protest.

'There'll be another convoy along the road today,' Bob told them calmly. 'So we better start collecting some missiles.' They looked at him cautiously. 'Stones and that,' he suggested.

'Stones?' Mick said dismissively. 'Great! Stone-age men against the paramilitary? What chance do we have?'

'More than if you sit here on your backside,' Bob answered with a look of scorn. 'Call yourself union men!'

'Aye, he's right. And I've got more than stones,' Dan spoke up, a sickly grin on his pasty face. Out of his pocket he drew an object and flicked it open.

'Bloody hell!' Mick exclaimed. 'Give it here, you daft bugger!' He leaned over and wrested the knife from Dan's grasp. Securing the blade, he put it in his back pocket. 'We don't want that kind of trouble, man.'

Dan gave him a surly look. 'That's typical of you, Mick Todd. You talk a good fight all the time but when it comes to a scrap you're just good at running away. I'm not afraid to use a weapon on the pigs!' He grabbed at a dandelion in the grass and thrust it childishly under Mick's chin. 'Aye, you're yeller, just as I thought.'

Mick flushed at the accusation of being a coward. He knew Dan was just lashing out to save face, but he was furious nonetheless. More furious perhaps because he was still smarting from his ignoble flight from the trouble. He had watched Marty being carted off and done nothing to try and help him. Mick's control went as he lunged at Dan and knocked him back in the grass.

Immediately, John and Eddy seized him and pulled him off.

'Steady on, lads!' Eddy warned. 'It solves nowt to scrap among ourselves.'

Mick sank back, ashamed once more.

The men lapsed into silence again and watched Bob as he stood up and climbed through a hole in the fencing. When he re-emerged, he thrust out a fist in Mick's direction.

'If you want to fight, then take this,' he challenged. Mick looked at him inquiringly. Bob's eyes seemed to be assessing his worth.

Mick put out his hand. 'Give us it.'

Bob placed a large stone on his palm. 'This time we fight back,' he said quietly, but with all the authority of an order.

The day was warm and before returning to the picket, they trooped off into the housing estate to buy cans of pop and sandwiches. But as they descended the hill once more, Mick could see that the situation had grown far worse. The road was lined with instant response unit vans and the front lines of police were equipped with full riot gear. His stomach twisted at the sight of the glinting blue helmets and perspex visors and shields arrayed like a military force against them. And beyond them they could see and hear the impatient stamp and whinny of horses - the mounted police.

'The gates are completely blocked off now,' John said in dismay. 'We'll not get anywhere near them.'

'Aye,' Eddy grunted, looking worn out. 'Maybes we should gan back up the road and wait for the bus.'

'No,' Bob scotched the idea. 'Sooner or later they're going to try and get another convoy in again. We've got to be there to stop it.'

'Aye,' Mick agreed grimly, 'we came here to do a job. We're not ganin' to run away twice in one day.'

They carried on down the road towards the crowds ahead. As they neared the other pickets, they picked up a rumour that Arthur Scargill had been arrested earlier in the day. It fuelled their anger and pent-up frustration at their failure to stop the blackleg lorry drivers from reaching the plant.

'What's happening now?' Eddy asked, as he shared a cigarette with a man in the crowd.

'Summat's up,' the man replied. 'I think they're going to try and clear the road any minute. I can hear the lorries revving up in the plant.'

A few minutes later a loud-hailer ordered the pickets to retreat. The jostling began again. Lines of riot police began to advance. The barrage of noise grew louder and the pickets shoved in return. Suddenly a stone came whizzing over Mick's head from the back of the crowd and landed with a clang against a riot shield. A shower of other stones followed. Mick ducked instinctively.

'Bloody coward!'

Mick turned to see who had spoken. It was Bob.

'Not much of a Todd, are you? Think more of saving your own skin than standing up for your family and marras, don't you?' he taunted.

Mick looked at him in astonished fury. He had no idea why this man had suddenly taken against him. How dare he question his loyalty to his family and friends? Mick had a fleeting painful thought of Carol struggling to make ends meet without complaint, losing her job because of the strike, yet doing all she could to help feed and look after mining families. And he thought of sweet, loving, demanding Laura having to suffer because of scabs who drove over picket lines and police who colluded with the Coal Board and Government to break their strike. He seethed inwardly at the injustice of it all and for being attacked by one of his own kind.

'Don't lecture me, you bald bastard! I haven't seen you do owt but talk a good fight so far!'

Another loud-hailer warning crackled out over their heads. If the stone-throwing continued they would use the mounted police to break up the crowd.

Bob's eyes glinted challengingly at Mick. 'Watch this then, Toddy!' He drew back his arm and flung the piece of brick he had been nursing over the heads of the pickets into the ranks of police. Mick stared after the missile, horrified. Then something inside him snapped and he did something he thought he would never do. Spurred on by the man's scorn and livid at their impotency, he hurled his larger stone, shouting his fury at the top of his voice.

Moments later, the lines of shield-carrying officers broke ranks and the mounted police came charging through, swinging long batons as they bore down on the pickets. Mick stood paralysed by the sight and noise of mounted men on the move like some medieval army sweeping all before them. Then there was a scramble of men around him trying to get out of the way and he was knocked into the ditch.

There was nowhere for pickets to go except back up the road they had just come down, pursued by horses, or over the wall into the nearby field where police with dogs were waiting for them. Mick scrambled to his feet in frustration and ran along the road, but very soon the horses were among them, scattering the miners while the riders bludgeoned them with truncheons. Mick, who had lost sight of his friends, suddenly saw Dan being knocked to the ground. He ran over to help him as he cowered in the grass with his arms over his head.

By now the mounted police had ridden past and were galloping up the far hill, but other police on foot were running up behind, kicking and punching and arresting as they went.

'Get up lad!' Mick shouted to Dan as he pulled on his arm. He saw the terror on the young man's face. 'Stick with me.'

There was mayhem around them as Mick tried to run along the side of the wall and avoid their pursuers. Behind the riot police trundled the vans ready to receive the arrested. Up ahead, Mick saw the mounted officers turn at the top of the hill. With sickening realisation he saw that they were going to charge down on them once again.

'Quick, Dan, over the wall!' he ordered.

As Dan heaved in panic, Mick gave him a shove up and hauled himself after him. Just as they were about to jump down the other side, a voice shouted, 'That's the one!' and someone caught at his legs and yanked him backwards. He heard Dan scream as he was pulled back too, and then Mick was falling, landing with a thud on his shoulder. Pain ripped through his upper arm. He looked up to see a helmeted officer coming at him with his truncheon and rolled out of the way. The weapon caught him on the leg.

Beside him he could hear Dan crying as he was kicked in the stomach and groin.

'You're going to lose this one, you hairy bastard!' Mick's attacker yelled. 'And so's your bastard leader, Scargill!'

Mick felt himself being pulled up by his hair and thought his scalp was coming away from his head. He felt blind fury and punched out wildly in defence, roaring, 'You'll never beat us, you fascist pigs!'

He must have caught the man under his visor, because for a moment he staggered back and let go. Mick turned to Dan's attacker and threw himself at the uniformed legs, bringing the officer down in a tackle. But moments later he was stunned by a whack to the ear and hunched up in agony as another truncheon rained down on his back.

He was dragged up by an arm round his neck and someone jabbed fingers in his eyes. Mick felt sick at the sudden blinding pain and could not see what was happening to Dan. Two men dragged him towards one of the waiting vans. Around him, Mick was aware of fighting, but something was trickling into his eyes and blurring his sight. He was thrown on to the van floor and then his captor gave him a final kick in the back before slamming the door shut.

Mick lay for what seemed like an age, his head throbbing and body aching from the blows. Then he pushed himself up, wincing at the movement, and tried to focus in the gloom of the van. Someone else was in there with him. Mick could clearly hear his sobbing.

He reached over and touched the man's shoulder. Dan's swollen face looked up at his own.

'It's all right, lad,' Mick tried to reassure him, but Dan seemed beyond comforting. He shook and cried until an officer came back and handcuffed them. They could hear the noise of battle outside and the charge of men on horseback once more. It was hot in the van and Mick's throat was parched. They sat on in silence, not quite believing what was going on outside. At last, the noise gradually began to subside.

The door opened once more and three men were bundled into the van.

'Mick,' a voice cried out in surprise. 'Is that you?'

Mick blinked in the sudden light. It appeared to be the policeman at the door who had called his name. The man climbed in.

'By heck, you're in a bit of a state.' He squatted down beside him and pulled off his helmet. Only then did Mick recognise Carol's brother, Simon. His boyish fair face was wincing in concern at the sight of his brother-in-law. 'That's a shiner you've got. Wait a minute.' He searched about and from somewhere produced a bottle of water. He poured some over Mick's face and the cut above his eye. 'Here, take a swig,' he said.

'Give a drink to the lad first,' Mick answered, nodding towards Dan. He had gone very quiet with his head hunched between his knees, but when Simon touched him on the shoulder he jerked up in panic.

'Drink,' Mick ordered. Dan obeyed, gulping greedily at the warm water. 'Pass it round, Simon,' Mick said, gesturing with his bound hands. Finally, Simon held the bottle to his lips and Mick felt the water trickle down his swollen throat. 'Ta,' he gasped.

'I wondered if I'd ever come across you,' Simon said. 'Never thought it would get this bad, mind.' He began to chat as if they were on some outing, asking after Carol and Laura. He burbled on and on as if in relief to be out of the chaos of the past hours. 'You must come round and see our new house sometime,' he said. 'Not that we're there much at the moment. Kate complains she never sees me these days. But the extra money comes in useful.' He caught Mick's look. 'Sorry, I didn't mean . . .'

The door banged open and an officer stuck in his head. 'You; out!' he ordered.

Simon grabbed his helmet and jumped out of the van without another word.

'Friends with a copper,' one of the pickets muttered and spat on the floor. 'Not an undercover agent, are you?'

'He's me brother-in-law,' Mick answered without emotion.

There was silence and then one of the others said, 'It's like a civil war, dividing families. There's a copper lives in our street. Went to school with him - canny lad. Now me kids are scared of him, call him names behind his back. How can we ever go back to how it was before?'

'We can't,' the other answered simply.

Silently, Mick agreed. After the violence he had witnessed today, he could not imagine going with Carol to visit Simon's new house. However amiable Carol's brother was, his house was renovated with money earned on overtime fighting pickets while they struggled to eat. He felt the bile of bitterness flood his throat and nearly choke him. Nothing would be the same again.

Shortly afterwards they were driven away.

Chapter Nineteen

Carol sat holding Linda like a small child while she cried into her neck.

'It's OK, cry all you want,' Carol crooned. Denise sat in the chair opposite, her legs curled beneath her like a cat, observing.

'I was so frightened on me own,' Linda wept. 'It was terrible when he left. . .'

'It must have been,' Carol sympathised. 'But you're not on your own now; you've got your family around you.'

Linda pulled away. 'It's all their fault in the first place. Me dad going on at Dan all the time to marry us. And Mam didn't stick up for us either, like she should've done.'

'Your mam's always stood by you,' Carol reminded her gently, 'and your dad was thinking of the baby.'

'Everyone thinks about the baby but no one thinks about me,' Linda wailed. 'It's ruined me life - I wish I'd never got pregnant. Dan doesn't want a bairn and now he doesn't want me because of it!'

Carol held her young sister-in-law close. 'It doesn't help getting all upset. Everyone's under a bit of strain at the moment, but it won't go on for ever. Dan will come round to the idea in time and you two'll be back together.' Carol was not sure if she believed her own words, but all that mattered just now was that Linda calmed down. She sent Denise into the kitchen for water and coaxed Linda to go and lie down on Laura's bed.

'I don't even know where Dan is,' Linda sobbed as Carol covered her with Laura's pink eiderdown. 'I haven't seen him for a week.'

Carol suspected that Dan might be away picketing with Mick, but said nothing.

Later in the day, she persuaded Linda to see her mother and hurried down to the Welfare to fetch Lotty. Her mother-in-law climbed on her moped and rushed straightaway to see Linda. When Carol got back, having collected Laura from school, she found them cuddling on the settee together sharing a precious packet of custard creams, as if there had been no rift. Denise had left.

Carol marvelled at how Lotty could lose her temper one minute and forget and forgive the next. She never carried grudges or nursed slights as her own parents did, bringing them up years later as evidence of their child's worthlessness. Lotty scolded and fussed and loved and forgave in equal measure - a tiny woman with an enormous heart, Carol had learnt.

'Linda must have her old bedroom back for as long as she wants to stay,' Lotty announced. 'Eddy will have to move out and find somewhere else in the meantime.' She gave Carol a direct look.

'He can come and kip here,' Carol offered at once, knowing that's what Lotty wanted.

'Thanks, pet.' Lotty smiled at her and touched her hand briefly.

It was while they were carrying Linda's belongings over to Septimus Street that news of trouble came through. Charlie came rushing down the lane to meet them.

'Come inside,' he urged. 'Some of the pickets are back.' Only then did he notice Linda. 'What's going on?' he demanded.

Lotty silenced his questions. 'I'll explain in a minute. Tell us what you know.'

Charlie came straight to the point. 'Some of the lads have been arrested.'

'Mick?' Carol asked anxiously.

Charlie shrugged. 'We don't know who or how many, but it looks likely. John Taylor said it was like a battle. Marty Dillon was nabbed early on and John thought he saw Eddy being taken away. If they're not back by this evening, then . . .'

Carol felt her insides twist. At once, Lotty put her arms about her. There was no need for words.

Linda gave a mirthless laugh. 'At least Dan won't be with them. He's too much of a coward to get himself in trouble. He'll be at home eating his mam's three-course meals.'

Charlie shook his head sadly. 'Sorry, Linda, pet, but Dan went off with them three days ago - I saw him go. I had no idea you'd fallen out, he never said.'

Linda gawped at her father and then burst into tears. 'You made him go, didn't you? It's all your fault, all this stupid picketing. You've spoilt everything between Dan and me. I'll never forgive you!'

'Hush, lass, you mustn't speak to your father like that,' Lotty chided. She gave her husband a sorrowful look. 'She doesn't mean it, Charlie.'

But Carol could see the hurt in Charlie's tired eyes. He got up abruptly. 'I have to get back. I'll let you know if I hear anything.'

He bolted for the door and instinctively Carol went after him. 'I'll walk down with you, see if there's any news. Come on, Laura,' she called to her daughter who was tussling with Dougal. The girl followed, looking perplexed by all the arguing, and gripped Carol's hand tightly. The dog went to Charlie's heels without being called.

As they went out through the yard, Carol noticed Laura clutch at her grandfather's hand too. Charlie grasped it and Carol felt a pang of sympathy for her tight-lipped father-in-law having to shoulder the worries of them all. Once, he would have sparked back with his youngest daughter for being cheeky but he was too preoccupied and careworn to argue with her now.

They hung around the hall waiting for news, until Laura was nearly asleep on her feet. None came. Eventually, Lotty, who had come down to be with them, persuaded Carol to take Laura home.

'If he'd been arrested, he would have got a message to us by now,' Carol fretted. 'What if something's happened to them on the way home?'

'We'll hear something soon,' Lotty assured her. 'I'll come home with you if you like.'

'But you've got Linda to worry about,' Carol said.

'Our Val's come round so she's not alone. Haway, let's get Laura to bed.'

So Carol allowed Lotty to take control, but later she insisted that she was all right and that Lotty should get back to Linda. She sat for a while in the darkening sitting room, the television flickering in the corner for company. Then pictures of the confrontation at Orgreave came on the late news and Carol strained to catch sight of Mick. When there was no sign of any miners from Brassbank, she swiftly turned it off.

A timid knock on the door startled her from anxious thoughts. Denise's ghostly face peered out of the dark.

'I heard about the arrests. Thought you might like some company.'

Carol smiled and pulled her in. Thanks, Denise.'

She knew she did not have to make conversation with Linda's old friend, because the girl was comfortable with silence. They shared some homemade biscuits that Denise's mother had made and watched a late film together, wrapped in blankets as the room grew chilly.

Carol must have dozed off; the telephone ringing startled her awake. She jumped to answer it.

'Hello?'

'Carol, it's me, Simon.'

'Simon?' Carol repeated confused, and then realised it was her brother. She felt disorientated; she had not spoken to him in weeks.

'It's about Mick,' he said hesitantly. 'Have you heard from him?'

'No. What do you know?' Carol demanded, heart racing. 'Tell me!'

'I saw him this afternoon. He's been arrested.'

'Oh, God! Where is he?'

'I haven't seen him since - since he was picked up. They were taking him to the local police station. But from what I hear most of them have been moved on.'

'Where to?' Carol tried to make sense of it all. 'And why?'

'They'll have to appear before the magistrates. Maybe at this very moment, I don't really know.'

'At this time of night?' Carol was incredulous.

'They'll sit through the night if necessary.'

'Oh, Simon, what's he done?' Carol asked in fear.

'I don't know.' Simon was guarded. 'There were dozens of them. They'll be up on riot charges probably. Listen, I have to go. I just didn't want you worrying.'

'Worrying? Of course I'm damn well worrying! What are they going to do with him? When will he come home?'

'I don't know. He was OK. If there's anything I can do, let me know.'

She wanted to laugh. None of her family had come near them since the start of the strike to see if they were coping. Simon had steered clear, not wanting to get involved or anger his parents. Anything for an easy life, Carol thought. 'And what can you do for me, Simon?' she challenged. 'Get him released?'

'Sorry, Carol, I really am.'

'Don't hang up on me! Simon!'

The line went dead. Carol slammed down the receiver. 'Damn you!'

Questions crowded into her mind. What was her brother doing there? Had he arrested Mick? Who else was with him? All she knew was that her worst fears had been realised and her husband was in police custody. Carol sat down shaking. She was living a nightmare; things were beginning to slip out of her control.

There was another quiet knock on the back door. Denise went to open it. Pete Fletcher padded into the room like a lean panther. He looked concerned. 'I heard. I was worried about you.'

Without thinking, Carol rushed across the room and hugged him. He understood the situation. He might be able to do something for the men. Pete was sympathetic and considerate and solidly there in the midst of all the turmoil. She felt his wiry arms go round her in a warm hug. She wanted to cry, but forced herself not to succumb. Suddenly she was embarrassed by her show of emotion and pulled away.

'Sorry. I've just heard that Mick's going before the magistrates' court on riot charges.'

Pete squeezed her arms. 'Poor Carol. I'll stay with you until you hear more.'

Carol shook her head. 'I must go down and tell Charlie. Denise.' She turned to her and saw the watchful expression under the curtain of black hair. 'Could you stay here, in case Laura wakes up?'

Denise nodded.

'I'll walk you down to the hall, then,' Pete offered at once. He didn't like the way the silent friend was giving him black looks.

'Thanks,' Carol smiled at them both.

They set off down the dimly lit lane. Pete put an arm round her shoulders.

'You should've called me. I could have made some inquiries,' he said softly. 'I really do care.'

Carol felt suddenly uncomfortable. She found his touch too intimate, too unsettling, his voice too sensual. Moving away from him, she answered, 'So you say. But you haven't done much for our cause yet, have you, Pete? Where are all the articles you promised, telling our side of things?'

It was too dark to see him flush. 'I have to get things past the editors first - they aren't always on the same side as the journalists.' He put out a hand and touched her arm. 'But I am on your side, Carol. I want to help you all I can.'

'All I want is for Mick to come back to me,' she told him bluntly.

They walked on in silence, acutely aware of the space between them.

Mick sat sweating on a crowded bench in the stifling holding room. Men were packed in all around, some with torn clothes and serious gashes and bruises to their heads and faces. No one came to attend to them. Hardly anyone spoke. There was a feeling of stunned exhaustion about them all. A young Scot next to him wept quietly, tormented by how his family would be worrying. Another boy had fainted earlier with the heat. They had been charged with nothing and yet their photos and fingerprints had been taken and their pockets emptied. Shoelaces, belts and earrings had been removed. Mick worried about Dan's knife which had been found on him.

Later, a solicitor came and insisted they were transferred to an exercise yard where they could breathe and move about more easily. It was at this point that Mick was taken away to be interviewed.

He was put in a stark room with a plainclothes policeman who did not give his name or say a word. They sat for ten minutes until another plainclothes officer came in. The interrogator lit a cigarette and blew smoke at Mick.

'You're from Brassbank in County Durham. How did you get down here?'

'On a bus,' Mick said wearily.

'Whose bus?'

'Proud's. They're local—' Mick suddenly broke off. Why did he want to know that?

'Where did you stay last night?'

Mick did not reply. He was certainly not going to get the kind Kirkups into trouble.

'You've done a lot of picketing, haven't you?'

'Have I?' Mick scowled.

'How do you get your instructions?'

'Who the hell are you?' Mick snapped. 'I demand my right to a phone call. Me wife doesn't know where I am.'

The man smiled. 'Ah, yes, your wife.' He picked up the photograph of Carol and Laura confiscated earlier. Mick's stomach twisted at the sight of the two of them on a swing smiling straight at him. 'We'll make sure she's told where you are. Nice kid. What's her name?'

'Laura,' Mick said automatically, then felt suddenly vulnerable that this man knew his daughter's name.

'I remember when my little girl was that age - can't see enough of them, can you? Pretty wife too. Must be awful having to go away from them so often. Do you really think there's any point picketing away from home?' His voice had become sympathetic, confiding. He almost whispered, 'Geordies like you aren't troublemakers, not like the Scots and the Yorkies. You're naturally law-abiding, hard-working, salt of the earth. You don't owe these people down here anything. All they've done is get you into trouble.'

Mick stared at him hard, resenting the man's patronising air. Not for a moment was he taken in by the crude attempt to set him against his comrades. *Unity is strength*, he heard his father's voice echo in his mind.

'The police have caused the trouble,' Mick answered bullishly.

The officer drew back and paused while he smoked. When he spoke again his tone was more businesslike. 'How are you managing without any money coming in? You must be in debt by now. Three months' wages down the can. You'll never make it up again. Admirable loyalty.' He shook his head sorrowfully. 'But is it deserved? I mean, are you picketing for yourself or for this leader of yours, Scargill?'

Mick was drawn. 'For all of us. It's one and the same thing.'

The two officers smiled at each other as if he had said something amusing. 'I disagree with you there. You see, Scargill doesn't care about your welfare. He's not a real union man like Gormley was. Gormley got results, he knew how to negotiate. Your Scargill's just a political wrecker. He's using you for his own political ends, manipulating you to try and bring down the Government.'

'Read that in the Tory press, have you?' Mick laughed in scorn.

'What newspaper do you read?' the man asked him quickly.

'Local one.'

'Does it tell you how Scargill lives in the lap of luxury while you struggle to pay your mortgage and eat? Does it tell you that your precious leader has a chauffeur while you foot soldiers are having to sell your cars because you can't afford to run them any more? No, of course it doesn't. Because you'd all go back to work tomorrow if you knew how you were being led by the nose.' He leaned closer, eyeballing Mick. 'How do you feel about Arthur being paid out of union money - *your* subs - when you're not even getting any strike pay?'

Mick felt contempt for the man before him and his attempt to demonise their union president. He could see how such arguments were being used every day to alienate the public from their cause, but he had met Scargill in person at the Quarryhill rally and did not doubt the man's sincerity in trying to save their jobs. They needed a strong leader to stand up to the forces ranged against them, embodied in men like the detective in front of him.

But the man had needled him. Mick answered, 'The union would be bankrupted in weeks if everyone got strike pay. But we're not in this for the money; we're in it to save the future of our industry. If the Government hadn't rigged the benefits against our families, we wouldn't be in such debt. But we're prepared to suffer to keep our pits open. People like you should be grateful that the miners of this country are willing to stand up and fight for our coal instead of supporting a government that brings in foreign coal at any price. Shut down our pits and that's British coal gone for ever.'

His questioner gave him a dismissive look as if he was not worth listening to. 'Lots of miners secretly believe there should be a national ballot but are too afraid to say so.'

Mick snorted. 'How the hell do you know what miners really think? You wouldn't be asking me all these questions if you did.'

For the first time the interrogator let his annoyance show. 'You lost a lot of public sympathy by striking without one,' he snapped.

'We had our mandate for strike action,' Mick answered staunchly. 'If we waited for the Tory press to give us their blessing, no buggers would ever go on strike at all. Miners have always stood up for what they believed in and fought for their rights. If they hadn't, we'd still be in the dark ages of private pits and no union representation.'

The officer rounded on him. 'What do you vote in general elections?'

'What do you think?' Mick replied.

'Are you a communist, Todd?'

'I'm a socialist - and a Newcastle supporter,' Mick said mockingly.

'Your father's a communist, isn't he? A delegate.' He thrust his face close, threateningly. 'He organises the Brassbank pickets, doesn't he?'

'What's this got to do with me father?' Mick was growing impatient too. How did this man know about his family anyway? 'And why have I got to listen to a Tory political broadcast? Am I being charged with holding political beliefs that don't agree with yours?'

'Oh, you'll be charged, don't worry.' He stubbed out his cigarette violently in the metal ashtray. 'Breach of the peace, threatening behaviour, carrying an offensive weapon. I'll throw the lot at you. You're in the shit, Todd!' Turning, he stormed out of the room.

Late that night they were herded on to buses and confined in narrow metal cells until they reached the magistrates' court. To Mick's dazed amazement he saw crowds of supporters thronging the building and shouting encouragement to the men as they were escorted away. It lifted his spirits.

He was crammed into a dark old cell with a dozen others and waited again. It was the endless dead time of hanging around that was the worst to cope with, Mick thought. Dan kept close by him all the time, but said nothing. Finally they were led out along a dingy corridor and up into the courthouse. Three other men emerged from a cell behind them. As they climbed the steps, they passed other miners descending.

'Mick, lad!' a familiar voice called.

Squinting in the dimness, Mick recognised his uncle. 'Eddy! What's the score?'

'Doing us in job lots, marra. Magistrates get to bed quicker that way,' he joked.

They were herded on and Eddy disappeared into the gloom below. But just the sight of his cheerful uncle gave Mick the strength to hold up his head and face what lay ahead. As they entered the court, Dan mumbled suddenly, 'Thanks for sticking up for me today.'

Mick glanced at him in surprise. That's all right, marra,' Mick smiled and went ahead.

It was over quickly and without much formality. They were handed out charge sheets in the court and hardly questioned. All sixteen were dealt with at the same time and released on bail on condition that they did not go within one mile of Orgreave or visit any premises of the Coal Board, British Steel or the Central Electricity Generating Board. A curfew from eight till eight was also imposed.

Mick was too tired and too relieved to be released to think about the restrictions imposed on them, until they were outside.

That's an end to picketing for us,' Marty Dillon sighed.

'And to any social life,' Eddy grimaced. 'Not that I can afford one now.'

'Hey,' Marty laughed unexpectedly, 'if we cannot gan on any Coal Board property then half of us cannot gan home the night! It'll be a tent in Captain Lenin's garden for you and me, Eddy.'

'Aye,' Eddy agreed, 'tucked up by eight o'clock with a few cans from the Captain's cellar. By! Do you think we could gan back to court and ask them to extend our bail?'

Mick broke into their fantasising. 'Anyone thought how we're going to get home first?'

Dan stood shivering beside him. He had not spoken a word since they had been transported to the court. But he nudged Mick and gestured towards a group of police standing at the bottom of the court steps. They were in shadow.

'What's wrong?' Mick asked.

Dan grunted, 'That's him, isn't it?'

Mick peered again into the dark. Something about the way one of them was standing, the glint of street light on his bald head ... It was Bob, the miner who had befriended them at breakfast, now an age ago. But he was chatting casually with the policemen around him, sharing a joke. All at once, Mick's incomprehension over Bob's aggressive behaviour at Orgreave became clear. The man had attached himself to their group and drawn information out of them about their families and village as skilfully as any detective and later he had been the one to incite them to violence on the picket line. Was it possible he was a policeman? One of the *agent provocateurs* that were rumoured to be at work amongst them?

Mick swore in fury. 'I'm going to have it out with him, the bastard!'

Eddy stood in his way and Marty caught his arm.

'Haway, man. We're in enough trouble as it is,' Eddy warned. 'Let's just get out of here.'

Before Mick had time to protest there was a shout across the street. Someone came running towards them through the crowd of onlookers.

'It's Sid!' Eddy cried in delight.

'All right, marras?' Sid asked them cheerfully.

'What you doing here?' Mick asked in amazement.

'Come to collect you buggers,' Sid answered. 'Borrowed Dimarco's van. Been hanging around for hours. Wouldn't let me in the court.'

'You've been inside them enough recently,' Marty teased him. 'Time you gave someone else a bit of the limelight.'

'Dimarco's given me some sandwiches and cans for you to scoff on the way back,' Sid told them.

'Now you're talking,' Eddy grinned.

'Did you come all this way on your own?' Mick asked, walking beside his friend.

'Na, Freddie Burt's with us.'

'Hurry up then,' Marty said, quickening his step, 'else there'll be nowt left to drink.'

Mick smiled and clapped Sid on the shoulder. 'Thanks, marra.'

'Fancied a trip out,' Sid answered. 'Breaks the boredom. But you'll soon find out about that now you're picketing days are over.'

They arrived back in the early hours of the morning, as grey light was seeping into the sky over the North Sea. Mick had to be woken and he felt stiff and disorientated as he climbed out of the van outside the Welfare Hall, yet he was thankful to smell the freshness of an onshore breeze and see the familiar outline of Brassbank's steep streets huddled around him. They tramped into the hall and there was a yelp of delight and welcome from the tired lodge members and family relations who had kept vigil all night.

Charlie came up and clapped his son on the shoulder and Lotty threw her skinny arms round her son in relief.

'Have you eaten anything? By, look at that black eye! Have they tret you badly?' she fussed over him.

'I'm all right, Mam,' Mick smiled wearily. 'Where's Carol?'

A voice spoke behind him. 'She came down earlier. She'll be relieved to see you safely back.'

Mick turned to see the journalist, Pete Fletcher, smiling at him, his face fashionably unshaven. Mick's immediate reaction was disappointment that Carol was not here to meet him, he had somehow visualised her being there. Then he felt annoyance that this outsider should be the one to tell him.

Lotty added quickly, 'She had to get back to let Denise home - she was minding Laura. She only went an hour or so ago. You get yourself off home and we can hear about it all when you've had some sleep.'

Mick nodded. He was utterly exhausted. He was too tired and too confused by the day's events to make sense of them yet. The memory of the riot and the arrest, the interrogation and the series of dismal cells appeared jumbled in his mind, each nagging for attention like toothache.

'Aye, I'll see you in the morning,' Mick said, turning to leave.

Pete padded after him. 'Good to see you back, Mick. Perhaps I could call and interview you at some stage. Carol thought it would be a good idea.'

Mick's irritation rose. 'Listen, all I want to do is gan home and see me wife. Just stay out me way till I've had some kip, do you hear?'

The two men held each other's look but Mick could not make out what the reporter was thinking behind his spectacles. Mick turned away first.

By the time he reached home he felt deflated and almost too tired to speak. He found Carol asleep on the settee under a blanket, her brown hair spread across a cushion. As he approached, she woke up and at once flung her arms round him.

'Mick! I was so worried.' He heard the tears in her voice and hugged her tight.

'I know,' he whispered and kissed her head. 'But I'm back now.'

It was too dark for Carol to see his bruising, but he winced when she touched the cut above his eye.

'What have they done to you?' she asked angrily.

'Nothing that can't be mended,' Mick assured her. But black memories of the day sprang up at once to plague him. He held Carol tightly to him as if she could keep them at bay. 'Come on, let's get to bed before Laura's awake.'

Carol kissed him tenderly. 'I'm proud of you, Mick. They can say what they like on telly about you lads. But when this is all over they'll be calling you heroes not criminals. You stood up for us all today and that makes me so proud.'

Mick kissed her swiftly and then turned away in case she saw the tears in his eyes. If only she realised that it was her who gave him strength. It had been the thought of her that had kept him going all day and made him hold out under interrogation. And he wondered fearfully what it would take to break that strength. To what further lengths would they have to be pushed before it was all over?

Chapter Twenty

'Look at this!' Mick waved the letter at her, his unshaven face livid.

Carol paused from packing Laura's sandshoe bag with her shorts and T-shirt for the end of term sports day. Blustery clouds raced past the kitchen window and she wondered if the rain would hold off until the afternoon. Laura was hopping about excitedly at the thought of the races and games in the football field and Carol so wanted the children to have a fun afternoon. She wanted it for the parents too, the mothers who could not afford any other treats for their children and the fathers with endless time on their hands this summer.

'Don't just ignore me,' Mick shouted again. 'It's from your bloody father!'

At the sound of Mick's raised voice, Laura scarpered outside and went to wait for Louise and Mark to pass by. Carol knew that Mick's bad temper upset the girl and she felt annoyance at his thoughtlessness. She took the offending letter irritably.

It was an invitation to Mick to return to work, promising generous bonus payments and holiday entitlement if he did so. There had been similar persuasions in the national newspapers, with full-page advertisements enticing the men to go back. But this letter had her father's signature on it and Carol felt her blood boil.

'Just ignore it,' she said, crushing the letter into a ball and throwing it towards the empty grate. 'It's not worth the paper it's written on. You shouldn't take it so personally, all the men will have had one.'

'Course it's personal.' Mick paced around the room. Carol noticed that his muscly body was turning to flab with too little exercise and too much stodgy food at the soup kitchen. 'I can ignore it, but will all the others?' he demanded. 'People are getting desperate for money. Marty says they're putting their house up for sale before they get repossessed.'

Carol could feel the cloud of anxiety hanging over her husband. 'People will manage. We're getting in funds all the time from other unions and sympathisers - even from abroad. And we've got the trip to London coming up.'

Mick swung round. 'You're not going away again, are you?'

'What do you mean again?' Carol snapped back. 'I've never gone away overnight before. Anyway, I told you about this last week.'

'You're out all the time for the Women's Group - shaking buckets in Durham, picketing workshops. I don't know where you are half the time.'

'I always tell you where I'm going,' Carol protested. 'It's you who doesn't listen any more.'

'You don't know what it's like being cooped up here all day with nowt to do,' he complained, 'while you go swanning off.'

'I know exactly what it's like,' Carol replied. 'I've been doing it long enough. Except when you used to come home the house would be tidy and the washing done and your meal on the table. What do I find when I get back from tramping round town rattling a bucket and taking abuse in the streets? A pigsty, that's what! Why can't you lend a hand a bit more instead of moping around feeling sorry for yourself?'

He glared at her. 'That's not my job.'

'Well, it is now,' Carol sparked back. 'And I am going to London. I've been asked to speak. I thought you would've supported me.'

'And who's going to look after Laura while you're away?' he demanded.

Carol gave him a look of despair. 'If you can't look after your own bairn for two days then you're not the father I took you for.' She turned and stuffed Laura's shorts roughly into the bag. 'But if you can't be bothered, she can go and stay with her nana.'

Carol marched out of the house before he could shout at her again, trembling from the argument. She was mad at Mick for his jealousy and lack of co-operation over her involvement with the support group; after all, she was doing it for him and the other men. Ever since the arrest Mick had sunk into despondency, withdrawing into some silent, bitter world of his own where she could not reach him. Why did he not busy himself with small tasks like some of the other men, mending prams and children's toys or helping wash up at the hall? She was tired of coming home to unwashed breakfast dishes and cigarette ash on the carpet and Mick slumped asleep in front of a blaring television. Of course she was sorry for him after what he had been through, but her patience with him was running out.

Gripping Laura's hand, Carol walked her daughter briskly to school and attempted to put him out of her mind. She imagined instead what she might say when she stood up in front of a hall of people in London to speak for the first time.

Mick sank back in a chair and buried his head in his hands. Why did he lash out at Carol all the time like that? he questioned himself harshly. He wanted her to understand how he felt and yet the words always tumbled out like an attack, aggressive and critical. He could see that she was working hard for their cause and yet he resented the time spent away from him, enjoying herself with the other women, keeping busy while his hands ached with inactivity and the boredom drove him near to despair.

Once she had made him go collecting with the other women, but he had been unable to banter with the crowd the way they did. He seemed to have lost all confidence in himself since the traumatic events at Orgreave two months ago and to leave the house at all now made him feel nervous and brought him out in a sweat.

Charged with riot offences, the men had all elected to take their cases to the Crown Court where they could have their day in court and set the record straight on what had happened. But that could take months and Mick had the threat of what might happen hanging over him like a black cloud. It kept him awake at night, so that he fell asleep during the day and felt constantly tired. Worse, the words of the interrogator would come back to him like snakes wriggling into his mind and poisoning his reason with doubts.

You'd all go back tomorrow if you knew how you were being led by the nose.

He went over to the fire and picked out the pit manager's letter, reading it again. Carol would be disgusted with him if she could see him now, or know the temptation he felt at the thought of going back to work and earning again. He dreamt of the day he could begin to pay off their sea of debts. They owed the bank and the building society, the electricity board and a finance company who still owned the washing machine. They had not renewed the licence on the TV and he had borrowed from Eddy without Carol knowing. The car had gone back to the HP company two months ago.

And this month he had finally uncovered the old motorbike from its gloomy shroud in the yard and taken it for a last spin along the coast, relishing the power at his hands and the wind in his face. It had sold for well under its value, but it had cleared their gas bill, bought Laura's summer clothes and shoes and paid for Linda and Dan's wedding.

That had been another bone of contention between Carol and him, when Linda had dumbfounded them all by announcing her marriage to Dan.

'Why does she have to have such a big reception?' Carol had demanded. 'We can't afford it.'

'We can with the bike money. And Mam and Dad can't afford to give her anything. Besides, you can't not invite half the family.'

'You can if there's a strike on,' Carol answered.

'We all need a bit of a party to cheer us up,' Mick had said and hidden his own concern that the wedding plans were getting out of hand.

'Why do Fay and Vic have to be invited?' Carol demanded. 'I mean, that really sticks in me throat.'

'Do you think I'm happy about your sister and that smarmy git coming to a family wedding?' Mick had shouted. 'It's Dan's parents have insisted on having them, not mine. You know as well as I do that Vic's a cousin of Dan's.'

'No one can ever say no to Linda, can they?' Carol had sighed.

Mick had silently agreed, but the wedding had gone ahead anyway with a heavily pregnant Linda squeezed into one of Val's hire dresses at a civil ceremony. Afterwards there was a disco at the Comrades Club.

'Grand to see the pair of them happy together at last,' Val had commented. 'Dan seems a lot closer to the family since all that bother at Orgreave.'

Mick had heard Carol agree and say it was thanks to him sticking by him that had given Dan his change of heart. Mick was not sure what had made Dan come round, but he did seem to be making an effort to do the right thing by Linda and the unborn baby. Perhaps the marriage would stand a chance, as long as Dan's sour-faced parents didn't make trouble, he had thought, watching the open disapproval of the Hardmans. They had kept among their own friends, talking to Vic Proud and denigrating the strike in voices that all could hear, yet they were happy to take the hospitality that the Todds had struggled to provide. Carol had made excuses to leave early and Mick had been happy to go too, no longer sure that he could control his temper.

He looked down at the crumpled letter in his hands with Shannon's signature on it and felt a swell of self-disgust rise up inside him. How could he even think of breaking the strike? he thought miserably. Shannons might be scabs but Todds would never be!

Violently he tore up the letter again and again until it was like confetti scattered about the carpet. 'Oh Carol!' he cried out loud. 'I need you!'

Then he crumpled to his knees and cried silently for the first time since he was twelve years old and Nana Bowman had died. He was gripped with a pain that would not go away.

Before Carol left on the bus for London she went to see Eddy who had moved back in with Lotty and Charlie after Linda's wedding.

'I'm worried about Mick,' she told him. 'He's changed so much since the arrest. I can't talk to him any more without him biting my head off. Everything I do just seems to annoy him. Can you do anything for him, Eddy?' she pleaded.

Eddy looked thoughtful. 'It's hard for him, Carol. With the curfew and that.

148

They've put conditions on us that make us feel like prisoners in our own homes, and we've been convicted of nowt yet.'

Carol nodded. 'I know. It's hard lines on all of you. But that's no reason to take it out on me.'

Eddy took her hand and squeezed it. 'He's not angry with you, flower. He's angry at the people that have done this to us - angry at himself for being so useless now.'

'But he's not useless; there are still things he could do, only if I suggest them he thinks I'm getting at him. Please help him, Eddy. I don't know what to do. Will you keep an eye on him while I'm away?'

Eddy nodded and smiled. 'Don't worry about him. You gan off and preach the word to the southerners. Raise some money to send the bairns on holiday.'

Carol smiled and kissed his cheek in gratitude. 'Ta, Eddy. I will.'

'Ta-ra, pet.' He gave her a wistful smile and Carol was aware of him watching her go until she was out of sight down the lane.

Lotty brought Laura to the bus station to see her off with Joanne and June and Lesley and Denise, who had surprised them all by volunteering to go. It was the first time Carol had been away from Laura for more than a night and she found it strange and a little upsetting, pangs of guilt mixed with worry about how she would cope without her. Laura had made a big fuss at first until Lotty had promised they could make biscuits together and go for a picnic in the park.

'I don't want you to go, Mammy!' Laura cried and clung on to her at the last minute. 'Why can't I come?'

Carol swung her up in a tight hug and kissed her. 'I'll bring you something back from London,' she promised. 'And we'll go there together when you're a big girl.'

Laura started to cry.

Lotty took her and said, 'She'll stop as soon as the bus is out of sight.'

Carol knew she was right, but somehow that made her feel even worse. Perhaps Mick had a point and she shouldn't be going away quite as much; she was needed more at home.

'Haway, Carol,' June shouted behind her. 'There'll be no seats left at the back of the bus if you don't hurry up.'

'Go on,' Lotty urged, 'you've important work to do.' Then she smiled, 'Enjoy yourself. We can manage here, so stop feeling guilty.'

Carol gave her a quick kiss, fondled Laura's head and climbed on the bus. She watched them out of the window until the bus pulled up the bank towards Quarryhill and Brassbank was hidden in the dip. But she was prevented from crying by Joanne who thrust a cup of tea in her hand, poured from her flask, and June who led them in a rendering of their new song, sung to the tune of 'Blaydon Races'.

Oh, me lasses! You should have seen us ganin',
Passing the folks at road blocks, just as they were standin'.
We gan on to the picket lines and serve the lads with dinners,
We're the Brassbank Women's Support Group - And we're going to be the winners!

They were met off the bus by Carol's Auntie Jean who put them all up in her cramped flat. They stayed up long into the night, talking and reminiscing and telling Jean all the news from home. Then Lesley told them they must all get some

149

sleep and they bedded down on makeshift beds on the floor and sofas.

The next three days were an exhausting round of meetings and fundraising events organised by local labour groups and union members. When Carol first got up to speak she was terrified, her heart hammering and mouth going dry, so that she thought her words would never come out. But somehow, faced with a sympathetic audience of ordinary women who had just the same concerns as she did, she found herself meeting the challenge and relishing it. But on the first occasion, her mind went frighteningly blank.

'We're glad to be here today - with you all. I just want to say . . . We've come today - to - to ask . . .' Carol swallowed and licked her dry lips, trying to remember what it was she had planned to say. She glanced at her friends on the stage beside her and saw June point to the 'Save our pits' badge she was wearing. June winked in encouragement. There was a restless murmur in the hall and children ran up and down the aisle, chasing each other.

Carol cleared her throat and began again. 'We need your help, not just to save our pits - your pits, the nation's pits - but our communities and way of life. Some of you might be asking, why do we want to save jobs that are dirty and dangerous? How can we want to pass them on to our sons? Yes, it's true, miners' work can be difficult and dangerous. But they are proud of the work they do. It gives them a purpose to get up at all hours of the night, or go underground when the sun's shining and everyone else is out of doors. No other work gives a man such comradeship, such reliance on each other. Grafting hard down the pit gives a man dignity.'

Carol looked around at the faces in the hall. They were listening now, attentive; the children had been hushed. Somehow, in the few minutes given her, she must make them understand what it was like to live in Brassbank and other such villages, to show them how much was at stake.

'But it's not just for the men that we're fighting, it's for all of us. The pit gives our village its lifeblood; it's the reason Brassbank exists. Our families have been together for generations, living and working beside each other, helping each other out in difficult times. We might fall out from time to time, like any big family, but we rally round when we're needed. Mining families have always looked after their old and sick, their widows, their bairns, long before the welfare state. And it's the women who are the backbone of our communities. We're the ones who have to manage when things are tight, when disaster strikes. Our mothers and grandmothers did it before us - held the village together.'

Carol looked directly into the faces watching her, urging them to understand.

'And we're the ones coping now, making meals for hundreds of men every day, sending out food parcels, helping young families survive, getting baby food to new mothers. We even have time to do a bit of picketing and marching at rallies. Because women can turn their hand to anything if needs be!'

There were cheers of agreement to this and a few claps. Encouraged, Carol continued.

'But we can't do it alone. We need the help of our friends in other unions, other women's groups, in the Labour Party. We've been bowled over by how generous ordinary people have been, paying a bit extra out of their wages to help our funds. It all gets put to good use. It might be that little bit extra to feed a family though the week that keeps the man from giving in and going back to work. There's big pressure on now to force the men back with promises of extra pay

150

and bonuses, to break their will. Some families are at the end of their tethers after five months without wages. But the women are keeping them going, keeping them strong. We don't want our men to give in, because this might be our only chance to fight for our way of life.

'If the strike is broken, then the men are broken, and the Coal Board and Government can do anything they wish in future. If they close our pit, they'll kill off our local businesses and the jobs they bring, the value of our houses will fall and our children will have a life of unemployment or be forced to leave. Who will look after our old people then? Our large family will be broken up. Brassbank and villages like ours will become ghost towns.'

Carol glanced again at June and saw she had tears in her eyes.

'But we're not going to let that happen!' she said with resolve. 'We're going to fight for our livelihoods for as long as it takes. We've been called criminals and worse than muck by the media. Thatcher's now calling us the "enemy within" as if we were trying to wreck the country that we love. That really makes me blood boil! Well, we're not the enemy! We're not the ones trying to butcher our mining industry and bring in foreign coal. British industry was built on the back of the coal British miners have dug out for generations. Countless lives have been lost in the process, but we've borne that cost, that suffering, without complaint.'

She looked at her friends. 'We're decent, honest, hard-grafting people who want to work for a living and do the best for our families. We're not asking for fat salaries, or the high life, or to live in mansions. We're asking to stay as we are, in the communities where we were born and brought up. We're not the enemy, we're the real Britain! The ordinary people with decent values that our parents' generation fought for in the last war. Please help us today to carry on fighting for what's right, for justice - for our children!'

As Carol stood back, the audience came to its feet clapping their approval. She felt Joanne's hand squeeze her arm and as she turned to the others, her vision blurred as the tears sprung to her eyes. June was crying too.

'You bugger!' she said. 'You'll cost me a fortune in tissues if you speak like that every time.'

Lesley soon had them organised into taking buckets round for a collection and the money began to pour in. Carol was touched once again by the generosity of complete strangers and it gave her renewed hope. One middle-aged woman caught her attention.

'I'm glad I heard you speak. They never tell you on the telly what it's like for the families. My husband Harry says the miners have been making a fuss over nothing, says they just like to fight. But now I can tell him different.'

Carol smiled and touched her arm. 'Thanks. Tell as many people as you can.'

She noticed that Denise was talking to everyone as she moved along the rows and she declared with pride at the end that she had the fullest bucket of change.

'You're scaring them with all your black clothes,' June joked. 'They're handing over all their money 'cos they think you've just come from a funeral.'

'If you're jealous of my success, I'll lend you something black to wear,' Denise answered with a rare grin. The idea of the vast June squeezing into Denise's skinny black T-shirts or leggings made the rest of them fall about laughing. June gave the girl a playful swipe and then hugged her.

151

At the end of the three days Carol was exhausted and her voice almost gone.

'By, we'll get some peace on the journey home,' June teased.

'You mean you'll be able to natter all the way without being interrupted,' Carol croaked back.

They said their farewells to Jean at the bus station.

'Ta for everything,' Carol kissed her aunt. 'It's been like old times, kipping in your flat and staying up late with a bottle of wine.'

'Doesn't that seem like a lifetime ago?' Jean mused. 'You've certainly changed. Seven years ago you would yawn at the very word politics. Now you're making speeches like a hardened campaigner. Perhaps we'll see you elected for Brassbank one day.'

Carol laughed and climbed on the bus. She had never considered such a thing. It had not even occurred to her that what she was doing was political. The thought intrigued her. Her father had always accused her of having no ambition in life, of idling through it aimlessly, relying on others to support her. Now, perhaps for the first time, she was doing something positive, responding to the challenge set before her without thinking of it as work.

She had got involved because Lotty had asked her to and because she needed to fill the emptiness left by Val laying her off at the dress shop. But it had grown into more than just a supporting hand for the men. She had found a new confidence and a sense of purpose that she had never had before. She enjoyed the company of the others in the group and they were having fun as well as helping the cause. Being away from Brassbank, she could stand back and see herself differently. During the last few days she had reaffirmed her love for her village, for her family. They meant the whole world to her. Yet she had tasted a new independence that gave her strength and a cautious belief in her own ability.

She thought of Mick and Laura and felt a sudden impatience to be with them again. Talking about the men to others over the past days had brought home to Carol how much Mick must be suffering. He had too much time to dwell on too many worries. Somehow she must see him through this dark time. She had to be strong for him as he had been strong for her so many times in the past.

The bus swung down into Brassbank in the early evening, the raucous singing of the women breaking off as they shouted out familiar landmarks and called out excitedly as they passed their homes or those of friends and family.

Carol wondered if Lotty would bring Laura to meet her, secretly hoping she would but knowing her sensible mother-in-law would probably have her ready for bed by now.

They scrambled off the bus, the driver helping them heave their cases down.

As Carol turned, she heard her daughter shriek her name and moments later felt Laura's body hurtle against hers and skinny arms wrap themselves round her waist. Carol lifted her up in a joyful hug and covered her face with kisses.

'I thought you'd be in bed,' Carol laughed as Laura began to burble.

'I wanted to stay up to see you. We've been to the park five times and I can skip up to ten and we've been out in a boat with Uncle Eddy!'

'You and Nana?' Carol asked in amazement.

'No, with Daddy,' Laura said as if her mother was being quite stupid.

Carol swivelled round and saw Mick standing back, waiting for them.

'Aye,' he nodded, 'we have. But it was six times to the park and not five.'

For an instant they stood awkwardly staring at each other and then Laura piped up, 'And Daddy's done the hoovering and ironing but he's burnt a brown mark on me school dress. And he's made a fish pie with the fish I caught in Captain Lenin's boat.'

'The fish we caught at the fish shop,' Mick corrected, flushing with embarrassment.

Carol laughed and stepped towards him. 'I'm impressed,' she smiled and kissed him on the mouth.

Briefly Mick's arms went about her. 'I've missed you, pet,' he murmured. Carol revelled in the feel of his arms as he held her, realising how much she had longed for his comforting touch.

She hugged the two of them. 'Me too,' she answered. 'The bus couldn't get me up the road quick enough.'

Mick gave his familiar, boyish smile; the one Carol had not seen on his face for weeks and had missed so much. He picked up her case.

'Aren't you going to tell Mammy the other news?' Mick reminded Laura.

'Oh, yes; Auntie Linda's had a baby boy.'

Carol gasped. 'Now you tell me! When did this happen?'

'Two days ago. She's still in hospital, but doing grand.'

Laura babbled excitedly, 'Daddy said we had to wait for you coming home and we'll go and see him together. Nana says he's called Calvin.'

Carol raised inquiring eyebrows.

Mick shrugged. 'Not a Todd name,' he laughed.

Carol exclaimed, 'Trust all the excitement to happen when I'm not here.'

'That'll teach you for ganin' away,' Mick answered.

She shot him a look but he was grinning. 'Well, I'm back now. Tomorrow we'll visit the pair of them.'

Smiling happily, she linked her arm through Mick's and clutched Laura's hand tightly. They walked home together.

Chapter Twenty-One

Are you sure you'll manage?' Carol asked.

'Course I will,' Mick insisted.

They were sitting on kitchen chairs in the back yard, soaking up the August sunshine. Mick's face was tanned and his thinning fair hair bleached and Carol saw how the past weeks of beachcombing for coal and helping in his father's allotment had toned up his body once more. He sat stripped to the waist and suddenly she realised how much she still wanted him.

Despite the happiness of her welcome home, these past weeks had been difficult. Mick had tried his best to help around the house and entertain Laura, but he often lapsed into brooding silences which unnerved her, so that she kept out of his way. She had found herself spending most of her time out of the house helping the Women's Group and delaying her return home until it was time to put Laura to bed. She had spent long hours helping Pete Fletcher with his radio documentary - too long perhaps. Now it was time for the children's holiday, paid for out of donations, and she had yearned for it to come, eager for a break from home, but most of all from Mick's reproachful looks.

Yet as the moment arrived, she was engulfed in guilt at her wish to be away from him.

'I feel bad about leaving you again,' she said, stretching out a hand to touch him.

He flinched away from her. 'Don't be. You and the bairn deserve a break.'

'So do you,' Carol sighed. 'I wish you could come with us.'

Perhaps her tone was half-hearted because Mick answered in a flat voice, 'No. The money's been raised to send the bairns on holiday, not the lads.'

She wanted to take his hand but dared not. 'I'll make it up to you when I get back,' she promised and then blushed.

Mick gave her a long, hard look and then glanced away, uncertain. The sadness in his eyes cut at Carol's heart and made her persist.

'Or now,' she suggested softly.

They looked at each other in silence, Carol steeling herself for rejection. Although Laura now slept in her own bed, Carol was frequently too tired for lovemaking by the time she got to bed and Mick seemed to have lost all interest. He would sleep curled up and turned away from her like an animal in hibernation. She had never felt so lonely as in these past weeks, even though Mick was around more than ever.

A hint of his old smile flashed across Mick's face. 'It's not even teatime,' he said, pretending to be shocked.

Carol smiled, encouraged. 'We're already packed and Laura's over at your mam's. What else is there to do?' she teased.

For a long moment he did not move, his blue eyes scrutinising her face. Perhaps he feared she was not serious, or maybe he no longer wanted her.

He was on the point of answering when the latch went on the back gate and the words died on his lips. Carol was left not knowing what Mick had wanted.

'Hiya! Anyone at home?' a voice called.

'One of your bloody committee,' Mick muttered.

Carol ignored the remark but was hurt by it. Kelly's bright face appeared round the yard door.

'Ha!' Kelly laughed. 'Sunbathing again. It must be nice having nowt to do.'

Mick jumped up. 'No, it bloody isn't,' he scowled and brushed past her. 'I'll gan over to Mam's and fetch Laura.' Then he was gone.

The moment between them was shattered and Carol felt a sudden annoyance at Mick for his rudeness and at Kelly for spoiling what might have been. Why did Mick always make it so obvious that he had no time for her friend? Carol sighed heavily.

'Sorry,' Kelly said as the gate banged closed. 'I didn't think.'

'Oh, nothing suits him these days,' Carol replied bleakly, 'it's not just you. Sit yourself down and have some of Lotty's elderflower cordial.'

'No, ta,' Kelly grinned. She moved about the small yard restlessly and Carol wondered why she was on edge. She was pleased to see her old friend. They had drifted apart and made different lives for themselves, but Carol still enjoyed her company. She noticed how well Kelly looked. She had lost that gaunt, pallid appearance of the past few years and her red hair gleamed in a long bob.

'I'm coming on the kids' holiday,' she blurted out.

'You are?' Carol exclaimed.

'Don't sound so shocked,' Kelly pouted. 'Joanne's had to pull out at the last minute because Mark's got chickenpox - covered in spots this morning. She asked Sid if I would go.'

'What does Sid say?' Carol asked. 'And what about work?'

'I'm due holiday, so I've cleared that at work. Sid doesn't mind,' Kelly said with a dismissive wave. 'He's going to help Joanne out with Mark. Spends most of his time round at his sister's any road. Wouldn't be surprised if he came down with chickenpox in sympathy.'

Carol ignored the snide remark. Sid and Joanne had always been close and Sid had worked alongside his brother-in-law, John, down the pit since they'd left school. Perhaps he felt more at home at his sister's than in his own house, Carol thought, but kept it to herself.

'Well, it'll be a laugh having you along,' Carol smiled. 'Didn't think you'd fancy two weeks of looking after kids, mind.' She gave her friend a suspicious look.

Kelly laughed and paced across to the gate again. 'Still a kid meself, I am. Least that's what Sid's always telling me. And I can't wait to get away from this place for a bit of fun. It's been deadly round here since the strike started.'

Carol snorted. 'Well, just remember you're there to give the bairns a good time.'

Kelly shot her a look and then quickly turned away. 'Boring old cow!' she teased.

Carol made a face back. 'Haway! Let's smoke your cigarettes before Mick gets back.'

Kelly laughed. 'Keeping secrets from your husband. Naughty, naughty.'

'And what secrets do you keep?' Carol challenged.

Kelly turned puce and seemed flustered by the question and Carol wished she had not asked.

'From your husband or mine?' Kelly quipped back, her tone cool as she glanced into the back lane.

Carol was baffled by the reply, but before she could ask what she meant, Kelly changed the subject. 'How's little Calvin?'

At the mention of Linda and Dan's baby, Carol felt a nagging anxiety. She was not at all sure the young couple were coping. Calvin was a fractious baby who slept fitfully and bawled with croup after feeding.

Linda had refused to breast feed him despite the cost of powdered milk, determined to regain her figure as soon as possible. Every time Carol had been over to see them at the flat she had found Linda in tears and the baby crying and Dan nowhere to be seen. Dan's mother was often there, criticising without offering practical help, while Lotty was too busy with the soup kitchen to give the support she would like.

Carol sat up, reaching for Kelly's handbag and rummaging for cigarettes. 'I must go over and see Linda before we leave tomorrow, I'm worried about her.'

Kelly shrugged dismissively. 'If she wasn't prepared to look after him properly she shouldn't have had him.'

Carol winced at her condemnation. 'She's doing her best under the circumstances,' she defended her sister-in-law.

Kelly turned away again to wave at someone far up the lane. 'Too late for a fag, Laura's back.' She hurried to snatch her handbag from Carol. 'I must go and pack.'

'Wait, Kelly,' Carol stopped her. 'Will you do me a favour? Drive me over to see our Linda this evening. I've been trying to persuade her to come on the trip but she won't leave Dan.'

Kelly sighed with annoyance but nodded. 'I'll pick you up at eight.'

'Ta,' Carol smiled.

Then her friend darted out of the gate with a clatter of high heels.

Kelly parked her father's old Datsun outside the block of flats on Whittledene Rise Estate. They could hear Calvin bawling from the bottom of the stairwell. Kelly grimaced and let Carol go first. At first she got no answer from her knocking, then finally Linda came to the door and peered through the gap allowed by the chain. Her face was swollen from crying and her fringe hung limp in her shadowed eyes.

'Let us in, Linda man,' Carol told her.

The darkened flat was strewn with dirty clothes and unwashed dishes and smelt of soiled nappies. In the gloom Carol found Calvin in his carrycot and picked him up. His Babygro was soaking and his skin felt clammy and cold as she peeled the urine-smelling garment off him.

'There, there, little man,' she crooned. 'We'll soon get you changed.'

'Into what?' Linda howled. 'I've run out of nappies and I've nowt to buy new ones with.'

Carol turned. 'What about the towelling ones Lotty gave you?'

'They're all in the wash,' Linda shouted. 'I don't have anything clean to put on him.'

'Linda,' Carol chided.

'Well, what am I supposed to do now the electric's been cut off? I can't do the washing - I can't even cook. We have to go to bed in the dark. I can't warm up the baby's milk. Oh, Carol!' She burst into tears.

Carol thrust the baby at Kelly and rushed over, putting her arms round her sister-in-law's shoulders.

'I'm sorry, pet. How long have you been without electricity?' she asked gently.

'Two days,' Linda sobbed.

'Where's that bugger, Dan?' Kelly demanded, surveying the squalor with distaste as she attempted to rock Calvin in her arms.

'I don't know,' Linda cried, 'probably back at his mam's. We had a terrible row. He called me a slut. The baby kept crying and I had nowhere to dry the nappies. All we had to spend went on baby stuff. Then they just cut off the electricity. We haven't paid anything for months. Dan said he couldn't stand it any longer.'

'Typical man!' Kelly fumed. 'Instead of giving a hand he's pissed off back to his mam's.'

'Why didn't you tell us what was going on?' Carol said, hugging Linda to try and stop her shaking.

'I didn't think he'd really leave us, not with the baby to take care of,' Linda sniffed.

'When's the last time you had something to eat?' Carol asked.

Linda shook lank hair out of her exhausted eyes. 'Don't know.'

'Well, you can't stay here,' Carol said briskly. 'Kelly's got her dad's car; we're taking you back with us.'

Kelly nodded. 'I'll gan and get some fish and chips for us all while you get packed up.'

'And see if they've got nappies in the corner shop,' Carol said, looking at her nephew's skinny body. 'New-born's or the smallest they've got.'

Linda pulled away in panic. 'But I can't go. Dan might come back. He'll not know where to find us.'

Kelly snorted as she rocked Calvin vigorously. 'Don't be so daft. The bugger's not going to come back now.'

Carol was more gentle. 'He'll know you've gone to your mam's or us. We can let him know anyway.'

'Eeh, look,' Kelly said with a sudden triumphant smile. 'Calvin's stopped crying.'

Carol watched her red-headed friend bending over and cooing to the half-undressed baby. It surprised her how comfortable Kelly looked with a baby in her arms, for she had never shown any interest in babies since their girlhood when they had knocked on neighbours' doors and asked to push their bairns out in prams. And that had only been a game to see who could win the bonniest baby in the poshest pram. Suddenly, Kelly looked up and caught Carol watching her. She gave her a strange look and for a moment Carol thought she might cry, then she walked across to Linda and plonked Calvin in her lap. At once the baby began to wail again.

'You sort him out,' Kelly said brusquely and turned away. 'I'm not his mam.'

It took an hour to clear some of the mess and bundle dirty clothes into a bin liner to take with them. When it grew too dark they gave up. The hot food seemed to revive Linda and the baby calmed down with a bottle, after they had put him into dry clothes.

As they drove back to Brassbank, Kelly insisted, 'You and Calvin are coming on the holiday with us.' Linda protested weakly, but Kelly silenced her dissent. 'You need a break and the bairn needs a bit of pampering. There'll be plenty to fuss over him while you and I hit the high spots, isn't that right, Carol?'

Carol laughed. 'I knew you weren't coming for the sea air.'

'I can get enough of that at home,' Kelly declared.

'High spots?' Linda smiled for the first time. 'All I want to do is sleep.'

'Sleep during the day then, high spots at night,' Kelly compromised.

Carol felt Linda relax against her and lay a weary head on her shoulder. Calvin lay peacefully in his carrycot on their knees, lulled to sleep by the car's motion.

Kelly broke the silence just before they descended the hill to Brassbank.

'It's terrible what this strike's doing to people,' she said, suddenly serious.

'Aye,' Linda agreed. 'I wish they'd all gan back to work and then me and Dan could start again.'

'It's not that simple,' Carol said. 'If they went back now with nothing won, all the suffering will have been for nothing.'

'What do you know about suffering?' Linda complained. 'You've got Mick. You haven't suffered like I have.'

Carol caught Kelly looking at her in the rearview mirror and expected her friend to defend her. But Kelly glanced away saying nothing and Carol felt a stab of hurt. Kelly was acting strangely; there was something going on that she could not fathom. They said no more until they reached Septimus Street, Carol trying to shake off the uneasiness she felt at Kelly's moodiness.

Lotty and Carol stayed up late washing baby clothes and drying them off as best they could, in time for Linda and Calvin to join the trip. In the morning, dozens of people turned out to see the coachful of excited children off on their seaside holiday, ecstatic at the thought of playing on clean sandy beaches and bedding down in dormitories in the hostel that had been paid for by members of the seamen's union.

All the Todds were there to see off Linda and Carol and their children. Carol hugged them all, even a bashful Charlie. Eddy was there, cracking jokes and doing a trick for Laura with a fifty pence piece. He made it disappear up his sleeve and then magicked it out of his nose.

'You spend it on your holidays,' Eddy told Laura as he pressed the coin into her small, eager hand.

Mick kissed Carol quickly, self-consciously, like a brother would do. With all the late-night washing, Mick had been fast asleep when Carol had got to bed and in the morning neither had referred to her attempts at intimacy. It confirmed her fear that he did not want her and the cold emptiness she felt inside deepened.

She watched him swing Laura into his arms and hug her goodbye. 'I'll miss you, pet,' he told her with one of his rare smiles.

Carol felt tears of sadness prick her eyes that he had not said so to her. She turned away quickly, swallowing the affectionate words she had wanted to say to him.

Everyone else seemed infected by the children's anticipation and the crowd around the bus chattered merrily in the morning sun. They had all worked so hard to enable the children to have this break and to send some of the older ones on a camping trip to Weardale. There was a feeling of optimism among the villagers that something positive had been achieved for their children after the months of having to deny them so much.

For a long time after the bus had moved off up the bank towards Quarryhill, Carol strained to catch a glimpse of Mick standing surrounded by his family, waving, while Laura pressed her face to the window and waved back. All the way down to Whitby, Carol could see Mick in her mind's eye watching her go and wondered why the sight should make her feel so bereft. She told herself she should be happy that he was content to see her and Laura have this longed-for holiday and that his earlier depression seemed to have lifted a little. The cold anger that had erupted in bouts of shouting had been less frequent since her return from London. Yet in their physical relationship, things had never been so bad and Carol found it frightening how quickly their passion had withered. For the first time she contemplated what it might be like living apart from Mick, something she would never have dreamed of before. Of course she would never leave him - at least, not while the strike was on. But how long could she cope with the bad atmosphere and lack of love? If only Mick would talk to her about how he felt!

And how would he cope with the empty hours now they were gone? Carol worried. She hoped that Eddy would keep an eye on him and knew that Lotty would spoil him. Yet some doubt deep inside gnawed away like a termite, telling her she should not be leaving him, not now. Was she frightened for him or of the freedom that these two weeks offered her? Why had she not told Mick that Pete Fletcher would be covering part of the holiday for another radio feature? She hardly dared admit how pleased she was that the journalist would be there. He was so easy to talk to and it was sometimes a relief to confide in someone outside the family and close neighbours.

But Mick had complained of Pete hanging around her 'like a bad smell' and Carol had decided to avoid another row by not mentioning the reporter at all. She told herself to stop feeling so guilty; she had done her best for everyone these past months and needed a holiday. Lotty had said she should go; the older women could run things while the younger women were away. Still, Carol could not shift the feeling that she was somehow deserting them.

A bright and blustery North Sea burst into view as the bus trundled down from the North Yorkshire moors and the compact old fishing town of Whitby appeared before them. Kelly swung along the bus and nudged her with an elbow.

'It's a holiday, not a bloody funeral!'

Carol sighed and smiled. Shaking off the feeling of gloom that had gripped her on the journey, she turned to share Laura's excitement at their arrival.

'Look, Mam,' the girl cried, wide-eyed. 'Look at all them buckets and spades hanging up outside that shop. Can I buy one with Uncle Eddy's money? Please, Mam!'

Carol did not have the heart to tell her that Eddy's money would not be enough.

'Course, you can,' she smiled and hugged her tight. Today, she was not going to let money worries spoil the magic of this holiday for her special daughter. For two weeks she was not going to worry about anything at all.

Chapter Twenty-Two

The first week of the holiday flew past, with frequent trips to the beach and walks along the cliffs. One day they went to Scarborough, on another they explored the moors and took a steam train ride. The days passed, exhausting but happy, and the women grew closer than ever as they revelled in the change of scene and the freedom from daily chores.

Every day, Carol made herself ring Mick for a few minutes to report on the day's events, though she was aware they both found talking over the telephone awkward. At first he sounded cheerful enough and said he was keeping busy, but at the end of the week Carol had the impression something had happened that he did not want to talk about.

'It's costing to ring every day,' Mick said testily. 'Spend the money on Laura.'

'What's wrong?' Carol asked.

'Nowt's wrong,' he answered with irritation.

'I can tell something's bothering you,' Carol persisted. 'Is it one of the family? Has something happened?'

'No! Nowt's happened. Just enjoy your time off while you've got it.'

'Mick, I'd rather you told me now what's going on.'

'I'll see you in a week's time, Carol,' he cut her off sharply. 'Don't keep ringing. Give Laura a kiss from me.'

And then he rang off, before her money had run out. Annoyed, Carol almost rang straight back, but knew she would get no more out of him at this distance. Mick had never been easy conversing over the telephone and always left her to answer its insistent call, rather than pick it up himself. She sighed with frustration, resenting that the holiday had now been tainted with worry about what might be happening at home.

Carol wished that the holiday was not passing so quickly. She had felt the strain of overwork and the emotional roller-coaster of the past months ebbing out of her tense muscles this past week. She had not laughed as much for ages as she had done with the other women and they all looked forward to that peaceful time in the evening when the kids were in bed and they could share a bottle of wine and a packet of cigarettes on the steps of the hostel in the fading light. They had all been more patient with the children than at home where the children had whinged with boredom and got under their feet. It delighted Carol to see Laura and her friends thriving and lively in the daytime and sleeping soundly at night. But another week and they would be gone from this haven; it would all be over.

As she came out of the booth in the hostel hallway she heard a voice speak her name. Turning, she found Pete Fletcher standing right behind her, his pleasant face smiling. He stepped forward and brushed her cheek with a kiss.

'Good to see you, Carol. You're looking great.'

So he had come! She felt guilty at how pleased she was to see him, still smarting from Mick's surliness.

'Hello, Pete,' she answered breathlessly, blushing at his kiss. He looked lean and tanned in his casual clothes, his chin unshaven and eyes sensual behind his glasses. 'I thought perhaps you weren't coming.'

'I find it difficult to stay away,' he said, his voice full of dangerous meaning. Then he laughed 'I've got to finish the radio piece, remember?' He touched her shoulder. 'Everything all right at home?'

Carol looked away, embarrassed that he might have overheard her being cut off.

'Aye,' she said briskly and stepped away from him, aware of her pulse racing. 'If you're looking for the kids, you better come and join us for tea. It's Laura's turn to serve out the fish fingers.'

'That I can't miss,' Pete joked and followed her in.

Carol noticed how at ease he was moving around the tables, chatting to the children and adults alike. Laura was especially pleased to see him and boasted that he had been a visitor at her house and slept on the settee. When Pete said she could be on radio, Laura nearly burst with importance. After tea, he promised her and a group of her friends an ice cream.

'Stop spoiling her,' Carol complained half-heartedly.

'You can come too,' Pete teased, 'but only if you agree to eat ice cream with me.'

Carol told herself she was only going to keep an eye on the children.

They walked along the top of the cliffs, past the grander hotels, and looked down on the harbour bustling with tourists. Smells of the sea and fish suppers wafted up on the evening breeze. The children scampered ahead, running along benches and jumping off with shrieks of delight.

'Where've you been for the past week?' Carol asked.

He smiled his sensual smile. 'Don't suppose that means you've missed me, does it?'

'No,' Carol lied. 'I was just being polite.' She pulled a face at him and he laughed softly.

'I've being doing some follow-up interviews at Greenham Common,' Pete explained.

'Got a thing about women's groups, have you?' Carol laughed.

'Maybe,' Pete smiled, 'or maybe just some women.'

She shot him a look and saw he was teasing. Nevertheless, she felt uncomfortable, surprised and annoyed to find that the remark excited her. She changed the subject quickly.

'Do you know if anything's happened at home since we came away? I haven't heard any news for days. It's been a bit of a relief not knowing, really.'

Pete looked serious. 'There's a big push on to get the men back to work. It was bound to happen. Summer will be over soon. Coal stocks are probably lower than the NCB are letting on. But they know some people are cracking.'

'So what's new?' Carol was dismissive. 'They try and bribe the men back to work every month.'

He laid a hand on her arm. 'Carol, this time it's serious. It's only a matter of time before someone at Brassbank goes back.'

'Don't say that!' Carol turned on him angrily and shook off his hold. 'The strike's solid where we are. We've all worked so hard to keep it that way.'

Pete nodded. 'I know you have and it's impressed me no end. But it's like trying to turn back the sea. You're up against the might of the state and all it can throw at you. Haven't you seen the adverts in the papers wooing the men back with

161

lumps of cash? And the TV - every night showing a map with the numbers going back to each pit.'

'But they just invent the numbers!' Carol protested.

'Maybe they do,' Pete said calmly, 'but that's part of the propaganda game. It's not the truth that counts, it's results. It's *winning*.'

'God, you're so cynical,' Carol exclaimed.

Pete took hold of her arm more forcefully and pulled her round. 'And you're so naive, Carol. You speak out about justice and fairness but that's not how you'll win this battle. You've got to play them at the same dirty game. Win at all costs. People like Charlie Todd know that. It's going to get a lot rougher once the trickle back to work gets going. Anything you've seen so far will be a kid's picnic in comparison. That's when we'll see who's really got the fight in them.'

Carol thought of Mick and shuddered. Being arrested and charged once had nearly finished him; she doubted he could take another mental beating. She was aware of Pete's hands on her arms. The feel of them burned into her skin, making her shake.

'So you think what I've been doing is a waste of time?' she challenged him.

'Not at all,' he answered, his face now very close to hers. 'But you can't influence enough people by speaking to the converted in provincial halls. You need to get your message out to a wider audience - TV, radio, press. Make your own propaganda, make people sympathise.'

'But the press hate us,' Carol said bitterly. 'They call our men criminals and bully boys.'

'We don't all hate you,' he said, his voice low and intense. 'That's why it's important to do features from the women's point of view, and the children's. That's where I can help with this radio programme.'

Carol looked into his earnest, intense face. 'You do want to help, don't you?'

He gripped her tighter. 'You know I do,' he said in his soft, persuasive voice.

Carol felt her legs go weak. Then Laura came bounding up to them.

'Come on,' she cried with impatience. 'You said you'd buy us ice creams.'

Pete relaxed his hold on Carol and smiled. 'Ice creams coming up.' But as Carol turned from him, he murmured, 'And perhaps a drink for the grown-ups later? To discuss propaganda, of course.'

She caught his quizzical smile and felt her insides lurch in a way she knew they should not.

Mick tore up the latest letter to arrive from Ben Shannon, urging him to return to work, and escaped up to the allotment where he found his father sitting in a faded deck chair, a book unread in his lap. It made Mick furious to think that they were all being hounded to get back to work, as if they could be bought off. But rumours had been spreading all week that some were ready to cross the picket line in Brassbank and had been in secret negotiation with management. Now every time Mick saw a small huddle of men in the corner of a pub or in the park he wondered if they were plotting betrayal. Would they be capable of such a thing? Which of those around him would be the first to crack? Eddy? Sid? Dan? John Taylor? Marty Dillon? Himself?

Mick tortured himself with speculation, knowing that that was exactly what the forces against them wanted the miners to do. They were trying to divide them with suspicions and doubts, tempt them with money and promises of no reprisals. It made him sick to the core. And then Carol had rung, full of happy talk of their holiday, and Mick had felt resentful and excluded and bereft without her and Laura. They might as well have been on the other side of the world, so far away did they seem from the tensions at home. So he had been short with her and cut her off. He had immediately regretted it and wished she had phoned back so that he could make it up to her. Why was he incapable of ever telling her how he really felt? If he could just explain how difficult it was not working, filling the endless hours, and how much the fear of the court case weighed upon him. If only she could understand how helpless he felt watching her grow in confidence and purpose as she coped with the strike far better than he did. It made him feel angry and useless, until he had no confidence in himself any more - not even in bed. It wasn't that he didn't want to make love to her, rather that he was frightened that he couldn't.

He yearned to hear her voice again, but after twenty minutes of staring angrily at the mute telephone, he made his way up to the breezy allotment, perched above the village on the cliffs. It was easier being with his father who understood better what he was going through, what all the men were going through. With Charlie he did not have to explain.

'Who can it be?' his father brooded. 'Or, worse, who can they be?'

Mick knew he was sifting through his mind to find the potential scabs. His father would take the betrayal personally, blaming himself for any crack in the solidarity at their pit. They were his men, members of his lodge, marras below ground. If just one of them turned scab, Mick knew that Charlie would be torn apart by the act, whatever the reason. His feelings ran too deep. His loyalties were as rock solid as the seams of coal beneath them; his memories stretched back into early childhood and the betrayal of his father in 1926. To scab would be incomprehensible to him and Mick knew his father would show no mercy to a weaker man.

Mick squatted down on his haunches. 'We'll soon know if it's true.'

'It is true.'

They both swung round at the sound of another man's voice behind them. Mick flushed at the sight of Ben Shannon leaning over the fence, watching them from the lane. He was dressed in casual clothes - fawn trousers, a polo shirt and Pringle jumper. Charlie eyed him without getting up from his chair.

'Delphiniums looking grand, Charlie,' Ben spoke with ease, 'not as many as last year though. Mine have come up better.'

'We're having to grow more food this year,' Charlie replied with a snort. 'Not a problem that's ever bothered you.'

'No,' Ben agreed. 'Can I come in?'

To Mick's annoyance, Charlie nodded and it suddenly struck him that Carol's father must have been up here before. Charlie seemed unperturbed by the manager's appearance; perhaps he had visited for years. There was no stiffness to their conversation; they were more like old boyhood rivals still vying with each other. Mick listened in astonishment.

'So, are you going to tell me whose arms you've twisted to gan back to work?' Charlie asked.

'No twisting,' Ben replied, picking off a raspberry from the nearby bush and tasting it. 'This strike's gone on long enough. You've gained nothing by it,

Toddy, and we've lost millions. My job is to get things cracking at the pit as soon as possible and safeguard all our jobs.'

'Bollocks, man!' Charlie cried. 'You're not on local telly now, so stop sounding like a Tory minister.'

To Mick's surprise, Ben Shannon laughed. He drew out a handkerchief and wiped his raspberry-stained fingers. Then his jowly face grew serious.

'Listen, Toddy, we go back a long way, you and I. We've seen the pit through many disputes in the past, but this one's different.'

'Aye, our future's on the line with this one.' Charlie was bullish.

'It doesn't have to be. Brassbank isn't on any closure list. We'll see out our days here, and young Mick after us. But only if we can get back to work and put this damaging dispute behind us. You've all been conned by Scargill. It's not your fight.'

Mick was at once reminded of the insistent arguments of the detective who had interrogated him months ago. It made him furious.

Ben turned to him with a smile of understanding. 'And you, Mick. This strike has landed you in trouble when you've always been hard-working and peaceable. I can help you out of this mess, help Carol and Laura too. If you agreed to come back to work, we could overlook the fact that you're facing charges for riot offences, no matter what happens when it comes to court. Imagine what a relief it would be to have the shadow of court and prison lifted from your shoulders. Imagine Carol's relief. You shouldn't have to be suffering like this. My daughter shouldn't have to be suffering either, it's not what she was brought up to expect.'

Mick looked at his father-in-law with stony-faced contempt and said nothing. Ben rocked back on his feet, instantly annoyed by his insolent silence. He spoke in a harder voice, the threat barely concealed.

'If you choose to turn your back on my offer, I can't guarantee you anything, I'm afraid. And with a criminal record, well, look what happened to your grand-father. He hardly worked again after twenty-six.'

Mick glanced at his father and saw the appalled look on his face. 'Leave my lad alone, Shannon,' he growled.

'You can't divide us against each other like a herd of stupid sheep,' Mick was scathing. 'I know what game you're playing and it stinks! And don't think you can try and get round me dad either, just because you went to school together. We all know how you turned your back on your own kind, how your father was a scab. My grandfather might have been a ruined man because the private coal owners wouldn't take him back after he'd gone to prison, but at least he didn't betray anyone - not like the Shannons!'

Ben turned a livid red. To Mick's surprise, Charlie intervened. 'That's enough, lad.'

But Ben was riled. 'I can see he's as hot-headed and ill-tempered as-you, Toddy,' he said in fury. 'I can't imagine what my daughter saw in him. Turned her into a common drudge.'

This was too much for Charlie. He jumped out of his seat. 'You can say what you bloody well like about me, but don't you insult my son or your daughter like that! You've never given a toss about what happens to Carol. But I can tell you she's been happier with our Mick and with my family than she ever was with you. Carol's a Todd now,' he said with defiance, 'and she's proved herself one of us a hundred times over. She wants nothing to do with you.'

Ben was apoplectic. 'Well, don't be so proud of your precious Todd credentials,' he snapped back, his look vicious. 'I bet you haven't told Carol about the skeleton in your family cupboard. Or Mick for that matter.'

The two men stared at each other in hot fury.

'What's that supposed to mean?' Mick demanded, unnerved by his father's abrupt silence.

Ben spun round and gave a cold, deadly smile of triumph. 'You haven't told him, have you, Toddy?'

'Leave the lad alone,' Charlie replied, his throat tight with rage. 'Nobody asked you to come here.'

'Well, I think it's time the boy knew all his family history,' Ben continued, aware of gaining the upper hand at last.

'What you on about?' Mick asked him impatiently. There's nowt in our family to be ashamed of.'

'Well, that's where you're wrong,' Ben turned on him with all the aggression of a savaging dog. 'Your father is still deeply ashamed of his part in your grandfather's arrest, isn't that right, Toddy?'

Mick looked at his father and saw with shock that he had tears in his eyes.

'I'll tell him, not you!' Charlie shouted, then turned to his son. He struggled to compose himself. 'Your grandfather was arrested for breaking the windows of Shannon's house—'

'I was cut by flying glass, got taken to hospital,' Ben interrupted.

'Because Shannon had scabbed,' Charlie glared.

'I know all that,' Mick protested. This is old history.'

'My father was arrested and found guilty and went to prison,' Charlie continued in a strained voice.

'But he was innocent, wasn't he, Toddy?' Ben goaded him.

'How would you know?' Mick demanded.

'It's true,' Charlie said, his face trembling. 'I was the one who threw those bricks. I wanted to injure old man Shannon so badly. He'd stopped me from seeing me pal, Ben. And he'd got me father that angry he was going out of his mind. I wanted to kill him!' Mick heard a sob catch in his father's throat.

'Instead you got me,' Ben added, his eyes bright with anger or some other emotion Mick could not fathom. 'But your father protected you, didn't he? Took the blame. Damn idiot! And hardly did a day's work again because of it. Because of you, Toddy. Not because of me or my father. We weren't the cause of your father's misfortune or your family's hardship, or his early death. You've blamed us for that all your life, when all along the fault was yours. Stupid little runt that you were!'

Mick watched in horror as his father crumpled into his deck chair, buried his face in his hands and began a deep, wounded sobbing that rose up from the pit of his being. He had never ever seen his father weep and it shocked him to the core.

Mick turned on Ben Shannon, more angry than he had ever been in his life. He would wipe the smile of destructive satisfaction off his face for good. He drew back his fist and threw a resounding punch into his face. Ben reeled back and hit the ground; he never even saw the punch coming. Mick advanced on him as he lay among the lettuce, stunned by the blow. Ben threw up an arm to protect himself and ward off his furious attacker.

Mick stood over him, restraining the urge to kick him senseless.

'My father was not to blame for what happened to me grandda or to his family,' Mick roared. 'It was men like your father who were to blame - the scabs who caved in to the bosses! If they had stayed out and stood firm with their marras as they should have done, your windows would never have been broken and no one would've gone to prison. The shame lies with your father. My father has no reason to be ashamed. Me grandda might not have thrown the bricks, but he as good as did. He knew what the lock-out had done to him and his son and all the other starving families in the village. I bet he was proud of what his son did!' Mick glared down at the cowering manager. 'So don't think you can intimidate us or set me against me father. I'm proud of me dad, always have been and always will be. He's ten times the man you are, Shannon. You? I wouldn't piss on you if you caught fire!' Mick stood back and turned away in contempt.

Charlie looked at him, his face damp with tears, yet there was admiration in his brown eyes. He stood up without a word and went to his son's side. They stood together, stocky shoulders touching, and watched Ben pick himself up hurriedly from the lettuce bed. His pale trousers were stained with soil and he winced in pain as he tried to answer back.

Giving up, he limped away, clutching his jaw. Dougal, Charlie's terrier, chased him down the path yapping aggressively. Together the Todds watched him retreat. Eventually they heard a car engine start up and listened as the car drove away.

Charlie put an arm round Mick's shoulders. 'I think you might have broken his jaw.'

Mick grimaced. 'I hope I did. He's had it coming for a long time. All the things he's done to Carol and said to us.'

Charlie looked at his son, his eyes bright. 'I wish you'd known your grandda Todd,' he said quietly. 'You're that like him. He would have been proud of you, just like I am.'

The two men smiled at each other. This strike was bringing them closer together than they had ever been before, just like Charlie had grown close to his own father in 1926. Then worry gripped Charlie, remembering how his own father had been so strong throughout the dispute, only to be beaten by it when it collapsed in defeat. All the fight had been bled out of him and never returned. That must not happen to Mick, he vowed, else he would never forgive himself.

Mick went back to Septimus Street with his father, not wanting to be on his own at home. There they explained to an aghast Lotty what had happened at the allotment.

'He'll probably have me done for assault,' Mick said with a fatalistic shrug.

'Well, they'll have a job getting past me if they try to arrest you,' Lotty fulminated.

Charlie smiled. 'And what am I going to tell Carol if you're both in the nick when she comes back, eh?'

Mick felt his insides twist at the thought of what Carol might say. He had let her down again, he thought bleakly. Assaulting her own father . . .

He stretched out on the settee and dozed while he waited for the knock on the door. The hours ticked on through the night, yet no one came to pick him up. He could not believe that Shannon would pass up the opportunity of having him arrested and punished for such a humiliating attack. But by early morning, nothing had happened. Exhausted yet restless, Mick decided to risk going with his father to the picket to see if he could help. He was already in such trouble, breaking his bail would make little difference, he told himself.

As they emerged from the back lane they heard a rumble of vehicles. They looked up the hill towards Brassy and stopped dead in their tracks. Charlie blinked and stared again as if he could not believe what he saw. Out of the dawn shone the lights of a solid line of vans as they snaked down the steep bank into the village, flanked by motorcycle outriders like some invading army. Police on foot ran ahead, shouting at a few early morning bystanders to get back in their houses.

'What the hell's ganin' on?' Charlie exclaimed.

Mick squinted into the gloom and saw a bus in the middle of the convoy. It was green and yellow, the colours of a Proud coach. In an instant he understood.

'Bastards!' Mick cried. 'They're bringing in the scabs!'

Charlie's stunned expression gave way to grim determination. 'Haway, then, lad. We'll be needed at the picket.' He set off at a run.

Mick did not hesitate but followed his father. A new purpose lit inside him as he rushed forward, one that he had not felt for weeks. He was prepared for anything, just as his grandfather had been. He would defend that picket line to the end.

Chapter Twenty-Three

Carol sensed the danger in what she was doing but could not stop herself. After several drinks with Pete at a snug old inn on the harbour, they took a walk along the beach in the dark, lit only by the spangled lights along the shore.

Pete listened while she talked and told him deeply personal things about her past, her early childhood, how she had felt excluded from the rest of the family in some inexplicable way. She talked of the directionless, empty years of her growing up, the scrapes she had got into with Kelly and her father's cold, furious contempt.

'Perhaps if he had really taken an interest in me or what I got up to, it might have been different,' Carol sighed. 'But I knew, deep down, whatever I did he wouldn't care, so I just kept on doing things I knew he wouldn't approve of, just to get back at him.'

'Like marrying Mick?' Pete asked quietly.

They had stopped at the end of the beach and were leaning on a large rock, gazing out to sea. All at once the sounds of the restless, murmuring waves jolted her back to that fateful evening on Brassbank beach where she had rescued Eddy from the water and met Mick for the first time. She tried to remember how she had felt about him then. Was it possible that she had made herself interested in him because she knew it would upset her father more than anything she had ever done before? Surely she could not have been that calculating.

She closed her eyes tightly and remembered. The look of Mick's handsome, surly face, the watchful, vivid blue eyes, his strong body glistening wet from the sea. No, she had hungered for Mick Todd from that moment, Carol knew. Nothing could have prevented her falling in love with him, whatever his family.

Carol opened her eyes and turned to look at Pete. 'I married Mick because I loved him,' she told him simply, 'and for the first time in me life I felt I belonged somewhere - with Mick and his family. I'll be grateful for that till me dying day.'

Pete's look was searching. 'But do you still love him?'

Carol looked away, confused. Being so close to this sensual man in the dark with the sea sighing around them, filled her with longing. She knew she could tell him anything and he would understand, would keep it secret between themselves. Pete was so self-contained, so private, yet so receptive to her need to talk and explain. No man had ever given her the chance to express herself as Pete Fletcher did. For some reason he seemed to value her opinion and care about her in a way that other men did not, not even Mick.

'Things are difficult between Mick and me,' Carol whispered, 'I can't deny it. It's been such a hard year for him. But all marriages go through rocky patches, don't they?'

Even as she spoke her inmost thoughts, she felt disloyal to Mick. She turned away, but Pete stopped her with a hand on her shoulder, pulling her round gently to face him.

'Why don't you admit it?' he urged in a low voice. 'It's been a terrible year for you, Carol. You're the one taking the brunt of all this suffering, you and the other women like you. I've watched a beautiful, spirited woman gradually buckle under the weight of worries that she's carrying, including the guilt that she doesn't love her husband any more.'

'Don't!' Carol cried, trying to pull away from him. That's not true.'

'Admit it, Carol,' Pete persisted. 'It's not the strike that's wrecking your marriage. The strike's the only thing that's keeping you together. You have nothing in common with Mick any more. The spark's gone, hasn't it? I've stood by and watched him hurt you with his indifference. God, how I've wanted to step in and protect you, hold you tight; tell you that someone does love you. I bet it's crossed your mind to leave Mick, though you'd never admit it. But you won't leave him while he's fighting for his job, for the pit, isn't that it?'

'No! I've never thought such things,' Carol gasped in horror at the suggestion. Suddenly he let her go and she clutched her arms about her to stop herself from shaking and tried to control her erratic breathing.

Was it possible that Pete had seen the truth of their situation before she had? She thought back to the past months of rows and silences, petty bickering and cold shouldering; the lonely nights when Mick had taken himself off to Laura's empty bedroom or drawn away from her when she'd tried to touch him in the dark. On occasion, Pete had slept on the settee downstairs and might have heard the footsteps moving about in the night, the doors closing.

Pete reached out for her again, but did not touch her. 'Sweet Carol,' he murmured, 'don't torture yourself. I'm sorry. I should never have said those things. I never meant to upset you like this.'

Suddenly Carol found herself weeping. She bowed her head and moved towards his comforting arms. Pete enfolded her, stroked her hair and murmured reassurances. How she had ached for physical contact, for hugs and embraces like this.

'I've been so lonely,' she sobbed.

'I know,' Pete whispered and kissed her forehead. 'I've wanted to step in and hold you a hundred times.' He tilted her chin up and gently kissed her lips.

'We shouldn't. . .' Carol gulped, feeling the longing flare inside her.

Pete kissed her again, a longer, lingering kiss that made her hunger for more. His hands moved round her back, pressing her closer so that she could feel the thud of his heart against her chest.

'I love you, Carol,' Pete said, caressing her face with soft kisses. 'I want you.'

Carol shuddered and closed her eyes, feeling her insides melt.

'You want this too, don't you, my love?' he whispered, beginning to kiss his way down her neck.

'I don't know . . .' Carol faltered.

'Let me love you, Carol,' Pete said, his voice as seductive as his fingers as they moved over her skin, setting it tingling with delight. 'Let me make love to this wonderful body of yours.'

Carol felt light-headed at his erotic words. She should not be letting this happen, yet at that moment she did not know how she could stop.

Suddenly, something very cold rushed at her feet. She yelped and jumped back.

'Ah, the bloody tide's coming in!' Pete shouted, hopping backwards to save his shoes.

At once the sexual energy between them was broken. Carol burst out laughing at his undignified hopping.

'That's the North Sea for you, a real passion killer. Now if we'd been beside the Pacific, just think what might have happened.' She was already making light of their embrace, her self-control returning.

Pete looked put out. 'How can you laugh about it?'

'I'm sorry,' Carol smiled with regret, 'but we can't let that happen again.'

'Can't we?' Pete asked wistfully.

'No,' Carol was firm. 'Maybe I'm not happy with Mick, but I'd never leave him for anyone else, no matter how sexy.' She flashed a smile, then fell serious once more. Anyway, I've Laura to consider too.'

'I know,' Pete sighed. They began to walk back up the beach. He put out a finger and ran it down her arm. 'Don't know how I'm going to keep my hands off you though.'

Carol shifted away before she weakened again. 'No more, please.' Her smile was kind but her green eyes held a warning. She quickened her step. 'Time I got back to the hostel.'

'Can I walk you there if I promise not to touch?' There was a mocking note in his voice.

Carol nodded.

He chuckled, 'So I'm sexy, am I?'

Carol gave an impatient sigh. 'Men and their egos. That was off the record, so don't go quoting me on it.'

They walked through the town, where everything had quietened down. Carol had not realised how late it was.

'I'll be locked out of the hostel,' she grimaced.

'Have to come to my hotel after all,' Pete grinned. She ignored the remark.

They arrived at the hostel to find it locked and in darkness. After a moment's hesitation, Carol picked up some pebbles from the path and began chucking them up at a first-floor window.

'It's Kelly's room,' she whispered, 'though knowing my luck she'll still be out on the town.'

But moments later the window was thrown up and Kelly stuck her head out.

'What the . . .?' Kelly peered into the dark.

'It's me,' Carol hissed. 'Can you come down and let me in?'

'Dirty stop-out!' Kelly peered long enough to notice the man standing at Carol's side and then disappeared.

'Better go now, eh?' Carol told Pete.

Pete smiled and kissed her quickly on the mouth. 'I admire your loyalty to Mick. But you know that I won't be far away if you need me, don't you, Carol?'

She pushed him down the path. 'Go.'

'He's a lucky sod,' Pete whispered and blew her a kiss as he disappeared into the dark.

There was a fumbling with locks and then Kelly's head appeared round the door.

'Where's he gone?' she asked.

'Who?' Carol countered.

'Don't give me that butter-wouldn't-melt expression,' Kelly snorted. 'Haway in and tell me what you've been up to with that reporter of yours.'

'He's not mine,' Carol hissed.

Kelly put her finger to her lips. 'Shh! My room. Tell all. Then I've got a secret for you that'll knock your socks off!'

Carol looked at her friend's animated face and felt a pang of misgiving. She knew that Kelly had been keeping something from her for ages, but now that her friend was going to confide in her, she was frightened of what she was about to discover. She would much rather have crawled into her bed to ponder what had happened to her tonight. But Kelly would never allow her to get away with that, so with reluctance she tiptoed after her red-headed friend and steeled herself for the interrogation.

The small picket on the gates was no match for the convoy that swept towards them down the main street of Brassbank and on towards the pit. But Charlie went among the men, encouraging them to stand firm and block the bus that trundled towards them. Mick strained to see if he could recognise any faces, but the windows were covered in wire mesh to resist assault and all he could glimpse was an anonymous figure wearing a black balaclava to conceal his identity.

The pickets rushed into the road to halt the bus, but a loud-hailer warned them to stand back from the road. Mick ran alongside the vehicle and battered his fist against the side. Even the driver was wearing a helmet. Mick realised with a shock that it was Kelly's father, Ted Laws. For a moment their eyes met and then Ted looked away quickly and revved the engine. Mick thought how Sid, Ted's son-in-law, had sacrificed everything not to cross the picket line, even to the point where his marriage to Kelly seemed shaky. Yet here was old man Laws actively breaking the strike by bringing in the scabs who cowered in the bus not wanting to be recognised. Worst of all, Mick realised, if Ted was the driver it confirmed that the bus belonged to Vic Proud, his own brother-in-law.

He swore and hammered the side of Proud's bus in his fury. 'You'll not bring them in, Laws!' he roared.

A policeman rushed up and pulled him away from the bus, but Mick was stronger and threw him off. As the bus edged forward, Mick hurled himself into the road in front of the bus. There was a screech of brakes and shouts.

A local officer, a cousin of Lotty's, came forward and held up his hand to the bus driver, then turned to Charlie.

'Call your lad off, Toddy, will you?' he asked. 'We don't want any trouble.'

'Looks like you're set on trouble with this army of occupation you've brought in,' Charlie challenged him.

George Bowman looked uncomfortable. 'It's back-up from other forces,' he said in a low voice. 'Either we take care of this ourselves or the boys from the south will take over the show. Neither of us wants that now, do we, Toddy?'

'We have a right to talk to the lads on board,' Charlie was firm, 'that's what the picket's here for.'

'And it's my duty to see that they get safely into the pit,' Bowman said wearily.

'Since when has it been your duty to protect scabs instead of striking miners?' Charlie demanded. 'What happened to impartial policing?'

Bowman glared impatiently. 'Toddy man, I haven't come here to argue with you. I'm not interested in your politics, I'm just doing my job.'

'The very fact you're here protecting strike breakers is a political act, George,' Charlie told him, 'so don't pretend this isn't political. Everything's political. You're being used by the Government against your own people, George, just like the police were in twenty-six when your own father was a pitman. Doesn't that bother you? Don't you sometimes wonder what your father would've done? He'd have been standing on this side, George, with me, or lying down in front of the bus with Mick, wouldn't he?'

George Bowman looked down at Mick stretched out in the road in his worn-out jeans, his gaunt face resolute. By now other men had joined him, while a steady flow of miners and onlookers had come out of the dark to gather at the pit gates, defying the men in uniform. George had a lifetime of experience among these people, his own people, and knew the lengths to which they would go to protect their own. They were loyal, stubborn and would tolerate great suffering for what they believed to be right. For a moment, Mick Todd seemed to embody all that George Bowman respected in the Durham miner and he would not see the lad harmed.

Abruptly, he turned on his heel and waved at the bus. 'Back her out!' he ordered.

There was a moment of confusion while all around took in what was happening, but George ordered his men to fall back.

Charlie looked up the hill where the convoy of police vans waited to be called upon. They were not called. Ted began to back the bus down the street, until he reached the opening to a back lane where he could turn.

George came up to Charlie again and said with a grim look, 'This is just a reprieve, Toddy. These lads will be back.' He jerked a thumb towards the riot vans. 'I can't stop them any more than you can. But there's been no trouble in our village, and I'd rather keep it that way. Speak to that lad of yours, won't you? I might not be here to save his skin next time.'

Charlie nodded and smiled briefly and George knew that was the nearest he would get to a thank you from Lotty's husband. He turned and led his men away, wondering whether he had acted foolishly after all these years of careful policing. He was too tired to ponder his decision; all he knew was that the situation had been too volatile and he would not go into retirement with blood on his hands.

Mick was hauled up and clapped on the back.

'Well done, lad,' Stan Savage congratulated him.

'You've turned the buggers back!' Frankie Burt crowed.

Mick grinned with triumph, but his father broke into the shouts of victory.

'Like Bowman said, they'll be back at the next shift,' Charlie warned. 'We'll need a bigger picket to see them off next time. So gan and put the word out now!' He turned to Mick. There was no need to speak of his pride in his son again; it lay like an invisible bond of strength between them.

Lowering his voice, Charlie said, 'We need to know who was on that bus and where the pick-up is.'

'Aye,' Mick nodded grimly. 'Leave that to me.'

Chapter Twenty-Four

Carol was stunned when Kelly told her.

'Pregnant?' she cried.

'Aye,' Kelly grinned, 'isn't it great? It's what I've always wanted really.'

'Well, yes,' Carol stammered, 'of course it is. It's just I didn't think you and Sid were, you know . . .'

Kelly stared at her an instant and then started to laugh. 'Hell no, it's not Sid's baby!' The dawn light was already fusing the room with a pearly glow and Kelly's face shone with happiness.

Carol sank down on the bed. 'I don't think I want to hear this.'

'Haway,' Kelly mocked, 'don't come on all virtuous with me, not after you've spent half the night on the beach with that journalist with the tight little arse.'

'I told you nothing happened between Pete and me,' Carol protested too hotly.

Kelly smirked. 'Oh, aye? I bet Mick wouldn't see it that way.'

Carol gave her friend a warning look. 'Don't you dare go telling him tales.'

Kelly pouted. 'Forget Mick. Now do you want to hear who the father is or not?'

Carol sighed, 'Not really, but you're obviously going to tell me anyway.'

'I thought you would've guessed by now,' Kelly grinned. 'We've been seeing each other on the quiet since last year. We've just been waiting for the right moment to leave our partners but with the strike and that—'

'Oh, Kelly man!' Carol exclaimed. 'He's not married an' all?'

'All the best blokes are now, aren't they?' Kelly answered defensively. 'But this is the excuse I've been waiting for to leave Sid - now I'm pregnant with this bloke's baby. Once he knows, there's no way he'll stop with his wife any longer.'

Carol stared at her friend as if she had gone mad. But Kelly looked radiant. This was the reason why her figure had filled out to its former roundness, why she was happy in a way she had not been for years - she was carrying the baby of a man she really loved. Carol had always suspected her marriage to Sid had been a sham, something Kelly had done because all her other friends were getting wed and she did not want to be left out. Perhaps if she and Sid had managed to have a bairn . . . Carol had often wondered what difference a child might have made in bringing them closer together. Her mind spun to think of how Sid would react to the news that Kelly was carrying someone else's child while he had longed for Kelly to settle down and give him a family.

'Are you telling me this lad doesn't even know you're pregnant yet?' Carol asked in disbelief.

'You're the first person I've told.' Kelly smiled her secretive smile. 'You should be honoured.'

'Kelly,' Carol was impatient. 'How do you know he won't go off the deep end with you? Does he want bairns? He might already have a family.'

'He has.' She looked unconcerned. 'He's got two daughters.'

Carol's heart began to pound. She felt unexpected fear clutch her stomach. 'Who is he?' she whispered.

Kelly gave her a look of triumph, like a cat that had just finished a bowlful of cream. 'You know him. It's your brother-in-law. Victor.'

Carol gawped. Her ears rang as if blocked by sea water. 'What? Vic? No! You must be kidding!'

'No, I'm not.' Kelly sounded miffed.

Carol felt the hysteria rising inside. It was too absurd to be true! Unexpectedly, she found herself laughing.

'Why's that so funny?' Kelly was hurt. 'Why is it so unbelievable?'

She was right, Carol instantly realised; it was quite believable. Vic; with his string of suspected infidelities, his go-to-bed eyes and wandering hands and that sensuous mouth with the moist kisses. Vic the boss; with his money and position of power over impressionable, unhappy Kelly, wooing her with his brashness, his cash and his empty promises. Kelly must have been easy prey, Carol thought with disgust, keeping her happy with secret dates while Fay kept order in their expensive home, entertaining his clients and bringing up his children.

'I'm just as good as that stuck-up sister of yours,' Kelly continued. 'She gives him a hard time for everything. His life's a misery with her. Spends his money like water, won't do anything in bed—'

'Shut up!' Carol suddenly snapped. 'I don't want to hear whatever Vic's been mouthing off about Fay just to get you into bed. Kelly man! I didn't think you'd fall for all that rubbish.' Carol thought with distaste how her brother-in-law had even tried it on with her when she had gone to him for help. 'Vic's a womaniser; he's always done exactly what he wants. You're not the first one to be taken in. Why do you think they had a string of nannies that never stayed? But he's never left Fay for anyone. They've got too comfortable a life together. He's probably living off her business at the moment anyway. Why should he leave her now?'

'Because we love each other!' Kelly shouted. 'I'm having his baby. I'll tell Fay about it and then he'll have to act. He's dying for the excuse to leave her, he told me so. We're going to live in their cottage up in Weardale. I've been there; it's got big open fireplaces and rugs on the floor like summat out of Ideal Homes. Vic says she can keep the house in Brassy, he doesn't care about all that, and I can't wait to get out of the place. We've planned it all.'

'Oh, Kelly.' Carol did not know what to say.

Kelly's face was pleading like a small girl's wanting approval. 'I thought you'd be pleased for me. Isn't it time I had a bit of happiness?'

'But it's all such a mess!' Carol cried. 'What about Vic's girls? And Sid? It's such a step to take. Don't you think you better find out what Vic thinks about you being pregnant before you throw everything away?'

Kelly looked close to tears. 'I know what he'll think. But I'll ask him tomorrow and then you'll see how serious we are about this.'

'He's here in Whitby?' Carol asked in astonishment.

Kelly nodded. 'He's been staying at a hotel down the coast for the past three days, but he's ganin' home tomorrow.'

Realisation dawned on Carol. 'That's why you came on this holiday, isn't it? You arranged it at the last minute to get away and be with Vic.' Carol stood up. "And I thought you'd come because you wanted to help out with the bairns. But you weren't thinking about them at all, were you, Kelly? You were just thinking about yourself as usual.'

Kelly's eyes blazed. 'Bloody hypocrite! You've used Laura as an excuse to come on the trip and get off with your fancy journalist. Don't you lecture me about Sid when you're going behind Mick's back. Well, me and Victor are different. We're

174

not just having a dirty little affair.'

Carol was stung. What was the use of repeating that she was not having an affair? Kelly's accusations were not so wide off the mark anyway; she had come very close to the edge with Pete.

'I would never leave Mick for anyone,' she said hoarsely.

'Well, more fool you!' Kelly answered angrily. 'He's no saint.'

Carol sprang forward and grabbed Kelly's wrist. 'What's that supposed to mean?' She flinched at the bitterness in Kelly's flushed face.

'Well, he walked out on me when I needed him. No man's going to do that to me twice!'

'You weren't even engaged,' Carol replied. 'How can you say he walked out on you?'

'He ditched me when he got me pregnant, that's why!' Kelly screamed.

Carol let go of her, falling back as if she had been physically struck. '*Pregnant?*'

'Aye! I was carrying Mick's baby and then we finished . . . and . . . and I decided to get rid of it. I didn't know what else to do.' Kelly crumpled on the bed and burst into tears. 'Oh, God, I wanted that baby! I still dream about it.'

Carol felt winded. Why had Kelly or Mick never told her about this? She should have been told. 'Mick knew about the baby?' she asked, shaking Kelly on the shoulder.

Kelly sobbed, 'I never told him outright, but he must've guessed. Why else would he not want me? He scarpered that quick. I tell you, no one's going to take away this baby. Even if Victor won't have me, I'm going to keep it!'

Carol shuddered. If Mick had guessed Kelly was pregnant, then he had been a coward to desert her and leave her to make the choice alone. She felt sick. Surely Mick could not have been so callous? But then he had been young and many lads his age shirked such responsibilities. Still, she felt somehow betrayed by the shocking news, to learn such a terrible secret about someone she thought she knew everything about. It was as if she no longer knew the man she was married to.

All at once she wanted to escape from the claustrophobic room and Kelly's vitriolic outburst. Their shouting had probably woken half the hostel. Had Vic stolen in and made love to Kelly right here while they had all been out on the beach for the day? Carol forced the image from her mind. She should have been back in her room with Laura and four of the other girls, but her bed would remain cold and unslept in for she could not bear to creep to bed as if nothing had happened. She had to get out.

Her thoughts rushed to Pete. He had told her he would be there for her when she needed him. She needed him now, she thought in desperation. Learning this about Mick, she wished she had given in to Pete on the beach. He at least did not pretend to be someone he wasn't. He did not want her as a wife or a mother or a skivvy in the kitchen standing in support behind her man. Pete simply wanted her for herself, as she was, with no demands or expectations.

'Carol?' Kelly was sitting up, sniffing. 'Where are you going?'

'Out,' Carol gasped and stumbled towards the door.

'Don't go!' Kelly pleaded. 'I didn't mean to tell you those things. I'm sorry . . .'

Carol lunged through the door and shut it behind her, not able to bear Kelly's pity after her insults. She rushed back down the stairs of the silent hostel and let herself out into the street. A blast of cold sea air hit her as she emerged on the path and a watery pink sun was already emerging over the lip of the sea as she ran down the street.

Mick went round to Ted Laws' house later in the day. He knew Ted would not answer his knocking so he walked straight in. Ted was standing at the sink in his vest peeling potatoes and Mick hesitated a moment at the sight of the vulnerable, grey-faced man who had lost his wife so long ago Mick could not remember her.

'What you want?' Ted growled and spat into the sink.

'You know what I want,' Mick answered calmly, blocking the doorway.

'Bugger off out of here,' Ted grumbled.

'Who are they?' Mick demanded.

'I don't know their names.'

'How many of them?'

Ted shrugged. 'It's dark when I pick them up. I just drive the bus.'

'Two? Four? Twenty-four?' Mick questioned.

Ted sighed, seeing Mick was obviously not going to give up. 'Three. There're three of them, but I don't know who. They keep their faces covered.'

Mick's look was contemptuous. 'Shit! They're bringing in scores of police from all over the country just for three bloody scabs who daren't even show their faces.'

'Aye, well, people have to make a living,' Ted lashed out.

Mick advanced on him. 'We all want to make a living, Mr Laws. But you have to stand by your marras. If you don't stand up for what's right together then you haven't got anything.'

Ted gave his smoker's cough and spat into the sink again. 'I just drive a bus. It's me job. Proud tells me what to do and I do it. I didn't have a job for six years until he gave me one. I'm fifty-five. If I lose this one, who's ganin' to give me another one at my age, eh?'

'And is it right to let a man like Proud frighten you into doing his dirty work? He doesn't care about you or any of us. He only thinks about making money for himself, making a fortune out of the misery of others, out of us lads on strike. He's probably got contracts to bring in scab labour to all the pits in the north, knowing Vic Proud. And you're breaking the strike by bringing those lads in an' all.'

Ted stabbed the chopping board with the paring knife. 'I don't belong to any union so I can cross any picket line I like!'

Mick gave him a long despairing look and saw him flinch away. 'Your missus used to work in the pit canteen, didn't she, Mr Laws? She'd have known what a picket line was for,' he said quietly and turned to go. As he reached the front door he heard Ted call after him in a tremulous voice.

'I pick them up at the back of the police station. They come by taxi. That's all I know.'

Mick heard him sob, so did not go back into the kitchen. Ta, Mr Laws,' he replied and let himself out of the house, leaving Ted the dignity of crying unobserved.

Mick determined to wait up all night if necessary to catch the strike-breakers. He would attempt to talk them out of scabbing before they boarded the bus. The police would not let the pickets near them, but he might stand a chance before the bus joined the convoy. At the very least he could find out who they were and then his father could go round and try to talk some sense into them at home. Besides, he could no longer bear to stay in his house alone. Eddy called to see if he fancied a half-pint at The Ship.

'I think I'll go over and see how Grandda is,' Mick told his uncle.

'I'll come with you then,' Eddy said, amiable as ever.

'You don't have to keep watch over me day and night,' Mick smiled. 'I'm not going to do anything daft.'

'No, but I might,' Eddy grinned, 'so you've a duty to keep an eye on me.'

Mick laughed. 'Mam's told you to follow me, hasn't she?'

Eddy shook his head. 'No, but Carol did.'

Mick flushed and pulled on his leather jacket. Eddy clapped him round the shoulders. 'Listen, lad, I'm not blind. I can see things aren't champion between the two of you, but I know that Carol cares about you. Things'll work themselves out once this is all over. If you love each other as much as I think you do, it'll come back with time. You don't just stop loving someone overnight. But you've got to show Carol you care too.'

Mick shrugged him off, embarrassed by talk of such personal feelings. 'Did you get that off one of your Johnny Matthis records, Eddy?' he teased.

Eddy laughed and dropped his arm. 'Haway, you cheeky bugger. Did I ever tell you about the time I met Johnny Matthis in a club in Soho?'

'Aye, and he was a waiter named after the famous singer.'

'Spoiling me punch line again,' Eddy complained.

Mick grinned and followed his uncle out into the lane.

Cutting across the park where a game of bowls was taking place in the dying sun, it took them fifteen minutes to reach Arthur Bowman's retirement cottage, built by the miners' union in the thirties. The house was in shadow and no smoke rose from the chimney, even though Grandda was still getting his pensioner's entitlement to free coal. The small, neat garden in front was a riot of late blooms but there was no sign of the old man pottering about his domain.

'Maybe it's dominoes night,' Eddy shrugged.

'No, he's always in on a Monday night,' Mick answered, puzzled.

They went inside and called, but there was no reply. Searching the small house, they found it empty and chill. Mick shivered, then something brushed his leg and he sprang back.

'It's Smoky,' Eddy laughed at him, bending to stroke Arthur's old cat. Smoky dribbled with delight and gave his bronchial purr. 'You wheeze louder than the old man,' Eddy said, scratching it behind the ears. 'Are you going to tell us where he is then?'

The cat meowed and then circled Eddy's legs.

Mick went back out of the house with impatience. 'Talking to the cat's not getting us anywhere.'

'Smoky knows where he is, don't you, boy?' Eddy insisted, following the cat into the garden.

'Smoky's a girl,' Mick snorted.

'No wonder she likes me then,' Eddy grinned. The cat jumped up on the garden fence and leapt out of sight into the dense undergrowth behind, which hid an old railway line that had once run to the pit. Eddy looked set to follow.

'We'd be better off asking a neighbour,' Mick said and went to knock at the

177

bungalow next door. Mary Hunt, the talkative widow who was working for the Prouds to earn some money for her striking family, came to the door.

'He'll be down the old railway track like he usually is,' she told them.

'Why?' Mick asked.

'Hunting for coal, of course,' Mary replied. 'He's at it most evenings when it starts to get dark.'

'But he doesn't need to do that.'

'What else is he going to get a fire going with?' Mary demanded. 'He gives his ration away to that family down the hill with the five bairns. I knew he wouldn't have told his own family. That's Arthur for you.' She seemed pleased to know something they did not. 'I told him he ought to stop, they're policing the line now, but he won't listen.'

'Haway and let's look for him,' Eddy said. 'Ta very much, Mrs Hunt.'

They climbed a fence at the end of the lane and jumped into the gloomy undergrowth of brambles and nettles, cursing the stubborn old miner.

'Thinks he's Robin-bloody-Hood,' Eddy muttered.

'Aye, and at his age with a bad chest. Daft old bugger,' Mick agreed, wincing as a bramble tore into his arm.

'Gan canny,' Eddy warned, 'we don't want you running into any coppers either.'

They searched for twenty minutes without finding him, as the evening sky dimmed to a deep violet and a stiff onshore breeze rustled the bushes around them. The old track was long overgrown, though Mick could remember it in the sixties, busy with rattling coal trucks trundling off to the staithes further up the coast. Grandda used to tell him they were taking coal to the large power stations in the south-east - 'Bringing light to the heathens of the south,' he had often chuckled. As a boy Mick had been forbidden to go near the line which belonged to the Coal Board and he knew he was trespassing now and breaking the conditions of his bail.

He pressed on grimly, angry that the thought should worry him. For what use was a deserted railway line to anyone but blackberry pickers and old men like Grandda Bowman trying to do his best for his destitute neighbours?

As they reached the brow of the embankment, just where it dipped gently down towards the pit, Eddy gave a shout.

'There he is! Down in the cutting.'

Mick peered and saw the frail, stooped figure of his grandfather bending over and digging the weedy cinder track with a garden trowel. He was working methodically along one side of the cutting; bending, digging, lifting some small nugget of coal dropped twenty years ago and then pausing before shovelling it carefully into an old shopping bag on wheels. After a moment's rest he began again, inching his way up the line. Smoky was with him, circling the operation like a watchful pit deputy. As Mick and Eddy drew closer, they could hear the old man chatting to the cat as he worked, his breath coming in laboured wheezes like a squeaking bellows.

Mick felt a lump forming in his throat at the sight. He remembered Grandda telling him how they had gone on to the pit heap to steal coal during the lock-out in '26 and how his cousin Albert had been caught and fined and gone to prison because he could not pay. And they had thought those bad old days had gone for ever! Hadn't his grandfather already had more than his share of hard times?

'It's not right,' Mick fumed. 'He shouldn't have to do this, Eddy.'

His uncle nodded. 'Aye, and your nana would spin in the cemetery if she knew he was using her tartan shopping bag for carrying coal.'

They descended into the shadowy cutting.

'Haway, Grandda!' Eddy called. 'You've done enough thieving for one night.'

The old miner jerked up in fright; he had not heard them approaching. For a moment he did not recognise them and Mick wondered if his grandfather's mind had wandered into the past as he worked.

'Oh, it's you, lad.' Arthur coughed with relief. 'For a minute I thought you were coppers.'

'Guilty conscience,' Eddy teased. 'Come on, give us that bag and we'll get you off home.'

'I'll just sit here for a minute and catch me breath.'

Mick, seeing he was tired out, tried to help him on to the grassy bank, but he squatted down stubbornly on his haunches and pulled out a tin of snuff. Dabbing the brown powder on to the back of his hand, he held it to his whiskery nostrils and snorted it in. A few seconds later he gave an enormous sneeze that sent Smoky leaping for cover.

'By, you oldtimers know how to enjoy yourselves,' Eddy chuckled.

'Who told you I was here?' Arthur asked.

'Smoky,' Eddy said.

'It was that interfering wife, Mary, wasn't it?' he grumbled.

'Mam would go light if she knew you were down here,' Mick scolded.

'Don't fuss over me, lad.'

'The place is swarming with police since morning, Grandda,' Mick said more gently. 'You shouldn't be out here.'

The old man turned to look at him and Mick could see the desolation in his face. He shook his head. 'I've lived through this all before, bonny lad,' he sighed. 'Did you know they turned the hoses on us to knock us off the spoil heap for picking dross? I swore I'd never let it happen to me own bairns. But I never thought to see me grandbairns suffering ...' He broke off, unable to finish, his eyes filling with tears.

'Haway, Grandda,' Mick said, reaching out to take his arm. 'Let's get you back.'

As they heaved the old man up, a flash of light darted at the end of the cutting and Mick heard voices and the tramp of feet. He glanced towards the bend where the old line disappeared into the colliery yard and saw two dark figures walking towards them.

'Coppers,' he hissed to Eddy.

'Bloody hell, that's all we need,' Eddy groaned. 'You get yourself out of here sharp, Mick.'

'I'm not leaving Grandda here with this coal.' Mick was adamant.

'Haway then and get him up the bank. The fence looks broken at the top,' Eddy urged.

But Arthur had stopped still, his face ashen in the twilight. Mick saw fear tense his features and felt the claw-like grip on his grandfather's hand tighten on his arm.

They'll have us,' he gasped. 'They'll have us, our Albert!'

'Grandda, it's Mick,' he tried to reassure the confused widower. 'Take his other

179

arm, Eddy.'

They heaved the trembling man between them, abandoning the shopping trolley, and began to clamber up the embankment. But the old man tripped and fell, scrambling on his hands and knees in his haste to get away. His breathing was heavy and erratic. 'Don't leave me, Albert.'

Mick heaved him up again, while Eddy searched in the dark for a way through the fence. They heard shouts further up the line and the two policemen began to run towards them, flashing their torches along the bank.

'Hoy! What you up to?' one demanded. 'Stop! This is private property!'

'Over here, Mick!' Eddy called.

Grandda cried, 'Don't leave the coal!'

Mick hauled his grandfather to the fence and thrust him at Eddy who was holding the broken fencing back to let them through.

'I'm going back for the bag - they'll trace it to Grandda,' Mick panted.

'Leave the sodding bag, man!' Eddy cried. But Mick was already scrambling back down the line. He grabbed his grandmother's prize shopping bag, but he had miscalculated just how close the policemen were. A moment later, he was dazzled by a torch shone in his eyes.

'It's Mick Todd.'

'Grab him!' the other cried.

'I'm not running,' Mick answered sharply, shaking off the young man's hold, then realised it was Carol's brother. 'Simon!'

'What the hell are you doing down here?' Simon asked him.

'What does it look like?' Mick said.

'Looks like you're stealing from the Coal Board,' the older man answered. Mick did not recognise him as a local man. 'Do you know this thief?'

'He's my brother-in-law,' Simon answered, embarrassed.

'Not the one who thumped your old man?' the officer crowed.

'That's just rumour,' Simon said stiffly.

'Too soft to press charges, I'd heard,' his colleague said with contempt. 'Don't know why he wants to protect scum like this.' He jabbed his torch at Mick's face, blinding him for an instant. 'Who else was with you?'

'No one.'

'Lying bastard! Get up the bank, Shannon, and see who they are.'

Simon hesitated an instant and then ran up the embankment, finding the gap in the fence with his torch. Through on the other side he saw Eddy Todd crouching in the grass with old Arthur Bowman. He knew the retired miner from his childhood; he was some distant relation of his mother's, according to Carol. The old man was whimpering and Eddy tried to shield him from the harsh light. They said nothing.

Simon switched off his torch and turned away. He scrambled back down the bank.

'Whoever it was, they've gone,' he told his colleague.

Mick caught the briefest of glances from Simon and knew he had saved his relations.

'Well, we've got this one,' the other policeman said with harsh satisfaction. 'Let's get him up the police station.'

'Just a warning would do, wouldn't it?' Simon suggested. 'I mean, it's just a bag of dross he's got, probably not even his.'

The other man gave him a sharp look. 'You're too pally by half with these people. You better remember who your mates are, Shannon. You stick up for your fellow officers, not riffraff like this hairy yob. Get it, Shannon?'

'Yeah, you're right,' Simon replied evenly. 'It's just he's a relation of Superintendent Bowman. Why cause embarrassment when there are more important fish to catch?'

But the other officer advanced on Mick, blinding him again with his torch. 'I thought I'd seen you before. You're that lunatic who lay in front of the bus this morning, aren't you? Well, you haven't got Bowman here to protect you now!' He looked triumphant. 'We're here to do a job and we're going to do it. Get him back up the line and into the van.'

Simon threw Mick a look of apology. Mick said nothing, only thankful that his grandfather and Eddy were safe.

He sat around for an age at the police station waiting to be questioned while forms were filled in and they took his fingerprints and photograph. But the inspector made it plain he thought it was a waste of time and Mick was finally released in the early hours of the morning without being charged. Exhausted, but worried about his grandfather, he made his way through the empty streets back to the retirement cottages.

The house was in darkness and Mick was about to leave, thankful that the old man was sleeping peacefully, when Mary Hunt startled him by appearing on her doorstep.

'By, what a carry on!' she whispered loudly. 'Your mam's been over, worried sick about you. And poor Arthur!'

'What about him, Mrs Hunt?' Mick asked.

'Poorly bad he is. Taken him off to the hospital. Heart attack. Your mam's gone with him. Poor Lotty, worried stiff. I told him he should never have gone down the cutting, but he wouldn't listen.'

'It's not your fault, Mrs Hunt. Don't you worry yourself. Grandda's a tough old boot, he'll survive.'

But as Mick turned away and headed off to Septimus Street, his heart was full of dread.

By the time he reached his parents' house, his mother was already back from the hospital in Whittledene. Auntie Val was there too, sobbing into Eddy's shoulder.

'Your father tried to find you,' Lotty told him, her eyes red from crying. 'Grandda died in the ambulance. They tried to revive him, but he never came round again.'

Mick went across and put his arms about her shoulders as she sobbed in grief. He was numb with shock.

He should have been with his grandfather - would have been with him if he had not gone back for the bag of coal. Perhaps it might never have happened if he had been there to help Eddy.

'I should've been there!' he cried in anguish.

'No, son,' Eddy tried to calm him, 'it was always going to happen.'

'Eddy's right,' Charlie agreed. 'All that humping coal up the railway line was too much for him.'

Mick spun round, his face haggard. 'I'll tell you what was too much for him, being chased by the coppers like a criminal. He thought he was back with his

181

cousin Albert in twenty-six. He was terrified for his life. That poor old man. He should've been left in peace to enjoy his retirement. I can't take any more of this!' Mick cried.

'Listen to me, lad.' Charlie rushed to him and gripped him tight. 'None of us will have any peace any more because of what they're doing to our village.' His face burned with fury and determination. 'We've lost too much already in this strike but we've got to win it, else we've lost everything. We owe it to your grandda to come out of this fighting. And that means stopping those lads going into the pit in a few hours' time.'

Mick looked at him through his pain and guilt and rage and something inside him snapped.

'I know where they get on the bus,' he said hoarsely. 'And I'm bloody well going to stop them!' He turned and blundered out of the house before they could stop him.

'Oh, Charlie!' Lotty wailed.

As Charlie moved to follow, Eddy sprang up. 'I'll go.'

'Both go,' Lotty urged. 'If anyone can calm our Mick down, Eddy can. Val will stay with me.'

The sisters watched from the window as the men disappeared into the dark.

'Look at that,' Val gasped in disbelief. 'You're being watched.'

Lotty peered and saw a panda car parked at the top of the lane. The lights were out, but a figure sat inside. Whose house were they watching and for whom were they waiting? For the first time she felt real fear at what was happening.

She clutched her sister's arm. 'Oh, Val, I wish Carol was back. I'm really scared what Mick might do. If only Carol was here!'

Chapter Twenty-Five

Carol got as far as the steps to Pete's hotel. She sat on them for several minutes, undecided, fighting with her conflicting emotions. She felt hurt and betrayed by Kelly's revelation and yet it was something that had happened before she and Mick had gone out. Was it fair to blame him for that? And what if he really had not known about their baby? Surely if he had he would have stood by Kelly and married her? It was the way Todds were - loyal.

So what was she doing about to seek comfort from another man? How could she act so disloyally, no matter how wounded she felt?

She wandered off towards the harbour and watched the fishing boats slip out in the dawn. Eventually she huddled on a park bench, smoked three cigarettes and then dozed until a light drizzle woke her.

Achingly tired and chilled through, she headed back to the hostel, with the uncomfortable thought that if Kelly had kept her baby and Mick had married her, there would have been no Laura. How different her own life would have been. She would never have had those first happy years with Mick, would probably never have stayed in Brassbank at all.

And battered though her spirits felt, Carol knew that she did not regret the course her life had taken. She belonged in Brassbank with Mick and Laura, with the Todds and her friends in the Women's Group. In that moment of clarity, she knew that her dangerous flirtation with Pete Fletcher was over. However strained her relationship with Mick, she was not going to give up and run away. Mick needed her and she would return to Brassbank determined to make things better between them. What had happened between him and Kelly was tragic, but it was in the past and none of them could do anything to change that. What mattered now was how she was going to deal with Kelly's affair with Vic and the explosive news that Kelly was carrying Vic's baby.

She lay on her bed for an hour before the girls woke up. She shivered at the thought of how outraged and hurt Fay would be, and yet, in a strange way, she felt sorry for Kelly too. Her friend was so troubled; latching on to a dream to escape a lifetime of unhappiness. And then there was poor Sid . . .

At breakfast, Carol tried to catch Kelly's attention but she avoided her. She was also aware of a coolness among some of the other women towards her and wondered quite what they had overheard the previous night, or what had been whispered about her when she had disappeared with Pete.

When Pete came to find her later in the morning, there was a tension about the group. The children were restless, cooped up indoors as the rain teemed down outside, so May and June led some of them off briskly for a swim. The weather had broken and suddenly for Carol the magic had gone out of the holiday. She began to feel unsettled too, her thoughts turning more and more to home. She became impatient for the holiday to end and for her and Laura to return to Brassbank. Yet there were five more days to go.

'Explain to me over coffee,' Pete suggested, aware that something had happened.

Carol was doubtful, but agreed, 'I'll meet you after the swim.'

Later, while Laura went to the pictures with the others, Carol told Linda to go and lie down while she pushed Calvin out in his pram. She met Pete across the harbour and told him of her terrible row with Kelly.

'Did you know she was having an affair with Vic?' Carol asked.

Pete shrugged. 'No, but it doesn't surprise me. Vic's always been greedy.' He tried to take her hand, but she pulled away. 'There's something else bothering you, though, isn't there?'

Carol nodded and told him of the revelation about Mick and Kelly's first pregnancy.

'Do you think it's possible Mick didn't know?' she whispered.

'Do you?' Pete questioned. Carol shrugged. Pete sighed. 'Does it really matter after all this time? Wouldn't you have married Mick anyway, even if you'd known? People make mistakes, Carol. Wouldn't it have been a greater mistake for Mick to have married Kelly out of pity? She wouldn't have been any happier in the long run.'

'I suppose you're right,' Carol nodded. She smiled at him. 'You've been very understanding, Pete. Thanks for your friendship.'

He regarded her a moment. 'That sounds a bit formal - and a bit final, somehow.'

'Aye,' Carol said quietly, 'it is. I think it's time you interviewed someone else, Pete, another group. I've got far too involved. It's not fair on you, or me family. I've been feeling too sorry for myself these past weeks, but now I've had time to think about a lot of things.'

'And you're going to stick it out with Mick,' Pete said in a tight voice.

'It's not just a matter of sticking it out,' Carol answered. 'We need each other, and Laura needs us both. We'll never get through this strike in one piece if we don't do it together, I know that much. The future's so uncertain, but I need to be back home to help see it through. I couldn't go anywhere else or be with anyone else while me family and village have their backs to the wall. It's where I must be.'

They looked at each other for a long moment.

'They're lucky to have you,' Pete said wistfully.

'No,' Carol answered gently, 'I'm the lucky one. Without them I have nothing.'

Calvin woke and instantly began to cry and they abandoned their half-drunk coffees. Outside in the rain, Pete gave her a sad smile.

'Will you say goodbye to Laura for me?'

Carol nodded. At the moment of parting, she could not find the words.

'I'll let you know when the piece is broadcast,' he said more lightly. Then, 'Take care of yourself, won't you?'

'Aye, and you.' Carol swallowed hard. They did not touch.

She turned abruptly away, shooshing the fretful baby, and wheeled him quickly across the bridge. She thought for a moment how different her life would be if she took the future that Pete held out to her - easier, more comfortable, more varied, more exciting. But ultimately rootless. Her spirit would gradually starve without the nourishment of deep ties and bonds of family and community that made her who she was.

That afternoon, Carol rang home to speak to Mick, despite his order that she should not. There was no reply. She tried again each hour until after eleven that evening, but no one answered. She tried Lotty's, but no one was at home. She went to bed wondering where they were and lay awake for hours, anxious at what might be happening. Unable to sleep, she got up and went outside for a cigarette. Dark-headed Denise appeared silently from behind and startled her.

'I've been helping Linda with Calvin's late feed,' she explained.

'You're a good friend to our Linda,' Carol smiled and offered her a cigarette.

'She needs them with a husband like hers,' Denise said with a grimace. 'She should've left Dan before he walked out on her. Do you know she's been ringing him all week at his mam's?'

'Never?' Carol was amazed.

'Aye. Says he wants her back now and that she's going to gan back to the flat after the holiday instead of to her mam's. Needs her head examined.'

It was the first time Carol had heard Denise criticise Dan so openly. 'She hasn't told me any of this,' she said, a little hurt.

'No, well, you've had your mind on other things recently,' Denise said, giving her a guarded look.

Carol blushed and changed the subject swiftly. 'Have you heard any news from home? I'm worried something's happening we don't know about.'

'No, but I don't think they'd tell us, would they? In case we decided to come home early.'

'Aye,' Carol sighed, 'that's true. I'm getting no reply from anyone.'

'I wouldn't worry. They'll be working hard at the Welfare, that's all.'

Carol felt reassured by the girl's common sense. Denise had grown up before her very eyes these past months. She stubbed out her cigarette and turned to go in.

'I'll tell you something strange, mind,' Denise added.

'What's that?'

'Kelly's not back.'

Carol tensed. 'She'll be having a last drink somewhere.'

'No,' Denise frowned. 'She hasn't been here all day. Went off in a taxi when you lot went swimming and hasn't been back. Took all her clothes. Do you think she's gone home?'

Carol's heart missed a beat. If she had, then she and Vic were probably dropping their explosive news this very moment. She tried to imagine her family coping with such an unforeseen crisis, but could not. It would be one scandal too much for her parents.

'Oh, Denise,' Carol fretted, 'I wish we were all home. I just have this feeling . . .' She shrugged helplessly. How could she begin to explain her dread at the unknown?

Mick stormed through the deserted streets of Brassbank with Eddy and Charlie running to catch up with him. He would not be calmed. Inside he boiled with fury and grief for his grandfather, dying in fear and pain, haunted by past ghosts and the dread that history was repeating itself.

'Look behind you, man Mick!' Eddy hissed. 'We're being followed. They'll pick you up before we get anywhere near the bus.'

Mick glanced behind and saw the police car crawling behind them, further up the street but near enough to let them know they were being watched. Mick stopped.

'You're breaking your bail again. They could nick you any time. They're just waiting to see where you'll lead them,' Charlie reasoned. 'Come home and get a bit of kip while you can.'

Mick's shoulders drooped suddenly. They were right, there was nothing useful he could do by letting the police chase him around the village. They would never let him get anywhere near the pick-up point.

'Will you go later and find out who they are?' Mick pleaded with his uncle. 'Ted says he picks them up behind the police station.'

Eddy sighed. 'If you promise to gan home and keep your head down, I will.'

Mick turned round. Ta, Eddy.'

The three of them walked back to Septimus Street together and Lotty settled her son on the settee under a blanket. Charlie left for the Welfare Hall to organise the picket. Later, when the others were asleep, Eddy slipped out the front door, knowing any patrol car would be watching the back.

There were signs of activity everywhere as he drew closer to the police station. They were obviously gearing up for a large presence to see the working miners into the pit. Today would be their greatest battle yet. He did not see any way he could get nearer the police station without being seen. Giving up, he was about to turn back down the hill when a pale green metallic Granada slipped past him and stopped at the junction ahead. It struck him immediately as familiar. Right opposite him, the driver wound down his window and flicked out a cigarette end. Eddy only saw his face for seconds but long enough to recognise Dan Hardman, driving old man Hardman's car.

An instant later and he had turned at the junction and disappeared into the station yard.

Dan! Eddy whistled in shock. What would Charlie and Lotty say when they knew their son-in-law was strike-breaking? And Mick? He had always stuck up for the young miner and taken him under his wing on picketing duties. Why had he not come to talk to Mick or any of them before taking such a drastic step? Eddy felt he was carrying a lead weight as he turned for home and ran off down the back street with his terrible news.

Mick was already up drinking tea with Lotty. Their sadness was palpable. For a moment he debated whether to tell them what he had seen, but his face must have betrayed him.

'Who did you see?' Mick asked at once. 'It's someone we know, isn't it?'

Eddy let out a long sigh. 'I couldn't get near enough, but I did see someone driving into the police yard. It's possible he was there for another reason. I mean, I didn't see him actually getting on a bus . . .'

Mick was on his feet. 'Who, Eddy?' he demanded.

'Dan.'

Lotty gasped, but Mick said nothing. He could not speak. His whole face was gripped in disbelief. Then his fists tensed up and he felt his throat fill up with bile.

'Not Dan,' he choked. 'Not without telling me first.' He smashed a fist on the table and knocked over his mug of tea. 'Stupid little bastard!'

'Mick!' Lotty cried, rising to calm him.

'I'll make him change his mind,' Mick growled and made for the door.

'Eddy, go after him,' Lotty pleaded. 'I'll go and tell Charlie.'

But Mick was gone and running up the lane before they could scramble out of the house. Eddy cursed himself for having told what he had seen. He should have realised what an emotional state Mick was in; his nephew could not cope with this extra shock.

Mick ran until his lungs heaved for air in the drizzly dawn, making straight for the pit gates. Dan had been accepted and helped by the Todd family, even when he had not wanted to stand by Linda and the baby. But Mick had helped him see sense and accept that he had responsibilities; they had talked about how Linda would go back to him after the holiday. Mick had worried about Dan staying with the Hardmans who were so against the strike, but he had thought Dan could stand up to them. Mick had said Carol and the Women's Group would help the young family in every way they could, and the union would help them too. Dan had agreed to swallow his pride and come down for free meals at the Welfare, and there would be food parcels for baby Calvin. But all the time Dan was secretly going behind their backs and planning to betray them by returning to work! Mick fumed. Dan had rejected them and taken the bribes of men like Ben Shannon to save his own skin. He was beyond contempt! He would pay for his treachery, Mick swore. He had not spent the last six months watching his family lose everything, seeing Carol drifting away from him and the village reduced to poverty just for his selfish brother-in-law to smash their unity and render the sacrifices futile.

As he raced towards the picket, Mick's anger and bitterness overwhelmed him. Relief would only come by giving Dan Hardman his punishment.

Charlie had gone early to the picket. They had expected reinforcements from out of the area but they had not arrived. Rumours were spreading that the top of the village had been sealed off and the flying pickets had been turned back miles away from Brassbank. The streets echoed with an eerie quiet. It was too quiet, Charlie realised. There was no early morning bustle common to the pit village; people had been frightened off the streets by patrols of police on foot and the anonymous vans gathering on the hill.

Then, out of the dark, the convoy began to move. Engines revved and motorcycles roared, shattering the tense silence. The men around him shifted and braced themselves for trouble; some began to shout.

'Clear the road!' a loud-hailer called. 'Stand back! Stand back now!'

The pushing and shoving started. As the bus came into view, the scuffling broke into fights. Van doors flew open and police in riot gear jumped out, charging at the miners to clear them off the road. The bus was not going to stop today, Charlie realised; it was hurtling towards the gates. Men fell back and the gates behind them clanged open. Soon it would all be over and they would have sustained an important symbolic defeat - the day Brassbank solidarity broke and scab labour signed on at the pit.

From somewhere there was a sudden splintering crash. Charlie looked up at the passing bus and saw a brick had smashed the front windscreen. The rest of the bus was impregnable, the windows protected with wire mesh, but the front was now shattered. The bus veered into one of the gates, narrowly missing several men, and crashed to a squealing halt.

There was confusion everywhere. Men shouted, surged forward. Police swarmed around the immobile bus.

'Get the door open!' someone yelled. 'Let them out!'

As police formed a human barrier, the bus door hissed open and the hooded travellers clattered quickly down the steps. There was uproar at the sight of them. Beyond, Charlie could see Ted Laws standing dazed by the driving seat, his head bleeding.

Men surged and jostled to reach the strike-breakers, screaming their hate. But the first two bulky men were swiftly out of the bus and running for the safety of the pit yard. Only one slighter built man was hesitating, petrified by the sights around him.

'Come on, hurry up!' an officer bawled.

Suddenly Charlie saw Mick move up behind the officer and hurl him out of the way.

'Hardman, I'll have you!'

The masked figure hesitated a moment longer, then Mick was lunging at his head and pulling his balaclava off to reveal Dan's ashen face. Mick knocked him off the steps. There was pandemonium: Mick shouting incoherently, Dan screaming. But the police were soon on the miners, pulling them apart. Charlie saw one kick Mick in the back, making him release his grip on the terrified Dan and then lay into him with a truncheon.

Charlie went to his son's aid, still stunned by the sight of his son-in-law unmasked as a scab. He threw himself between Mick and the policeman, taking the blows of the truncheon upon his own back and head. Mick, who was doubled up on the ground, was able to scramble to his feet. He looked dazed and confused. A moment later, someone pushed Charlie out of the way and several policemen seized Mick, dragging him back with them into their ranks.

Charlie turned to see Dan, blood dripping from his mouth, being bundled beyond the pit gates. After him ran Ted Laws, escaping his immobile bus, clutching his bloodied head. The gates closed and the men fell back. As Charlie looked to see what had happened to Mick, some of the miners turned on the bus instead, wreaking their revenge and frustration on the vehicle that had brought in the scabs.

'Proud's are bastards!'

'This one'll not bring in any more scabs!'

'Turn it over!'

Makeshift missiles, bricks and debris from the waste ground around, rained on to the bus. The police fell back from the volatile crowd, their main mission accomplished. The security cameras put there during the week, watching like unblinking eyes above the pit gates, would identify the offenders later.

Eddy appeared at Charlie's side, gawping at the sight of the bus being battered. Several men were now trying to heave it over. At the third attempt they succeeded.

'They've got Mick,' Charlie said, full of anger, kicking the ground.

Eddy nodded. 'I saw. Did he smash the window?'

Charlie shrugged. 'I didn't see who did it.'

'He'll be for the high jump now, mind.'

Charlie swung round, glaring furiously. 'I know that! And all for that bloody Hardman boy and after all Mick's done for him. I tell you now, Eddy, Dan Hardman will never cross my doorstep again.'

'Watch out!' Eddy cried, pulling Charlie back with him.

A flash of vivid light lit the dawn sky and then flared crazily. The bus was on fire. The two brothers leapt back to safety, cursing the way things had spiralled out of control. A siren wailed in the distance and Charlie looked up the hill to see the riot police regrouping, extra men pouring out of the back of instant response unit vans. Charlie knew they would be powerless to defend themselves. He had heard so many tales of violence around picket lines from the travelling pickets but he never thought it would come to Brassbank. They would always be solid behind the strike, Charlie had believed. They were Durham men who had proved themselves for generations as loyal to the union asto their own kin.

But as the dark waves of police swept down on them once more, Charlie's faith was shattered. And the spectre of 1926, buried in his childish memory for so long, rose up to haunt him. His own father had defended him then, but just now he had been powerless to protect his own son from arrest.

'What do we do now?' Eddy asked, quite at a loss.

Charlie answered with bleak determination, 'Remember the lodge banner, "Never Stand Alone". That's what we do, Eddy, we stand with the others.' He stepped forward, fists bunched, his square face set. 'And we fight!'

Chapter Twenty-Six

The news reached the women in Whitby later that day. Sid rang them from Joanne's to tell them of the picket line trouble and several arrests. Carol spoke to him briefly.

'Sorry, pet, but Mick's been arrested - his dad an' all.'

Carol was stunned. 'But what happened?'

Sid explained quickly about the return to work of three Brassbank miners. 'Mick stopped the bus going in the first day,' Sid told her proudly. 'But there was all hell on this morning. Mick had a go at one of the scabs. They say it was Dan Hardman.'

Carol gasped. 'Never!'

'Listen; don't tell your Linda until things are clearer, eh?' Sid suggested. 'We're sending a bus down to collect you all tomorrow.'

'I wish I could be back sooner,' Carol said, trying to control her voice. 'Is Mick all right?'

There was a pause, then Sid said, 'We're trying to find out where they're holding him. We'll know more by the time you're back.'

Carol could not speak. She felt faint at the thought of what might happen to Mick now. And Charlie arrested too. What a blow to their resistance.

Just as she was about to ring off, Sid asked, 'Can I speak to Kelly a minute?'

Carol's stomach lurched. So Kelly had not gone home yet. Where on earth could she be?

'Sorry, Sid, she's out,' Carol answered.

Sid grunted. 'Well, tell her I'll see her at home tomorrow.'

Carol agreed and rang off quickly. All the women were gathered in the dining room talking about the news. June was in tears because her husband Frankie was one of the arrested. May came over and hugged Carol.

'We'll stick by you, pet,' she comforted.

Carol wanted to cry at her kindness. 'Oh, May. What about poor Lotty?'

'The sooner we all get home the better,' Dot said. 'The men need us there more than ever.'

'Aye,' May agreed. 'Look what happens when we go off for a fortnight. They get themselves into bother, that's what! They're worse than the bairns.'

Carol wondered how she was going to get through the night waiting for the journey home. They had all packed and most of them were watching the TV with the children, or sitting out on the steps chatting quietly. The temperature had suddenly dropped with the onset of wet weather and Carol shivered in the dampness as she shared a cigarette with Denise. Summer was abruptly over.

'Will you look at that!' May exclaimed.

They turned to see a large yellow Dodge pulling up outside the hostel.

'Isn't that Uncle Eddy?' Denise asked.

Carol was on her feet and running down the steps to meet him. 'Eddy!' she cried and hugged him dearly as he climbed out of his huge battered old American car.

'Thought you'd find it hard waiting till the morra,' he smiled, 'and Lotty wants you back sharp.'

Carol had no idea how he had afforded the petrol to come down and fetch them, but she was thrilled to see him and hear that Lotty needed her.

'And can you take Linda and Calvin too?' Carol asked.

Eddy nodded. 'Aye, it's best if they come home now.'

Carol noticed the tension in his face but asked no more questions. She raced back into the hostel to fetch Laura and their luggage. When she emerged again, Eddy was sitting in the middle of a throng of women, answering their questions with his usual light banter. He was obviously not going to add to their worries while they were away from their husbands, Carol observed with fondness. Neither did he repeat any rumours about Dan being a scab in front of the others.

Linda became tearful as she said goodbye to Denise and seemed reluctant to go, but Eddy humoured her into the back of the car with the baby and Laura. As the sun set over the moors, the other women waved them away and promised to meet up as soon as they got home.

It was only in the privacy of Eddy's car that he began to tell them of the traumatic events of the past days. When he told them of Grandda Bowman's death, Linda burst into floods of tears and Eddy had to pull the car into a lay-by while they calmed her down. Later, when they were on the road again and Linda and Laura had dozed off in the back, exhausted from crying, Eddy told Carol what had happened subsequently.

Carol wanted to cry herself when she heard how Dan had betrayed them; she understood how Mick had lost all reason.

'Charlie and me were caught up in the scuffle after the bus was burned but I was sent home. The others are being kept in. They'll be up before the mags tomorrow.'

Carol's heart was leaden. She knew Mick was in real trouble this time. He had assaulted Dan Hardman and probably caused the bus to crash in the first place. She should have been there! Perhaps she could have stopped him. And dear Grandda dead. She wanted to weep.

They arrived back in the village after dark, but before they were halfway down the hill, Eddy was stopped at a roadblock.

'You can't take a vehicle down here,' the policeman told them.

'But we live down there,' Eddy said, 'in the rows.'

'Sorry,' the man looked apologetic, 'there's no traffic allowed on the lane up to the pit. You'll have to park here and walk down.'

Carol sprang out of the car and faced him. 'We've got a bairn and a two-month-old baby in the back! What do you mean we have to walk?'

'There's been a lot of trouble today, we're just making sure it's peaceful from now on,' he explained. 'I can get someone to help you carry things.'

'You've no right to stop us moving about our own village,' Carol said, furious. 'What are you, the bloody Gestapo?'

'Carol,' Eddy intervened, 'we're in enough bother as it is. Get in and I'll park the car.'

'Don't be so soft!' Carol said with contempt. 'He's no right to stop us driving to our own homes.'

Linda and the children began to stir in the back. 'What's wrong, Mam?' Laura said in alarm.

Carol glared at the policeman who was answering a crackling radio.

'Haway, Carol,' Eddy appealed to her, 'Lotty doesn't need you arrested an' all.'

Carol swallowed her fury and got back in the car. Eddy parked in a back lane and they trudged down the hill to Septimus Street, Carol carrying Laura while Eddy humped their cases.

Lotty was waiting up for them and both Linda and Carol fell into her arms with relief. There were tears and talk well into the night and Linda was finally told about Dan's return to work and Mick's attack. She howled with distress and woke Calvin and Laura. Carol could not comfort her daughter who screamed for her daddy and wailed that she would never see him again.

'You shouldn't have taken me on holiday, Mam,' Laura sobbed. 'It's all your fault! I want my daddy!'

Eventually Lotty managed to calm the child and she lay down on the bed beside her granddaughter, while Carol slept fitfully on Laura's other side. In the morning, still exhausted, Linda insisted she was going to return to Dan and rang his parents. Dan had been discharged from hospital but was off work with concussion. Reluctantly his father agreed to come and pick her up with the baby later.

Lotty was close to tears. 'Please stay with us, pet,' she pleaded, 'at least until your father comes home.'

'He might not be coming home,' Linda snapped. 'Any road, you're all against me and Dan now. How can I stay here after what Mick did? I'm going back to Dan. He's the one who needs me.'

'Let her go,' Carol said, exhausted and resigned. 'We can't run her life for her for ever.' She looked at the fretful Calvin and thought how wrong it was that he was having to drink watered-down condensed milk for some of his feeds because they could not afford the baby formula. At least if Linda went back to Dan, their baby might have a better chance of survival. There would be a wage coming in, Carol thought with a twinge of resentment, and for the first time glimpsed why Linda might be leaving.

She said, 'You go up and have a wash. I'll give Calvin his bottle. Then Eddy can take you over to the Hardmans'. There's no need for Mr Hardman to come here.'

Linda looked at her with suspicion but did as she suggested. Lotty sat down and wept while Carol cradled Calvin.

'Oh God, I can't bear it!'

'It's probably for the best that Linda's gone when Charlie gets home,' Carol said. 'He might take it out on the lass. Linda will come back if she needs us.' But silently she doubted whether Linda would ever return to Septimus Street, or whether she would ever be accepted there again. She knew that Dan certainly would not. She hugged Calvin tighter.

They listened to the sounds of Laura kicking a ball against the back wall, like she so often did with her father. It made Carol want to weep for her young daughter, frightened and confused by what was going on. But she knew she had to be strong for them all, stronger than she had ever been before. Lotty's courage was crumbling in the face of her father's sudden death and the arrests of her husband and son. Carol had to carry the burden for them all until her mother-in-law recovered.

'Here, Mam,' she said gently, holding out Calvin, 'take your grandson for a bit of a cuddle.'

Lotty blew her nose and put on a brave face, then took the baby in her arms.

'Oh, you poor little lamb,' she crooned as she rocked him close to her, 'what sort of future will you have?'

Mick was silent. He had learned from experience. He would not be tripped up by his questioners like before. It was all he had to fling back at them: defiance, silence.
'Where do you live?'
'Who are your next of kin?'
'Are you related to Charlie Todd?'
'You're a union activist, aren't you?'
'Your wife's mixed up in politics, isn't she?'
'Did you throw the brick?'
'You're a dangerous man. You could have got people killed. Did you ever stop to think of that?'
'How long had you planned your attack?'
'You've got a record of violence, haven't you? You're up on riot charges, aren't you?'
'You're an out-and-out criminal, masquerading as a striking miner, aren't you, Todd?'
'You're a piece of scum!'
'You're going away where you belong - among the rest of the filth.'
Silence. Mick answered no questions and reacted to no insults. He did not even confirm his name. He sat mute throughout and the more angry and impatient his questioners became, the more powerful he felt. They thought they had him beaten. But he - Mick Todd, son of Charlie Todd, grandson of legendary Michael Samuel Todd - was not beaten, would never be beaten.

In the afternoon, Eddy drove Lotty and Carol over to the magistrates' court in Whittledene. The other women had arrived back from Whitby and Denise had come straight round to Septimus Street. She had swiftly seen the state of things and taken Laura off to the park with a promise of a trip of Dimarco's on the way back. Paul Dimarco was well known for giving the children of the strikers free treats without them asking.

The court was packed with press and relations of the accused. Carol noticed with a jolt that Pete Fletcher was there among the reporters, but she glanced away when he tried to catch her eye. Lotty squeezed her hand and began to tremble when Charlie was led into the dock along with Frankie Burt and two others. There was a buzz among the press at the sight of him. The lodge deputy was a force to be reckoned with in Brassbank; he had masterminded much of their union resistance and here he was up on criminal charges.

The men were charged with minor riot offences, pleaded guilty and given suspended sentences of a year. Angry murmurings broke out in the courtroom, but Lotty clung to Carol in relief that Charlie was being released.

'Licence to give him hell for a year, that's what the suspended sentence means,' Eddy muttered to Carol. 'He'll have to stay squeaky clean.'

She could not speak, for her eyes were riveted to the sight of Mick being led out alone, between two police guards. He still wore the grubby clothes he had been arrested in and his hair looked unkempt, his unshaven face bruised and unwashed. But he stood defiant, composed, his blue eyes fixed on the magistrates, showing no fear. A huge lump formed in Carol's throat at the sight of her husband, so brave yet so alone.

He was charged with assault and criminal damage and remanded in custody pending trial at the Crown Court. He had broken his bail and would not be bailed again. Carol watched him standing there, erect and expressionless, silent throughout. And then he was being led away and the court broke out in noisy protest. They were all bundled out of the courtroom. Outside there were local television reporters pressing around them for interviews. Carol caught a glimpse of Pete Fletcher, but he was holding back and did not approach them.

'How do you feel about your husband's arrest?'

'How are you managing, Mrs Todd?'

'What do you think of Scargill and the strike now?'

The questions rained in on Carol as Eddy tried to steer her to the safety of the car. She was shaking with distress and rage. She wanted to speak back at them and say all the clever things she had said to rally people to their cause in the past. But she could not utter a word. All she could think of was Mick, somewhere in the building behind her being led away to a cell or a waiting security van to take him off to prison.

Prison! They had talked about it in theory before. They had even talked of it with pride when harking back to Mick's grandfather's heroic spell in prison in 1926. But this was reality. Mick, her once happy, uncomplicated, law-abiding husband, would be locked up like a common criminal while he awaited trial. The unthinkable had happened.

Carol hardly remembered getting home. Charlie and Lotty and Eddy were there and some of her friends came round to comfort and reassure her that he would soon be released. But all she could feel was a numb unreality.

Finally Eddy came back with some whisky from The Ship and poured her a large tot, then Lotty put her to bed. Carol passed out with fatigue sometime in the middle of the night, vaguely wishing she would never have to wake up.

The days passed in a blur. Carol insisted on staying with Laura at Dominion Terrace, feeling closer to Mick that way. She longed to see him, but it took Charlie a while to find out when she could visit him at the new high-security prison between Whittledene and Durham. Meanwhile, the trickle of returning miners continued and the battles grew more bitter.

The village seemed gripped by tension and suspicion. Police from other forces patrolled their streets, going into shops and harassing the wives of strikers, dropping lewd comments and making obscene gestures. Paul Dimarco put up a sign of protest, telling police on picket duty they would not be served in his cafe. One officer marched in and tore down the sign and deliberately knocked over a large bell jar of sweets from the counter, which smashed on the tiled floor.

At the pit gates the new police waved five pound notes at the pickets and walked by them in the late summer sun eating ice creams.

'When's the last time your kiddies had one of these?' one mocked.

'Carry on striking,' another crowed, 'the overtime's getting me a holiday to the Caribbean. Pity you'll never be able to afford a foreign holiday again,' he laughed. 'Bet your wife and kiddies love you for that!'

With each day that the convoy brought workers to the pit, relations in the village grew worse. By the weekend the place seethed with angry young miners, hanging around outside the chip shops and the pubs. But everywhere they gathered, vans of police turned up to move them on, harass them off the streets, taunting them into retaliation so that they could bundle them into the waiting vans.

Each night a patrol car sat outside the Todds' house and watched. Charlie was convinced the telephone was tapped and refused to answer it. Officers policed the back streets and the beach with dogs, chasing off the children who tried to pick coal from the tip.

Carol kept to the house, not wanting Laura to witness the intimidation or be frightened of the police. After all, her Uncle Simon and Auntie Kate were police officers and Carol did not want her mind turned against them because of what had happened to Mick. Yet inwardly she was bitter and hoped she would encounter neither her brother nor his wife around the village.

Finally Eddy managed to scrounge the petrol to take her out to Ridley Prison to see Mick, but on the way there, the ancient Dodge broke down and they were left stranded along a wet country lane until the local garage came to tow them away. Eddy had to abandon the car there, for he could not afford to have it repaired and he and Carol forlornly made their way home on the bus.

It was that night that Kelly appeared on her doorstep in a terrible state. Carol let her in quickly. She knew that Kelly had returned to the village on the same day as the trip from Whitby, but nothing seemed to have happened - no big scenes, no running off with Vic. She was back at home in the Birches with Sid, as far as Carol could tell, though she had not seen her to speak to until now.

Kelly crumpled on the settee in floods of tears. Carol went to get her a drink of water and closed the sitting-room door in case Laura was woken by the noise.

'Tell me,' Carol said gently, sitting down beside her friend and taking her hand.

'It's f-finished,' she sobbed. 'He's finished with me!'

'Victor?' Carol asked.

Kelly nodded.

Carol sighed. 'You told him about the baby then?'

Kelly nodded again.

'And he didn't like it?'

Kelly sniffed and said bitterly, 'He offered to pay to get rid of my baby - his baby! Said it didn't have to spoil things between us, we could go on as before. Think of it? I could never do that again. I want this baby so much. God, I hate him!'

'Aye, of course you want it,' Carol said, disturbed at the reminder of Kelly's abortion and thoughts of Mick's past. 'So he brought you back to Brassbank after you told him?'

Kelly blew her nose. 'He said he had to get back because there was trouble at work. He was just going to leave me there at his hotel to make me own way back! I said I'd make a big stink about our affair if he didn't take me with him, said I'd go straight to Fay and tell her what he'd done.' Kelly shuddered at the memory. 'He got really nasty. Said he'd sack me dad on the spot if I breathed a word of it and I'd be out the door at work too. Said he'd have me picked up by the police if I went anywhere near his house or family. Then he pushed me in his car and drove me back to Whitby and dumped me down the street from the hostel. It was just as well the bus hadn't already gone, 'cos I didn't know anything about the trip coming back early.'

Suddenly she turned to Carol. 'Oh, Carol, I'm so sorry! I've never even asked about Mick. And here you are with him in the nick and all I'm doing is giving you an earful of my troubles.' She put out her arms to Carol and they hugged in reconciliation.

'I tried to get to see him today but Eddy's car broke down,' Carol gulped, 'but we're hoping he'll be allowed out for Grandda's funeral.'

'I can take you next time he's allowed visitors,' Kelly offered at once.

'I don't know when that'll be,' Carol answered forlornly. 'But ta anyway.' She squeezed Kelly's hand. 'So what happened when you got back?'

Kelly gave a shuddering sigh. 'The first few days were all right. I went back to the office and Vic was hardly there. There's a load of work on with getting men back to work—' Kelly broke off, with a wary look.

'I bet there is,' Carol answered bitterly. 'Go on.'

'I thought Vic might change his mind about us, then - oh, Carol it was terrible!' Kelly began to shake. 'Just this morning, me dad comes in and tells Victor that he doesn't want to drive any more buses into the pit, he wants to be put on the London run. Said he was sick of what he saw. Victor went berserk, called him all the names under the sun, even blamed him for the bus being set on fire. Then he sacked him on the spot. Well, I argued back at him for once and he told me to get out an' all. I just flipped. Ran out with his car keys and drove his BMW up to Brassy.'

'Oh, no,' Carol dreaded what she was going to hear.

'Your sister was at home having a facial done. I think I screamed a lot at her about me and Victor and the baby - I don't really remember. Finally Victor turns up in a work's van and hauls me away, denying it all to your sister, of course, but I think she got the message.'

'That was a really stupid thing to do,' Carol said. Her sister would be beside herself with hurt and humiliation.

Kelly started to laugh hysterically. 'Aye, it was, wasn't it? But she did look a sight in her cucumber face pack!' Then the laughter dissolved into sobbing once more. 'Oh, Carol! What am I going to do? I've got nothing now. I've lost me job, I've lost Victor. And I loved him so much, it really hurts.'

Carol shoved a tissue at her. 'Does Sid have any idea what's been going on?'

Kelly shook her head. 'I don't think he does. He's always round at his sister's. I haven't told him yet about being sacked. Me dad's the only one who's guessed about Victor, but he won't say anything.'

'So you haven't lost everything,' Carol said more briskly. 'You have a baby on the way that you want to keep, and you have Sid.'

'I can't stay with Sid after what's happened,' Kelly said unhappily.

'You don't have much choice,' Carol answered, 'and staying with Sid's the best one, if you ask me. He'd make a smashing father and he's always been as keen for a bairn as you have, hasn't he?'

'Aye, but I don't love him any more.'

Carol grew impatient. 'You love your baby, don't you? Well, the least you can do is give the bairn a loving father who won't disown it before birth. And the least you can do for Sid is to give him that happiness too. It's either that or admit what you've done and go back to Mafeking Street to live with your dad.'

Kelly gave her a petulant, frightened look, like a child being told off. 'I couldn't do that.'

'Well then, what have you got to lose by pretending the bairn is Sid's? That's if it's physically possible.'

'I could lie about the dates a bit,' Kelly said, with an embarrassed smile.

Carol felt relief. Her friend was a survivor. Perhaps it would work out for her and Sid after all. Yet she thought how little they would have to give the baby if the strike lasted till Christmas, as everyone was now predicting. They would need all the help and support they could get. Carol buried her anger at Kelly for her futile affair with Vic. Her contempt for her brother-in-law, though, would not be so easy to suppress. She wondered briefly if she should go and see Fay, but she could imagine how she would be rebuffed. They had not spoken for too long and none of her family had come to comfort her when Mick had been taken away to prison, she thought with resentment.

She put an arm round Kelly. 'I'll volunteer for babysitting and anything else I can help with, you know that.'

Kelly grinned at her tearfully. 'I don't deserve a friend like you. I've never brought you anything but trouble.'

'Aye, I know,' Carol laughed. Then added more seriously, 'But you were a good mate to me when we were growing up. At least I had someone to go off the rails with.'

Kelly hugged her tight.

Arthur Bowman's funeral was delayed a further week while the Todds fought for Mick to be allowed to attend. On a bright September afternoon, with a hint of autumn in the air and the first chestnuts beginning to fall, Mick was brought under guard to the Methodist Chapel in Good Street.

Laura was at school and Carol had not told her that her daddy was going to be there in case she had hysterics again. The girl was constantly flying into tantrums and alternately biting and kicking her then clinging to her, fearful of letting her out of her sight.

Carol was able to sit next to Mick, but she felt his distance and he did not respond to her smile of encouragement. He sat there, his hair cropped and his face once again shaven, looking boyish, not saying a word. Mick's calmness alarmed her, but his composure broke as the coffin was lifted by Charlie and Eddy and Sid and Stan Savage. Outside, the colliery band struck up the miners' hymn of Gresford in tribute to the old face worker and the chapel filled with singing. Carol heard Mick sob.

She slipped her arm through his and held it tight, ignoring the way he stiffened at her touch. Then the tears came, pouring down his face, and his body shook. Carol wept too. She wept for the old man and for them all, united in their pain as the strains of the band rang out in the sunny street, rallying their spirits.

They filed out together, but Mick's escort kept close beside him as they made their way up the hill to the cemetery. There, under a rowan tree bright with autumn berries, Arthur Bowman was laid to rest beside his wife, among so many of the folk of Brassbank with whom he had lived and worked. Lotty and her sister Val were bowed in grief, comforted by Charlie and Eddy.

All too soon, Mick was being led away. Carol caught his hand before he went and they hugged each other awkwardly. Yet he looked at her for a long moment and she thought she saw tenderness in his blue eyes, which gave her courage. He was telling her to be brave. Then he was being hurried out of the cemetery and out of her life again.

Carol stood feeling quite alone in the autumn sunshine, wondering how much more she would have to endure.

Chapter Twenty-Seven

At the end of September, after a month on remand, Mick was found guilty of assault and criminal damage at the court in Durham and sentenced to ninety days in prison. He was sent back to Ridley where he continued his mute defiance of non-cooperation which landed him in solitary where he was denied exercise and allowed no visitors.

Carol was desolate at the thought of not being able to see him and after a month she grew angry with Mick for his stubbornness, wondering if he was deliberately keeping her away. She threw herself into work at the Welfare kitchen and spent every hour of the day with members of the Women's Group so that she did not have to stay in the cold empty house at Dominion Terrace. At the weekends she took Laura blackberry picking and they made fruit pies with thin pastry which they took round to Septimus Street and shared with the Todds.

With October came the first of the really cold weather and the soup kitchen was busier than ever. Carol noticed how thin and tired many of the women looked, as they gave what meagre resources they had to their children and husbands first. She and Laura survived on endless vegetable soup and beans on toast; her daughter had given up asking for chicken or ice cream or sweets or bananas. On Sundays they went round to Lotty's for dinner and Eddy played football with Laura and taught her to whistle.

Carol knew that Lotty grieved deeply for her father, but it was Charlie who seemed to miss his company the most. He still took Dougal for a walk up to the cottages on the days he would have gone to visit Arthur and fetch him to play dominoes at the club.

'You know you can move in with us any time,' Lotty repeated every visit.

'Ta, I know that,' Carol smiled, 'but we're managing. I'm trying to keep things as normal as possible for Laura. Being in her own home is one way.'

Carol kept to herself the worries about how to pay for the winter clothes and shoes that Laura needed. The strikers' children were not entitled to free school meals or clothing grants as other poor families were; they had to manage as best they could by swapping second-hand clothes at the Welfare and begging for jumble from charity shops.

In the evenings, unable to afford coal for the fire, she and Laura would go to bed early wrapped in extra jumpers and sleep together in the double bed. She marvelled at how her daughter did not complain at their change in circumstances; it was she herself who nearly cried with despair when she had to bathe in cold water and leave her hair unwashed for a week at a time.

Then one day Laura came out of school crying. When Carol got her home she noticed a cut on the back of her neck where someone had scratched her.

'What's been happening?' Carol said gently, taking her on her knee and cuddling her.

'Nothing. I'm not going back to school,' Laura muttered. 'I'm going to be poorly tomorrow.'

'No you're not,' Carol cajoled her, 'you'll be just fine. But how did you get that scratch?'

'Sarah did it,' Laura admitted in a whisper.

'Sarah Lawrence?'

Laura nodded. Carol's heart sank. Sarah's father had recently gone back to work and his house had been daubed in red paint. She had heard from gossip around the school gate that the children of scabs were being picked on at school and no doubt Sarah was one of them. She felt sorry for the girl, but it made her angry that she had taken it out on Laura, one of her best friends.

'Have you been saying hurtful things to Sarah?' Carol asked.

Laura shook her head vehemently. 'No I never.'

'So why did she scratch you?'

'We were playing houses,' Laura sniffed, 'and Louise Dillon said to Sarah she should paint her house red and she was crying and Louise was calling her scabby, scabby Sarah. And then I said she could share my house and she hit me and said she would never come to my house 'cos me dad was a hooligan and a very bad man . . .' Suddenly Laura's face crumpled. 'And she said the police would come and take me away next because of what Daddy had done and put me in prison.' She burst into tears.

Carol hugged her daughter tight and tried to calm her, sick at the cruelty of children. But then they were only repeating what they heard the adults say; they could not be blamed for the awful bitterness that was tearing their community apart.

'It's not true, pet,' Carol reassured her. 'None of it's true. No one's going to put you in prison. You'll always stay here, safe with me. And your daddy is not a bad man; don't let anyone tell you so.'

Laura wiped her nose on Carol's shoulder and snuggled into her hold. 'Then why is he in prison, Mam?'

Carol sighed. 'It's difficult to explain in a way you'd understand. Daddy's been forced to do things he never wanted to do because of the strike. But he's only been trying to do the best for all the men at the pit, like Granddad Charlie and Uncle Eddy - standing up for them, for all of us.'

'Then is Uncle Simon wrong because he's a policeman? Louise Dillon says all police are pigs and they hate my dad and her dad.'

Carol wondered what else Marty Dillon had been telling his children. But he was still awaiting trial for the incident at Orgreave months ago and she knew from May that their eldest boy Rob was being hounded or picked up by the police every time he left the house. Rob was only fourteen and terrified by all the attention, but he was the son of an activist and the Dillons were under constant surveillance. No wonder Laura's friend Louise was turning into a playground bully.

'Uncle Simon doesn't hate Daddy,' Carol assured.

'What about Grandpa Ben and Grandma? We never see them any more. Is that because of what Daddy's done?'

Carol's heart missed a beat. Her daughter had not mentioned those grandparents for months and she had wishfully thought she did not even miss them. It would have made her feel less guilty for staying away and keeping Laura from them.

Carol swallowed. 'Your dad's got nothing to do with Grandpa and Grandma not seeing us. It's Mammy who fell out with them, I'm afraid.' When Laura did not pursue this, Carol was relieved. 'Anyway, I'll come into school with you tomorrow and help you make it up with Sarah if you want. Then you can be friends again. Is that what you want?'

Laura nodded.

'OK. Let's have some tea.'

'But if I make friends with Sarah, will you be friends again with Grandpa and Grandma? Then I can go and play in their garden and go on Grandpa's swings again.'

Carol felt her eyes sting at the sight of Laura's longing face. Life was so hard these days and yet Laura demanded so little; how could she refuse to let her see her own grandparents?

'I'll take you to see them soon,' Carol promised.

Later, as she tucked Laura into bed and the condensation on the window began to freeze, she felt a stab of guilt towards Mick. He might see it as a sign of weakening, of going behind his back to take Laura over to Granville House. But then Mick was not here, she thought with resentment, and she just had to get by as best she could without him. She had to make her decisions alone and stand by them.

Pulling on an extra pair of socks and a large jumper of Mick's, Carol snuggled in beside her daughter, wondering how life could have changed so dramatically in eight months. When would they ever live a normal life again?

As so often happened these days, Carol went to Lotty for advice. Her mother-in-law was still as busy as ever, spending long hours in the Welfare kitchen and riding around the village on her moped muffled in scarves and Eddy's old donkey jacket, visiting families and finding out their needs. Yet Carol noticed the tired lines of strain etched into her face at the end of the day.

'Laura wants to see her other grandparents,' Carol confided as they peeled an endless mound of potatoes one morning.

'Have they ever got in touch with you since Mick was imprisoned?' Lotty asked tartly.

'No,' Carol admitted, 'but this is about Laura.'

'Yes,' Lotty sighed, 'I'm sorry.'

Carol asked cautiously, 'Do you think I'm being disloyal going to see them?'

'Oh, pet,' Lotty squeezed her hand. 'You could never be accused of being disloyal. You've done more than enough for our family, our village. I'll not blame you for going to see your own mam and dad and I'll not let others bad-mouth you either.'

Thanks, Mam,' Carol smiled. It seemed so natural calling Lotty that. She had never been as close to her own mother as she had grown to Lotty. What a disappointment we've been to each other as mother and daughter, Carol thought sadly and once again gave thanks for the way Mick's parents had made her their own.

That weekend, she braced herself for the walk over to Granville House. Laura skipped and chattered all the way, oblivious of her mother's apprehension. Carol half hoped that her father would be down at the pit offices, working. As they passed the end of the lane going down towards the pit yard, she realised how quickly she had got used to seeing the presence of police on their streets.

She no longer shivered at the sight of video cameras poised like birds of prey at the perimeter fence, training beady eyes over the colliery houses and their back lanes, far beyond the confines of the pit. The picket itself had become a part of the landscape; men huddled in donkey jackets stamping their feet to keep warm outside a crude shelter nicknamed The Alamo. Yet on reaching the gravel drive, Carol was shocked to see a constable positioned at the gate. Not recognising them, he came forward.

'Can I help you?'

'We've come to see Grandpa,' Laura piped up at once.

The constable hesitated, then stood back. 'Sorry, I didn't know . . .'

Carol flushed. 'We don't often come. Why are you here?'

'Well, it's these striking miners,' he said confidentially. 'Mr Shannon's had threats. Not that it seems to worry him; it's for Mrs Shannon, you know.' He smiled. 'You just visiting then? Bet you're glad you don't have to live in a hole like this.'

Carol went puce. 'I do live here and it's not a hole! Least it wasn't till you lot marched in and took it over.'

The young man looked at her in astonishment and then suspicion. She would have turned round and left at once, but Laura had dashed up the drive and was shouting back at her. 'Come on, Mam! I can see Grandpa in the garden.'

She followed her daughter, cursing herself for getting riled so quickly. She seemed to lose her temper at the slightest thing these days. She should not have let the constable's silly comment bother her.

Carol's heart lurched at the sight of Laura flinging herself at her grandfather and being picked up in a delighted hug.

'How's my favourite girl, then?' Ben said as he kissed Laura.

'What about Jasmine and Ngaio?' Laura giggled.

'They're not around to hear my secret, are they?' he laughed. 'What have you been doing? I've missed you!'

'What do you think we've been doing?' Carol blurted out.

Ben shot her a look, but continued to question his granddaughter. 'How's the new class at school? Uncle Simon says you can count up to fifty.'

'Sixty!' Laura corrected.

'Well, I can see you're going to be an accountant.'

'Uncle Simon rings me up. Why don't you, Grandpa?'

Carol saw her father redden. 'I must do that,' he blustered. 'Let's go into the house and raid the biscuit barrel. Grandma's going to be thrilled to see you.'

'And can I have some ice cream? And then can I go on the swing?' Laura bubbled with excitement.

'Anything you want,' Ben beamed.

It was too much for Carol. 'Laura, pet, go and have that swing now while I talk to Grandpa.'

The girl looked between them in confusion and seemed about to protest, but Ben put her down. 'Quick swing, then a special tea.'

Laura ran off happily. He turned to face Carol.

'Dad, how do you think that makes me feel? You spoil her rotten for an hour and then what? She's got to go back to living on baked beans in a house without heating - without her daddy. You don't have to buy her affection.'

'I haven't seen her for months,' Ben protested. 'Why shouldn't I spoil my own granddaughter? It's not my fault you're living in the state you are.'

202

'No, it would never be your fault, would it?'

'Well, it's not. You know I would give you money if you asked for it. There's no reason for you to live in squalor.'

'You know I couldn't take your money! Not while my family and neighbours are suffering like they are. Not while Mick stews in prison. Have you enough money to pay everyone's debts?' Carol looked at him squarely with angry green eyes. 'All the money in the world wouldn't make up for what's happened to the miners. It's never been a fight over money; it's always been over jobs and the future. That's why we have to see it through. That's the only reason we put up with all the hardship. When will you ever understand?'

Ben was riled. 'It's you who doesn't understand! If the men don't go back to work, there won't be a future for any of us at Brassbank. I've lived and worked here most of my life. I dragged your mother back here from Newcastle so that I could be manager of this pit because to me that was the best job in the world. I was so proud to be in charge here.' His brown eyes blazed. 'And I was proud to work with men like Charlie Todd because they don't come much better than him. You won't believe me, but I even admired your husband Mick before he went and attacked Dan Hardman. The idiot! He punched me too, did you know?'

Carol was taken aback by her father's outpouring. 'No - when?'

'Just before he lay down in front of Proud's bus and stopped the workers coming in,' Ben grunted. 'I went to see Charlie in his allotment - I often did before the strike. I suppose I was trying to get him to see sense as I saw it. But we argued and I said things I shouldn't have. Mick stood up for his father and hit me. It was just like seeing a young Charlie standing over me again.'

Carol was astounded. 'But you never did anything about it?'

Ben shook his head. 'I'd asked for it. In a way I admired Mick for standing up to me. I'm not the sort to go blabbing to the police about a personal fight.'

'Charlie never said anything,' Carol answered, the anger draining out of her.

'How is Mick?' Ben asked at last.

'I don't know,' Carol said in a small voice. 'They won't let me visit him until he stops his non-cooperation. He'll serve out the full three months at this rate.'

Ben sighed. 'I'm sorry. It's not the way I would have wanted it.' He waved Carol towards the house. 'Come on; let me spoil you too for just one afternoon.'

Carol gave in. Ben called to Laura who came rushing over like a frisky puppy. Carol thought how skinny she looked; as if a sea breeze could lift her off spindly legs and blow her away like the autumn leaves. She would put principles aside for the afternoon and allow Laura to gorge herself on treats. There was no point in living beyond the day.

Her mother was quite flustered by their sudden appearance and she fussed around them, talking incessantly about everything but Mick and the strike. After half an hour, Ben could stand it no longer and took Laura back out in the fading light to pick a turnip to make a lantern for Halloween.

Immediately Nancy began to talk about Fay. Carol knew she had been bursting to speak of the affair since her arrival.

'I can't imagine what Vic was thinking of! I mean, that Laws girl has always been so common.'

Carol grew annoyed. 'Stop it, Mother. Kelly's still a friend of mine.'

Her mother humphed. 'Anyway, is it true that she's pregnant?'

Carol contained her anger. 'Yes, she's having Sid's baby.'

Nancy snorted. 'How do we know it's not Vic's?'

'It's none of our business, Mother. You keep your suspicions to yourself. They don't do anyone any good.'

'Oh, I wouldn't go telling anyone, it would reflect too badly on Fay. She's distraught about the whole thing, of course. Blames you for not stopping it in its tracks.'

'Me?' Carol said in amazement. 'How was I supposed to know what was going on? And even if I did, how could I have stopped it?'

'Well, you know Fay,' her mother blustered.

'Aye, still blaming her little sister for everything. Does it never occur to her that her precious Victor might be the real villain?'

Nancy sighed. 'Anyway, they're staying together for the sake of the children. It's the best way. And perhaps it wasn't all Vic's fault. Maybe Fay made him unhappy.' She shrugged.

'Don't go making excuses,' Carol retorted.

'And don't you go getting on your high horse. No marriage is perfect and people do sometimes make mistakes they regret.'

Carol blushed, thinking of how attracted she had become to Pete Fletcher when she was feeling sorry for herself in the summer. She had been unhappy, vulnerable, close to being unfaithful. . .

'How is Mick?' Nancy asked suddenly.

'Thought you'd never ask, Mother,' Carol said sarcastically.

'Well, you know I don't approve—'

'No,' Carol cut her short, 'so don't say any more. He's Laura's father and you'll not say a word against him, do you hear?'

Nancy looked at her strangely, Carol thought almost in fear. 'Don't be cross with me, Carol. It's just I've always wanted more for you than this. It's the reason . . .' She shrugged and gave up trying to explain.

'The reason what?' Carol asked, suddenly aware something deeper was running through the conversation.

Nancy gave her a frightened look. 'I'm being silly as usual, take no notice.' She jumped at the sound of footsteps running along the hall. 'Goodness Laura, you startled me!'

Ben appeared behind her, chill air still hanging around them like cloaks. 'Your grandma's such a bag of nerves all the time,' he joked. 'Jumps at her own shadow. She'll be no fun at Halloween.'

Laura looked concerned. 'It's all right, Grandma, I'll shine my lantern and chase the witches and goblins away. Then you'll be safe.'

Watching her mother, Carol saw tears spring into her eyes. It was such an unusual sight, she felt disturbed by it. What was it about their conversation that had begun to upset her?

With the lantern, they set off into the dark back to Dominion Terrace, Laura promising they would call again soon. Carol was not so sure it was a good idea but decided to keep quiet for the moment.

In early November Carol got word from Ridley prison that she would be allowed to visit Mick. There were passes for three people and Carol asked Mick's parents to go with her. Yet she was torn about whether to let Laura go with her, deciding that it would probably be too upsetting if she did. But the girl picked up from adult conversation what was going on and demanded to be taken.

'She's going on about it all the time,' Carol told Lotty. 'I'm going to have to take her.'

'Well, it might cheer Mick up to see her,' Lotty replied with a smile of understanding. 'Charlie won't mind giving up his place for her.'

Lesley Dimarco gave them a lift in the van on the day of the visit. They waited nervously in a canteen run by volunteers. Carol looked at the other visitors with apprehension, but they seemed just like her: distracted mothers trying to put on a brave face while keeping their bored children under control, wondering what they were going to say to their husbands when the time came.

Eventually they were shown into the interview room, secure and anonymous with Perspex tables. Mick came in with the other prisoners. There was an eruption of chatter and children's wails, a scraping of chairs. Carol went to Mick and kissed him. Laura was suddenly shy and clung to her mother.

'Say hello to your daddy,' Carol ordered. But Laura was overwhelmed.

Lotty gave him a hug and then they all sat down. Carol saw the muscles in Mick's neck working, as if he was trying to say something.

'See-through tables, eh? Must be to stop us passing love notes,' Carol joked.

Laura clung to her neck and peered with one eye at Mick.

'How are you?' they all said at once.

'We're champion,' Lotty told him. 'Father and Eddy said to ask after you. Keep your pecker up, Eddy said.'

'And you?' Carol asked again.

Mick nodded. 'I'm fine.' His voice sounded hoarse, as if it had not been used in a long time. 'The other lads - they're all right.'

'I've brought you some books to read and some chocolate.'

'What did you do that for?' Mick was suddenly angry. 'You can't afford chocolate, Carol. Take it back for the bairn. We get better fed in here than you do at home. Three meals a day. One of the warders keeps reminding me,' Mick added bitterly.

Carol gulped, feeling suddenly weepy. She could think of nothing to say. Lotty took over and began to chat about the soup kitchen and people in the village. But Carol had the impression that Mick was not really taking it in.

The time dragged and Laura shifted restlessly, asking to be taken home. Lotty picked her up swiftly. 'We'll wait for you outside while you say your goodbyes.' She removed a protesting Laura.

When they were gone, Mick said, 'You shouldn't have brought her here. She shouldn't see this.'

'She was that keen to see you,' Carol tried to explain.

'It's best if you don't visit again, Carol. I'll be out at the end of the month, any road.'

'Aye,' Carol agreed, putting on a brave smile, 'you'll be home soon.' But inside she felt desolate and more unhappy than when she hadn't been allowed to visit.

They said a brief goodbye and Carol stumbled out of the room, blinded by tears. She ached for the man she left behind and yet feared that he no longer loved her. What would it be like when he was released and had to come home? she wondered fearfully.

Mick went back to his cell. The familiar smell and claustrophobia made him nauseous. It seemed so much more oppressive now that he had seen his family. He felt completely exposed as if he had been stripped and searched and scrubbed down all over again. It was the ultimate humiliation to have them see him like this, so helpless. He could stand being in prison, had found to his surprise that he could make friends among the other men; they were not beyond the pale, as he had imagined. They were ordinary men with feelings like himself.

As long as he could keep his old life at bay, he had been able to cope with confinement. But their coming here had shattered his defences, left him naked and vulnerable to feelings. How he had longed to see them! But watching Carol sitting there with a frightened Laura, he had been seized with guilt that they were having to cope alone without him. How could he ever make that up to them? And now he had sent them away feeling wretched and unwanted and it tore at his heart.

He sat down and pulled a grubby notepad from under his pillow. He began to write. The pad was full of letters he had written to Carol and never sent, telling her about life in the prison, the other men, the time dragging without her, feelings that he could not express to her in words. It made him feel better to write them down. Perhaps when he got out he would show them to her and it might make up for what he had done. Maybe one day Carol might forgive him.

Chapter Twenty-Eight

Carol wanted to look attractive the day Mick was released from prison in late November, but she was full of cold and her top lip was marred by a cold sore. She went round to Val Bowman's for a hot bath and hair wash and Val trimmed her mane of shaggy brown hair, yet to Carol it still looked dry and without lustre.

'You look grand,' Val tried to reassure her, 'a sight to gladden his eye.'

She insisted on giving Carol a soft jumper with sequins stitched on the shoulder that had been salvaged from her failed shop. Val had finally had to close her business the previous month and was trying to sell the lease on the property, without success. 'The jumper's much too small for me,' Val told her.

Carol was touched. Val must have so many worries of her own, but she managed to hide them behind her usual cheerful expression. 'I'll wear it for the Christmas party - if not every night in bed!' Carol grinned.

'You'll not be needing extra jumpers in bed once your Mick's home,' Val teased her.

Carol blushed and looked away. What was it going to be like with Mick back once more? Part of her longed for his return, yet part of her dreaded it. They would be like strangers. And how would they be able to afford to feed him too?

She and Laura had got used to their quiet, close existence without him; a routine of calling round at the Welfare after school where it was warmer than home, then going to bed after tea and reading stories under the covers to Laura's teddies and dolls. At weekends they would visit Lotty for Saturday tea and her parents on a Sunday afternoon.

Carol shuddered to think what Mick would say about her regular visits to Granville House. They were short visits and made for Laura's sake, and the conversation never went beyond the trivial, but even Carol found herself looking forward to the teas where she could satisfy her craving for sweet cakes and biscuits as much as her daughter did. It was as if a truce had been declared between herself and her parents. She never mentioned Mick and they never mentioned the strike. She often thought how much better their relationship might have been if the strike had never taken place.

At times, watching her father playing patiently with Laura, she felt almost fondness towards him. Why had he never been able to accept her in the same easy, unjudgemental way? They had wasted too many painful years being at odds with one another.

And thinking of Mick now, Carol determined that she would try her utmost not to waste their future together. Lotty would collect Laura from school and they would be waiting for him with a special tea of mince and potatoes, apple crumble and custard. The mince had been a donation from the local butcher who supplied the Women's Group with cheap meat and had heard that Mick was to be released. She would go with Charlie and Eddy to fetch him in Dimarco's van.

Quelling her nerves at the thought, Carol chatted excitedly with Val about the preparations for the children's party at Christmas and the adults' disco. With all the strife in the village since some of the men had returned to work, there was a determination among the Women's Group to make this Christmas as happy as possible for the striking families.

'We raised over two hundred pounds at the pie and peas supper,' Carol told her, 'and the raffle's selling well.'

'That's great,' Val nodded, 'and Lotty tells me you've been writing to your supporters in London too.'

'Aye, they've promised money to buy presents for the kids. And Charlie reckons we might get help from the miners in France - the lodge's been in touch with our twin town. Mind, it's going to take so much organising to make sure every bairn gets something this Christmas.'

'You'll manage,' Val smiled. 'It's nothing short of a miracle what the Women's Group's done for the village up till now.'

Just before Carol was due to leave for the prison, she got an urgent call from Joanne. Her neighbour Sheila was in a terrible state. She was a quiet woman, too shy to join their group, but they had taken a special interest in her because she had produced one of their 'strike babies', as they affectionately called the newborns. Joanne had found her weeping alone in the house with her young baby.

'The baby was blue with cold,' Joanne said on the telephone. 'Sheila's been using rags as nappies. I heard the bairn crying through the wall and couldn't stand it any longer. Her husband doesn't like us interfering, but I don't care. Can you come round and help? I can't calm her down.'

Carol went immediately. She rang Charlie and told him to go without her; she would meet them all at Septimus Street. She took the last of the week's house-keeping from the drawer in the sideboard and stopped to buy disposable nappies and baby milk on the way.

'Sorry, Carol,' Joanne whispered when she arrived, 'I just thought you'd be able to cope with her.'

They changed the baby's urine-soaked clothing, covering his sore bottom in protective cream, and made him up a bottle. Sheila had been trying to feed him herself, but her milk had dried up soon after she had left hospital. Then Joanne wrapped him up snugly in the pram that the group had bought for Sheila and took the baby out into the crisp wintery air.

'I'll take him up to school and bring your Sandra home with Mark,' Joanne assured Sheila as she left.

Carol held and comforted and listened to Sheila's cries of despair for over an hour. She was near to breaking. They had sold everything worth selling to pay for baby equipment and now, without telling her husband Tom, she had borrowed money from a lender who had come round the doors, and she did not know how she was going to repay the man.

'And I just keep looking at me bonny baby and thinking how I can't give him anything.' Sheila broke off sobbing again. 'Sometimes I wish I was dead.'

Carol hugged her. 'You mustn't say that. Listen, how much do you owe this moneylender?'

Sheila sniffed. 'It started as just a loan of fifty pounds. But now with the interest, I owe him over a hundred and fifty. Tom'll kill me if he finds out what I've done!'

'No he won't,' Carol said gently. 'The group'll try and help you out. We'll see what we can do about paying off this man. In the meantime, we'll make you up some extra parcels of baby stuff for little Harry. Looks like you could do with a bit of feeding up, an' all.' Carol looked at her. 'Why don't you bring

Harry down to the Welfare during the day for a bit of company?'

'Oh, I couldn't do that,' Sheila said in panic. 'Tom wouldn't want it. He likes me at home. He doesn't approve of the women getting together like you have, thinks you're all getting above yourselves.'

Carol bit back a retort about Tom's views, thinking that she must find a way for Sheila to get out more or at least be visited by some of the group more regularly. She should not have to shoulder these burdens alone and Carol was thankful that Joanne had intervened when she did.

Sheila must have seen the look on her face, for she added quietly, 'I don't think like he does. I might have at the start but now I think it's grand what you're doing. And you with a husband in prison. I couldn't have stood Tom going to gaol. But I don't want him going back to work either, not before everyone else. That's why I borrowed the money.' She crumpled into Carol's arms again.

'I know. You've done your best, don't blame yourself. Now let us help you a bit, eh?'

Carol stayed with her until Joanne got back with the children.

'Sandra can come in and have tea with us this afternoon,' Joanne offered. 'You get yourself off home, Carol.'

But Carol was worried about leaving Sheila on her own. 'What time will Tom be back?' she asked.

Sheila shrugged. 'Not till late. Stops out all day somewhere.' Her look slid away from theirs. Carol wondered if Sheila's husband was being unfaithful and felt real anger at the man for causing his wife such pain.

'I'll look after Harry for an hour then,' Carol insisted. 'You go and get some sleep.'

Sheila hardly protested. Soon Carol discovered there was no electricity. She sat in the dark, with Harry huddled inside her coat trying to keep him warm.

Sheila slept on and Carol did not like to wake her.

Later she gave Harry a cold bottle of milk and changed him again by the light of a candle, thinking she would go straight to Charlie and sort out their reconnection in the morning. She thought with frustration of Mick arriving at Septimus Street without her, but there was no telephone in the house to let them know of her delay.

The door banging open startled her. Tom, a man she knew little about except that he had come from Cumbria to work in the pit and married Sheila, stood before her, stony-faced.

'What the hell are you doing here?' he asked, startled and then indignant. 'Where's the wife?'

'Don't worry, Sheila's getting some sleep,' Carol answered civilly, 'and Sandra's having her tea next door. I'm just helping out for an hour or two.'

'Helping out?' he grumbled. 'We don't need your help. We can manage on our own.'

'It seems to me Sheila could do with a helping hand,' Carol said, trying not to sound too critical. 'It's difficult at the best of times with a new baby and Joanne was just keeping an eye.'

Tom advanced on her, smelling of stale beer. 'That nosy bitch from next door? I don't need lasses from the bloody Women's Group telling my wife what to do. So the pair of you can just piss off!'

Carol was shocked. She felt like dumping the baby and running, but steeled herself to stand up to him. She could not leave him drunk and in a foul temper alone with newborn Harry and the unsuspecting Sheila.

'I said I'd wait until Sheila woke up,' Carol said, standing her ground. By now Harry was crying again.

'I don't want you in me house!' Tom shouted, seizing her by the arm and dragging her towards the door.

Carol struggled to shake him off and hang on to the baby at the same time. Panic filled her throat. She cried out. 'Watch the baby!'

Tom swore at her foully and smacked her on the side of the head. Carol ducked away.

Sheila appeared in the doorway behind them, her exhausted face pale and terrified in the candlelight.

'Please don't,' she whimpered.

Tom veered round at the sound of her voice, distracted for a moment. Carol staggered over to the pram and put Harry down still yelling. Tom was shaking his wife and swearing at her for allowing strangers into the house.

'Leave her alone!' Carol cried and rushed over to push him away.

Tom threw her off with a punch in the face. Carol fell back, the pain shooting from her eye into her head.

Someone must have heard the screams because there was a hammering on the front door and when no one came to answer it, it was flung open, letting in a gust of icy wind that snuffed out the candle.

Carol was crouched on the floor, dizzy and sick from the punch, unable to see who had come to their rescue. Then arms seized her and pulled her up from behind. Men's voices argued and a scuffle that she could not see took place. Sheila was wailing in distress.

As her good eye grew used to the dark, Carol saw Tom being manhandled down the corridor by two or three other men. She recognised Sid and John. There was a lot of shouting. But then a voice spoke her name and she turned to see who had yanked her up off the floor.

Mick's cropped head of hair was close to hers.

'Oh, Mick!' Carol gasped and felt she would faint. His arms came round her in support and she fell against his broad body. She hugged him tightly and buried her face in his shoulder. She began to cry with shock and relief and could not stop. He held her and stroked her head and whispered that she was going to be all right.

'I've missed you so much!' she cried.

'Me too, pet,' Mick told her and kissed her head. 'Let's get you home.'

It was then Carol saw Sheila crouched on a chair by the window, clutching a whimpering Harry.

'Mick,' Carol stopped him.

He read her mind. 'They can come home with us tonight if you want,' he agreed resignedly.

Minutes later, Joanne was there with Eddy who had come round with Mick to find her. Joanne insisted that Sheila and the children should stay with her and John.

'You and Mick need some time together,' she told them firmly.

Carol was relieved, but wondered anxiously if Mick had agreed to have the family so that he would not be left alone with her. She dismissed her fears quickly. It was all too easy these days to conjure up worries where they did not exist.

Tom had been taken away by the men to sleep off his drunken rage elsewhere. They would deal with him in the morning, John Taylor said; he was a man at the end of his tether.

Carol and Mick returned home, awkward with each other once the initial thrill of being reunited was over. Lotty had put Laura to bed and she was already asleep, drained by the excitement of seeing her father again. Carol was thankful that her daughter did not have to see Lotty bathe her swelling eye with icy water.

'I hope people don't think you did this,' Carol teased Mick. But he seemed upset by the suggestion and she wished she had kept quiet.

Lotty left quickly and they went to bed. Mick held her while she told him of the busy preparations for Christmas and tried to describe what had happened over the months of his absence. Mick said little. She did not know what he was thinking or feeling. When she tried to ask him about prison, he clammed up.

Carol told herself to be patient and that she would discover more in time. Her heart beat faster at the thought of lying with him again, but soon he was turning over and telling her goodnight. She lay for a long time, fighting back tears of frustration and loneliness. It was in these dark hours of the night that the fears kept at bay during the day flooded into her mind, leaving her anxious and sleepless.

But she must have fallen into an uneasy sleep eventually, for she woke before dawn to find the bed empty. In a panic she sat up, calling out Laura's name. Then she saw a figure curled up on the floor under a blanket and realised that it was Mick. He was back. He should have been beside her in their bed.

Carol lay back, stifling a sob of despair. She could hardly bear to think of more endless months without intimacy with Mick. Once they had made love regularly, without thinking. Now she found those times hard to remember. It was like looking back on the lives of two different people. But then that's what they were, Carol thought bleakly. Whatever the outcome of the strike, neither of them would ever be the same again.

The three weeks leading up to Christmas were hectic. Carol had never been so busy and was thankful to be occupied. The women went fundraising round the shops of Durham and Whittledene, clanking buckets and forcing themselves not to look into the packed shops filled with gifts and clothes they could not afford. Carol shed tears when an old lady came up to her with a box of biscuits.

'I'm just on a pension, but I want you to have these. It's not right what they're doing to you,' the stooped pensioner said. 'I wish I could give you more.'

They spent long hours at the Welfare, preparing and cooking meals and making up food parcels and sorting out donations of presents for the children's party. Carol and Joanne and May called on all the businesses in the village for contributions to the Christmas party and the raffle. When Carol suggested they approach Proud's, the others were horrified.

'We're not going begging to that man!' May snorted. 'He's making money hand over fist out of the strike.'

211

'Exactly,' said Carol, 'so he can repay a bit of it to those that need it most.'

'You'll get nowt out of him,' May declared, 'and I'm not going to give him the satisfaction of saying no.'

But Carol went and found Vic in his dingy office at the bus depot. She noticed that the secretary that had replaced Kelly was middle-aged and motherly and wondered whether Fay had had a hand in picking her.

Vic seemed pleased to see her, as if nothing had happened over the past year. He did not refer to their last stormy meeting and she did not allude to his affair with Kelly. She would play his game.

'You never come to see us,' he chided.

'I'm too busy, just like you,' Carol replied evenly.

'We miss seeing you. The girls are always asking to see Laura,' he smiled.

'We haven't moved,' Carol reminded him. 'Bring them round,' she suggested, knowing he never would.

Vic gave a charming shrug. 'Perhaps when this little difficulty is over, we can all get together again.'

Carol was rendered speechless. Little difficulty! Did he really see it as no more than that? And then it struck her that that was probably how Vic did see the strike. He saw it only in terms of how it affected his business.

It had taken a hammering when no buses were needed to ferry the men to the pit from the outlying areas, and the day trips and holiday bookings had suffered from lack of cash among the miners. But he had overcome this by securing lucrative contracts to bus in the scabs; the little difficulty had turned into a business opportunity. The social consequences of the strike were not his concern, Carol realised, and he would not be swayed by appeals to his conscience. So how was she going to get money out of him for the striking families?

'When this is over,' Carol said lightly, 'we'll all have to go on living beside each other. You'll want the holiday business back again once the men are working, won't you?'

'Go on,' Vic said, intrigued. He had been expecting a tirade.

'So it might make good business sense to be seen to be generous this Christmas towards the miners.'

'I can't get involved in your politics,' Vic said uneasily, 'this Women's Group thing.'

Carol stayed calm. 'No, not for the strike fund as such. But you could make a donation to the children's party - to the families' Christmas fund.' She looked at him levelly. 'It might get a mention in the local paper.'

A grin spread slowly across Vic's bearded face. 'Yes, I like that idea. Publicity too, not anonymous. It might give Proud's a lot of good will in the future.'

He laughed. 'God, Carol, you're wasted in this place. I think I married the wrong sister.'

Carol hid her distaste at that remark. She forced a broad smile, telling herself the more she pandered to his vanity, the more money she could squeeze out of him.

'We're looking for a hundred pounds,' she said lightly. Her heart hammered, for she knew from Kelly how he hated to waste money giving to charities. He would bargain down to forty or fifty at the most, she suspected.

He was giving her one of his flirtatious looks. 'I'll tell you what,' he smiled. 'I'll double the amount if you do something for me.'

Her stomach began to churn, hoping it had nothing to do with Kelly.

'I'll give the kids' party two hundred pounds for a Christmas kiss from you,' Vic laughed softly. 'One big grown-up kiss on the lips, of course.'

Carol felt sick at the suggestion. She was revolted at the thought of kissing this man. But for two hundred pounds...

Carol crossed the room and came round his desk. 'Write out the cheque first,' she said, still smiling. Vic chuckled and did so, handing her the precious piece of paper.

Then he patted his knee for her to sit down. Carol forced herself to perch on his lap and stiffened as he put his arms round her.

'Relax,' he murmured, pulling her towards him. He fastened his moist mouth over hers and pressed hard against her, forcing his tongue between her lips, round her teeth and into her mouth. He made a sucking, grunting noise as if he would devour her and Carol thought she would retch. When his hand slipped round to squeeze her breast, she pulled away.

'Time's up,' she breathed.

She could see his eyes were full of lust, his cheeks flushed.

'We could do this again,' he smiled, squeezing her thigh as she stood up. She turned away before she betrayed her revulsion. 'Or are you still involved with my old mate, Pete?'

Carol felt herself go puce at the mention of the journalist's name.

'I was never involved.'

Vic gave his infuriating laugh. 'That's not what Kelly told me.'

At the mention of Kelly, Carol almost turned on him to give him a mouthful. But she checked herself just in time. He might cancel the cheque.

'Thanks for the donation,' she said, smiling once again.

Then she was out of the office, rushing past the disapproving secretary who had probably listened to everything and into the cold, wet December half-light. She ran down the street, clutching the cheque and gasping for fresh air. She felt dirty and cheap, hating herself for what she had done, hating the man who had humiliated her and hating the strike for making the sordid little episode necessary.

She gave the cheque to Joanne who was amazed and thrilled with the amount. But Carol did not stay to take the praise. She went home and changed her clothes and scrubbed her face and hands and teeth in icy cold water. She was thankful that Mick was out and she did not have to explain. He would be walking the cliffs and coastal paths on his own. It was as if he could not bear to be confined indoors since his three months in prison. Both Eddy and Sid had rallied round and tried to take Mick fishing, or for a rare half pint or a game of pool, but he made excuses not to go, preferring his own company and the stormy seascape.

Later, forcing herself to think no more about Vic's predatory kiss or his smirking insinuations about Pete Fletcher, Carol went back to the Welfare Hall to help.

The week before Christmas, Carol got a call from Laura's head teacher asking her and Mick to come and see her at school. 'Do you need me there?' Mick asked, growing agitated. He paced the room restlessly.

Carol lost her temper. 'Aye, I do need you there! You're the bairn's father, Mick.

Or have you forgotten?'

'Of course not,' he snapped.

'Well, I sometimes wonder,' Carol cried. 'You disappear all day, you do nothing with her at weekends, and you don't even pick her up from school. I have to do that when I've got a hundred other things to be doing. And where are you? Roaming round the countryside like bloody Heathcliffe or summat. I don't know where you go or what you do. I just know you're not here for Laura - or me!'

They faced each other, Carol trembling from her outburst. She had kept the resentment bottled up for so long, but now it was out. Mick's look was harrowed. It made her want to take back her angry words, yet she would not apologise. It was like having a lodger in the house, not a husband, and it was time he knew how she felt.

Mick struggled to say something. Eventually he simply nodded and muttered, 'I'll come.'

They walked up to the school in the early afternoon in tense silence. Carol noticed how people glanced round at them in surprise at seeing them out together. Even others have noticed our estrangement, she thought unhappily. She wondered what Mrs Little wanted to say to them. Maybe she was worried about the state of Laura's clothes or was going to offer free school dinners at last. Carol glanced around the playground to see if she could spot her daughter, but it was too crowded.

Mrs Little was a smartly dressed woman with short, greying hair and a brisk, kind smile. Carol had never talked to her for more than two minutes before. Mrs Little sat them down in her office.

'Is anything wrong?' Carol asked, seeing that Mick was going to remain silent.

Mrs Little did not answer directly. 'How are things at home, Mrs Todd?'

Carol was going to shrug off the question, then decided to be truthful. 'Difficult. We're only just managing. Some weeks we don't.' She avoided Mick's look.

The head teacher nodded in sympathy. 'I see that among so many of the families here.' There was a pause. 'Has Laura been ill recently?'

Carol looked nonplussed. 'Ill? Well, she seems to have a permanent cold - her nose is always running. And she's had a couple of mild attacks of asthma, but I think that's because of the old paraffin heater Mick's parents have lent us. We have it on when she's back from school, but she doesn't like the fumes. Trouble is, if you open the windows then the house is freezing again.' Carol stopped, realising she was gabbling.

But Mrs Little just nodded in understanding. 'So nothing that would keep her off school for several days at a time?'

'No, of course not. She loves school, she doesn't like to miss it,' Carol insisted.

'That's what I thought.' Mrs Little smiled kindly. She leaned forward in her chair and spoke gently. 'This term we've had a big problem with truanting. The children are very unsettled by what is going on - they show it in different ways. I'm afraid Laura has been absent from school three times now in the past two weeks, yet I've had no note from you.'

Carol was stunned. 'But I bring her to school myself.'

Suddenly Mick was vocal. 'The bairn's only five! She can't be skiving off school!'

'I know, it's a shock,' Mrs Little said. 'Does she come to school with anyone else on some days?'

Carol flushed. 'Well, there have been a few times recently when she's gone up with the Dillon children - when I've had to leave the house early.' She gulped. 'The oldest lad, Rob, sees them into school before he goes on to the comp.'

'It seems he must have been taking them off somewhere else instead,' Mrs Little said glumly. 'Louise Dillon has been truanting as well, as far as we can make out.'

Carol and Mick looked at each other in disbelief. Carol thought he was going to blame her for failing to see Laura safely into school. But he had washed his hands of all responsibility towards their daughter since his return from prison and she would tell him so.

Mick was angry. 'We'll have it out with her as soon as we get her home.'

'Please, don't be too hard on her,' Mrs Little cautioned. 'There's bound to be a reason. I thought we could call her in now and have a quiet chat together.'

Carol heard the warning in her voice. 'Yes, we'd like to see her now, wouldn't we, Mick?'

Mick gave her a stormy look. Mrs Little went out to fetch Laura from her classroom.

'Don't go losing your temper with her,' Carol hissed.

'A truant at five!' Mick muttered. 'What's our family coming to?'

'Aye,' Carol snapped back. 'Just ask yourself the same question!'

Laura came in cautiously behind her head teacher, clutching her hand. Carol thought she looked terrified and wanted to reach out and hug her, but was inhibited by the formal surroundings. Laura did not attempt to go to either of them, preferring to sit on Mrs Little's knee and answer her questions in a mouse-like voice.

'You know you should have been in school, Laura?'

The girl nodded.

'Your parents thought you were here,' Mrs Little said gently. 'It's not fair to make them worry, is it?'

'No,' Laura whispered.

Mick blurted out, 'So where the hell have you been, Laura? Where's Rob been taking you?'

Laura cringed at his anger, burying her face in her hands. Mrs Little held on to her tightly.

Carol leaned forward and touched Laura. 'Tell us, pet. We're not going to be angry.'

'Well, I am,' Mick shouted. 'My lass isn't going to nick off school at her age and get away with it. She should be told what's right and wrong.' He glared at the teacher and at Carol.

Mrs Little ignored his outburst. Gently but firmly she pulled Laura's hands away from her face.

'I'll not let anyone hurt you,' she promised.

Carol felt her heart jerk at the reproof. She could not bear the look of misery on Laura's face. Crouching on her knees in front of her, she urged, 'We'd never hurt you. Tell us why you haven't been to school. Tell Mammy.'

Laura looked at her, her face tear-stained. 'It was Rob said we should d-do it,' she whispered.

'Do what?' Carol asked, holding her hand.

'Go up the woods, round Brassy church. He said we should. But not to tell.'

Carol exchanged anxious looks with the head teacher. She dared not look at Mick's furious face.

'Rob's been taking you into Brassy woods?' Carol echoed.

Laura nodded.

'Why, pet?'

They held their breath.

'It's secret.'

'Mammy can keep your secret,' Carol whispered.

'We've been getting it from there. Rob's got a barrow. He takes it and hides it in his dad's shed.'

'Takes what?' Carol asked in confusion.

'The sticks and everything. We find them and put them in his barrow. He's going to share it out. Says he'll bring some round to our house when it's dark so the pigs don't see.'

Carol was dumbfounded. 'You mean you've been collecting firewood instead of going to school?'

Laura nodded. Then her face crumpled and the tears streamed down her peaky face. 'I'm sorry, Mam! I thought it would make Daddy happy. He doesn't like sitting at home with us 'cos there's no fire. I did it for D-Daddy!' she sobbed.

Carol looked across at Mick. His face was appalled. He was staring at his daughter as if for the first time, yet she would not look at him.

Mick slipped off his chair and went to hold her. Mrs Little let go.

'Oh, pet!' he cried. 'Don't be sorry. It's your dad who's sorry . . .'

Carol saw the tears spring into his eyes as Laura's skinny arms went round his neck. They clung to each other in a fierce hug and cried. Carol's vision blurred as she looked up gratefully to Mrs Little. What a terrible burden for a small girl to carry! How had they not seen how unhappy they were making her with their lack of love towards each other? How frightened and desperate she must have been to miss school in order to try and please them with the firewood!

Mrs Little got up quietly. 'I'll go and make a cup of tea for us all.' Then she left them alone to weep and hug one another in reconciliation. Carol could hear young voices beyond the door, practising carols for the end of term service.

Mick looked at her. 'I'm sorry, Carol. I've left you to cope on your own for too long. I'm going to help you now, I promise.'

Carol smiled through her tears and gave him a kiss.

Then for the first time in days, she saw Laura's anxious face break into a beautiful smile.

For the last week of term, Mick took Laura to school and picked her up. As the preparations for the Christmas socials grew more frantic, he came to the Welfare to help out. He and Charlie went with Paul Dimarco to the cash and carry to buy bulk amounts of food to keep the village going through the holiday period. The soup kitchen would close after Christmas Eve until the New Year and they had to make sure the striking families would have enough to tide them over.

Carol and the committee spent long hours compiling lists of family numbers and ages and pinned them to a street map of the area. They asked the parents who came to the hall to write down requests from the children as to what they most wanted for Christmas.

'We can't promise they'll get it,' Carol told them, 'but we'll do our best.'

Laura still had her heart set on a puppy, but said some clothes for her teddies would do instead.

Carol and the other women stayed late into the night, sorting out parcels of clothing and presents. There were so many in need and yet so little of any value to go round. Some evenings Lotty would bring them in a bottle of cheap wine and they would sit around drinking out of tea cups, sharing each other's worries and making one another laugh.

When she got home Mick would be waiting up for her instead of being already asleep and would ask how preparations were going. He seemed reluctant to let Laura out of his sight since the revelation about her truanting and was content to stay at home while she worked at the hall.

The day before Christmas Eve, Charlie and Mick came rushing into the Welfare kitchen, waving their arms in excitement.

'We've got a message to go down the docks,' Charlie shouted. 'A call's just come through. There's a container of stuff come from France!'

They waited all day for the men to come back from the port. As dark descended, there were shouts of concern as a hearse drew up in front of the hall, until May shouted, 'You bugger, it's Eddy driving!'

He had borrowed it from the funeral director who drank at The Ship and it was full of boxes. Behind, Charlie drove up in Dimarco's van. They all rushed out laughing to help unload. When they began to unpack the boxes of gifts from French trade unionists, the women were rendered speechless. They gasped at the generosity of their friends abroad. There were brand new toys of all descriptions - bikes and scooters, dolls and roller skates, games and footballs, clothes and books. There were hundreds of pounds worth of toys.

'That's not the end of it,' Charlie told them, almost overcome. There's another van load to collect.'

'Hearse load, you mean,' Eddy grinned.

Carol felt her throat tighten at the thought of their kindness. She had felt they were battling alone so many times recently and morale had been badly damaged by the trickle of pitmen back to work. At times she had questioned if they were right to carry on when there was so much suffering in the village and in countless other villages across the coalfield. But these generous workers in France thought they were right. They had not given up on them as some at home had done. They were not alone.

Carol went over to Charlie and gave him a hug, unable to speak for emotion. For once he could not reply, only patted her back.

'Haway, then,' said Lotty briskly, 'get yourself back for the rest of the stuff. We've got some parcelling up to do.'

For two days they kept the children out of the hall while they sorted out presents and decorated the canteen for the party. Mick and Sid scaled ladders tying streamers and balloons, while Charlie and Stan Savage wrestled with the boiler that was threatening to pack up. Eddy had volunteered to dress up as a clown and entertain the children, while Captain Lenin was to make an appearance as Santa. Mick and Sid had gone over to Quarryhill and persuaded an old marra of theirs to bring his disco equipment for the evening party. He had agreed to do it in return for a few free pints. A London support group had sent up money to buy in some kegs of beer and bottles of wine so that everyone would have a free drink this Christmas.

In the evening, Mick helped Carol take some of the French presents around to families after children were in bed and they were rewarded with smiles and tears from fraught parents wondering how they were going to get through Christmas Day with nothing to give their children.

By the time Laura was getting dressed for the party, Carol was as excited as she was. Normally they would have bought their daughter a new dress for the season, but Carol had lengthened the one from last year. It looked tight round the armpits and Carol thought Laura was going to protest, until Mick came in.

'What a little princess!' he exclaimed, lifting her up and swinging her round.

'Don't crumple me!' Laura complained and then giggled suddenly as he pretended to drop her.

Carol came back wearing the soft sequinned jumper of Val's and a shortish black skirt. She had dashed on some eye-liner and lipstick and pulled a brush through her hair, without any more time to spend getting ready. But Mick whistled in appreciation for the first time in an age and made her blush.

'I like your jumper, Mam,' Laura said with approval. 'Isn't Mam pretty for her age?'

Carol and Mick laughed.

'Very,' Mick agreed, grinning.

'I'm only twenty-six, you cheeky pair!' Carol retorted. Yet how much older she felt at times.

She bustled Laura out of the house and told Mick to hurry and change and meet them down at the hall, but she went with a lighter step to think that Mick was more like his old self.

The children's party was a huge success judging by the level of noise and laughter. Eddy had them screaming with giggles when his tricks went wrong and Carol was not sure if he deliberately messed them up or was just a hopeless magician. The women supervised the teas and she and Sid organised the games, while Kelly stuffed herself full of leftover jelly and ice cream. The pregnancy was showing, but Sid had broadcast this to the world long before. As far as Carol could see, they had settled into a truce, though she'd been too busy of late to discover how Kelly was feeling about her decision to stay with Sid.

Finally Captain Lenin rolled in with his white beard and booming chuckle, wearing an enormous Santa suit and carrying a sack of small gifts. Some of the younger children ran screaming to their parents, but were soon coaxed back with the promise of something from the sack.

By seven o'clock the hall was emptying of tired party-goers and the committee began to clear the hall for the adult disco. Carol was nearly asleep on her feet and would have liked nothing better than to slink off home with Laura and put her to bed instead of Lotty. She wondered where Mick could have got to and was vexed he had not turned up to help with the party.

When they had finished resetting the tables, Carol slipped out for a cigarette and went home to say goodnight to Laura. There was no sign of Mick at home and Carol wondered if he had gone off to the pub with Eddy after the party.

Lotty confirmed this. 'Said he wanted to see the Captain about something.'

Carol sighed in annoyance. 'I hope he's not going to get stuck there all evening with Eddy and not turn up at our disco.'

'He won't.' Lotty seemed sure. 'You get yourself back to the hall and have a drink.'

But Laura was too excited and would not go to bed. She knew that she would not be getting as many presents as usual, but thanks to donations from abroad, Carol was able to promise that Santa would come. Just then the front doorbell rang.

It was Eddy. He put a finger to his lips and whispered, 'Go and open the curtains in Laura's bedroom.' Then he swept into the sitting room, shouting for Laura.

'I've just come to say goodnight to me favourite girl,' he called, his craggy face grinning.

'Uncle Eddy,' Laura said, jumping up and down on the settee, 'do you think Santa will come tonight?'

'Only if you get to bed now like a good lass,' Eddy bargained. 'I'll give you a carry upstairs.'

He gave Laura a piggy-back and dumped her down on her bed. Carol was standing at the window peering down into the back lane.

'Laura, come here quickly,' she whispered, 'but don't make a sound.'

The girl scampered over to the window and gasped. There in the lane below was Santa carrying a sack on his back, his white beard gleaming in the soft street lights. In the wondering silence that followed, they could hear his boots clearly tramping down the lane.

Laura's eyes were wide in awe. 'Is that the real Santa?'

Carol nodded, smiling at Eddy.

'Will he be coming back here?'

'Of course he will. But you'll have to be in bed and asleep first.'

Laura leapt into bed, thrilled by what she had seen, and buried herself under the covers with her teddies. Carol kissed and hugged her.

'Mam,' came a muffled voice.

'Yes?'

'Santa wears pit boots just like Daddy, doesn't he?'

Carol glanced at Eddy and stopped herself from laughing. 'Aye, just like. Get to sleep now, pet.'

Downstairs they chuckled at what Mick had done. 'It was all his idea,' Eddy told her. 'He's borrowed the clothes off Lenin. He's going to walk round the village until the bairns are asleep.'

Carol was overwhelmed by Mick's gesture towards the children. It made up for so much of the painful months when she thought he no longer cared about her or anyone else.

'You get yourself off to the dance now,' Lotty told Carol, seeing that she was near to tears. 'Have a grand time and don't come back until they kick you out, do you hear?'

Carol kissed her mother-in-law gratefully and set off into the cold night with Eddy.

'It's strange,' she told him. 'It's been such a terrible year and yet this is the happiest Christmas Eve I think I can remember.'

Eddy swung an arm about her shoulders and gave her a hug. 'I know what you mean. As Grandda Bowman used to say, "The more you put into it, the more you get out".' He mimicked the old man's wheezy voice.

'Canny old Grandda,' Carol said with a wistful smile. 'We'll miss him this Christmas.'

Eddy surprised her with his reply. 'I think old Arthur's still with us,' he said quietly.

They found the hall packed and noisy, filled with smoke and laughter and people out to enjoy themselves. The Women's Group banner was displayed above the kitchen hatch and Carol felt a surge of pride. Kelly came over complaining that Sid would not let her drink alcohol.

'Get us a vodka, won't you, Carol man? This is not the Christmas to sign the pledge.'

Carol laughed. 'I'll get you a glass of wine, diluted with soda.'

'Oh, ta! Call yourself a friend?' Kelly groaned, but steered Carol over to the bar anyway.

After the buffet of pies and sausage rolls, pickles and crisps, the DJ made an announcement.

This evening has been organised by the luscious ladies of Brassbank Miners' Women's Support Group. Let's all put our hands together for the girls, eh, lads?'

There was loud applause and whistling.

'Now, before we get down to some serious boogie,' he continued, 'we have a request from the ladies themselves. They've asked me to kick off with a special song that's dedicated to their men. So here we are. This one's for all the Brassbank lads who've stuck it out through thick and thin - "You'll Never Walk Alone".'

Carol glanced around, wishing Mick was there to hear the tribute, for he had sacrificed more than most during this strike. The women joined hands as the music filled the hall and May and Val led them in the singing.

Carol saw tears on the faces of both men and women as more and more linked arms around the room. Suddenly she caught sight of Mick standing in the doorway, his face red and pinched from being out in the cold. She went straight across to him and drew him into the singing crowd. People stood aside to let them through. As the tribute continued Carol clung to Mick, knowing he would hate the attention but determined he should be acknowledged for what he had done. The song grew to a deafening crescendo as they sang out the chorus with all their hearts.

Tears streamed down Carol's face as she held Mick and saw the look of love in his eyes as he smiled at her. Around them, the closeness and strong friendship that bound them all together in that hall was palpable. For a brief, heady moment Carol felt it and knew that everyone there felt it too.

At the end, Sid grabbed the microphone.

'Somebody here needs a special mention tonight. Let's all give a big hand for Mick Todd. He's been a credit to our pit and our lodge. Just like on the rugby pitch, or down the pit, Mick can be relied upon to back his marras. No one's taken as much of a hammering as he has. But he's still the right side of the picket line!'

There was a roar of approval and deafening applause. Mick pulled Carol into his arms and stood holding her in front of the others. He was telling them in his bashful way that he could not have done it without her.

The clapping continued and people came up to shake him by the hand and fetch them drinks. The disco began and they moved to a table with Sid and Kelly and Joanne and John. Friends crowded round to chat and shout above the strains of Band Aid. But Mick did not let go of Carol's hand. She revelled in his closeness and thought she would burst with pride in him.

She knew she would remember this night as long as she lived.

Chapter Twenty-Nine

When they got home that night, exhausted but elated by the evening, Mick took Carol to see what he was hiding in the back shed. There, curled up in a box with blankets, was a small black puppy. It lay fast asleep, making little sighing sounds. Carol stared at Mick in amazement.

'Where did this come from?' she asked.

'It was payment in kind,' Mick grinned.

Carol gave him a suspicious look. 'Oh aye?'

'I've been doing a bit of gardening for Mrs Hunt and some of the other pensioners up by Grandda's. I wouldn't take any money, but they knew about Laura wanting a pup. So they clubbed together and got this young 'un off the dairyman at Brassy. I think its pedigree is about as dodgy as the Todds' but it seems canny enough.'

'Mick, it's smashing,' Carol said, stroking the tiny puppy gently. It snuffled and stirred. 'It's even got a red collar like Laura wanted. She'll be over the moon.' She put out a hand to touch his face. 'So that's where you've been spending your days, gardening for the old folks?'

Mick shrugged with embarrassment. 'Some of the time. I need to be out doing summat. I can't stand being idle.'

Carol put her arms round him. 'Aye, I know. I can see how hard it is for you not working.'

Mick rested his chin on her wavy hair. 'And it made me feel close to Grandda, being up there. It's like I've said me proper goodbyes, not chained to a warder like at the funeral. . .' He broke off.

Carol raised her head and saw his eyes glistening with tears. It was so unlike Mick to say what he was feeling. She felt very close to him at that moment. Gently, tentatively she kissed him on the lips. He drew back an instant and then kissed her in return - a longer, more confident kiss.

'Let's go to bed,' Carol whispered.

The bedroom was icy and the light harsh and Carol suddenly froze with the awkwardness of the situation, as if they were two strangers forced to share the same changing room. Mick, who was removing his jeans, looked over at her.

'Do you want to get undressed or put more clothes on?' he joked.

Carol laughed, reassured.

Mick came over and helped her undress quickly. 'Haway, before we get frostbite.'

Naked, they dived under the pile of covers, dampish from the cold. They rubbed each other to warm up and started to kiss. Carol almost cried at his gentleness and the tender way he stroked back her hair, kissing her face and neck and breasts.

'I've missed you,' he whispered.

'So have I,' Carol croaked. 'I thought I'd lost you.'

'Never!' Mick answered vehemently and hugged her against him.

They kissed eagerly and with passion. They revelled in the feel of each other after so long and the old familiar intimacies. Carol clung to Mick and told him that she loved him, her whole body coming alive again.

'I love you too, pet,' he assured her.

She could hardly believe how happy she was. She had the old Mick back once more, vigorous, tender and loving. They made love again and then lay wrapped in each other's arms, reminiscing about how they had met and the time they had taken off impulsively on the motorbike and disappeared to Weardale, scandalising their families.

'It seems that long ago,' Carol sighed, 'another lifetime. Will things ever be that simple again?'

'We'll come through all this,' Mick encouraged. 'One day we'll buy another bike and gan off round the country. You can introduce me to all these new friends you've made through fundraising.'

'And Laura comes too,' Carol reminded him.

'Aye, of course,' he agreed. 'We'll have a sidecar for her - and any other little Todds that might come along.'

Carol blushed. They had not talked about another baby for years and she had not known whether Mick still hankered after another child.

'Do you still want more bairns?' she asked quietly.

'Aye, I do,' he answered, searching her face. His blue eyes were anxious, questioning.

'So do I,' she whispered. 'But we can't afford one now even if we could manage to have—'

Mick kissed her hard on the lips, silencing any doubts. 'If we're lucky enough to have another bairn, we'll manage,' he assured her, 'just like Sid and Kelly will. There's enough family around to help.'

Carol felt uncomfortable at the mention of their friends; it raised so many unanswered questions about Mick's past with Kelly.

'Mick,' she asked tentatively, 'why did you finish with Kelly when you did?'

He gave her an astonished look that made her unease grow. 'Why ever are you asking me that now?'

'It's just Kelly still seems bitter about it.'

Mick snorted. 'Well, she shouldn't. She was the one finished with me! Me pride was a bit hurt, if I'm honest. One minute she was wanting to get serious, the next she never wanted to go out with me again. She's a strange lass, I never really knew what she wanted. But I never led her on. I told her I couldn't love her. And I didn't.' He touched Carol's face. 'You're the only one I've ever loved, or ever will.'

Carol kissed him tenderly, convinced he knew nothing of making Kelly pregnant. Kelly had resented Mick for not loving her and nursed her bitterness all these years over something he knew nothing about.

'But it was all that long ago, why are you dragging it up now?' Mick asked.

Quietly she told him of Kelly's affair with Vic and the probability of the baby not being Sid's.

'Do you think I did the right thing persuading her to stay with Sid?' Carol asked, still unsure.

'Time will tell,' Mick sighed, shaken by the news. 'But I'm glad you did, for Sid's sake. It's given him new hope after such a hard time. It doesn't make me think any better of Kelly, mind.'

'It's Vic I blame,' Carol replied. Yet she felt a great burden had been lifted from her, now that she had shared the secret. She knew Mick would tell no one else.

'Let's just think about ourselves for tonight, eh?' Mick hugged her.

'Aye,' Carol smiled and kissed him. 'And we should go and fill Laura's stocking before that puppy starts barking and wakes her up early.'

Christmas flew by with family visits and walks along the cliffs. Laura was enchanted with her new puppy, and brought all her friends round to see him. After a week of mopping up after the small dog, they named him Puddles and Carol's enthusiasm began to wear off. He was an extra mouth to feed too, but she was not going to spoil Laura's enjoyment by saying so.

Mick was much more his old self and went out with Eddy and Sid for games of pool and darts, as well as taking Laura to the park and spending time with his parents, chatting and teaching Laura dominoes so she could beat her grandfather. Carol took Laura to see her parents while Mick was playing rugby. He would not go to see them and she would not force him. Kate and Simon were there, but to Carol's relief Vic and Fay were holidaying in Spain. Laura came away with money for a new pair of boots and a Snakes and Ladders game.

It was like a period of calm that came as a gift during a stormy season and Carol wished it could go on for ever. But soon Laura was back at school and the soup kitchen was operating again. There was a feeling of anti-climax among the women and Carol noticed that many of them seemed exhausted after having kept their families going all through the holidays.

When they met in each other's houses, there were anxious stories about mounting debts and tensions with husbands over how Christmas was to be paid for now it was over. Despite trying their best to provide for everyone, the holidays had brought unforeseen expenses and the strain on the Women's Group and the strike fund were great. Carol and Joanne mounted a further fundraising effort, but soon found that sympathy for their plight had waned. Shopkeepers in Whittledene were openly hostile to them collecting outside their shops and moved them on; while shoppers complained they had their own families to take care of.

Taking refuge from the cold in one cafe, Carol was rounded on by the proprietor.

'You've got a cheek asking for money!' he fulminated. 'I wouldn't give a penny to the miners. They're nothing but a bunch of violent thugs. I'm sick of watching them every night on the telly. They should get themselves back to work and do some honest toil like the rest of us. I run a business and get no time off - that's what hard work really is.'

Carol flared with anger. 'That's just what they want, to get back to work! And don't you tell us about hard work. Pitmen graft harder than any men I know.'

The man was scornful. 'I don't have a rich union to give me months off work when I feel like it. If I went on strike, this business would go down the drain.'

Carol was up on her feet, despite Joanne tugging on her arm to sit down.

'The union's had most of its funds taken off it, you ignorant man! The miners have never had a penny in strike pay. We've had to live off charity for nearly a year. Imagine what that does to proud men? They've been on strike for principles, not money. And it's been no holiday. For some of us it's been a year of hell!'

His face had gone livid at her answering back. He gesticulated at the door. 'You can tell you're a bolshie miner's wife. You deserve each other! Well, you'll not get charity here, so bugger off!'

'I wouldn't stay and drink your tea anyway, it would choke me,' Carol answered with contempt.

As she stormed to the door, followed by Joanne, she heard his wife shout from behind the counter, 'Well, I hope they all lose their jobs and end up on the dole. That'll teach them!'

Out in the street, Carol shook with anger and hurt. Not since the rally in Mansfield at the beginning of the strike had she experienced such hostility.

'And these are local people,' she gasped at Joanne. 'They've grown up among us, they know how the area has depended on the pits.'

They caught the bus home, the fight gone out of them. Carol worried about the implications of public opinion swinging away from them. Perhaps people had grown tired of caring or were too caught up in their own lives to realise what was being lost on their very doorstep. She had a brief, crazy thought about what the area would be like without any pits at all. No, that was unthinkable! Even if they lost the strike, the big pits would still survive and there would be jobs for some. But the vision scared her. And reaching home she realised that, for the first time, she had let the thought of their losing the strike enter her head.

January was a bleak, dark month of just getting by. Carol felt permanently cold, her hands often numb, her feet sore with chilblains. Laura's attacks of asthma grew more frequent and alarming; Carol's trips to the surgery with her became regular. Twice she met Kelly there, looking sallow and unwell and anxious about her unborn baby whom she felt was not moving enough. She still had two months to go. Carol went to visit her later and found her huddled in a duvet in front of the TV.

'We're going to lose the house,' she said, nearly in tears. 'We might have to move in with Dad again - not that he can afford to have us since he's still out of work. Oh, Carol! All that we've worked for down the toilet. What sort of future will our baby have?'

Carol put her arms round her in comfort. 'If we cave in now, we'll have no future to offer our bairns at all. As long as we stick it out together, we have a chance of offering them something.'

Kelly threw her off, instantly angry. 'Sod your strike! That's all you ever think about. I just want Sid to get back to work so we can afford to buy this baby some clothing when it comes. We've got nothing left, nothing!'

Carol stayed until Kelly had calmed down a little, worried that she was making herself ill. But Kelly remained touchy about anything she said, so she decided to keep away for a bit.

The pressure on the men to return to work was now intense. Each received a copy of Coal News to urge them back to work.

'Think what all this is costing!' Mick shook the management newspaper indignantly. 'They've spent a fortune trying to break us.'

'Aye,' Eddy grunted. 'Funny how there's always money for some things.'

Police patrolled the coal tips and people caught picking the coal were prosecuted. Then February came and negotiations re-opened between the union and Coal Board and their hopes of a just settlement were raised once more. But by the middle of the month the talks broke down again.

Charlie came round. 'They're giving us nothing,' he said grimly. They won't even discuss an amnesty for the sacked miners.'

Carol was alarmed at this. There were so many men who had been hauled through the criminal courts like Mick and many of them had been sacked on the spot, even if their offences had had nothing to do with Coal Board property. Some had been ruthlessly dismissed before their cases came to court. So far no disciplinary action had been taken against Mick or the others at Brassbank and for that she was sure they had her father to thank. But there was no knowing what might happen to them if they lost the strike. The news was full of the growing numbers flooding back to work.

They make up the figures,' Charlie complained. 'They don't tally with the numbers of men we know are still on strike.'

'At least Brassbank's nearly solid,' Mick said. 'There's still only a handful going in.'

Carol thought sadly of Dan and Linda. They had not seen them since Mick's arrest. Linda had never even brought Calvin back to see Lotty; they had quite cut themselves off. Carol knew that Lotty was deeply wounded by the family split, but her life was with Charlie and there was little she could do to heal the rift after all these months. Even Denise, Linda's best friend since childhood, did not know where Linda was living. She had gone once to look for her at the old flat in Whittledene Rise but found it occupied by someone else. It was obvious neither Dan nor Linda wished to be traced while the strike continued.

Unexpectedly, the next day, Sid came rushing round in a panic.

'They're taking Kelly into hospital. She's got high blood pressure and they're worried about the baby.'

'I'll come with you, if you like,' Carol offered. 'Mick can meet Laura from school.'

Sid accepted with relief. 'I don't like hospitals and all that.'

They saw Kelly briefly in a side ward, before she was taken away for tests.

'I'll come back and see her tomorrow,' Carol promised Sid.

But early the next morning, Sid rang to say that Kelly had gone into labour during the night and the baby had been born six weeks prematurely.

'She's in special care,' Sid told Carol. 'Kelly'll stay in with her till we see . . .' His voice broke off.

'If she's a fighter like you, she'll be just fine,' Carol assured him, then remembered that the baby was not Sid's. 'What's she called?'

'Sally Mary, after Kelly's mam,' Sid said proudly. 'She's that small but she's a little picture. Perfect...' he was overcome and Carol rang off quickly, saying she would visit soon.

It was a couple of days later that she and Joanne went to visit the maternity wing in Whittledene hospital, promising Laura that she could go the next time. They found Kelly sitting beside Sally's incubator gazing at her baby.

'She's lovely,' Carol said with tears in her eyes, staring at the tiny crinkled infant wearing a knitted doll's hat. Her arms and legs were long and thin, with delicate miniature fingers and toes. She looked too fragile to touch. Joanne was full of wonder too.

'This is from the Women's Group for my special niece,' Joanne smiled, handing Kelly a small parcel.

Kelly seemed embarrassed, but opened it to find a bundle of baby clothes knitted from unravelled old jumpers that they had been working on since

Christmas.

'Looks like they won't fit her till the summer,' Carol laughed.

'Ta very much,' Kelly mumbled and then started to cry.

Carol gave her a hug. 'You don't know whether to sing or cry for the first few days, do you?'

'And my brother's on cloud nine,' Joanne laughed. 'You've made him really happy.'

Carol glanced at Kelly, knowing she must be thinking how this was really Vic's daughter. How difficult had it been for her to carry on the pretence? Carol wondered.

'Carol,' Kelly sniffed. 'Do you know . . ?'

'What?'

Kelly shook her head. 'Oh, nothing. Just thanks.'

Carol regretted that she was not on her own with Kelly so that she could have spoken of what troubled her. She was obviously inhibited by having Sid's sister there.

They chatted about the birth for a few minutes and then Kelly said she wanted to go for a bath.

'It's great round here - hot water whenever you want it. And the food's smashing.' Suddenly Kelly was her old animated self and Carol felt a touch jealous.

'I'll bring me sponge next time,' she joked.

Kelly hurried away without replying.

Carol was holding a meeting at her house to discuss a fundraising social. There was more need for food parcels than ever. Mick and Eddy had gone round to see Sid and take him down to The Ship for a pint as they had not celebrated Sally Mary's arrival yet.

May had brought a bag of broken biscuits and Joanne some of John's homemade rhubarb wine saved for a special occasion.

'Well, we can all have a sip to toast young Sally Mary,' Joanne said.

After a glass each, everyone was chatting merrily and laughing at the week's troubles. Carol described her visit to see the new baby and how pleased Kelly had been with their knitting.

'It cheers everyone up having a new bairn around, doesn't it?' June declared.

Suddenly they were startled by the door swinging open and Mick and Eddy stamping in, drenched from the rain.

'Boots, lads,' Lotty shouted.

But Carol could see from Mick's face that he was in no mood for teasing.

'Whatever's wrong?' she asked, getting up.

'It's Sid,' Mick said, struggling to speak.

'What's happened to him?' Joanne asked in alarm.

Eddy explained. 'He wasn't there when we went round. So we went round to Ted's to see if he knew where he was. Sid was there. He was just leaving.'

'For the hospital?' Joanne asked, puzzled.

Eddy shook his head. 'To go on night shift.'

There was a stunned silence in the room. Then it erupted.

'Never?'

'Not Sid! He'd stay out for ever!'

'It's that Kelly's driven him back.'

'And after all we've done for them!'

Carol went to Mick. 'But he's stuck out for so long. Why is he doing this now?'

Eddy spoke quietly, while the remonstrations went on around them. 'Said he's done it for the baby. He won't bring Kelly and the bairn back to no heating and no food. He's had enough.'

'We've all had enough,' Carol snapped. 'But we would've supported them, Sid knows that.'

'The baby's changed all that, it seems,' Eddy answered tiredly.

Carol was filled with guilt. It was she who had persuaded Kelly to stay with Sid and pretend the baby was his. Now Mick's staunchest friend was prepared to cut himself off from them all and betray them for the sake of a daughter who was not his. Carol felt sick with disgust at Sid and Kelly for their weakness and at herself for allowing the charade. Should she tell Sid about Vic being the father in order to bring him back on strike? she wondered wildly. But that would be to shatter lives further. Suddenly, Carol realised Mick could have told Sid himself but had not. Mick had spared his friend that humiliation, but at what a cost! Sid had crossed the line. The damage was already done; she saw that in the haunted look on Mick's face.

'He was me marra, Carol,' Mick said, still in shock. 'Me best marra. I'd have done anything for him.' Carol put her arms round him, wishing she could protect him from this deepest of hurts. But she felt him stiffen. 'And now he's a *scab*. He spat the word out as if it poisoned him. Joanne, hearing the venom in his voice, buried her face in her hands in shame and wept.

Things changed after that night. Mick was even more determined to fight on with the majority of the Brassbank men. But there was a hardness about him that had not been there before, grown out of the bitterness he felt at Sid's betrayal. It was far worse than anything he had felt for Dan, Carol knew, and it seemed to eat away at him.

They soldiered on, but none of the Women's Group went to see Kelly. Carol wanted to go but felt it would be too disloyal to Mick. Sometimes she wondered if news had filtered back to Victor about his child and whether he knew of the havoc he had caused. She imagined he would not care.

News on the strike was bleak. After the recent talks broke down, there were appeals for mass pickets because of the fear of more returning to work. And by the end of February there were angry scenes again at Brassbank pit gates as the police battled to bring in the scabs.

Then rumours began of an orderly return to work. Mick went off to the lodge meeting where a vote was to be taken on whether to continue to strike. Carol waited nervously for his return, but he came back buoyant that their pit had voted to stay out.

Charlie went off to the delegates' meeting in Sheffield the first weekend in March. Carol and Mick watched the TV for news. There were angry scenes outside the NUM headquarters when the delegates emerged. They had voted by 91 to 89 for a return to work, despite the determination of pits like Brassbank to carry on.

Carol and Mick sat in disbelief. The reporter was telling them the strike was over. The miners' leaders had capitulated. There would be no amnesty for sacked miners. Thatcher was claiming it as a 'famous victory'.

'It can't be true,' Carol said, stunned. 'The media have got it wrong again, they must have!'

Mick said nothing, just bowed his head as if someone had punched him unconscious. They sat there for an age, while Laura played with Puddles, unaware of the crisis. The telephone rang, but neither of them answered it. It went silent. Laura looked at them in surprise.

'Have you gone deaf?' she asked, grinning cheekily.

Carol looked at her daughter through a blur of tears. A whole year of suffering for nothing! She wanted to feel anger, to lash out at the people who had done this to them. She wanted to feel pain, grief, pity, to cry out her hurt - anything that indicated she was still alive, still felt something. But she felt nothing. Carol sat there, unable to speak, unable to put her arms round her husband to comfort him as she had done so often, unable to smile at her daughter and pull her over for a cuddle.

There was just emptiness, a gaping nothingness in her heart. And it was the most terrifying feeling she had ever experienced.

Charlie returned with instructions from the delegates' conference to advise an orderly return to work. Carol knew he had not voted to end the strike and the duty of telling them all to march back was a painful one. She had never seen him so subdued. He escaped to his allotment for most of Monday, the day before the march back to work.

'We'll make it a proud march back,' Lotty declared. 'We'll all be there to support you. The world will see that we're not broken - we'll have our heads held high!'

Carol wished she could summon the same fighting spirit but was too overwhelmed by the anti-climax of it all. She thought of Sid and the others who had returned just two weeks earlier amid such hatred and wondered if they regretted their decision now.

That night she held on to Mick tightly. Only then did a strange relief come over her. Tomorrow the long strike would be over and the men would be back at work. They could at least begin to pay off their debts and life could get back to some semblance of normality.

'Oh, the group had planned such a party for the end of the strike,' Carol sighed. 'We've been dreaming of this day all year, but now there's nothing to celebrate.'

'We just have to look ahead,' Mick murmured. He kissed her tenderly. 'It'll be strange going back underground after so long. Though what it'll be like now . . .'

Carol knew he was thinking of Sid. If there were families like the Todds and Shannons who still did not speak to each other because of enmities created in the 1926 lockout, she shuddered to think of what the legacy of this bitter year might be.

'Hold me,' she whispered.

That night they made love with a tender desperation, trying to blot out the world beyond their cold bedroom. At least she had Mick, Carol thought as they held each other tight and drifted into sleep; she would always have Mick.

They gathered in a wet dawn. Hundreds of them were ranked behind the colliery band and the proud scarlet banner depicting former union leaders and their lodge motto, 'Never Stand Alone'. The Women's Group walked beside them up the pit lane under their own flag, in solidarity with the men. Carol noticed how the muddy ground still bore the hoof marks of the mounted police who had protected the convoys of scabs in recent days.

The lane looked stark and bare in the grey light; the ditches churned up and stripped of the thorny trees that had given the pickets some shelter in the early days. But the band thumped out their stirring music and there were smiles of pride as well as tears on the faces of those who marched.

Mick was up at the front, holding one of the banner poles, and Carol thought how just a year ago she could not have dreamed of her husband getting so involved in the struggle. But then neither could she have imagined how committed she had become. Being involved in the Women's Group had been like stepping into a new world for so many of them. They had travelled the country, stood up and spoken in front of halls full of strangers, run committees, handled large amounts of money, organised massive food relief every week and catered for hundreds every day in the cramped Welfare kitchen. They had learned so much without even realising it, Carol thought.

She could not imagine the group breaking up and the women just returning to their domestic lives like before. She dreaded such an outcome. She determined that they must keep in touch and find new projects. There would still be a need for food parcels during this next month, she thought as she marched forward with Lotty and Joanne beside her. They still had a job to do.

Villagers lined the road clapping them as they marched past and the children cheered them and ran ahead. At the pit gates the band played 'Gresford' and they all stood together, thinking about the many men they knew who had worked at Brassbank in the past. Carol saw tears on Lotty's face and knew she thought of Grandda Bowman. She squeezed the older woman's hand and found Lotty hanging on to her tightly. She wondered if Charlie thought of his own father, excluded from this same pit and dying young.

It was as if in that moment the thoughts of all of them rose and mingled with the emotional music. And under a pewter sky, massed together on the spot where Mick had been arrested, they stood as one family. They were united in their sorrow and disappointment, yet proud in defeat. Carol, watching the faces around her, knew that few regretted what they had done. In a strange way, she would not have missed this year for anything, despite its sacrifices. They had come much closer to each other than ever before. Lotty had often likened it to the spirit of the war.

Something special had happened here in Brassbank this last year that no politicians or Coal Board accountants could measure, and Carol was glad that she had been a part of it. Looking at Mick holding the lodge banner aloft with such pride, she felt a huge lump constrict her throat and the tears came at last.

Chapter Thirty

After the men filed through the pit gates, Carol and her friends walked their children to school. It was comforting to chat together and have others around her. Nevertheless, anxiety began to mount in her at the uncertainty of what would happen now. It was like the nagging feeling she got recently when she woke in the night for no reason and began to sweat with worry without knowing why.

'You all right, Carol?' Joanne asked her in concern.

Carol nodded.

'Well, you don't look it,' May was forthright. 'You should get yourself home for some sleep - you look washed out.'

But Carol shrugged it off and went home via Lotty's. Her mother-in-law was mending a pair of Charlie's trousers.

'Haven't had time to do this till now,' Lotty smiled in pleasure at her appearance. She put down her sewing. 'Let's be wicked and make ourselves some tea. I'm feeling at a loss this morning.'

They sat and drank tea in the kitchen for an hour. Carol was thinking it was about time she stirred herself to go home and do something, when they heard the sound of heavy boots crossing the back yard. The two women looked at each other in alarm; the men could not be back already.

Charlie and Mick walked in. They stood in silence looking at the women.

Lotty said, 'What in the world's happened?'

Mick glanced away from Carol. 'We've been sacked,' he said in a dead voice.

'Charlie?' Lotty gasped, her hands flying to her mouth.

'It's true,' he nodded grimly, waving papers at them. 'Gross misconduct.'

'For what?' Lotty demanded.

'For standing up on the picket line, of course, and getting a criminal record,' Charlie growled.

'Let's see that,' Lotty said, seizing the letters from her husband, as if she did not believe him. She picked up her reading glasses.

Carol stared at Mick. She could think of nothing to say. This was her worst nightmare, the fear that had been lurking in the back of her mind.

Lotty's hands dropped into her lap in defeat. She handed the letters across to Carol without a word. Carol scanned the letter of dismissal and gasped. They had been signed by her father. A cold rage seized her. He was not going to do this to them, not after everything else they had endured!

'I've got to gan back up there to represent the other lads,' Charlie said resignedly. 'Marty Dillon's been suspended till his court case is heard. Frankie Hurt's been sacked too.'

'Oh, poor June!' Lotty said in distress.

Charlie made towards the door. 'I'm coming with you,' Carol told him, jumping up.

'What for?' Charlie asked.

'To give me dad an earful, that's what!' Carol declared.

Mick spoke for the first time. 'That won't help us. And I'll not have you making a fool of yourself to your father - not on my behalf.'

But Carol could not stay there and do nothing. She was at the limits of her endurance and this news was the final blow. She picked up her worn jacket and ran out. Not waiting to see if the others followed, she headed down the lane towards the pit.

At the gates she demanded to be let in to see the manager. There was a lot of activity in the pit yard and it was still heavily policed. She was told to go away.

'Then I'll stop here till he comes out,' she replied.

They turned their backs and ignored her. Carol stood around in the cold, damp air, growing angrier by the minute. She watched the picket hut being demolished and every sign of the strike being swept away in a morning. Even the brazier the pickets had huddled round was tossed into a skip still smouldering. Charlie appeared and went back into the pit yard, telling her to get off home. But Carol could not bear to return and face Mick. She had no words of comfort left, only a deep, burning fury.

In the early afternoon her father drove out of the pit yard. She ran at him, shouting, and hammered on the car for him to stop.

He wound down the window. 'Get in,' he said curtly.

They drove in stony silence along the Quarryhill road until the turnoff to Granville House.

'I don't want to come in,' Carol told him as he parked in front of the house. 'I just want you to explain why you're trying to crucify my family.' She glared at him.

He turned to face her in the car. He looked old. 'I had no choice.'

'Of course you have a choice, you're the manager! Or so you've never tired of telling me.'

'Listen, Carol. This is between you and me. We've been told to take a tough stand against the criminal element,' Ben said stiffly.

'You mean the Government's told you to get rid of the activists?' Carol said with scorn. 'You know the Todds aren't criminals.'

'Mick's been to prison, for God's sake!' Ben lost his temper. 'I should've sacked him long ago.'

'So why didn't you?' Carol demanded. 'So I'd still bring Laura to see you?'

He did not answer.

'You let us go on all these months thinking Mick still had a job and yet all the time you planned to get rid of him. He was one of your hardest workers, you've said so yourself. You've deceived us all!'

'I didn't mean to,' Ben grew agitated. 'I hoped it wouldn't be necessary. If he'd come back to work sooner like Dan or Sid Armstrong—'

'Like Sid?' Carol was contemptuous. 'You know Mick would never have crossed the picket line. He'd rather die.'

'What do you expect me to do, Carol?' Ben said impatiently. 'Is there any point to this outburst, or have you just come here to argue as usual?'

She looked at him long and hard, trying to control her frayed temper. When she spoke again, it was with a quiet, intense voice.

'I'm appealing to you to take Mick and his father back on,' she said. '*Please.* They've gone through enough. I lost Mick for three months while he was in prison. The courts punished him for what he did to Dan. Don't punish him twice by taking away his job. It's all he's got. Mick lives for the pit, you know that.' Carol's voice wavered. 'And I don't think I could bear him not working again. I've had it up to here, Dad,' she said, touching her forehead. 'I can't take any more.'

Ben saw the tears in her eyes and it struck him deep inside. He did not know if he loved or hated this young woman sitting beside him; he had felt both emotions. They had argued and disagreed all her life. But he was in awe of the way she pleaded now on her husband's behalf; he had thought her too proud. And at that moment he was in no doubt of the strong love Carol had for Mick Todd. At the time he had thought she had only married Mick to defy him. Now he was ashamed of such a thought.

Would that his own marriage had been half as happy, he thought sadly. He knew Nancy did not stay with him out of love, merely security. Yet perhaps even he was no longer that secure. He was full of disillusion about how the strike had been handled and hijacked by the politicians and he feared for all their futures, but he could not say this to his daughter.

'Carol,' he said, feeling very tired, 'I never wanted things to turn out like this. Brassbank is my life too. I know how Mick feels about the pit. But I'm under pressure. There's a new manager being brought in under me, one of the new breed, from outside the industry. There's very little I can do about the sackings.' He saw the look of despair on her face and knew he would never be forgiven. 'Look, I'll see what I can do about Charlie. His sentence was suspended. There might be some leeway there. But Mick,' he steeled himself to be firm. 'I just couldn't get away with taking him back on. There would be uproar. He put a man in hospital.'

'For half a day!' Carol protested.

They lapsed into tense silence.

Then she fixed him with her green eyes, always so sensuous and dangerous, but now ringed with fatigue. 'Just tell me this. Would you have taken him back on if he'd scabbed, despite his criminal record?'

Ben flushed, offended by the question, yet knowing she deserved a truthful answer.

'Probably,' he admitted. 'We were under enormous pressure to get anyone back to work.'

'That stinks,' Carol said bleakly and opened the car door. 'Aren't you just a little bit ashamed of the way your own men have been treated?'

Ben could not answer. He was stung by her words. She was right. Deep down he was ashamed that hardworking men like Mick would never work in the pits again, penalised for remaining loyal to their union and sticking to their principles. He had worked with such men all his life and he was not one of those who branded them troublemakers, only those who did not know them called them that.

Carol was climbing out.

'Let me give you a lift,' he urged, wretched at making her so unhappy. He felt this time he was losing her for ever.

She shook her head and began to walk away.

Ben forced himself to call out, 'I'm sorry, Carol, I really am.'

She looked at him one last time. 'Don't say it to me, Dad, say it to Mick. He's the one who's just beginning his real sentence.'

As Carol walked away she saw her mother staring out of the sitting-room window. She had been watching them in the car but now darted away out of sight. How sad, Carol thought with detachment, to be so afraid of your own husband

and so estranged from your own daughter not to be able to come out and greet them. But then her mother had run away from situations all her life.

Carol wandered out into the road, not knowing where she was going.

She had no recollection of getting to the beach and yet some time later she found herself sitting by Colly's Leap, watching the fierce tide throw itself against the rocks. The light was already trickling out of the sky behind the rush of clouds and Carol knew it must be late afternoon.

Alone, she finally let go. The pain and anger bottled up for so long came gushing out in bitter sobbing. She shook and heaved and cried, quite unable to stop herself. She had been strong for so long and now she was beaten, not by the strike but by the thought of what came after it. While it continued, she had had a purpose. Now she had none. She ached with weakness and exhaustion. She wanted to sleep for ever, but she did not know how to stop crying.

The search party found her just before dark, shivering on a rock, unable to speak. Mick and Eddy raised her gently to her feet and helped her along the beach to the path through the dunes. Carol was vaguely aware of Charlie and Stan being there and Marty Dillon. She fell asleep in the warmth of someone's car and remembered nothing else until the next morning.

She awoke in her own bed at home, her head pounding and body shivering with aches and pains. Her nose streamed and she either burned with heat and threw the covers off or grew cold and shivery again.

Lotty was there from time to time, with hot lemon drinks and once with Joanne. The doctor came and went, but Carol could not find the strength to speak to any of them. She slept a lot, woke confused, heard voices below, dozed and then sank into oblivion once more. Sometimes she heard Laura's plaintive voice asking to be let in, then someone shooshing her away. In a detached way she knew she should have called out to her daughter, but she did not have the energy. She wanted no one's company, not even Laura's. Yet at times she was aware of a comforting presence. Someone who came and went and sat beside her in the silence, held her hand and wiped her sweating face with a damp cloth. After several days of not knowing or caring what day of the week it was, she woke feeling less feverish.

Mick was there, sitting in the corner reading a newspaper and doing a crossword. He looked up and smiled.

'Feeling any better?' he asked. 'I've made some soup if you could manage it - well, I've opened a tin of your favourite,' he grinned.

Carol felt slow tears run down her cheeks at his kindness. He was across the room and holding her in his arms at once.

'Hey, I'm not that bad at cooking,' he teased.

Carol laughed and cried at the same time. She felt like a small child with no defences left, a weak baby who cried at whim.

'Oh, Mick,' she whispered tearfully into his neck, 'I've let you down.'

'Never.'

'But I have. Look at the way I've gone to pieces. I'm a right mess. I've been no use to you or Laura.'

Mick held her tight, kissing her forehead. 'You were strong for me for a whole year,' he said. 'You were there when I needed you most, even when I gave you a hard time. I'll never forget that, Carol,' he said, his voice full of emotion. 'Now all

I want is for you to get better. I couldn't live without you, pet,' he whispered.

Carol dissolved into tears again. 'But Mick, how will we manage now with you out of work? It worries me so much.'

'We'll get by somehow,' he was adamant. 'Now, I'll fetch some soup. And I'll let Laura see you after school; she's been pestering to get in for days.' He stopped at the door and turned. 'Me dad's been taken back on at the pit,' he said, his eyes gleaming. 'So has Marty Dillon. His charges were dropped and the case thrown out of court.'

'Thank God,' Carol sighed. But she could not tell what Mick was thinking. She felt a deep sense of sadness for him, for he now stood apart from the men he had fought beside all year. They would be working all the hours that they could get to pay off their debts. Mick would never be a part of that camaraderie again.

Carol spent the next few weeks close to the house, while Mick took care of her and Laura. She marvelled at how he coped with his enforced domesticity. Lotty was one of the few people he allowed to come and visit her, as she found it hard to face old friends; she had lost her appetite for sociability. Her confidence had quite gone.

From Lotty she heard how the atmosphere at the pit was low, with the men being threatened with dismissal if they caused trouble with any of the scabs.

'Charlie's been put on night shift for the first time in twenty years,' Lotty told her. 'He's not best pleased at that. And Eddy's been moved to another part of the pit, but they're not going to guarantee the same wage. There's war on.'

Eddy came by one spring afternoon with a bunch of early daffodils for her.

'Pinched these from your dad's garden on the way back from The Ship,' he grinned. 'By, I thought Shannon was a dragon, but this new bugger!' Eddy mimicked the new manager's southern accent. *'You've been calling us bastards for the past year, now you're going to find out what a bastard I can be!'*

Carol laughed as Eddy made jokes about the grim conditions at the pit.

'Poor old Sid got a nasty surprise the other day. Someone shit in his bait tin.'

Carol grimaced. 'That's disgusting.'

'Well, he shit on Mick, didn't he?' Eddy replied.

Carol was surprised by the sudden bitterness in his voice. 'Are you very unhappy?' she asked gently.

Eddy looked suddenly glum, his cheerfulness unmasked. 'It's not the same any more, flower,' he answered sadly. 'There's that much bad feeling. That's what the scabs have really done to us, robbed us of the old comradeship, of having a good laugh.'

Carol had never heard him speak like that before; Eddy had always been so flippant about everything. Life was always a joke. But she saw the sadness in his eyes and her heart went out to him.

'Things'll get better again.' Carol tried to sound convinced. 'We'll start fighting for the sacked miners to be set back on.' As she spoke, she felt the surge of interest in the outside world return. 'Lotty says the women still meet now and again - we'll take up the cause of Mick and the others.'

Eddy smiled at her wistfully. 'By heck, you're a Todd to your fingernails,' he said, his eyes shining. He came over and briefly kissed her on the head. It was an unusual gesture for Eddy. He left her looking after him in surprise.

Spring turned into summer and outwardly the village returned to its old routine. Clanging and sighing came from the pit and the sound of men's boots was heard once more tramping down the streets. People began the lengthy process of paying off arrears on mortgages and electricity. Some suffered the trauma of bailiffs calling to impound furniture against debts that could not be repaid, with the bailiffs shaking their heads at how little there was to take away. Others put their houses up for sale or were repossessed. This happened to the Dillons who found themselves and their family of five back in a cramped two-bedroomed colliery house, paying rent to the Coal Board.

'It's the house me Auntie Anna used to live in,' May told Carol. 'Hasn't had any mod cons put in since she died, as far as I can see. I told Marty we'd open it as a museum and make some money that way.'

Carol heard the rumour that Vic Proud was buying up many of the houses at knock-down prices and had set up his own property company, but as she no longer visited her parents, the news was only second-hand. It made her sick to think how her brother-in-law had profited so much out of the strike and left a trail of unhappiness. She no longer saw Kelly or baby Sally Mary as they and Sid had moved out of the village to some outlying estate where they could live anonymously. Carol would have liked to have news of them, but she did not contact Kelly and Kelly had never tried to contact her. There was too much bitterness between their husbands.

Despite the campaign to win an amnesty for the sacked miners, Mick remained without work at the pit. He was blacklisted from any other pit in the area too. Charlie was growing old before their very eyes at the treatment to his son and at his impotence to do anything for him.

They were living off benefits and Carol knew how much that ate at his pride. They had debts that they could never repay without the help of the family. Yet Mick did not complain. The other men had paid him a wage out of their own for the first two weeks, but Mick had given it to the strike fund to provide food parcels for others. Then, before the end of the season, the rugby club had put on a special benefit match and raised several hundred pounds on his behalf. Mick had been overwhelmed and too overcome to speak at the presentation in the club house. He had split the money with Frankie Burt and it had helped pay off the washing machine and the gas bill. But finally they had to put their own house up for sale and themselves on the council waiting list.

Mick went to the Job Centre every day to look for work and walked into Whittledene and trawled around the factories, but got nothing. He had a prison record; no one wanted to know him. His only hope was that the Coal Board would have a change of heart towards the sacked men.

As Carol's strength returned, she realised it was she who must now look for work. After a week of searching, Paul Dimarco took pity on her and offered a part-time job in his cafe, washing up and clearing tables.

'Well, I've done plenty of that this past year,' Carol joked. The pay was meagre, but Carol's confidence blossomed again at getting out of the house for a few hours and among the company of others. Soon she was serving behind the counter and helping Lesley make sandwiches and snacks and her hours were increased. With help from Eddy and Mick's parents, they were just able to pay their mortgage each month, but they did not like to be in debt to them so the house remained on the market.

By the autumn there was more money around again in the village and Paul was confident that his business was going to survive. He had extended so much credit to people during the long strike year that at times he thought the cafe would fold. Carol marvelled at his optimism and ability to carry on when things were so tight and still be cheerful to his customers.

'My family have survived a world war, several major strikes and a move from Whitton Grange,' Paul told her with a proud grin, 'and we're still in business!'

Carol glanced up at the old photograph of the handsome, moustached man with his pretty dark-haired wife and family, which Paul kept above the counter.

'Your grandda would be proud of you,' Carol smiled.

'Aye, maybes,' Paul admitted and Carol knew the remark pleased him.

Autumn came and although Charlie and Eddy grumbled about conditions at the pit and the lack of trust and consultation with management, there was much activity, with new expensive machinery brought in and a high-security wall built round the yard.

'At least they're investing in Brassbank,' Lotty said optimistically. But no one discussed the pit much for fear of upsetting Mick.

He had taken to going off on long walks again like he had following his release from prison. Carol knew from the state of his worn-out boots and trainers that he roamed for miles. But she did not criticise him as she had done before, because she knew it kept him sane and at least he was not wallowing in self-pity or drink like Tom Fowler. Tom, who had been sacked for daubing a colliery house with anti-scab graffiti, had been banned from most of the pubs in the village and his wife, Sheila, had left him and taken their young children back to her mother's in Quarryhill.

They spent a quiet Christmas at home, going to Lotty's for their tea. Eddy, who had moved back into a flat on his own, was there, and so was Val, who had begun a small dressmaking business from home. But Carol knew they all thought of Linda and young Calvin and wondered how they were spending their second Christmas away from the family. It was heartbreaking for Lotty to know her grandson was growing up nearby and yet to be denied all contact with him. Carol had written to Linda via Dan's parents, pleading with her to bring Calvin to see his grandmother, but had heard nothing.

Carol looked for enjoyment in small events, such as decorating the cafe with tinsel and streamers and watching Laura play a noisy camel in the school nativity, but there were no parties like the year before and none of the togetherness and excitement of that demanding time.

The Women's Group had finally disbanded in the summer when their funds had dried up and their attempts on behalf of the sacked miners had proved fruitless. Most had gone back to a quiet existence, but Denise had surprised them all by enrolling on a business course and had taken herself off to Sunderland. Carol noticed how many of the group came into the cafe to chat just before Christmas, as if they, too, felt something was now missing from their lives. She mentioned it to Lotty.

'Let's have a night out,' Lotty suggested, 'just us lasses.'

'Sounds expensive.' Carol was cautious.

'Well, I'll invite them round here,' Lotty said, undeterred. 'Send Charlie out for the evening.'

Carol was amazed at how many of them came. Among the sixteen were May and June, teasing each other mercilessly, Denise and her mother Evelyn, Maureen Savage and her daughter Angela who was pregnant, Lesley and Dot, Val who brought a huge flagon of wine and Joanne who came with her old neighbour Sheila.

'She hasn't been out since the Jubilee,' Joanne teased, 'so I said she had to come.'

Denise put on her 'Frankie Goes To Hollywood' cassette and soon the room was throbbing with noise and laughter as they all swapped news.

'How's the course?' Carol asked.

'Brilliant,' Denise enthused and talked nonstop about it for the next twenty minutes, her long earrings jangling as she moved her now close-cropped head of hair.

Joanne had news of Kelly. She still visited Sid, although it caused friction with her husband, John.

'It's like fireworks between the pair of them when I go round,' Joanne said. 'It's back to how they were before the baby - maybe worse. Mind, they both think the sun shines out of Sally Mary, so they'll probably stick it out for her sake.'

Carol was saddened to think Sid's sacrifice had been an empty one. He had crossed the picket line for the sake of someone else's daughter, only two weeks before the strike crumbled. But he would not be remembered for his months of solidarity or his arrest at the power station, he would be remembered as one of Brassbank's scabs. Having known Sid for so long, she knew that he would be tortured by the shame of it for the rest of his life.

The conversation turned to lighter things. They ended up with a sing-song like old times and promised each other they would do this more regularly. June became tearful. Her husband was odd-jobbing, part of the 'black' economy since being sacked.

'I miss the times we had,' she sobbed into May's shoulder.

'Haway, June man, you'll shrink me blouse!'

Joanne took June's other arm and they marched her into the night, skidding in their high heels and giggling their way home under the frosty stars.

Carol stayed on late, helping Lotty clear up. 'Thanks a lot. We all had a good night.'

Lotty smiled, but looked at her in concern.

'Everything all right at home?' she asked.

Carol sighed. 'As good as it's ever going to be, I suppose. I just feel that sorry for Mick. He's only in his early thirties and yet all he can look forward to is a lifetime of doing the odd bit of gardening for people. It's so unfair.'

Lotty put a hand on her arm. 'I know, pet. But he's got his health and he's got you and Laura. I thank God for that. We'll just have to hope things get better. Maybe after another year the management might relent.'

Carol was filled with warmth at Lotty's affectionate words. Whatever else had come out of the strike, she was grateful for the closeness with her mother-in-law. Their friendship was as strong as ever and no one could ever take that away from them.

Then just as 1986 seemed to be passing without incident and most of the villagers were once more settled in their lives, Carol picked up disturbing rumours at the cafe that were circulating the village.

'It's about your dad,' one woman from the pit canteen told her. 'They say he's retiring early.'

Carol flushed with embarrassment that she was hearing such news from a woman she hardly knew.

'Aye, and Granville House is going up for sale.'

Carol was shocked to think her parents might be leaving Brassbank for good and she was surprised by how much she minded. There had been no contact between them for a year now and yet it hurt not to be told by them in person.

After work she rushed round to Septimus Street to see if Charlie had any further news. She burst in to find Lotty in tears at the kitchen table, Charlie and Eddy standing beside her, at a loss as to how to comfort her.

'Whatever's the matter?' Carol cried, rushing to Lotty's side.

The older woman could not speak, she was so overcome. Carol looked at the stony faces of the men.

Finally it was Eddy who spoke. 'There's just been an announcement to the lads,' he said hoarsely. 'They want to close the pit.'

Carol was stunned. 'Never in the world!'

'Aye,' Charlie confirmed the terrible news. 'They're putting it in for review procedure. Unless there's a miracle, Brassbank will close this summer.'

Chapter Thirty-One

The next weeks were ones of rumour and uncertainty. At first the village drew together again in their determination to fight the closure. Lotty and Carol re-formed the Women's Group and after Easter they went every day to the pit gates with their banner and placards declaring. 'Save Our Pit' and 'Coal Not Dole'.

Carol watched her father driving in every day as he worked out his final month, but he never stopped to speak to her. She knew from the For Sale sign that Granville House still had no buyer. She wondered where they were intending going and almost rang on several occasions, but could not summon the courage. Laura had stopped asking about her grandparents, aware that to do so brought a sharp response from her parents. Carol wondered if they would contact her before they left and was bereft at the thought that they might not.

Even communication with Simon had lapsed. He had rung at Christmas to wish them well and sent Laura a present but said it was difficult to get over to see them now that he was working in the south of the county. He and Kate had bought a place in Durham, far from the village, and Kate was expecting their first baby. As for Fay, Carol neither saw nor heard from her sister. She lived on in her isolated luxury in Brassy, ten minutes but a world away from Brassbank. So much had changed irrevocably in the past two years, Carol thought in bewilderment.

There was a rally in the village with visiting speakers and the local media came to cover the event. After the coverage, Carol got an unexpected visitor.

'Pete?' she gasped on opening the door. She stood there foolishly.

'Can I come in?' he asked with a wary smile.

Her heart began to hammer. Mick had just gone out on one of his walks and Laura was at school. She stood aside.

'Course, come in.'

She busied herself making coffee, while Pete sat down at the kitchen table.

'I've been working in London since last year,' he told her, 'but I saw the piece on the news and decided to come up. I was wondering if there was anything I could do to help.'

Carol glanced at him over the steaming kettle. 'I don't think so,' she said quietly, 'not unless you've got the ear of some energy minister.' She pushed a mug of coffee into his hand. 'We're doing everything we can.' She paused and looked at him. 'Why have you come back after all this time, Pete?' It was unsettling.

He put down his coffee. 'I wanted to see how you were - how things were around here.'

'They're OK. It's hard on Mick not working. But me and Mick are fine.' Carol wondered if she saw disappointment in his face. He looked so attractive sitting casually astride her kitchen chair. But she was not going to allow her old feelings for him to surface again. She must give him no cause for hope. 'Whatever happens to the pit,' she added, 'we want to stay here and make the most of it. Brassbank's our home. I hope it always will be.'

Pete gave a wistful smile and nodded. 'That makes it easier, then.'

'Makes what easier?' Carol asked.

'Going abroad. I've been offered a contract with an Australian radio station.'

Carol's eyes widened. 'Australia! By, you've done well.'

Pete shrugged. 'Not really, but it should be fun. My career here never really took off as I hoped. Doing all that stuff on the strike - no one really wanted to know. The plight of miners' families wasn't commercial enough, touched too many raw nerves.' His smile was self-mocking. 'But then you knew that.'

'You tried and that's what counts.' Carol was generous. She bolted down her coffee. 'Anyway, I've got to get to work. Then I'm on duty at the pit gates this evening.'

Pete smiled broadly and took her hand. He kissed it. 'You never give up, do you? I love you for that.'

Carol withdrew her hand quickly, colouring at his words. 'Off you go,' she ordered briskly, 'before the neighbours start talking.'

They smiled at each other. She thought Pete was going to kiss her, so she stuck out a hand. He held it for a moment.

'Bye, Carol.'

'Ta-ra, Pete, and good luck in Australia.'

He went and she tidied up quickly, wanting all trace of him gone. She still felt guilty about her weakness for him during the strike. Perhaps if things had been different and there'd been no Mick or Laura . . . Carol dismissed the daydream. With a twinge of regret she knew she was unlikely to see Pete again. Just as she was drying up the two mugs, Mick came back unexpectedly.

He looked at her flushed guiltily and noticed the two coffee mugs.

'I saw him leaving in his car,' Mick said in a voice full of suspicion. Carol knew he had never trusted Pete Fletcher, had always been jealous of his interest in her and the Women's Group. Perhaps there had been rumours circulating nearly two years ago about her and Pete.

'He just called in, out of the blue. He's going off to Australia. Got a job at a radio station. That's why he came - to say goodbye.' She could hear herself gabbling, like a teenager caught doing something illicit.

Mick said nothing. He crossed the kitchen and picked up his haversack with the flask of tea and the corned beef sandwiches that he had forgotten.

'Will you be back for tea?' Carol asked, feeling wretched.

'Aye,' he answered stonily and was gone.

After Ben Shannon retired there was extra pressure on the men to take redundancy. Large, attractive packages were being offered, but only if the men agreed to go now on management terms.

'Look how they can find all this money in the industry for buying men off,' Charlie railed, 'but not for keeping the pit open!'

'It doesn't make sense,' Lotty said for the umpteenth time, 'after all the money they've poured into the pit recently. It's a big modern super pit with decades of resources left. Why do they want to close it?'

'We're being punished for the strike, that's why,' Charlie said bitterly. 'All that new machinery lying around in the yard unused, I think it's just so the books won't balance, so the accountants can call us "uneconomic". We've flogged our guts out to increase production this past year, but what for? They'd rather import coal from countries that use child labour. What's happening to our country?'

Carol could see how upset he was but before she could think of something comforting to say, Eddy appeared in the open doorway. She had not seen much of him recently; he was obviously enjoying being back in his own flat again and resuming his bachelor life.

'Well, bugger them all, I say!' he grinned.

'What are you looking so cock-a-hoop about?' Lotty demanded.

'I've decided to take redundancy,' he announced.

They gawped at him.

'You've what?' Charlie thundered.

'Aye, and I'm going to throw a git big party at the taxpayers' expense when I get me hands on it,' he laughed.

'We're the taxpayers too, remember,' Lotty snorted.

But Charlie was furious. 'Me own brother selling off his job before the pit's even closed? I don't believe it! Eddy man, that's not just your job you're selling when you take their redundancy money, it's the next generation's job. Can't you see how you're playing into their hands? They want us all to go without a fuss and not have the bother of finding us other jobs. But every redundancy taken is a job lost for someone else.'

Eddy gave a slow handclap. 'By, you'll make a smashing preacher if you lose your job.'

'Eddy!' Lotty remonstrated.

Charlie was purple in the face, but Eddy made an impatient gesture. 'Haway, Charlie man, I'm your brother not your lodge meeting. I've had enough. The pit's going to close any road. And I'm going to take some money and run. Have a bit fun after the last two years. I'm entitled to it, so why not?'

Charlie gave him a blazing look and stormed past him. 'I'm off to the allotment. I've nothing else to say to you,' he shouted.

'Good,' Eddy shouted after him. 'I didn't want to buy you a drink, any road, you miserable bugger. I'll go and celebrate and get pissed with someone else!'

Lotty sighed when Charlie had gone. 'Oh, Eddy. Did you have to stir him up like that?'

Eddy gave her a strange look. 'How else was I going to tell him?' he asked. 'Charlie, let's gan for a pint - oh, and by the way, you'll be pleased to hear I've thrown in the towel?' He looked at them both for a long moment with a helpless expression.

Carol saw his point. However he broke it to Charlie, his brother would feel let down. Eddy went before they could answer.

By midsummer they knew they had lost the fight to keep Brassbank open. All their appeals and publicity were not enough. There was a flood of men taking redundancy while others chose to be deployed at the few pits still open in the area. Charlie had been offered a job in a pit forty miles away where there would be no pit bus to take him or collect him.

'They want rid of the officials,' he told Lotty, 'but they're not ganin' to get rid of me so easily.'

'But the travelling,' Lotty was worried, 'and after a long shift.'

'It's either that or we have to up sticks and move there,' he said grimly.

But they both knew that they were far too settled in Brassbank to move at their age, even if they could sell their small terrace house. And for how long would his job be secure at this faraway pit? Lotty wondered. As it was, Charlie was being demoted to datal worker and his pay at the old level would only be guaranteed for a year. She had restless nights agonising over whether they would not just be better off taking the redundancy he was due. But Charlie insisted he would travel and accepted the job.

The week leading up to the closure was hard for everyone. Carol knew that Paul Dimarco was very worried about his business. It might be possible to recover from a year-long strike but not a permanent shutting down of the pit.

Carol went about that week straining for the familiar sounds from the pithead and breathing in the smell of coal fires as if she could somehow make them last for ever. Brassbank was the pit. The pit was its heart. Carol felt physically sick to think how all their efforts to save it had been in vain. They had stretched themselves to the utmost, yet all the hard work and endeavour had not been enough. In a week's time the pit would be closed and broken up, the shafts sealed off and their livelihoods buried for all time.

The finality of it all was worse than the ending of the strike. She felt a huge burden of weariness and disillusionment which she could not shake off.

Since Pete's visit, Mick had spent every waking moment away from home. Carol had grown resentful of his disappearances when she had been so busy campaigning for the pit. But he no longer had an interest. She understood how difficult it was for him not being one of the miners there any more, yet she was disappointed that he did not help. After all, the whole village would suffer once it closed. It was as if he was so wrapped up in his own solitary world that he did not care.

Sometimes he would return with a bag of coal and Carol knew he had been picking along the disused railway line. One afternoon she went up with a flask of tea for him and found him in the empty cutting.

'You don't have to pick coal any more, you know,' she said impatiently.

Mick seemed embarrassed that she had found him there. 'It's the only coal I can pick,' he answered shortly.

Carol bit her lip. She had not meant to upset him.

'It's so lonely for you up here, that's all I meant,' she tried again.

'I prefer to be on me own. Anyways, I don't feel alone . . .'

Carol saw him flush. 'Grandda?' she asked softly.

He nodded. 'Sometimes I can almost hear his cough and spit,' he said bashfully.

Carol's heart went out to him, yet it was upsetting that he chose the company of ghosts over hers. 'I don't think it's healthy for you being up here dwelling on the past like that. Why don't you come down to the pit gates and take your turn? See a few old faces. It would do you good.'

Mick gave her a bleak look. 'I've done me fighting, Carol. I've been knocked back that many times . . .'

'So have others,' she replied. 'If we all just gave up the fight, there'd be no point to life at all.'

Mick looked away so that she did not see his eyes glisten. 'It's over, Carol,' he said, his shoulders sagging with resignation. 'As long as Brassbank stayed open I had a chance of being set back on. Not now. I'll never work down the pit again. I've never wanted to do owt else, Carol, just work in the pit and provide for you and the bairn.'

Carol's heart felt leaden at his words; they were so final. She could not bear to be near him. She had come to find him for her own comfort, she realised, not his. But he had nothing of comfort to give. She yearned to put her arms round him and say things would get better, but she no longer believed that they would. Instead she turned from him swiftly.

'I'm off to pick up Laura,' she muttered and scrambled back over the dilapidated fence.

Mick looked after her until she was out of sight. Only then did he allow himself the weakness of weeping.

On the way back from school Carol took Laura to the park. She found Eddy sitting on a bench watching a game of bowls. He waved them over cheerfully, giving Laura a huge hug.

'Pooh! Uncle Eddy, you stink of beer!' she cried in disgust and wriggled away. Eddy laughed as she ran off towards the swings.

Carol realised he was drunk.

'Celebrating a bit early, aren't you?' she said drily.

'Never too early,' Eddy chuckled. 'I was sick of the pit any road. Good riddance, I say. I'm going to buy a new car and go on a holiday. Maybes I'll take you and Mick and the lass.'

'It'll take more than a holiday to put a smile back on Mick's face, I'm afraid,' Carol sighed. She told him about her argument with him in the cutting.

Eddy was suddenly sombre. 'I'm sorry, flower.' He put an arm round her. 'I wish there was something I could do to make things better. It doesn't matter about an old bugger like me losing his job but for a young lad like Mick it's criminal.' Eddy's mood was abruptly morose. 'I hate to think of you unhappy. You deserve so much more. You're a wonderful lass, the best. . .' His voice broke.

Carol laughed uncomfortably. 'You soft old sod!' she teased him. 'Don't worry about me. I'm a survivor.'

'Aye, you are,' Eddy said tearily. 'I don't deserve you.' She handed him a tissue to blow his large nose on. 'Carol?' he sniffed. 'Can I tell you something?'

Carol was in no mood for Eddy's maudlin confidences.

'No, but I'll tell you something.' She tried to sound bright. 'You're not too old to find another job. You could go anywhere - back to the Midlands maybes or even abroad. Or spend your redundancy on a little business, like Marty Dillon's going to do.'

Eddy forced a laugh. 'Aye, I could. Anywhere. The world is Uncle Eddy's oyster, eh?'

'That's more like it,' Carol smiled. 'I just wish Mick could be given such a chance.' She got up to follow Laura.

'Carol,' Eddy stopped her. 'You don't think I was wrong to take the money then? I keep wondering if I should have done what Charlie's done.' He sounded quite sober now.

Carol considered. 'Charlie's that involved in the union. For him there's only one choice. But I don't blame you for taking redundancy. You did all you could to save jobs during the strike. So don't feel guilty now, Eddy. There was nothing more we could've done to stop the pit closing. They probably had it planned before eighty-four.'

Eddy's lived-in face looked emotional. 'Ta, flower.'

She smiled at him and walked away quickly before he cried again.

He called after her. 'They were good, them days, after all, weren't they?' She turned to give him a quizzical look. 'Us fighting together in the strike like

244

one big family. By, we had a few laughs an' all, didn't we?'

'Aye, Uncle Eddy, we did!' Carol called back and grinned.

When she reached the swings and turned again, he was gone from the bench. She thought she heard his whistle retreating behind the hedge, some tune of Nat King Cole's.

The Women's Group held a party the night before the closure. They put on brave faces, recognising that this would be their last gathering.

Marty Dillon had taken redundancy.

'Well,' May blustered, 'it's the only way we can pay off our debts from the strike. Likely we'll move out the village. Marty wants to buy a fish and chip business. Doesn't even like fish!'

They laughed with her. No one was the judge of anyone else. They all knew how difficult the decision was. At the end of the evening there were tears at the thought of some of them moving away.

'What's it going to be like without the pit?' Joanne asked in fear. But no one could answer her. They could not imagine it.

The last shift down the pit marched there with the colliery band and waves of supporters. The women stood with their banner at the pit gates as they had done for the preceding months and clapped them in. There was a heaviness in the air which was not just from the thundery sky. The mood was reflective and sombre. This was the last shift of a pit that had been sunk in 1887, the last men in a line of pitmen who had worked in the county since beyond memory.

Tears and harrowed looks marked the faces of many. Then the men disappeared inside the pit yard and the band stopped playing. The musicians stood around talking quietly for a while, wondering what to do. Gradually they dispersed, carrying away their instruments, and the women folded up their banner and slipped away. Some would return to see the men come out of the pit at the final shutting of the gates with a couple of reporters from the local newspapers.

Carol decided not to put herself through the agony again. She had a sudden desire to go with Mick on one of his long walks. She did not have to work in the cafe until one o'clock. Perhaps she could accompany him for part of the way. She needed his company and she wanted to give him hers, after the last few days of tense silence between them.

Hurrying home after taking Laura to school, she found he had already gone out. Disappointed and a little angry, she stormed off to the cafe early.

'I don't expect you to pay me for this morning,' she told Paul in a tight voice. 'I just need to be doing something.'

'Champion,' said Paul in his easy way. 'You can start by making us both a pot of tea.'

He was such a kind man, Carol thought tearfully, and she was grateful that he did not ask questions. He was part of Brassbank and understood.

Carol worked on in the cafe. Laura had been invited round to a friend's for tea. Carol was touched at the way her friends tried to ease their strained finances by having Laura for meals. There was no rush to go home. At teatime the cafe filled up with the last of the shoppers and they watched the pitmen streaming up the road on foot and by car, for the last time. Some went to the window and the open door to wave them away with respect.

At half past six, Carol left to collect Laura. When they got home, the house was still empty. It was unusual for Mick not to be home for Laura, but then it had been a traumatic day for them all, Carol reminded herself. After her bath, Laura played out in the warm evening air for a while longer, reluctant to get to bed before seeing her daddy.

Carol grew impatient and then annoyed at his deliberately staying away. Finally she chased Laura to bed. She stubbed out a half-smoked cigarette in the back yard. It made her feel queasy. She telephoned Lotty.

'No, pet, he hasn't been here all day,' Lotty answered. 'He'll be off on one of his walks.'

'Mam, I'm worried,' Carol blurted out. 'He's never been this late before.' She did not want to admit how distant relations had grown between them again over the past month. 'I'm afraid he might have had an accident - up the old railway line, or somewhere no one would hear him.'

An unspoken thought too awful to contemplate lay behind her concern. Mick, too depressed by the future to carry on ...

Lotty must have heard the fear in her voice. 'I'll send Charlie up to look. He can call in at Eddy's and take him up too. I'll come round and keep you company till Mick comes back. He'll probably turn up any minute and be annoyed at all the fuss.'

'Thanks,' Carol answered.

She went upstairs to check on Laura. Something made her look in her own bedroom for the first time that day. In the twilight, nothing struck her as different. Then she spotted the bundle of papers on her side of the bed. Leaning across and snatching them up, her heart jolted to see they were letters written in Mick's heavy handwriting.

'Oh, God!' she whispered and tore at the rubberband holding them together. On top was a note that read;

'Dear Carol, it's time you read these. I wrote them in prison but never sent them. I'm sorry now I didn't. It might have made things better between us. I never meant to let you down. All my love, Mick.'

Carol's hands trembled as she sat on the bed and began to read the letters. They were chatty, full of details about his prison life and the other men. But they were more than that. They held tender messages for herself and Laura, endearments that Mick had never been able to say aloud. They told her of his inmost thoughts about the strike and his determination to stick by his principles whatever the cost. There was one, written after her disastrous visit, apologising for his rudeness.

It's not that I didn't want to see you and Laura. It's what I want most in the world, pet. But I feel ashamed of dragging you here to this place. I can't bear the looks on your faces, seeing me here. It makes me feel that bad that I'm not at home to help you. So it's better if you don't come. I can get through the time easier if I don't see the pair of you. Mind, I can picture you that clearly that you're with me every day. I cannot wait to be with you. Things will get better between us when I get out. I'll make them better. You're the one who keeps me going, Carol. I love you more than anything in the world. Take care of yourself and Laura. All my love, Mick.

Carol crushed the letter to her and sobbed aloud. Why had he never sent the letters? She agonised. It would have made such a difference. There had been so much misunderstanding between them, so many times when she thought he no longer loved her enough, and others when she had held back from telling him of her feelings for fear of being rebuffed. She had not thought him capable of such depth of feeling. This was the first time he had revealed it so completely. At least she was now certain of his love; it was not too late to make amends.

Carol looked at the scattered letters on the bed. Why had he decided to show her these now? Coldness crept into the pit of her stomach. She re-read the covering note. There was regret; a finality about the words. He felt he had let her down. Surely it could not be a note of farewell?

Carol sprang from the bed in a panic, her heart racing painfully. Mick had been gone all day, far too long. She searched the room to see if anything else was missing. No clothes or possessions had been taken; there was no suitcase gone. Part of her wished that he had. At least if he walked out on her, it would be proof he was still alive.

Real fear rose up in her throat, threatening to choke her. She ran downstairs. Lotty was coming in at the back door. There seemed to be some commotion going on in the back lane, but Carol was too distracted to care.

'He's left me all these letters,' she cried in distress, 'and he hasn't taken anything else with him!'

Lotty caught her by the arms and told her to calm down.

'What does he normally take when he goes on his rambling?' she asked.

Carol looked around wildly. 'A flask. His old bait tin ... in his haversack.'

They searched the kitchen but could not find them.

'Well, that's normal,' Lotty said, letting out a breath. 'He's taken a meal with him. That's not the sign of someone who's about to . . .'

They looked at each other, unable to speak of the horror in their minds.

'What does he usually wear?' Lotty said, more urgently.

Carol forced herself to think. 'Just jeans and T-shirt. And his old leather jacket if it's likely to rain.'

As she said this, her eye was caught by the back of the kitchen door. It was empty. For over two years, since the start of the strike, Mick's donkey jacket and a spare pair of overalls hung there, like a symbol of his working life. They had hung there so long, waiting for the day he would need them again at the pit, that Carol no longer noticed them. But it struck her like a blow to the stomach that they were now gone.

She pointed at the door wordlessly, making a terrified whimpering sound.

'His pit clothes?' Lotty asked.

Carol nodded. An image came into her mind of Mick, dressing in his old work clothes, packing his bait and swinging out into the summer's morning as if he was going to the pit. Except there was no work for Mick to go to; never would be again.

Carol's whole body was shaking with fear. 'I've got to go and look for him,' she cried.

Lotty stopped her. 'Not on your own. And you wouldn't know where to start. Let's call the police and report him missing first.'

Carol stared at her mother-in-law. She must be really worried to suggest calling in the police. Trust in the police in Brassbank was still fragile since the strike.

Lotty went to dial.

247

As Carol stood by the open kitchen door, feeling the space where Mick's clothes had hung, she became aware again of the noise in the back lane. Stepping out into the yard, she saw children calling to each other and running down the hill. She saw that what interested them was the coastguard helicopter clattering overhead. Her first thought was that the children should be in bed.

Suddenly she dashed out and stopped one of them. 'What's going on?' she demanded.

'Something's ganin' on down the beach, missus,' the boy said in excitement.

'What is?' she asked, blocking his escape. But the boy dived under her arm and ran off into the gloom.

Other neighbours had come to their doors and were peering into the sky and watching the activity.

'Must be some sort of rescue,' Evelyn Wilson suggested. 'Let's hope it's not someone's bairn been trapped by the tide.'

Carol went back inside. Lotty had just put down the telephone. All colour had drained from her face.

Carol's heart knocked like a hammer in fright.

'What is it?' she whispered.

'Sit down, pet,' Lotty said in a trembling voice.

Carol shook her head. She was rooted to the floor. 'What did the police say? Tell me!'

'A lad's reported seeing someone falling off the cliff, above Colly's Leap, just half an hour ago. He's gone in the sea.' Lotty's voice was faint.

'Someone?' Carol demanded.

'A man - a pitman. Lad says he was wearing pit clothes.' Lotty's hands flew to her mouth to control a sob.

Carol turned and made for the door at once.

'We don't know it's Mick,' Lotty cried. 'George Bowman's going to fetch you and take you down. You mustn't go on your own, Carol!'

'I can't wait for him,' Carol shouted back. Nothing could have kept her waiting a moment longer.

'Then let me get Evelyn to stop here with Laura. I'm coming with you,' Lotty insisted.

They dashed out into the lane. Lotty hardly needed to explain to Evelyn; their old friend agreed at once.

'Course you must go with Carol. If Bowman turns up, I'll tell him.' Evelyn waved them away. 'Eeh, the poor lass!'

Carol wanted to run ahead, but she slowed for Lotty. Her mind was in turmoil. Please don't let it be too late! she prayed. Please save him! If she lost Mick now she would never forgive herself for all the petty arguments and missed opportunities, for never telling him how much she needed him, not just over these past weeks but in the future, how she would always need him.

She had seen how depressed and withdrawn he had become again and yet she had been too busy fighting the pit closure to have any time for him. She flinched at the memory of Pete's recent visit and how hurt Mick had been by his appearance. Words she had spoken came back to haunt her. She had berated him for not helping fight the pit closure. *'If we all just gave up the fight, there'd be no point to life at all.'* But he had admitted defeat. *'It's over, Carol. I'll never work down the pit again.'*

The image of a pitman throwing himself off the cliff into Colly's Leap burned in her mind. It mustn't be Mick; please don't let it be Mick!

Then memories of happy times with him rose up to torment her as they hurried along the lane, past the empty pit and down the road towards the beach. What had happened to their hopeful plans to buy another motorbike and tour the country with Laura? To have another baby? But Carol knew they had been dashed when Mick had been sacked from the pit. Even then, Mick had still held some optimism, still soldiered on believing in a time when he might be taken back on at Brassbank. But his fragile boat of hopes and dreams had finally broken up with the closing of the pit. Carol realised now that she should have taken his desolation at the closure more seriously.

Scrambling in the half dark among the sand dunes, Carol sobbed at the thought of how much she loved him. It would be too cruel if Mick had chosen the very place they had first met - Colly's Leap - to end his life.

There was a small crowd of people already gathered on the beach. High tide was receding. Coastguards and police were milling around the rocks near the pool and an ambulance was standing by at the clifftop. A stretcher was being carried down the steep path.

Carol's stomach churned at the sight. There was a crackle of radio telephones and anxious murmurings among the onlookers.

They heard one of the emergency crew say, 'They're pulling the body out now.'

Lotty gripped Carol's arm to give her courage and suddenly Carol was thankful that Mick's mother had insisted on coming with her. She could not bear to face this ordeal alone. And it must be no easier for Lotty either, she thought.

She pushed through the crowd to the area of beach being kept clear by the police. She could see something being dragged over the rocks by the coastguards. The ambulance crew dashed forward.

'Please keep back,' an officer told them.

'It might be the lass's husband and my son!' Lotty cried at him.

'I'm sorry, it's a matter of waiting,' he apologised firmly. 'I could get someone to wait with you.'

Carol shook her head, unable to speak. She clung to Lotty as the minutes dragged by. There was a lot of commotion around the body and lights illuminated the scene like an eerie play. People became aware of the two Todd women huddled by the policeman, waiting in dread, and the rumours began to spread about the body's identity.

Then the urgency in the operation seemed to abate. The emergency crew stood back. Somebody was fetching a blanket, radio messages crackled. After some rapid talk, one of the police came over to Carol and Lotty.

'I'm sorry,' he spoke softly, 'they tried to revive him, but he was already dead when they pulled him from the water.'

Carol felt her knees buckle, but Lotty held her and the other policeman grabbed her arm.

'You don't have to identify him now. You can come in the ambulance—'

'I want to see him now!' Carol gasped and pushed forward.

They took her over. Her insides had never felt so cold, so leaden. But she wanted to see him, was desperate to touch him . . . Please God! Help me! she sobbed to herself.

Lotty clung to her beside the bundled form on the stretcher. As they pulled the blanket off his face, Carol could feel Lotty's warm grip supporting her, giving her strength in this worst moment of her life.

She gasped at the familiar face staring up at her. His skin looked clammy and grey, the green eyes staring but unseeing.

Carol heard Lotty cry out beside her in disbelief.

'Oh my God! Oh, no!'

Carol was bewildered. A first kick of relief went through her as the truth registered. It was not Mick.

Then shock stunned her once more. She knew the dead man at her feet.

It was Eddy.

Chapter Thirty-Two

Carol could not remember how long she remained on the beach that night, weeping with Lotty at what they had found. It may only have been a few minutes, yet it seemed endless.

Eddy's body was removed with swift efficiency and the crowd dispersed. She and Lotty were led to a police car. From somewhere the young vicar from Brassy, Steven Copeland, appeared to comfort them. Carol must have been shivering - she had rushed out in T-shirt and skirt - for someone put a blanket round her and gave her a mug of coffee.

She was quite numb now. Mick had not thrown himself off the cliff. She was guilty at her relief. But dear, kind Eddy was dead. The tears gushed again. Yet Mick was still missing. Where had he gone? And what had Eddy been doing alone on the cliff in his pit clothes? Was it suicide? She already heard murmurs around her that Eddy must have been drunk and fallen accidentally.

Then George Bowman was at her side, trying to tell her something.

'He's here, Carol,' he said gently.

Carol peered into the dark around the dunes as two figures hurried forward.

Charlie and Mick.

Carol fell into Mick's arms with relief. 'Oh, Mick, Mick!' she sobbed. 'I thought you were dead!'

Mick held her tight as if he would never let her go. 'I'm sorry, I'm sorry,' he kept repeating. 'I didn't mean to be gone so long. I'm sorry!'

She was aware that he smelt smoky, like a bonfire. But she did not care where he had been, just that he had returned.

Later, when the initial relief was over, they took Lotty and Charlie back with them to Dominion Terrace. Charlie was deeply upset by his brother's death. They all needed to be together.

'But where were you all day?' Carol demanded at last. 'You had us worried sick. And you took your pit clothes.'

Mick looked contrite. 'I went up to Grandda's, sort of to say me goodbyes. You were right; I was dwelling too much on the old man, the past. Anyways, I made a bonfire by the old railway.'

'Bonfire?' Carol was confused.

'Burnt me old work clothes.' Mick's face was grim, haunted. But his voice was strong, defiant. 'Well, I couldn't march into the pit with the other lads this morning so I had me own little protest up there, where I've been digging out me coal and pretending I was still a pitman for the past year.'

Carol leant over and hugged him quickly. 'Oh, Mick, I'm sorry. I should have understood.' She ached to think of him so cut off from his former marras, unable to share in their camaraderie. That had been the cruellest part of his sacking, she realised.

Lotty went and made some tea.

They talked on late into the night about Eddy and what could have happened to him. Charlie was ridden with guilt about arguing with his brother over taking redundancy. He had not spoken more than half a dozen words to him in the past week. He had called that evening to ask Eddy to search for Mick and been annoyed at not finding him in. None of them had seen him since the day before

251

last.

'I saw him on his way to The Ship two nights ago,' Mick said. 'He was canny, laughing and trying to get me down for a pint. He can't have killed himself. He must've been drunk. It's just a tragic accident.'

But Carol was not so sure. When she had last seen him to speak to in the park, his mood had been unstable. He had been guilty about the redundancy and trying to hide his hurt at the pit closing. And she remembered how he had been trying to tell her something. Why had she not listened to him properly? She was filled with remorse. If only she had let him speak his mind!

Eventually, Lotty took the shattered Charlie away. Carol and Mick went to bed. The letters were still lying scattered across the bedspread. Mick looked away shyly.

'They were lovely letters,' Carol said quietly. 'I'll keep them for ever.' She put her arms round him. 'Why did you choose today to show them to me?'

Mick regarded her with his piercing blue eyes. 'Because I finally saw how much I'd hurt you, taking meself off all day, cutting you off, when all the time you were working yourself into the ground to keep the pit and the village alive. I was that ashamed. I felt like I'd really let you down, Carol. The letters - they were all I could think of to give you. I don't have owt else.'

Carol kissed him tenderly. 'Thank you. They're worth more than anything else in the world you could give me.'

They went to bed and held each other through the night, unable to sleep as they remembered Eddy and how deeply they would miss him.

The funeral was delayed for a week while a postmortem examination was carried out. There would be an inquest later. Many people came to Charlie's door in Septimus Street to express their sympathy and it struck Carol what a popular man Eddy had been. Val was very upset and Lesley came round in floods of tears at the news, wanting to talk of the old days. Carol went with Mick to see Captain Lenin, knowing how bereft the publican would be without his close friend.

They sat with him in his nautical garden while he gazed out to sea, quite emotional.

'I know they're saying he was drunk,' the Captain sighed and shook his head, 'but he hadn't been in here all day. I was expecting him, but he never came. If you ask me, the pit closing was the finish of Eddy. He joked about hating it, but it was his life.'

Mick would not have this. 'Eddy left Brassbank a few years back, remember? He could have transferred to another pit again.'

'But he couldn't stay away from here, could he? He lived and breathed for Brassbank,' the Captain pointed out. 'Anyways, they found him in his pit clothes. What was he doing dressing up in them when he'd already finished? It's a strange, sad business.'

After a drink, he perked up a bit and they were able to talk about happier times. Captain Lenin recounted many of Eddy's favourite tales. They left him chuckling with tears in his eyes, looking out to sea where he and Eddy had so often gone fishing together.

'What do you think, Carol?' Mick asked as they returned home.

Carol shrugged. 'I'm not sure. But I do think Eddy was a lot more unhappy than we realised - he was just good at hiding it. I wish I knew what it was he was trying to tell me in the park before, you know ... I feel so guilty.'

The day before the funeral, Mick got a call from a local solicitor, asking him and Carol to visit his office. He was a young man called Andy Potts who had helped defend some of the arrested pickets during the strike. He showed them into his shabby office above two empty shops that had gone bust after the strike and gave them coffee out of brown, chipped mugs.

'Your uncle came to see me a week before his death,' Andy told them.

'Eddy?' Mick was surprised.

'Yes. He wanted to make a will. You and your wife Carol are the main beneficiaries.'

Carol and Mick exchanged astonished looks.

There are a few personal items which are to go to his brother and sister-in-law. But his redundancy money - it's in a building society account - it all goes to you two.' He showed them the amount.

'That much?' Carol gasped. 'Fancy Eddy doing that!'

'B-but why us?' Mick stammered.

Andy Potts knew Mick's situation well. 'I imagine he wanted to help you out. He spoke of you both very fondly. I think it upset him a lot to think you'd never work again.'

'Aye, that's right,' Carol agreed, 'he said as much to me.'

Mick was overwhelmed. 'You don't think this means he . . .?'

Andy shook his head. 'We can't assume this is the act of a suicidal man. He was quite urgent about wanting to make this will, that's true. But I think he would have used the money to help you out anyway. I'm sure that was his intention.'

'Oh, Mick,' Carol held her husband's hand tearfully. 'What a canny, canny man!'

The news of Eddy's generosity touched them all and lifted Charlie and Lotty's spirits. When they reached the Methodist Chapel on the funeral morning, they were overawed to see it packed to overflowing. Carol and Mick had decided to take Laura. Eddy had been so close to their daughter and they did not want her to feel left out. Better to confront death at an early age than to pretend it did not happen or could not be mentioned, they decided. It was the way of mining people from generations of experience, Carol knew.

Outside the chapel, Mick and Charlie took their places at the front of Eddy's coffin and carried him in, supported by Captain Lenin and Stan Savage, Marty Dillon and Frankie Burt. Carol and Lotty and Laura followed behind, with Val and the Dimarcos and some of Eddy's old marras from the pit.

Just as they were about to go in, a car drew up noisily at the gates. Two latecomers tumbled out.

Lotty's drawn face gasped at the sight. 'Linda?'

'Eeh, Mam!' Her daughter hurtled into her arms and burst into floods of tears. Carol saw Dan following nervously behind. She waved him to come in with them. Now was not the time for recriminations. It must have taken some guts to show his face in Brassbank for Linda's sake, Carol realised.

She went in beside the weeping Lotty and Linda. The chapel erupted in a loud rendition of 'Bread of Heaven' that wrung Carol's heart. How Eddy would have enjoyed the singing, she thought tearfully.

At the end of the service, as they filed out, she noticed with a jolt that her parents and Simon were standing near the back. She was astonished that her mother and father had bothered to attend. For a brief moment she caught their look and thought her mother seemed strained, even tearful. She was glad they had come. She gave them a weak smile and walked on.

'Look, there's Auntie Kelly and Uncle Sid!' Laura piped up.

Carol glimpsed their estranged friends among the large congregation and it made her think what a special person Eddy had been that he could inspire affection from all sides of a torn community. However briefly, Eddy had performed the miracle of bringing them all together. Perhaps some of the old hurts could be healed by it, Carol hoped suddenly.

As they emerged into the strong sunlight, the colliery band struck up a tribute. They all stood and listened for a moment in the airless, baking street as the coffin was lifted into the hearse by Eddy's family and friends. The jazzy strains of 'Unforgettable' by Nat King Cole filled the air.

Carol dissolved into tears. Eddy had been whistling that song the last time she had spoken to him. Mick came and put his arm round her.

'Do you remember when Eddy got a lend of the hearse to go and fetch the Christmas presents during the strike?' Mick said.

Carol smiled at the memory. 'Aye, and then he gave a lift to some of the pickets down to The Ship. Said it nearly gave Captain a heart attack when he saw the hearse roll up outside his pub.' They both laughed.

Suddenly Carol was aware of groups of mourners around them, talking about Eddy, laughing and telling jokes just as he would have wanted them to.

He was buried in the family plot in the large cemetery at the top of the village and then everyone was invited to the wake in The Ship. Charlie had hired the whole pub for the occasion and Lotty and Carol and Val had been busy preparing a cold buffet for days beforehand. The beer flowed and Mick kept playing Eddy's favourite hits on the old jukebox.

People spilled out into the sheltered garden and stayed all afternoon. Carol had an overwhelming sensation of Eddy being with them. She knew he would have approved of the brave attempts to be cheerful. But she was glad when she and Mick and Laura could leave and walk home alone. It was a hot afternoon and Mick took Laura off to chase the ice-cream van they could hear in the neighbouring street. Carol sat on a chair in the yard, kicking off her shoes and closing her eyes. The funeral had been a trial for them all, but she felt comforted by the day.

Still, she could not shake the doubts from her mind about Eddy's death. Perhaps they would never know if it had been suicide or not. It was easier to think of it as an accident, she thought in resignation. After all, Eddy had fallen into Colly's Leap before when drunk, so many years ago when she had first met Mick . . . She was jolted by a sudden thought. What if Eddy's first fall into Colly's Leap had been an attempt to end his life too? Carol's heart began to hammer. No! That was ridiculous! Eddy had nothing to be depressed about in those days, she assured herself. Still, the thought left her feeling queasy.

Hearing the telephone, she dragged herself wearily inside.

'Carol, it's me.'

For a moment she did not recognise the voice. It had been so long. 'Mother?' she queried.

'Yes, of course!'

'Well, don't sound so offended. I haven't heard you for that long,' Carol reminded her.

'Yes, I know, I'm sorry,' Nancy answered. Carol was surprised by the climbdown. 'Listen, I need to talk to you. Could we meet somewhere private?'

'Mother; we've just buried Eddy. Can't we leave it for a day or two?'

'Please, Carol!' Her mother sounded close to tears.

Carol did not know whether to feel annoyed or alarmed by her mother's sudden contact. 'Is it about leaving Brassbank?'

'No, it isn't,' her mother said, 'but it is important. Your father's gone out to the garden centre. He doesn't know I'm ringing you.'

Carol sighed. 'OK. I'll meet you in the cemetery. No one'll see you there.'

'Oh, I couldn't go there!' her mother said in panic.

'Well, the park will be busy. It's either that or you come round here,' Carol answered with impatience.

'Very well, the cemetery. In twenty minutes?'

Carol agreed and rang off. When Mick returned, she suggested that Laura go round and play with Louise. She was happy to do so after being with adults all day. They walked her round, and then Carol explained to Mick about the telephone call.

'I want you with me,' she told him. 'I don't know what it's about, she wouldn't say, but I can't face her on my own today.'

Nancy was waiting for them just inside the gates, her car parked discreetly under the high wall. She was horrified to see Mick.

'Whatever you tell me, Mick will get to hear anyway,' Carol defended him. 'We don't have secrets from each other and I'm not going to hide him away from you any more.'

Nancy nodded and began walking towards a secluded bench under a chestnut tree. They followed, Mick wishing Carol had not insisted he come. He had never felt comfortable with the haughty Nancy Shannon, even though she was a distant cousin of his mother's. Yet today she appeared nervous and upset; the air of superiority gone.

They sat down, Carol watching her mother twisting an embroidered handkerchief round and round in her hands. Her heavily made-up face was flushed and her faded eyes quite bloodshot with crying.

'This is very difficult for me,' she began, 'but I have to tell you. It's been such a burden for so long, Carol...' She broke off and wiped her nose. The twisting started again.

Carol felt Mick shifting uncomfortably beside her, itching to be gone. 'We haven't much time, Mother,' she said, a little irritated.

'I have a confession to make, a large one that I can't bear to carry alone any more.' Nancy breathed in deeply. 'I don't want you to stop me when I'm halfway through. So please just listen to me for once, Carol, without interrupting, will you?'

Carol sat, tight-lipped, remembering familiar scoldings.

Nancy sat bolt upright, her hands busy in her lap but her voice more calm.

'We were happily married at first, I suppose, your father and I. But I always expected us to move away from here. It was my dream come true when he began his training at one of the Newcastle pits and we could live in the city. We lived in a big semi with a nice, manageable garden and it was only fifteen minutes into the city centre and all the shops. I had that many friends, other young mothers like me with small children, and such a social life . . .'

Carol made an impatient gesture indicating she had heard all this before. Nancy scrunched up the handkerchief into a tight ball. 'So it broke my heart when he announced we were coming back here so that he could be under-manager. I'd married Ben to get away from Brassbank and here I was being dragged back with two little ones to that big cold house - impossible to heat in the winter—'

'But you loved that house, Mother,' Carol exclaimed.

'I hated it!' Nancy cried. 'It was so big and I had no neighbours, no social life. Ben was working all hours and never had time for me or the children. I was so unhappy - so *lonely*, Carol. I hated Brassbank.'

Carol heard Mick snort with impatience. But in a way, Carol understood. It must have been hard for the young, sociable Nancy to be torn away from the home and new friends she had made; to find herself stuck in an unwelcoming old house all day with small Fay and Simon and no husband around.

Carol put a hand on her mother's. 'Go on.'

Nancy's voice trembled. 'I had my own car, a little Hillman - my only escape. I used to take the children out on picnics. One day in the park I met an old flame, as they used to say, someone I used to go courting with before I married Ben. As youngsters we'd gone to dances in the Welfare and even into Whittle - it was still a small town then. He was fun. I'd forgotten how much fun. So I began seeing him again and the more I saw of him, the less lonely I felt. Your father didn't even seem to notice, so I just carried on, meeting out of the village, going off in the car. Or he would meet me on his scooter. Sometimes I'd leave Fay and Simon with my mother and pretend to go shopping. It went on all summer and into the autumn. I couldn't believe I was getting away with it, until. . .'

'Until what?' Carol whispered, dreading what she was about to hear.

'I got pregnant,' Nancy said hoarsely.

Carol's hand slipped off her mother's. It felt suddenly cold. 'It was with me, wasn't it?' she said.

Nancy nodded. Carol's heart knocked like a punchbag against her ribs.

'But this man,' Carol said in disbelief, 'are you telling me he's me real father?'

'Yes, I am,' Nancy said in a quavering voice. 'Sometimes I tried to tell myself that Ben must be your father but as you grew up, I could tell he wasn't. I just had to look at you to know - those green eyes!'

Carol's pulse was racing painfully. This was too much of a shock on the same day as the funeral. Why was her mother telling her this now?

'Who was he?' It was Mick who suddenly spoke, asking the question that Carol could not bring herself to ask. Something about his tone made Carol think he had already guessed.

Nancy turned and looked at Mick directly for the first time since their meeting. 'Carol's real father was Eddy - your Uncle Eddy,' she whispered.

Carol looked from Mick to her mother, horrified. 'Don't tell me this now,' she gasped. 'Not now!' She felt Mick's arm go round her shoulders.

'I'm so sorry, Carol,' Nancy whimpered. 'You should have been told before, you had a right to know, but I never had the guts to tell you. And I made Eddy swear he would never tell you either. I think that's why he went away down to the Midlands to work after you and Mick married because he thought living so close to you he might give the secret away. I messed up his life for him and now he's dead and it's too late to make amends!' Nancy broke down and wept.

Carol was shaking. She felt such a clash of emotions: disbelief, anger at her mother and Eddy for their secrecy, remorse that she could never hug Eddy and call him her dad. It felt like being lost in a maze - she needed to know so much more.

Gripping Mick's warm hand, she demanded, 'What happened when you found out about me? What did Eddy say? And what about Dad? You have to tell me, Mother!'

Nancy forced herself to stop crying and speak again. 'Eddy wanted me to go away with him. He said he'd get a job out of the area. They were beginning to close a lot of the old pits in Durham then and plenty of men were going down to Yorkshire and further south to work. He wanted us to go - start again with the new baby. Said he'd love to bring up the other two kids as well if I'd just give him the chance. He was very fond of Fay and little Simon ...'

Carol saw her mother's face contort in pain.

'I panicked,' Nancy shuddered. 'I was too frightened of the unknown with Eddy, of losing the security Ben gave me and the children. I knew Eddy could never give me the material things Ben could.' She looked at her daughter in shame. 'I loved your father - your real father. But never in a thousand years would I have had the courage to run away with him. Not like you. You had the courage to go with Mick - you were so like Eddy, you'd risk everything for the things you really wanted, things you believed in. He was like that in those days. But I wouldn't go with him. I told him he was never to come near me again.' Tears spilled down her cheeks as she faced the truth at last. 'I thought I was saving my marriage, my future happiness. But all I did was run away from the only man I could have been happy with. I ruined his life and then I ruined my own!'

Nancy sat and sobbed. Carol wanted to touch her but could not. She knew her mother had been brave finally to tell her the truth that had tortured her all these years. Yet she felt so bitter that her own mother had kept these secrets from her. All her life she had struggled to be someone she was not, to please her parents. She thought of all the times she had been the focus of her parents' anger and disappointment and for the first time she saw why. She was a constant reminder to them both of Nancy's betrayal and frailty. And Ben Shannon had to bring up a daughter who was really a Todd. No wonder he had resented her!

Now she understood why he had always favoured the other two above her. He must have known.

'Did Mr Shannon not guess what was going on?' Mick asked quietly. Carol knew he was deeply embarrassed by her mother's confessions, but he was asking for her sake, so that she would know all there was to know.

Nancy nodded. 'I'm sure he knew,' she whispered. 'I think he was the only one who guessed. But nothing was ever said. He never asked me outright, and I never confessed. But after you were born, things were never the same between us again. It's been an empty marriage - one of convenience to us both, I suppose.' She sounded so sad, so utterly empty.

Carol spoke fiercely with tears in her eyes. 'You could have left him. Why didn't you go with Eddy later, when you saw your marriage was a sham? It was my life you were ruining too. You could've done it for my sake!'

Nancy sniffed. 'I know, Carol. I know you've suffered because of what I did. I've hated myself at times for the way I've taken my guilt out on you. But it seemed too late to go off with Eddy afterwards. I thought the best thing for all three children was to stay with your fath— with Ben. And I had hurt Eddy so much already. He started courting Lesley Paxton and I thought he was happy. I expected them to marry, but they never did. I never realised until Fay's wedding just how deeply it had scarred him. He came to the house the day before to give her a present, but I sent him away. Well, imagine the questions that would've been asked. And Fay would never have wanted ...'

She stopped, seeing the look on their faces. Carol knew how Fay would have ridiculed such a gift. Her mother had made sure her eldest had turned into a social snob who would never make the mistakes she had. But poor Eddy, rebuffed once more. And the night of the wedding he had fallen - or thrown himself? - into Colly's Leap. She shuddered.

She had to ask. 'If you had your time again, would you have gone with Eddy?'

Nancy swivelled to look her daughter in the eye. 'Yes,' she croaked. 'It's my biggest regret. That, and never being able to tell Eddy again that I loved him, truly did love him . . .' She broke off.

Carol reached out at last and put her arms round her mother. Maybe one day she might forgive her for the wrong she had done, but at this moment all she saw was a grief-stricken, lonely, ageing woman who needed to be comforted. And she was the only one who could give her the comfort she sought.

They held each other and cried for their common loss. Carol was filled with unbearable sorrow that she would never be able to talk about these things with her real father. She had known Eddy as a kind, loving uncle and loyal, humorous friend. But how much more she would have liked to know him! Carol grieved. How cruel to have had this father taken from her before she even knew him as such.

Mick left them together, saying he would go and collect Laura. They must have stayed there another hour, talking and weeping and being silent while they struggled to sort out their feelings. They walked to Eddy's freshly dug grave, covered in floral tributes, and stood together as mother and daughter, united in understanding for the first time in Carol's life. Finally, when they heard someone come to lock the gates, they left.

Nancy stood by her car. 'Will you be all right?' she asked, unsure.

Carol gave a tearful smile. 'I was going to ask you the same.'

'We've found a house in Durham,' Nancy told her. 'We're moving out next week.' She looked worried. 'What will you and Mick do? Ben and I could help you out. I'd like to do something, help you get away . . .'

Carol shook her head. There's no need. Eddy's left us his redundancy money. It's enough to give us a new start.'

Nancy stifled a sob and got quickly into the car, muttering an incoherent goodbye.

'I'll come and see you before you leave,' Carol promised, 'and bring Laura.'

'Thank you,' Nancy mouthed, tears running in rivulets through her make-up. And then she was gone.

That night Carol lay awake for a long time in Mick's arms as they talked through the implications of Nancy's startling revelations.

'We're cousins,' Mick laughed in disbelief. 'By, Eddy was a dark horse!'

'So I've been a Todd all along,' Carol mused. 'I've never been a real Shannon at all.'

'Well, give old man Shannon some credit for bringing you up.' Mick was generous. 'You did live with him as his daughter for nineteen years.'

'Aye, I did,' Carol admitted. 'And I'll always think of him as me dad, I suppose. But it makes it easier to understand him, knowing about Eddy. He must have been very unhappy too.' Before they went to sleep, Carol added, 'Perhaps I'll go and talk to him, before he leaves. Put things right between us before it's too late.'

Mick did not try to dissuade her.

Two weeks later, Mick and Carol took Laura up to the high field above the allotments to get a view of the demolition of the pit. It was an eerie sight. The squat buildings of the pithead had already been bulldozed; equipment and furniture lay scattered among the debris of bricks and rubble, like flotsam from a shipwreck. There appeared to be no attempt to salvage anything.

Charlie had told them that millions of pounds worth of equipment and miles of copper wire had been left abandoned down the pit, never to be used again. It seemed such a terrible waste. All that remained above ground would be hurled down the shaft too in the haste to clear the site of any remaining trace of Brassbank pit.

'Other pits are just left to crumble,' Mick commented sadly, 'but they can't get rid of this one quick enough. It's like they can't bear the sight of it.'

Carol looked at the forlorn, windswept yard which had been such a hive of activity for as long as she could remember. Soon it would be a black, pockmarked plain like any other derelict industrial wasteland. Nothing would mark it out as the site of one of County Durham's largest pits, which had produced coal for the nation since 1887. Next year they should have been celebrating its centenary; instead there would be only commemorations and fading memories.

'It reminds them too much of how the miners stood up for themselves, that's why,' Carol said with emotion. 'I'm going to miss it all so much.'

It was the familiar noises that she would miss the most: the rhythmic hum of machinery in the distance, the clank and throb of the pithead and the clatter of coal trucks, the to and fro of boots down the back lane. And she would miss the bustle around the shops, the family bus trips, the socials, the routines, the neighbourliness. The silence would be such an empty silence.

Laura scampered off to play with the children of other watchers. They all awaited the blowing up of the pithead.

Mick's face looked bleak. 'We could leave. There's nothing here to keep us now. I'll go anywhere if it'll make you and the bairn happy.'

Carol looked at him tenderly, searching his handsome face.

'Or we could stay and try and help Brassbank survive,' she suggested quietly, 'take our house off the market. The landscape garden business you've talked about - you could start it here, maybe employ a couple of the other lads in time.'

His eyes lit at the idea. But he was doubtful. 'What about the business side of it?'

'I'll do the book-keeping. I could go to night classes. By heck, I handled thousands of pounds during the strike and balanced our books,' Carol pointed out proudly. 'And maybe I'll get involved in local politics too.'

'Is that what you'd really like to do?' Mick asked, excitement in his voice.

'It's what you'd love to do, isn't it?' Carol countered.

'Aye, but it's got to be for the both of us. It's your father's money, remember?'

Carol felt her eyes sting at the thought of Eddy's generosity. She spoke with quiet conviction. 'I want us to try and make something of our lives here in Brassbank. It's still our home. Some don't care if it dies; we're just numbers on a balance sheet. But I care about Brassbank and all our friends here - our family.'

Mick smiled. 'Aye, I know you care. But Mam and Dad would understand if we decided to go.'

Carol's heart beat faster. Perhaps this was the time. She took his large rough hands in hers and pulled him away, out of earshot of the others.

'It's not just your mam and dad,' Carol said quietly, 'it's our own family I'm talking about. Laura - and the bairn I'm carrying.'

Mick gave her a quizzical look, then gripped her hands hard. 'What did you say?'

'I think I'm pregnant, Mick,' Carol smiled. 'It's not confirmed, but I can tell by the way I'm feeling sick at the smell of things and everything tasting of metal. I know I am.'

Mick hugged her close and kissed her head. 'Oh, pet, I'm that pleased. I'm bloody pleased!'

Carol laughed. 'I knew you would be. But it's early days so let's keep it to ourselves, eh?'

'By, that'll be hard,' Mick groaned and kissed her, not caring if those standing nearby saw him.

Suddenly someone shouted and they turned to stare at the sight below. The gasps of the people were drowned by a muffled boom that shook the ground beneath them, and before their eyes the mighty headgear of the pit toppled and crashed as if in slow motion. The death-noise filled their ears and then the scene disappeared in billowing clouds of black smoke and grey dust.

Carol clung to Mick in awe. It was done. Brassbank's heart had received its mortal blow. There was no way back to the old way of life. Ahead lay the future as blank and frightening as the devastated land below them.

'Oh, Mick,' she whispered, the tears streaming down her face at the tragedy. 'I'm so glad I've got you.'

'You'll always have me, Carol, always!' he promised. And she heard the tears in his voice too.

As the smoke cleared and the debris settled, Laura came running back.

'Mam! Dad! Look, it's gone. The pit's gone!' She was wide-eyed, excited by the explosion, yet frightened by what it meant. Carol tried not to show that she was frightened too.

'What do we do now?' Laura asked.

Carol could see that Mick was too gutted to speak. She put out her arms and pulled Laura into their joint embrace. Wiping the tears brusquely from her face, she summoned a smile for her daughter.

'We go home,' Carol answered. 'That's what we do now.'

Lightning Source UK Ltd.
Milton Keynes UK

175547UK00002B/6/P